CALIFORNIA.
Where Trouble Wears a Pretty Face.
And Snow isn't Something You Ski on . . .

There was *Alex*, a stud who made driftwood sofas—and any woman within reach. *Catherine*, who gave the term rich bitch real bite. *Louis*, a towering Chinese homosexual bookkeeper who favored cowboy hats. *Orestes*, very old and very rich, using his children as perverse pawns. *Anatole*, trying to prove he was a man. His handsome brother, *Jack*, too macho to be true. *Ruth*, a redhead over her head into sexual chic . . .

And above all, there was *Dani* . . . the girl with the big blue eyes . . . if Brennen somehow lived long enough to find her!

"Powerful . . . I recommend it with pleasure!"

—ROSS MACDONALD

COCAINE
AND
BLUE EYES

FRED ZACKEL

A BERKLEY BOOK
published by
BERKLEY PUBLISHING CORPORATION

This Berkley book contains the complete
text of the original hardcover edition.
It has been completely reset in a type face
designed for easy reading, and was printed
from new film.

COCAINE AND BLUE EYES

A Berkley Book / published by arrangement with
Coward, McCann & Geoghegan, Inc.

PRINTING HISTORY
Coward, McCann & Geoghegan edition published August 1978
Berkley edition / November 1979

ISBN: 0-425-04456-4

A BERKLEY BOOK® TM 757,375
Berkley Books are published by Berkley Publishing Corporation,
200 Madison Avenue, New York, New York 10016.
PRINTED IN THE UNITED STATES OF AMERICA

This one's for my mother.
She waited longest.

CHAPTER 1

It was almost midnight Christmas, and the runt was spoiling my breakfast. We were the only two customers in the OK truckstop. He said nothing to me, just sat sniffling at the counter. He had the sniffles bad.

His hair was tied back in a ponytail. Patched blue jeans, a workshirt without buttons, raggedy hiking boots. The California highways were filled with hundreds just like him every summer. Some were raggier, almost all were taller. Just another rammy runt with a runny nose and a shirttail always hanging out.

He watched Kate Walker. "I knew a guy down in Berkeley," he told her, "who drew his own Christmas cards."

Kate was barely listening. She was busy stapling the Christmas cards that had fallen from above the windows. "That's a nice friend to have," she conceded.

"Yeah. Maybe." He wiped his nose on his jacket sleeve. "What he had was Santa Claus strung up on a crucifix and Jesus meditating in a full lotus at the Foot of the Cross."

She stared. "Why would he do something like that?"

"It was a protest against commercialism."

She went stern, then sad. "I guess Christmas means nothing to you."

1

"It means a lot." He turned away from her. "It means I gotta spend Christmas here."

Kate had taken a couple of business courses at the local junior college. She could cope with him, but she didn't need him. She decided she could finish stapling tomorrow and headed for the coffee pot.

The OK truckstop was tiny, even for Mendocino County. There were four stools at the counter and two tables on the floor. Generations of scrambled eggs had tarnished every fork, and the water glasses were plastic and discolored. But the eggs were ranchhouse fresh and the apple cider sparkled like California champagne. There were paper Santas on the windows, and artificial snow was swirled in Jack Frost designs on the plate glass. Opal and Kate Walker had put a lot of love in here.

The runt rubbed clean a patch on the steamed windows. I don't know what he hoped to see outside. There was nothing there. Oh, the parking lot had floodlights. Once in a while outbound semis went past us, their port and starboard running lamps like Christmas lights. The nearest town was three miles north, and redwoods went thirty miles in every direction. Even the stars weren't out.

It was raining outside, a downpour that had been pouring down for the past week. A typical Northern California winter storm—rain without lightning or thunder, just water falling from the heavens like Chinese water torture. Dull and grey.

During the Gold Rush, murderers received lighter sentences if they killed in the rain. Juries could understand how a weeklong rain could fray a man's nerves and turn his temper into a razor. The newspaper I had said this was already the coldest and wettest winter since the Gold Rush.

My mood was nearly as grey as all outdoors. A four hundred mile roundtrip with some second-rate presents. My youngest asking why Daddy had to drive back in the rain. Every man winches when he's being nibbled, and today had been a real bite.

Kate brought me the pot. "How was the omelet?"

"Great." I looked across. "I noticed that."

Her frown was long. "I wish he'd leave."

"Where did he come from?"

"His van broke down," she told me. "A wheel bearing I guess. He coasted this far. With the holiday, the garage can't get parts until Monday." She left to turn some bacon for tomorrow's rush.

Opal Walker came from the back room. She had stopped smiling years ago. Now she chain-smoked Pall Mall regulars. She seemed to be shrinking with the years. Her neck was bowed, she didn't move as fast as before, and her skin was tightening with wrinkles. She claimed her hearing was going fast, and her legs seemed to hurt more with every rainy season.

She saw me and came over with a fresh pot. "You got a full cup," she noticed. She pulled up a chair. "Then I'll sit down."

Opal Walker was first generation Oakie, one of the Dust Bowl babies. She and her husband had sweated and slaved and scraped to build a farm in the San Joaquin Valley. Thirty years ago, a drunk careened his pickup into a tree. Opal sold the farm, took the insurance settlement and her baby daughter, drove north from the Valley heat to these fog-bound coastal forests, and bought the first truckstop with a For Sale sign.

"How are the boys?" she asked.

"Real good," I said. "I spent most of the day cleaning up after them. They had a real good time."

"Your oldest, he comes in now and again. I always cut him an extra piece of pie."

"You shouldn't do that."

She sloughed it off. "My whole life is things I shouldn't do." She lowered her voice. "I think she's starving those boys."

"She just thinks they should be lean."

"Looks like starving to me."

"That's because you're raising granddaughters. And little girls eat more than little boys. Besides, I can't say anything. She won't listen to me."

She pursed her lips. "Since when?"

The runt was restless. He left the counter. He closed the front door behind him, and the paper Santa swayed. He cowered from the rain like a street urchin. He went around the building, heading for the restrooms out back.

Opal had a face that could stop a vulgar trucker. It fell when she saw the runt. She was old-fashioned and had little sympathy for snifflers. "Hope he didn't spoil your breakfast."

"On Christmas? How could he?"

"I knew I shouldn't've opened today."

"Throw him out into the rain."

She was tempted, but she couldn't. "It's Christmas."

"Lock the doors and turn off the lights," I suggested. "If he keeps it up, call the CHP."

"Michael." Her voice was as soft as it gets. "You're heading back when you finish. Could you . . . could you take him back with you?"

"Two hundred miles with him?"

Her eyes were pleading. "Kate don't need him tonight."

I thought it over. "I'll think about it."

She was grateful for that. That was more than she had expected. I drank some coffee and thought about that long dotted line to the city.

The runt came back and went over to his stool. He looked like her had washed with cold water. "This place isn't bad," he reconsidered. "This wouldn't be a bad place to build a cabin, if you got shelter from the rain and all."

Opal had her doubts he was smart enough to come out of the rain. "We like it here," she told him.

The runt turned her way. "Any jobs out here?"

She knew of none. "It's been too wet for lumber, and the few crops we get, well, the harvest's been over two, three months already. Most young men your age, they're either living off unemployment, or they've moved down to the city for the winter."

"What about that town up the road?"

That gave her pause. "There might be," she said slowly, thinking about the opportunities in a logging town of two thousand. "Maybe a checker down at the supermarket. But you gotta join the union, or know somebody. The donut shop might need somebody in the mornings."

"Do they make you cut your hair?"

She stared at him, then at his ponytail. "Around here you do what you want, and nobody makes you do anything different."

"But you don't get hired unless you got short hair."

"I didn't say that." She went off to wash my dishes.

"I can see it in your face." The runt snorted, looked back at the rain. He ordered another beer.

Kate went to the cooler.

He stared at the back of her head. "Are you married?"

She flinched, said nothing.

He was persistent. "The reason is, you're wearing a ring, but there's no cars outside, and I was wondering where your husband is, this being Christmas and all."

She turned away, hid her face from him.

I could see her reflection in the glass cabinets. She'd probably say there wasn't much to see. Just a big-boned woman with plain features and an Oakie accent. Add a couple of baby girls asleep in the house trailer out back, and a husband who skipped rather than pay child support, and Kate was no marriage prospect. But her life was nobody's business but her own.

I pushed back my plate and went over the runt. When he saw me coming, he became uneasy, afraid I might be the one to throw him out into the rain. He didn't want that. I was bigger than him.

"I hear you need a ride south."

He disbelieved his luck. "Are you going to San Francisco?" He slid off the stool. "Is that where you're heading?" Up close, his eyes weren't dilated. You could hide his pupils under a pencil point.

"When I finish breakfast."

He started rummaging for his bedroll and backpack.

"I live in Sausalito, and it's on the way." He was high enough to fly south.

I started having second thoughts. "What's the hurry?"

"I just gotta get back, okay?"

"What about your van?"

"I can pick it up in a couple days."

I was squirming, looking for a way out. I didn't see one. "Okay. Let's get going." Kate had a nice smile for me. Opal was grateful, too. She took away my check and wouldn't let me pay it.

He was already outside, watching his breath in the light.

The runt and I went back across the gravel apron to my car. The truckstop was set back like a gingerbread house a hundred yards from California 101. There was plenty of room for truckers and their rigs, but tonight the lot was an acre of puddles from the holidays and the rain. The gravel had seen too much oil from too many truckers, and the puddles were prisms in the floodlights. It was a miserable night.

He still yapped. "They don't make much money up here, do they?"

"They make a little," I told him. "There's lots of traffic during the summer. People from the city coming up to the lakes." I looked over my shoulder. The Walkers had just turned off their neon sign. "The state's going to widen the road next year." I thought about their second mortgage on the truckstop. "That'll help."

He had only contempt. "That'll help the pollution, all right." He snorted like a horse. "Bad enough they ruin the air, but they gotta clog up the roads, too."

My car was damp cold metal beneath the redwoods. It was stone cold inside. The runt settled himself against his window, on the edge of his seat, as if he didn't want to dirty his jeans. He didn't trust it, but it was shelter.

The car took its time starting. Soon enough we were heading south like the logging trucks. My wipers were worn and the rain plopped down like Nevada dollars.

The heater wasn't working right, and the windows kept steaming up. I kept my eyes peeled for mule deer jaywalking. I turned on the car radio to drown the grating of my worn wipers. There was nothing but Christmas music. I settled down for some serious driving.

A hundred miles later his sniffles were back.

He looked more normal. He looked miserable, a dim shape against the window, motionless, clinging to the edge of the seat. As far as I was concerned, he could perch there forever.

Ten miles later he was driving me crazy. He was still sniffling, still sitting like a gargoyle on a ledge. I listened to him. I wished he'd blow his nose.

I glanced over again. "There's no way we'll get there tonight. We'll be lucky if we make it by sunrise."

"I know that." He was miserable.

"If you want to sack out . . ."

He cut me short. "I can't sleep."

I had enough. "All right. What were you on?"

"Wha? I'm not on nothing." But he knew.

"I'm talking about before," I said. "When we left the truckstop. What were you on? Wanna walk?"

"Reds." He waited. "Seconal."

"Right. And you can't sleep." I asked the little liar what his hurry was.

He looked out his window. He didn't want his face seen. "I'm expecting a phone call." His voice was muffled by the rain and my wipers.

"Maybe she'll keep trying."

A startled sniffle. "How'd you know it was a chick?"

"It's Christmas."

He sniffled again, lost in his past. He had little future. They never hit this hard when he was younger.

I told him there was kleenex on the dashboard. He fumbled around like a man with a lit cigarette on his lap. When he found them, I went back to watching the road. I just missed a raccoon.

"Brennen."

I looked over. "How'd you know my name?"

He held up a business card. "It says you work for Pacific-Continental Investigations."

The bite went on. "I don't do that any longer." I knew I had to clean the car soon. It was getting to be a scrapbook.

"You're on your own?"

"I've always been on my own." I thought back over the years. "I just didn't always know it."

"How much do you charge, you know, to find somebody?"

"I'm not for hire." Saying it felt good.

"I can pay you for your time."

I said nothing. No sense rubbing salt in his wound.

"It's Dani. My old lady. She left me."

"Get a divorce. It'll cost you fifty bucks."

"This is different," he insisted.

"Sure."

"We're not married. Just living together."

I made a noise in my throat. He was another sickie who had forgotten what was normal. "She walked out the door, right? Why not say goodbye and start looking for someone who wants to stick around a while?"

"We got four years together already."

"Be grateful. Cut her loose."

"She's beautiful."

"They're always beautiful. If they stay."

He was a believer. "You know, she's got big blue eyes."

"And you're a sucker for blue eyes."

He shook his head. "She can't keep her eyes closed when she's sleeping. They're really freaky. They're so big, her eyelids roll back. Yeah, they roll back and she's staring at the ceiling. They're too small, I guess, or maybe her eyes are just too big, or something." He stared out the window. "Really freaky."

He was desperate. I hoped he wasn't dangerous. "She left willingly, right?"

"Yeah." His voice was small and distant.

"If she's so wonderful, why did she leave?"

"That's why I gotta talk with her."

Mmmmm. "Did she say why she left?"

"She said she loved me too much to stay."

I marvelled at that. Some guys'll believe anything. "You don't suppose there's somebody else, too, and she went to him."

"She would've told me if there was."

I made a face in the dark.

"It's not that way," he told me. "I was good for her. Real good. She was always alone until she met me. She didn't have to stay four years. That says something."

I told him to forget it.

"I can't. She means everything to me. I just gotta get her back. I don't know anybody else to turn to."

"If you want a private eye, there's plenty in the phone book. They're all better than me, anyway."

"Maybe you need some time to think it over."

"Sorry, pal. I quit playing detective, and there's no way I'm getting back into it."

"Hey, man, you gotta listen to me." He whined like a man kept from suicide. "The last thing I want to feel is that broken-up over anybody. It's a bummer being like this. I just gotta get her back. If I can just talk with her—"

"Forget it," I snapped. "I'm booked solid." I turned the car radio loud. Christmas music all over the car. *Jingle Bell Rock* and *White Christmas* were better than nothing.

We said nothing more to each other.

I dropped him off in Sausalito at sunrise. Well, it would've been sunrise, if it hadn't been for the rain. Sunrise was just a lighter shade of grey.

He scurried between the raindrops with his hands in his jeans and his collar turned up. More than rain fell on him. Forgetting him was the easiest thing in the world.

CHAPTER 2

The telephone caught me poolside at the cocktail hour. I set my beer in the soap dish, dangled my hand over the bathtub and caught the Princess by the second ring. "Yeah. Who's this?"

His name was Sam Khoury. He was a deputy coroner with the County of San Francisco. "I hope you're not too busy. We could use your help in solving a problem for us."

My vanity struggled against animal wariness. "Down at the morgue?" Animal wariness won.

"That's fine." Papers rustled at the other end. "We'll expect you within the hour. Goodbye."

"But this is New Year's Eve!" But he had hung up, of course. They never make it easy on you.

I raised both feet above the waterline and counted my toes and wondered what the coroner's office wanted with me. But there are no answers in a bathtub. If I wanted to know, I'd have to go downtown.

I soaked a few minutes more, doused my cigarette in bathwater, then hauled my skinny butt from the tub. Thirty minutes later I had my car pointed downtown. A lot of San Franciscans had today off, and the morning traffic was light. Fifteen minutes later I was pulling into a meter space at 850 Bryant Street. I plugged a couple of pennies in the box and got a couple of minutes grace.

I passed through the metal detectors in the Hall of Justice, then found the rear doors that take you to the morgue. The Coroner had his own building out back. His work begins where Justice leaves off.

Deputy Khoury had a hot little room to himself on the second floor. He sat hunched over his desk, surrounded by files and reports, flanked on one side by a desk-top computer. He was a little man, mean-faced, with slumped shoulders and red eyes. He wore a regulation suit and a regulation tie. The suit needed pressing, and the tie needed widening.

"You said you wanted to see me."

He didn't look up. "Any ID with you?"

I passed over my driver's license.

He played with the keyboard of his computer, wanting proof I was really Michael Brennen.

I lit a cigarette and waited. I wondered which computer net he was tied in with. NCII, CII, CHP or the local heat. I wondered how many warrants I had for parking violations, I'd hate myself if I turned myself in.

He was the salt of the earth. "That sign up there says no smoking." People like him kept the trains running on time.

I stubbed it out. "So what's this all about?"

He made a notation and gave me back my license. Then he threw an accident report my way, then went back into his files, making more little notes. I didn't want to wade through the thick file, but I didn't seem to have any choice.

Just after 4 a.m. this morning, when the fog hangs thickest on the Golden Gate Bridge, a black Jaguar driven by a fifty-year-old playgirl from Hillsborough stalled in the right lane around the curve from the tollbooths. The drunk left her car and began hiking back to the toll plaza for help. She didn't set out reflectors or flares. She turned off her lights to spare her battery.

Before the bridge district could send a tow truck, a VW microbus came through the toll plaza doing fifty miles per hour. It struck the disabled vehicle. The microbus stopped, but the driver's body sailed forward. His head punctured the windshield, the broken glass punctured his throat, and the steering wheel crushed what was left.

A state highway patrolman doing speed-trap duty on the other approach was the first to respond. Recognizing a fatality when he saw one, he notified his supervisor who signaled the Coroner's Office in San Francisco. A two-man team of deputies was sent out. They pronounced the VW driver DOA at 4:22 a.m. An inventory of personal effects followed them and John Doe to the morgue.

The CHP patrolman and his supervisor stayed on the scene. An accident report was made, photographs were taken, receipts were signed and countersigned, and the damaged vehicles were impounded and towed to storage. The supervisor noted strong alcoholic breath on the driver of the Jaguar. He advised the drunk of her rights and asked which drunk test she wanted to take—blood, urine or breath. The drunk became abusive and refused all three. She was arrested for Driving While Intoxicated, Resisting Arrest and Vehicular Manslaughter and taken to the women's drunk tank at the Hall of Justice.

Business as usual, as far as I could see. A lousy way to go, but business as usual. And yet the Coroner's Office wouldn't bring me down here just for an accident report. I re-read it and tried imagining I'd been there.

The poor stiff had been driving an eight-year-old microbus. Those vans are death traps. The engine's in the rear, and tin foil separates the driver and the road. You hit anything in one of those—a tree, a lightpole, another car, a fire hydrant—and it's all over.

When the fog hangs thick, the bridge seems more a very wide, low tunnel filled with lambswool. In that fog, the television scanners on the towers go bananas with conflicting shapes and images. And with every other floodlight on the bridge turned off since the energy crisis, striking a stalled Jag in the dead of night was easy.

Sure, it was a goofy way to go. Too goofy not to be

believable. If it weren't an accident, the CHP and the Coroner's Office were a bunch of silly-headed sorority girls. Which they aren't and never will be. They were always looking for weird details, crazy gimmicks, nutty problems. It gave them a chance to use up their cop equipment, and they're not about to let that precious junk gather dust. Not when the Feds think crime prevention means throwing money into every cop shop in the land.

I still had to ask. "It was an accident, right? It couldn't have been deliberate?"

Khoury's pencil stopped roaming paper. He twitched his nostrils, and the ends of his moustache twirled through space. I was trying his patience.

I got the message. If the lab boys found nothing suspicious, there was nothing suspicious to be found. If they were satisfied, then so was I. About the accident. Not about what I was doing here.

"So what am I doing here?"

"How well do you know John Wilmer Castman?"

"I never heard of him before. Why?"

"He's not a friend of yours?"

"He's nobody I know."

Khoury checked his file. "How about George Arthur Conroy?" He looked at me and looked back down. "Joseph Robert Crawford? James Walter Cheney?"

"Hey, I'm new to all this."

"You're a private investigator."

"I got a license, yeah, but so what?"

"Are you working on any case involving any of these men?"

"I'm not working." I raised my hand. "I swear to God."

He fished through the files, grabbing and throwing xeroxes at me. There was a fishing license made out to John Wilmer Castman of Napa, a library card for George Arthur Conroy of Sonoma, an ATD card for Joseph Robert Crawford of San Francisco, a vehicle registration card belonging to James Walter Cheney of Los Angeles.

"Like I said, I never heard of these clowns."

"He had these in his wallet."

"John Doe?" Then I understood. "Oh, no. It's New Year's Eve. I'm not going downstairs and ID a stiff for you."

"We know who he is," Khoury said.

"No shit."

He gave me an NCII teletype. A Washington State rap sheet on Joseph Robert Crawford (aka Joey Crawford) of Spokane. It had his fingerprint classification, his FBI file number, his birthdate, and his state of birth. When and where arrested, the aliases he had used, the penal code violation, and the eventual disposition of the case. Under the penal code number, somebody (probably a staff secretary) had checked the law library and translated the out-of-state code into plain English.

Joey Crawford had quite a resume. Auto theft with six months probation. Six months in county for simple possession. Charges dropped on credit card fraud by the telephone company. Sentence waived for Aid to the Totally Disabled fraud. All in Washington State, and none for the past three years.

"What do you need me for?"

"We found this in his wallet, too." Khoury threw down a business card from Pacific-Continental Investigations. It was torn in one corner, but still crisp. "This belongs to you."

"I took it. "Thanks."

"Where'd he get it?"

"How should I know? I give it out a lot. Free advertising. Good PR."

"Don't hardnose me. How did he get it?"

"I don't know." I hesitated. I still didn't want to go downstairs. "You got any pictures of him?"

He gave me a Washington State Driver's license. It was crumpled and torn, as if tucked away for years, and made out to Joseph Robert Crawford of Spokane.

I did a second take on the photograph. "Yeah, I know this clown. I picked him up the other night up north, in Mendocino county. His van broke down, and I gave him a lift down to Sausalito.''

He had his pencil ready. "When was this?"

"Christmas night. After midnight.''

"What was he doing up there?''

"I didn't ask. He didn't say.''

"How did he get your card?''

"It was on the dashboard. I don't clean my car too often. He found it, and he must've kept it.''

"Any reason why he'd want it?''

I tried remembering. "Yeah. His chick split on him. He took it pretty hard. He wanted me to find her. I told him no. That's all. I forgot about it, but I guess he didn't.''

"Any address on the lady?''

"That's what he wanted me to find out.''

"Okay. What's her name?''

"First name Dani.'' I spelled it out. "No last name.''

He looked up. "She isn't his wife?''

"They were just living together.''

"Screw her.'' He scratched her name.

"Why'd you scratch her? Somebody oughta call her, tell her Lover-Boy's dead.''

"Without a last name? How?''

He was right, but it seemed a shame. I suppose she'd find out someday. Maybe she wouldn't, though. How many people know what happened to their senior prom date? Same story there.

"How come you didn't take the case?''

He had a great sense of humor. "I'm not getting involved just because some chick walks out on her old man. I'm not even in the business any more.''

He was curious. "What do you do for money then?''

"Unemployment.'' I saw his face. "It's legit.''

His sneer could warp glasses. "Maybe you wanted to pad your claim.''

"How's a runt like him going to pay me? Give me a couple of lids, saying thanks a lot? Extra money is extra money, but I'm not crazy.''

He brought out a receipt. "Fifteen hundred sixty-two dollars. All cash. He could afford you.''

"Where'd he get that kind of bread?"

"Dope dealing. That's how most kids get it nowadays."

"Without proof, that's slander."

"We found paraphernalia in the wreckage."

I didn't think much of his evidence. Paraphernalia was cop talk, and cop talk can frame you anywhere except in court. Paraphernalia could be a syringe, a spoon, a pipe, an alligator clip, cigarette papers, dollar bills, soda straws or even candles.

Khoury was eyeing me. "You're not so old yourself."

"Oh yes I am." I stood up. "Too old to listen to this shit."

I left Khoury with his pencils, found my car and dead-headed home. There was more traffic now—the New Year's crowd was awake and outward bound. The announcer on the radio said rain was expected later this afternoon.

The mail was waiting for me at home. An overdue bill from Kaiser Medical wondering why I still hadn't paid for my firstborn's maternity care. My college alumni association asking for donations for an ice skating rink. An executive from *Playboy* offering me 17 issues for only 57 cents an issue. And a first class letter with no return address and my name misspelled.

I took the mail into the kitchen and started breakfast. Hot buttered bear claws and chocolate milk. I slit the first class letter and dumped it on the counter. I knocked over the milk carton when a thousand dollar bill fluttered to the floor. Chocolate dribble landed on it.

I held the bill beneath the hot water faucet. The ink didn't run. I found a magnifying glass. The red threads were all there, as were the dots along the President's nose. I never knew Grover Cleveland had beady eyes.

I went back to the letter. A sheet of notepaper inside. The words "Find Dani for me" were scribbled across it, followed by Joey Crawford's signature. A wallet-sized photograph was wrapped in the notepaper. The young woman who smirked at the camera's lens had big blue yes, all right. As blue as the bay at sunrise and larger han robin's eggs.

Were those eyes worth a thousand bucks?

A thousand dollars to do a job. Find a girl and the noney was mine. Even an implication that this was just . retainer. There might be more. The punk was saying e could buy me.

It didn't matter he was dead. That made no difference n the world. He'd been alive and well when he'd com->osed this silly little game, and maybe he even expected might keep the money and still refuse him. The housand dollars was throwaway money to him, but he .ad guessed it was enough to buy my attention. I owed .im nothing for this windfall, but he hadn't even dared.

Why should I play detective? I could keep the money .nd spend it on groceries and rent and spark plugs and aundry. I was still collecting unemployment from my .ast job. I wasn't in business for myself, and I knew I vasn't likely to start now.

Playing detective is like being a gravedigger. There's lways dirt to be dug up, people willing to pay to have it lug up. But what kind of a man wants to spend his life crounging for human rot six feet underground?

Shit, I knew the ropes. I could play the game. I know nost scams being used today. And wandering husbands vere always better off gone, and runaway wives should lways come back. Even the opposite is sometimes true.

But I was sick of tired scenes and cheap games. I vanted to be someone in my life, I wanted to be omething. Not just a peeping tom in lotus land. The ast thing I wanted was to go back on the streets again. I vanted no part of the detective game. The only way to vin that game is to quit.

I stared at the thousand dollar bill like some comic >ook hero with x-ray vision. I couldn't see inside it, and wanted to burn it up until even its ashes had vanished. f I kept it, I'd have to accept some responsibility along vith it. The thousand dollars was a sucker's game, and he runt had decided I was greedy enough to play.

I hate how money screams.

CHAPTER 3

Think of an opened clam, and you've visualized the small harbor town of Sausalito.

The bottom shell is Richardson's Bay, a dogleg of San Francisco Bay north of the Golden Gateway. Richardson's Bay is filled with salt water, seagulls and sharks, buoys and yawls, dinghies and schooners, houseboats and cabin cruisers. The top shell is Wolfback Ridge, part of the California coastal range. The freeway into San Francisco is the crest of the ridge, and the slopes below it are densely wooded and dotted with expensive homes for San Francisco commuters. The hinge between the two shells is at the base of the ridge, a two-lane black-topped road called the Bridgeway.

Downtown, the Bridgeway is lined with taverns and clothing stores, art galleries and restaurants. The drinks come watered, the seafood has been defrosted and microwaved, the clothing wears out just before the fad does, and the galleries sell watercolors of gulls and buoys.

The north end of town is further than most tourists can walk, so development there has been limited to serving the needs of residents. There are ship chandleries and marinas and yacht clubs, a couple of greasy spoons and a French laundry, a supermarket and a carry-out liquor store.

18

The houseboats are north of downtown, too. Like all waterfront towns, Sausalito has residents whose appearances tend to frighten the tourists. Of course the houseboat dwellers say the feeling is mutual. They resent being considered tourist attractions, even if they do resemble the remark.

I drove along the Bridgeway until I found the Mohawk gas station where I had dropped Joey Crawford last week. The gravel access road alongside led down towards the boats and dead-ended at the foot of the Waldo Point boardwalk. I parked behind a weathered kiosk, rolled up my window and locked my doors, then went for a stroll on a lonely pier in the rain.

The tide was nearly gone, leaving behind a foot or so of water, and the houseboats floundered in the mud. The round-hulled crafts looked like Noah's Ark after the waters receded, and the square-hulled ones like quake victims. With thunderclouds above them and the roiled waters of a gunmetal bay beneath them, the houseboats looked like a wino's nightmare.

I stopped halfway down the boardwalk. With the tide leaving, small sea critters found themselves high and drying out, and their last gasps made the mudflats stink like rotten eggs. I didn't know which houseboat belonged to my client. I could always come back later in the day; a six-hour wait for high tide shouldn't make any difference. I retraced my steps downwind to think it over.

The kiosk had a bulletin board on its backside, flanked by a row of mailboxes. I went over each mailbox. There was no Crawford scrawled on any one, and I didn't know Dani's last name, so I set about rifling the mail inside each one. There was no mail for Joey Crawford or for any woman named Dani. Which meant I might have to wait for the afternoon delivery and repeat the whole procedure. Even that was a gamble.

The bulletin board was a good guide to the Sausalito lifestyle. There were people trying to buy houseboats, trying to sell sailboats, wanting to crew to Bora Bora.

There were rock concerts and sailing schools and
organic restaurants and macrame lessons. There were
psychologies and theologies, philosophies and socio-
logies. And a yellowed card advertising Seascape Sofas
For Sale. Contact Alex Symons on board the *Mal de
mar*.

The *Mal de mar* was a converted riverbarge jammed
aft end first into a dismal little slip. The original
deckhouse had been jettisoned, and a more spacious one
built in its place with thick redwood beams for bracing.
There was a small deck aft and a larger one forward.
Large chunks of driftwood were strewn across the roof.

I went around the unpainted deckhouse and came out
on the canopied forward deck. A thirtyish young man in
white denims, rugby shirt and brine-soaked tennis shoes
was sitting on a wood bench. His hands were spotted
with grease, and he was having trouble rolling a joint. A
can of Olympia was beside him. Through an opened
window, I saw hanging ferns and a stereo speaker.
Someone inside was frying liver and onions. A portable
radio on the doorstoop played an afternoon jazz concert
from Berkeley.

"Alex Symons?"

He glanced up. "What can I do you for?" His face
was babyish, like a fraternity boy. He had sandy hair
and shaggy eyebrows and a moustache like an undercover vice cop. His hair was styled in an early Beatle,
and he wore his sideburns long. His suntan came more
from exposure than the sun. With his good looks, he
probably did well at the fern bars and body shops on
Union Street in the city.

"I saw your card on the bulletin board."

"Oh, glad to have you aboard." He set aside his
makings, rubbed greasy hands on a nearby rag and offered me his hand. He had a good grip. His hands were
rough and calloused, the hands of a carpenter. "How
about dousing your cigarette?"

I saw the bucket of kerosene by the bench. Scattered
around were tools and pistons and casings and plugs.

He had been overhauling an outboard engine. I made a move towards the port side.

"Not in the bay. Use the beer can."

I did as he wished.

He saw me eyeing his joint. "I was just about to go inside." Carelessly, he tucked it into a crumpled pack of Camels. "You here about a sofa?"

"What is a seascape sofa, anyway?"

"Driftwood with legs." He pulled a tarp from a sample and told me how he built his furniture. A friend in Oregon searched for sofa-sized driftwood along the coast, then trucked the hunks down to Sausalito, where Symons would router some space for cushions, then screw legs on both ends. A girlfriend would tie-dye swatches of muslin, sew them into cushions, then stuff with fiberfill. The price tag came last.

"How much does one run for?"

"A grand." He watched my eyes.

"Those tourists'll buy anything," I marvelled.

He made an effort to control himself, then threw the tarp back on. "You didn't come about a sofa."

"I'm looking for Joey Crawford's boat." I flipped open my wallet to my photostat. "I'm a private investigator. Joey Crawford was living with a girl, and about a month ago she walked out on him. I'm trying to find her." I gave him a photograph from Joey's letter. "Recognize her?"

"That's Dani." He hesitated. "I don't know what her last name is. She lives down the boardwalk on a barge like mine. What do you want with her?"

"Joey Crawford died this morning in an auto accident. His parents think she should know about it. They have no way to contact her, so they hired me to do it."

My little white lie sounded better than saying I was here because Joey Crawford hated sleeping alone. It sounded better than admitting I had no client, that Joey died before I could refuse him. Anyway, somebody should tell her.

"Did you know the guy she lived with?"

Again he hesitated. "I never knew his name."

"It was Joseph Robert Crawford."

"If you say so."

"But you've seen this girl before."

"Oh yeah. Mostly in the late afternoons. I work outside a lot. You have to, with driftwood, and I'd see her sometimes. Never in the mornings, always in the late afternoons, like she was on her way to work, maybe."

"Where does she work?"

He didn't know. "She might be a waitress or a barmaid on the Bridgeway maybe. Like I said, I never saw her in the mornings. Maybe she works in San Francisco."

"What did you think of her?"

"She's a fine-looking piece." He gave me his All-American grin. "Those eyes, you know, that's what it is. Big blue eyes. Jesus, they are something."

"How close did you get to them?"

"I bought her a drink once." He shook his head, a little too sadly for me. "Her boyfriend birddogged her everywhere."

"One drink? That's it?"

"Yeah. Down at the No Name. I ran into her one afternoon, told her I lived on a boat, just like she did, and I asked if I could buy her a drink. She said sure, so I bought her a drink."

"What did you talk about?"

"My furniture, mostly. She thought I could make money off it. Lots of people, not only tourists, like driftwood. The hassle is getting enough logs."

"What did she talk about?"

"That boyfriend of hers. All she talked about was him. It was a real shame. A waste of a good woman."

"Was she happy with him?"

"She was living with him."

"But you still tried."

"Sure. Why not?"

"What happened anyway?"

"Her boyfriend walks in on us. I finished my drink and went down the street. As simple as that."

"No hard feelings?"

"Hey, if she's not the one, she's not the one. Women are like the tide. They come in. They go out."

"Anything else you remember?"

"She drank Galliano. I don't see how that helps you, but that's what I remember the most. Galliano. Sitting at the front bar. Does that help you?"

"Hard to say. Anything else?"

"That's about it. Galliano and blue eyes."

"Did you see her after that?"

"Sure. On the boardwalk. I was somebody to say hi to."

"When did you hear she moved out?"

"When you told me." He looked up. "I haven't seen her around. Hell, there's lots of people, you don't see them every day, and later you find they moved to New Mexico or got run over by a truck or committed suicide. Some people, you never know what happens to them. You just don't see them any more."

"How about Joey? Seen him in the past month?"

"Sure. On the boardwalk. But not often. A couple of times."

"Did you ever talk with him?"

"Not really. We never hit it off."

"He stood in your way?"

"What's that mean? I wasn't about to bump him off. He didn't stand in my way. He stood in her way. Christ, she could've been a helluva fox, if only she didn't live with him."

"When was the last time you saw him?"

"Last week sometime. Just after Christmas. He said he was having trouble with his van."

"He didn't tell you she walked out on him?"

"Why should he? I only knew him in passing. We weren't good friends, or anything."

"He didn't ask if you'd seen her?"

"He didn't ask anything. I asked him how he was

doing. He said he was having trouble with his van. That's all we said."

"Can you show me her houseboat?"

He thought it over. "I guess so." He stood and started wiping the grease from both hands. Tucking a kerosene-soaked rag in his back pocket, he headed up the gangplank. I followed him. Behind us a girl inside the houseboat sang along with the portable radio. She didn't know how to sing.

The houseboats came in all colors, from unpainted wood to psychedelic rainbow. Most were converted tugs or riverbarges, but some were covered lifeboats and floating shanties. Some were shaped like gypsy wagons and Chinese junks, while others were single-storied summer cottages over shallow hulls. Some were designed in Mineshaft Modern with redwood shingles and barbeque decks, and a few were floating mansions with stained glass windows and stone fireplaces. There was even a derelict paddlewheeler dry-docked in the mud, green slime coating her bare ribs.

Joey Crawford's houseboat was a deepwater barge with a ferrocement hull. There were several portholes with brass fittings along the starboard side. The curtains behind the portholes were tie-dyed and drawn. A stovepipe from a fireplace looked like a misplaced nipple beside the diamond-shaped skylight.

We came single-file down the gangplank, squeezing past a ten-speed bicycle chained to the railing. The boat lurched sideways as we boarded, then settled deeper into the mudflats.

The houseboat had a single door, and there was a Yale padlock on it. I lifted the latch, checked the keyhole, then let it drop against the wood. I could open it, but I didn't need a witness to Breaking and Entering.

He was a mind-reader. "Take out the screws."

"You carry a screwdriver?"

"I got one back at my boat."

What the hell. "Go get it."

A minute later he was back. Two minutes later we entered the houseboat. It was warm and stuffy inside.

Joey had left the heat on and the windows closed. But then he thought he was coming back.

The room was split level, with the lower level a small dining nook that led to the galley. The living room was done with chocolate shag carpeting and seamless burlap wallpaper. There were bamboo shutters on a bay window, and potted ferns hung from exposed beams. The plants needed watering, and a pane of skylight glass was cracked and needed replacement.

A half-cord of wood and a stack of old magazines were near the stovepipe fireplace. There was a bookcase in one corner with rows of paperbacks, empty Galliano bottles and some of Dani's college textbooks. A battered tv sat on a cable spool probably stolen from the phone company. The houseboat had a fair stereo system, and a melon crate kept the albums together. Most were hard rock, some classical, and most had Dani scrawled on the back. A hatchcover coffee table was in front of a beige sofabed.

The galley was tight and compact—a woman or a sailor's design—with many built-in cabinets and all-electric appliances. The faucet was leaking, though, and the sink was crammed with dirty dishes. Most cupboards were bare, but one had a jar of unbleached flour and a bag of brown rice. A cookie jar held nothing but crumbs. The refrigerator held a bottle of locally produced carrot juice, a stale pack of natural cheese, a couple of cans of beer, three slices of luncheon meat, a post-dated quart of low-fat milk, a shrivelled orange, several potatoes growing new eyes, and a freezing compartment of beef pot pies.

The bathroom was a man's mess, with toothpaste rotting in the sink, hair in the shower drain, a ring around the tub, dental floss on the tile floor. There was one toothbrush, no tube of toothpaste, a chewed bar of soap, a stiff washrag. The towel racks were brass, maybe from the neighboring chandleries.

There were *Penthouse* magazines near the toilet. It was a chemical toilet and needed flushing. Like most sailors and would-be sailors, Joey (or Dani) insisted on

conserving water. I flushed it into Richardson's Bay.
Behind the toilet were several fuck books. Disfigured,
tattered, vulgar. I paged through a couple. Somebody
had a fetish for kissing cousins. Under the *Penthouse*
stack, I found a pink battery-operated vibrator. Maybe
that was their love life. Disgusted with the tool and with
my thoughts, I threw it back.

The bedroom was off the bathroom. Dani and Joey
had water on the brain, for a kingsize waterbed squatted
in a redwood frame beneath the only window. A down-
filled sleeping bag served as a bedcover. Rumpled sheets
and a single pillow.

A portable heater was on in one corner. I turned it
from automatic to off and the coils went from scarlet to
dull grey. A second-hand dresser was nearby with a few
science fiction books on top. Arranged around them
were a clock radio, a calendar for the next year, a
terrarium with flourishing marijuana plants, several
filthy ashtrays. The two bottom drawers held men's
clothes. There was a lot of empty space, very few
clothes. Dani had left Joey room to spare. I found
several packs of wheat-colored rolling papers in the
right-hand side.

"Got any weed on you?" I called.

Symons came over. His breath on my neck. "That
was the last of my stash. Why?"

"Just checking."

"Fuck you." But his heart wasn't in it, and he wandered off towards the kitchen.

He was an oddball. An over-the-hill frat boy with a
salt water fetish. Maybe he was a mellow fellow in love
with the sea. Maybe he just like playing the role. Maybe
he lived on the waterfront because women found
dockside life appealing. Maybe he could impress the
ladies. Some women confuse vanity and self-assurance.

I put aside my thoughts for something more tangible.
A food stamp authorization card made out to Dani
Anatole. It was two years old, but I now had Dani's last
name. The address on the card was on Pacific Avenue

near Steiner in Pacific Heights, the silk stocking district of San Francisco. An old-line family from the San Francisco society pages?

Dani had left some clothes behind in the closet. I checked them over, but they seemed like the stuff everyone leaves behind when they move from one place to another. Excess baggage that never makes it to the new place.

There was an empty knapsack on the top shelf. There were too many coathangers. A muslin laundry bag sat on the floor. I spilled out Joey's last laundry. Nothing there. Several pairs of boots were underneath. Hiking boots, cowboy boots, desert boots. I shook each one and wondered which were for formal occasions. A pair of socks fell out and bounced. I pulled them apart and found a wad of money wrapped with a rubber band. Several hundreds, a lot of fifties, and a helluva lotta twenties. The dough went into my jacket with my other souvenirs.

The houseboat had the same empty feeling my own digs have had since my wife split. Whenever two people have lived together too long and one suddenly leaves, the one left behind always spreads out his belongings to mask the emptiness. But the belongings never seem to fill the available space.

And then it hit me. Dani had left with no more than a carload of her belongings, but she had left behind too much. A modern young woman might walk out on her man, but she wouldn't leave behind her vibrator.

I didn't like the notion, but it had merit. She had taken her clothes, most food stores, all her cosmetics, her toothbrush. She left behind her record albums, her stereo, her college textbooks. She had left behind brass fittings, a kingsize waterbed, her knickknacks and decorations, her plants.

She had left behind her houseboat.

It had to be hers, not Joey's. Probably she had paid for it, with her own money or help from her wealthy family. It showed her taste more than his. She had

designed this living arrangement, and Joey was a tenant.
She prepared menus and probably cooked organic food.
When she left, Joey reverted to junk food.

She had left in a hurry. Maybe she had given Joey an
ultimatum to move. When he refused, she might've
decided to leave herself. Or maybe she had been un-
decided and left to settle her own mind.

Either way, it felt like she was coming back. Either
she'd re-establish the old arrangement or she'd divide
up the communal property. And the longer she stayed
away, the worse shape Joey was in. And from the feel of
things, if Dani did come back, he'd be leaving the way
he had come. Filling up the backseat with his things.

Joey had been more than a heartsick lover. He'd been
totally dependent upon her. She was his mealticket, and
he'd been living above his station. When she left, she
took his security, his livelihood, his future, his lifestyle.

He had been at wit's end, running scared, when he
mailed me a thousand dollar bill to find her. He had to
find her. He had no choice. Maybe only a private investigator could find her.

Joey knew the streets. He had been born a flight
above them in Spokane, had fallen through in Seattle,
had risen above them in Sausalito. Those who've lived
on the street always expect the worse. They always
hedge their bets.

Joey died carrying fifteen hundred bucks. At least
another fifteen hundred was in my jacket. Hard cash,
not a bank statement, not savings bonds. Maybe Joey
was afraid of an audit from the tax boys. Or, more
likely, an audit from a vengeful Dani, if part belonged
to her.

It felt like getaway money, the last of the stash, a
grubstake for a bleak future. And with Joey's criminal
record, it would be a long time before he could find
work. And with his record . . .

Joey had sold dope before. And selling dope was
easier than counting gas stations on the highway. Your
regular customers call back for their friends. And the
cash flow could account for the large sums, maybe even

his last errand in the city. If he had been smoking samples with potential buyers, he probably never saw the stalled car in the fog. I went back to the living room.

Symons was on his knees going through the record albums. There was a beer beside him. He had taken one from the refrigerator. He glanced up as my shadow reached him.

"Planning on playing some music?"

He shook his head. "His tone arm's probably set for high tide." Whatever that meant. "Wanna beer?"

My turn to shake a head.

He stood and dusted his knees. "Any skeletons in the closet?"

"Just clothes," I told him.

I waited until he lifted his beer and was pouring it down his throat. Then I sidestepped and suckerpunched him.

He folded like a switchblade and sprayed beer on the wall. Since he was off-balance, I grabbed the nape of his rugby shirt and shoved him headfirst into the wall. His head thunked against the burlap. Then I hauled him backwards onto the sofabed. He landed like a bear in a wallow.

His face was choking red, and his rugby shirt was white with foam. His lungs shuddered, and he sucked air before he found voice. "Why . . . why'd you do that?" His voice cracked like a teenage boy's.

"Joey would've asked you about Dani."

"He never asked nothing!"

I watched his muscles tensing. He was stalling for time, debating whether to move against me. I hoped he'd make that move. I wasn't sure I could topple him again, but I wanted to try. I was sick of listening to the hip wharf rat.

"He never asked me nothing!"

"He asked *me*, and I never knew him."

His beer can lay on the floor. I kicked it closer. It was an old-fashioned steel can. I grabbed it and crushed it in his face. A cheap trick, but his nerves sagged. He was a bundle of surprises.

"Let's start at the beginning, and I want the truth this time. I don't expect the whole truth. I don't think you could tell me that, not even with a gun at your head, but you can tell me enough so I don't break your head in two."

"I don't know nothing. Nothing, man, nothing."

I chucked the beer can at him. He didn't duck fast enough, and the steel lip gashed his right temple. He howled and clasped his hand over the wound. Startled, he looked back at his hand. It was covered with blood, shaking like a house of cards. He looked at me as if he wanted to swoon. Maybe he had never seen his own blood before.

"When was the first time you met her?"

"Last year. May or June."

"I can't hear you."

"It was last year. May or June." He looked around for help. There wasn't any. "They had a party, her and that guy she lived with. Everybody from the houseboats was there."

"What kind of a party was it?"

"Just a normal party."

"What do you mean by normal?"

"If everybody hadn't been invited, somebody would've called the cops, because the music was so loud. But since everybody was there, there was nobody left to complain."

I lit a cigarette and threw the match into an ashtray. The match covered a whitish etching in the glass. The etching was a leering dolphin in Victorian skirts clutching a parasol Mae West style. White lettering around the dolphin advertised the O. Anatole Fish Company of San Francisco.

"So you went to their party?"

"I didn't go. This chick came over. We stayed on my boat. It was a nice night. She didn't want to go out."

"The same one who's on your boat now?"

"A different one. She was a school teacher, I think."

"You're not sure?"

"That was last year. This one's an actress."

"And that's how you met Dani."

"Sorta. I saved her life that night."

"Oh yeah? How'd you do that?"

"Like I said, it was a nice night. I got up to take a leak over the railing . . ."

"What time of night was this?"

"I dunno. It wasn't that late. I think I saw the lights of the last ferryboat from the city. It was just coming in past Alcatraz."

"Then what?"

He almost touched his lips first. "I heard this racket coming from their party. People shouting and screaming. Like they were trying to get off in a hurry. I thought they were sinking, or maybe they'd lost their moorings." Symons looked at me. "If you've ever lost your moorings, it takes forever to get them back. So I zipped up and started up the gangplank. I was sober. I was straight. Maybe I could help. And then Dani ran past me, and she almost knocks me into the bay. Everyone else, they're still trying to get off the boat."

"So you chased her?"

"Yeah. Right behind her." He was almost wistful at the memory of his daring. "I caught up with her, too, down on the Bridgeway." His face sombered. "She was running down the middle of the Bridgeway, screaming her head off, cars all around her, all that Friday night traffic." He stopped to shake his head.

"What did you do then?"

"I chased her, grabbed her, tried pulling her back, out of the traffic. She started pulling me the other way, right back into the cars. I thought she was gonna kill me."

"Was she trying to commit suicide?"

He didn't know. He couldn't be sure. "Maybe she's suicidal when she's stoned. I've known crazier things to happen."

So did I. That was the problem. "What did she say?"

"She said she was a free spirit."

"A free spirit."

"That's what she said." He squirmed. "I told her she

was crazy. That she had her whole life ahead of her. But she kept tugging away from me. She kept saying she was a free spirit, lemme go, I want to run forever."

"Why didn't you deck her?"

"I tried, but she wiggled too much." He got sheepish. "I guess I'm not much good in a panic situation. I got her back to the curb, though, and a couple of guys from the party showed up, gave me a hand with her, and took her back to her boat. She was pretty wacked out."

"You didn't take her to your boat?"

"I had a chick on board. I couldn't ditch her and bring some maniac on board in her place. The last thing I needed was a suicide on my hands."

"After the party, did you try again with her?"

"Sure. A couple weeks later. That's what I was telling you before. Her boyfriend wasn't around, I got curious, she was good-looking, so I bought her a drink. I figured we had something in common, her running down the Bridgeway and me catching her."

"Did she remember it?"

"Not at first. When she did, she got embarrassed and walked out on me. She didn't even thank me."

"You don't walk up to a girl, tell her you saved her life, then expect her to fall all over you."

"Yeah, sure, but she didn't even thank me."

"And since then?"

"She won't talk with me. Just keeps walking out, like I'm poison. Like I'm a bad memory."

"Where did she go when she walked out on Joey?"

"I didn't know she had left."

"D'you think she might've left the Bay Area?"

"She might've. Sure, she could have. It might be an easy way to break up with him."

"Did she have any girlfriends?"

"I never saw any, but she probably did."

"How about boyfriends?"

He thought that was funny. "Joey wouldn't let her have any. He never let her outa his sight. He birddogged her everywhere."

"What about relatives?"

"I s'pose she's got some. She never talked about them."

Symons sat like a hound waiting for his master's kick. The blood on his temple had dried like a summer creek, and his rugby shirt wasn't white with foam anymore. He wanted me to believe he had "saved" Dani's life. That he had tried his best, but never scored with her. That he was a defensive clown, lonely and vain, who hadn't even scored with a warm telephone number.

Maybe he told the truth. Some seemed plausible. A lot didn't. A lot sounded too plausible, too traditional, too melodramatic. I knew a wealthy Union Street stud who told a jury he was a faggot to avoid a rape charge. They didn't believe him and sent him away. When he came back from Q, he was a flaming queen.

When I said we were leaving, Alex rose slowly, afraid I might suckerpunch him again, or throw something else at his head. But I wanted nothing more to do with him today.

We left in a single-file. I refastened the hinge screws as best I could. The padlock would keep out the curious and the nervous, but it was useless against the professional or the hungry. Dani was the only one who could improve the security.

I clambered up the gangplank. It creaked like splintering wood as it settled deeper into the mudflats. The noise spooked some seagulls and they scattered bitching into the airlanes.

I walked Symons to his houseboat. The drizzle had stopped, but off towards the Golden Gateway, against a wrinkled sky, storm clouds were rolling in like dull grey bandits. The sky was greyer for it, too.

The kitchen lights were already on inside the *Mal de mar*, and the sound of a woman singing softly to herself came through the half-opened windows.

I left Symons, hiked down his gangplank and scooted aboard. I peeked into his kitchen window. She was short and fat and naked. But she wasn't Dani, and she couldn't sing. I wondered if she were any better as an actress.

Symons hadn't said a word, but he was madder than a hooker in the rain. "Your're a fucking bounty hunter," he hissed.

I considered it. "That's as good as any."

He was shook. "You don't mind being called a bounty hunter?"

"That's what I get paid for."

"That's shitty," he said.

"Sometimes it is," I admitted. I left him standing there and made my way back to the parking lot. The tide had gone for good, and the mudflats were a backed-up toilet. I vowed I'd never set foot again on the Sausalito waterfront without a tide table.

I made a stop at the mailboxes. Anatole was the next to last box. I rifled it and found a surfboard catalog from Matzalan. I threw it back in disgust. I went for my cigarettes and found Dani's food-stamp authorization card, along with the money from Joey's boot. I counted it. Sixteen hundred forty-seven dollars. A lot of money for an unemployed hippie. But Dani and Joey could all wait until after lunch.

After all, they were buying.

CHAPTER 4

I took Bridgeway downtown. In the summer you can windowshop faster than drive, but the rainy season isn't the tourist season, and the downtown was deserted. Most of the shops were closed for mid-winter vacation, and the rest did business with a skeleton crew. There were even parking spaces by the town square.

I parked in the Trident lot and went across the planks into the restaurant. I had arrived before the noon crowd, and there were plenty of open tables. A cute little waitress in a t-shirt and no bra gave me a menu and a seat near the fireplace. I gave her my order and settled down with a cigarette.

I needed to find a missing person.

What makes a missing person? Someone vanishes and someone else misses him. Silly, but factual. It's a question of identity. What makes up a person? Is it his name, his haircut, his clothes, his home address, his occupation? All these are easily changed, of course, and people pick and choose what they want to alter this time around. The telephone directories changed a third of their listings every year. Change all those characteristics, and you're a missing person. Part of the Vanishing Breed.

I did have some luck on my side. At least I didn't think Dani was trying to jump totally underground.

Some disappear to avoid the whole show. They're willing to live on the periphery of the action. And the underground makes up a sizable proportion of all big cities. Dani had ducked below the surface, but I didn't think she had gone too deep.

It would be a different story if she were a criminal. Then the cops would be watching for her. And, given their patience, they'd find her. Cops have all the patience in the world. They don't bother with dragnets any more. There aren't enough loopholes left in society for anyone to escape unscratched. Sooner or later, everyone runs afoul of the Law. It might be a routine security check for a job. It might be a traffic ticket for a faulty taillight. The game is over once they check their files, run names through their computers, send prints off to Washington. But as far as I knew, Dani was nothing to the cops. Joey Crawford's death was accidental. His criminal record was ancient history. His file had been microfilmed and sent to the vaults.

And my best clue was a food stamp authorization card which was two years old. A good candidate for ancient history, too.

Doug Lacjak was a source who could help there. He was a lawyer with Legal Aid in the city's Department of Social Services. We had been friends ever since his landlady had Pac-Con investigate him during a prolonged rent strike in North Beach.

I gave him a call at work. The operator said he was on another line. I convinced her it was important, and eventually she transferred me to his line.

Doug answered quickly. "You picked a good day to call," he grumbled. "What's wrong with my day off? Why don't you ever call me on my day off?"

"I never need you on your day off."

At first he refused to run a computer check on Dani Anatole. Then he tried putting me off for a week. Finally he relented and said he'd get me a print-out. He put me on hold, and I settled back for the long wait.

I wondered what I'd do if Dani wasn't in the computer. I could always check new apartment listings. All I needed would be this past month's newspapers, and luckily I'm a lousy housekeeper. I have a closet filled with *San Francisco Chronicles* I'm too lazy to throw out.

I could haul out the December papers and section out the classifieds. That would be a large stack to whittle down, but the classifieds seem to change on Wednesdays and Saturdays only. That would leave me with a half-dozen problem children.

Even if I crossed out all apartments with more than three bedrooms, all apartments under a hundred bucks a month, and all apartments over five hundred, there'd still be too many to crosscheck. There were also flats and houses for lease and shared rentals and residence clubs.

I could make a telephone call to each listing, asking for Dani Anatole and posing as the credit bureau, the Kaiser hospital or All-State Insurance, the Triple-A, whatever. But if she were in San Francisco, it would be fishing for a needle in a haystack of six hundred thousand people. And she needn't be in the city, either. She could be anywhere in the nine Bay Area counties.

I watched my waitress bring my eggs benedict. I watched neighboring tables finish their meals and leave. I watched new tables being set up and new customers ushered to them. I watched my eggs benedict cool.

"You picked a great day to call."

"I'm sorry, Doug, but I needed your help."

"As long as it doesn't take too long . . ."

"What've you got for me?"

"I don't see how it can help . . ."

"Let me do the detecting, okay? Now, is Dani Anatole still on the dole in San Francisco?"

The phone said yes.

"No change of address?"

"Just the one on Pacific Avenue."

"Then she hasn't reapplied anywhere else?"

"Not yet. But it takes thirty days for the computer to process new applications and/or changes of address. Maybe there'll be a new listing next month."

"Oh joy. Back to square one."

"Something else, too. What if she changed her name?"

I had thought of that. I hoped she hadn't, but she might've. She wasn't running from the Law, but she was running from a nutty lover, and women on the run do change their names for less cause.

But I had to go with what I knew. Dani hadn't filed for reapplication nor for change of address in San Francisco or any other county in the state. Which meant she might still be collecting food stamps at that same address in San Francisco. Someone might be holding them for her.

My waitress came by and flashed me the evil eye. She needed my table. The lunch crowd was drifting in. I gave up my detecting and went to my eggs benedict. They were colder than a hooker's eyes.

CHAPTER 5

The house was a grey Victorian mansion stuck between two African consulates. There were many leaded glass windows, and a wreath of real holly encircled a wrought-iron door knocker. The door itself was rich mahogany, piano-width and sturdy enough to forestall the Second Coming.

The young black maid who answered the door chimes wore tie-dyed blue jeans and a Mexican peasant blouse. Dark nipples pouted like sharks against the fresh white linen. She eyed me like a doorman eyes a drunk. Maybe I was trouble. Maybe I wasn't.

I asked to see Dani Anatole.

"She don't live here."

"Then I'll wait until she does."

She pretended she hadn't heard me. "She don't live here."

I gave her a smile. "Maybe she'll visit."

"Maybe you better go away."

I gave her my photostat. She handled it as if it might wet her hand. She didn't like the law. Not even the hint of law. I took back the card before she could spit on it.

"Dani Anatole."

She told me to wait outside. I stepped into the hallway. She gave me another deeper foul look. "Maybe you'll wait here."

"Sure. Why not?"

She turned and left me alone.

The hallway went several yards, then split into two halves. One half went level on towards the kitchen and the pantry, while the other became a staircase towards the upstairs bedrooms. The doors to the living room were closed, and white curtains hung over the leaded glass panes. The doors to the dining room had been slid back into the wall. Though dinner was hours away, there was an eight piece setting of fine china and crystal atop a mahogany table.

I touched the wallpaper. It was real leather, and the seams were invisible. This was privacy that stretched back before the turn of the century. Security from the institutional wolves and street jackals who crave old money and the influence it can purchase. I wondered who dusted the money.

Several red tapers from the Christmas season were on a sideboard near the hall closet. They were subdued and tasteful, and their wicks hadn't seen flame yet. The morning mail was also there. I moved quickly and fanned the stack. When I saw the letterhead from the Department of Social Services, I knew my ammunition was good. Dani was still on the dole.

Then it hit me. Dani had a letter here, but there had been no mail inside the houseboat. Even though she had been gone most of December, that Matzalan catalog in her mailbox had been addressed to her, so she hadn't applied for a change of address with the Sausalito post office. Somehow she was getting her mail.

Joey wouldn't have needed me to help him find her if he had been forwarding it to her. If he had been saving it for her, there would have been a stack of mail, even if only junk mail or Christmas cards. He wouldn't have chucked it overboard, either, because he didn't know whether she was coming back.

The maid was gone long enough to announce me, not long enough to discuss me. When she returned, her face was blank and her chin was pointed at the carpet, unhappy with the news she carried. "Miss Anatole says you should come with me."

She led me past the staircase and ushered me into a tiny library off the hallway. It was a cozy room with a ceiling a mile away. The door closed silently behind me, entombing me with Great Literature.

There were two ladderback chairs and a long flat desk with a single drawer. A nearly filled bottle of Grand Marnier on a sideboard. Some poinsettias in decorator pots by the Grand Marnier were the only concession to the Christmas spirit.

I opened the desk drawer. Inside were a ballpoint pen, a Gucci leather checkbinder and a .25 caliber Baretta. The Baretta wasn't much larger than a track pistol, but the little bugger was well-oiled and fully loaded. It was easy closing the drawer on trouble.

Fifteen minutes passed, and then the library door reopened. In the hallway a woman wearing tennis togs was talking with a black man in tennis whites. She wore smoke-lensed sunglasses and carried a brandy snifter with amber liquid and ice cubes. The black man, who whispered with a cultured accent, as if he had learned it overseas, fiddled with the racquet in his hand. She told him to wait for her upstairs. He glanced at me as if I were a nuisance and said something even more indistinct. She laughed and squeezed his forearm. She watched him disappear down the hallway towards the staircase. She came into the library, closed the door behind her, and stood facing me.

She came right to the point. "What do you want with Dani?"

I stood. "You're not her."

"I'm Catherine Anatole. Her sister."

Thirty-five-year-old blondes are an endangered species these days, and Dani's sister was a real palomino. A big-boned woman with long legs and a golden mane. She had a tan that bordered on fanaticism. She was a show horse bred by money and the best it can buy. Even if she hadn't been born rich, money would've still gravitated her way. She had the beauty money always finds irresistible. And you didn't have to be a woman to resent all she had.

"Where can I find her?"

"She lives in Sausalito."

"She's collecting food stamps from here."

She stared and didn't blink. Then she lifted her golden butt onto the edge of the desk. She set her sunglasses beside her. "Are you from the police?"

She gained a decade removing those glasses. Wrinkles were already showing up around her eyes. Like her kid sister, Catherine had blue eyes, but hers had a washed-out look to them, as if they'd been bleached by a bright sun.

I've never understood what makes blondes think sunlight is good for their skins. Most are fair-skinned, and they peel and blister easily. It takes time for a woman like Catherine Anatole to acquire such a rich tan. In order to keep her skin from drying, she had kept it greasy with lotions. Too much sun had dried and brittled her hair, and her freckles were darkening like liver spots.

"This is a private investigation," I told her.

"I'm going to call my lawyer." But she didn't move. "What do you want her for?"

"I'm trying to locate her for a client of mine."

"How did you find out about the food stamps?"

"I was at your sister's houseboat earlier." I passed the authorization card in front of her eyes, but wouldn't let her get her hands on it. It was trump only if I kept it.

She scanned it as if it were a parking ticket. Only her eyes moved. "Who wants to find her?"

"I can't divulge a client's identity."

Her eyes caught fire. "The creep!" she hissed.

"Who's the creep?"

She was so angry, she couldn't think of his name. "That clown she's living with. *Was* living with. He's been calling every day now for the past four weeks."

"Why do you say *was*?"

"She left him. He's a creep. I knew he was a creep. I

told her that a hundred times. I'm glad she left him, and I hope she never sees him again."

"How does Dani feel about him?"

She tapped fingers on the desk. "She doesn't know what she thinks about him." It sounded honest.

"Why doesn't she go back with him?"

"Look, Dani's a grown woman. She makes up her own mind, and she's perfectly capable of making rational decisions. Since she's chosen to leave him, I feel it's none of my business to interfere."

"But you've interfered before."

"How would you know?"

"That's what families are for."

She shook her golden hair and snorted.

"Do you know where she is?"

"If she were here," Catherine said, "d'you think I'd still be mailing her food stamps to Sausalito?"

"You haven't answered my question. You already know she doesn't live in Sausalito any more. Food stamps come tomorrow, the first of the month. You've probably already received the vouchers in the mail. Will you be mailing them to her, or will you just save them and let her pick them up here?"

"You don't know Dani. You don't understand her."

I debated the idea. "Okay. Tell me about her. Just enough so I get a feel for things. Just enough so I know what kind of person we're talking about."

She was relieved. "Dani," she finally brought herself to say, "grew up with too much money. She's never had to face up to reality. She's stubborn. She does whatever she feels like doing."

"What about her folks?"

"They died when she was in high school." A hard line had formed at the edge of her mouth. She was traveling back in time, and like all time travelers, she was troubled by ghosts and memories.

"How did she accept their deaths?"

"I don't know. She never talked about it. Nobody said much anyway. Our grandfather took us in. He was running the family business then, a fish company. He didn't have much time to spend with her—with anyone, for that matter. He was just a man. A man doesn't know what's right for a woman. And he's her grandfather, too, so he just let her get away with murder until she went off to college.''

"Which college did she go to?"

"Mills. I don't expect you to know it. It's a private school for young women in Oakland. We thought it would be just the thing for her. For a while it was, but she went off to school at the wrong time."

"Why was it the wrong time?"

"The Sixties. You know how they were. Rhetoric and politics. You start questioning everything, and lose track of who you are. It's just a short-lived thing, or it should be, but it's very frightening to watch."

"How did it change her?"

She found it hard to say. "Dani rejected her family. We were parasites, robber barons. Not just great-great-grandfather, either, but all of us. Her wealth, her position, was a curse."

"You didn't agree with that," I said.

"Well, that is a little much. I mean, wealth and position can be a curse. You wonder what you did to deserve it, and it's easy to become paranoid. You can also be very lonely when you're wealthy. You have to resolve those problems, or money does become a curse."

Anywhere else in the world, Catherine Anatole would've been a fluke, an anachronism, a dinosaur. But in San Francisco she was a part of old San Francisco Society, a society dame.

And I was bored. "How did she escape the curse of money?"

"She dropped out." Catherine made dropping out sound like giving up. The thin line had crept back to her mouth. "She went to Seattle. A friend of ours runs a salmon cannery there. She went to work for him. Filleting fish."

"How did she like filleting fish?"

"What do you expect? She hated it." Catherine jutted her chin out with wounded pride. "Seafaring does run in our family."

"But you don't go to sea any more."

She tightened. "Dani had to prove that money wasn't an albatross around her neck. It's understandable, I think. You don't know how wealth can make you paranoid. People talk behind your back . . ." She changed course abruptly. "I'm very proud of her. She hated what she was doing, but she stayed there all those months. She made her mistakes, but she also learned from them. She's quite a woman."

"How long was she up there?"

"Six months. Something like that."

"Is that where she met Joey Crawford?"

The thin line grew thinner, if possible, as if she were smiling and biting a bullet at the same time. "They worked side-by-side on the gutting line. He was poor and worked with his hands. He caught the flu or something, and Dani nursed him back to health. It's a touching story." She still couldn't believe it.

"How long have they lived together?"

"Four years." Her voice had dropped an octave.

"Four years is a long time."

Her chin quivered. "Yes, it is, isn't it?"

I wanted to laugh at her frustration. For four years she had fought romance, interfering wherever she thought she could, and now she had been suckered out of victory by Dani's free will. "What made her leave Seattle?"

"She was ready to settle down," Catherine said. "She wasn't a little girl any longer. She was a woman, ready to accept a woman's responsibility."

"How did you hear she was leaving Joey?"

"She called me just before Thanksgiving. The family had a get-together planned. She begged off, saying she needed the time to think. She was thinking about leaving him."

"She didn't call the day she left?"

"No, she didn't. The creep called and asked if she were here. I said she wasn't." Catherine's eyes challenged mine. "It was the truth."

"Were you upset because she didn't call?"

"Of course not. She needed some time off by herself. I thought, if she didn't call me, she had a reason. Maybe she was afraid I might say I told you so."

"Which is how you felt, right?"

"I know that." She had gone waspish again. "Nobody likes admitting that they're wrong. Anyway, she called me a couple days later."

"What did she have to say?"

Catherine furrowed her golden brows. "She said she was tired of him, that he frightened her. His behavior was growing more and more erratic. She thought he was losing touch with reality. He was too possessive. She wasn't ready to give him what he needed. He felt she didn't care anymore, that there were other men in her life. He kept demanding more and more from her. He needed more and more reassurance. She just wasn't ready to give him that."

It was quite a litany of sins. I wondered why Catherine had gotten so involved in Dani's problems. Unless she was also talking about herself, as well as her sister. But I had no way of knowing, and hunches are always suspect.

"Were there other men?" I asked.

"I wouldn't know."

"Joey thought there were."

"Yes, he did," she said, bitterness rampant in every word. "I never could stand the little creep. I told her that, when she brought him back with her from Seattle, and she chose to ignore me. Luckily, since then, she's smartened up and left him. And that's all there is to that."

"I think there's more," I said. "More than just living with some creep. More than just a simple split-up. More than just ripping off the food stamp people for a lousy fifty bucks a month. Fifty bucks a month doesn't feed anybody these days, but that's between you and your conscience. That creep, well, he's a cold fish face up at the county morgue.''

Her eyes grew like a startled burglar's. "He's dead?"

"Oh yeah. You didn't know?"

"No. No. How could I? How did he . . . ?"

"The SFPD could explain better than I can."

Sure, maybe I could end the case right now, but maybe I couldn't. Dani was probably staying with friends or relatives. Her sister was only a single source of info, but her actions and reactions were clues to the Dani puzzle. A little melodrama helps draw blood sometimes.

"The police. Do they know about Dani?"

"They asked about her," I said.

"How did he die? Was it . . . murder?"

"The police don't confide in me," I lied.

"No. I guess they wouldn't."

I knew she didn't consider herself impolite, but she irritated me. It wasn't much of an irritation, sort of like a car parked in the fast lane.

Like many who belonged to Old San Franciscan families, she treated everyone as her inferior. Brusquely, incautiously, impatiently, as if money makes one righteous. She had the confidence that comes from a lot of old and dusty money. Her life was spent in leisure, and I was interfering with that leisure.

I didn't think it would be that hard to shake her self-assurance. Just treat her the way I'd handle a junkie. Kid gloves one minute, melodrama the next. Money and dope are first cousins, anyway. Like dope, money's beneficial in moderation. Too much and you lose track with reality.

The wealthy have the same fears as the junkie, and they cope with them just about as well. Their vanity makes them a hall of mirrors. Afraid of being misunderstood, they take offense easily, overreacting like a child throwing a temper tantrum. They're secretive and clannish, not realizing the mark of money is as noticeable as needle tracks on the beach. They think they know what you're saying about them behind their backs, and they're right about what you're saying, but they don't dare challenge you about it. What you say might threaten their security. So they hide their fears and worry a lot, which just makes them more vulnerable and more paranoid.

It was about time for a touch of that melodrama. "Did you know he was a dope dealer?"

"How do you know that?"

"He was busted for that. The cops told me that much."

"Oh, it could have been years ago."

"He had fifteen hundred bucks on him when he died. Another sixteen hundred in his boots on the houseboat. For a dealer, even, that's a lot of hard cash. For a runt on Aid to the Totally Disabled. . . ."

From her expression, she didn't understand.

"Another of his scams. He was busted for that, too. It's like ripping off food stamps when you don't need them."

"He's been doing that?"

"Probably. He didn't have a job, and nobody can live on welfare. Some people moonlight with a second job. Street punks moonlight, too. A couple of scams at the same time to supplement their income. Dope dealing was probably his specialty."

"You know a lot about him."

"I know his type. With his background, he could easily put small-time dope deals together. You'd be surprised how easy it is unloading a few pounds of weed on the streets. People want to buy it. They don't ask questions. Throw in some scams on the side, like welfare or ATD or food stamps, and Joey could make enough money to carry a bankroll like that."

"That little crook!" She was livid.

"He was streetwise. He knew how to survive out there. He'd been there before. He was only doing what came naturally."

"I knew he was a crook."

"You couldn't survive half as well as he did."

"You sound like you admire him."

"I knew where he was coming from."

"Is Dani involved in this?"

"That's hard to say. Dealers play games with other dealers, with pushers and smugglers. Some of those folks play rough when you interfere with them. They don't have to know you to hurt you. And if you've been messing with them, you're presumed guilty, and you have to prove your innocence. That is, if they let you prove it. Dani was close to that lifestyle. How close is a matter of speculation. Maybe you know how close that was."

She rose and walked around the desk to the sideboard and its bottle of Grand Marnier. With her back to me, she poured a large dollop in her snifter and gulped down more than she added.

I expected something from the gold woman with the Grand Marnier, but not the staccato of questions she unleashed. She wanted to know if the police might come to her house. She seemed annoyed that they might prowl her hallways and corridors. She said she had never been too keen on the creep. Dead, he was still causing trouble. She wanted to know if the Anatoles, especially Dani, could be kept out of this mess. She wanted to know how much that would cost.

"Are you trying to hire me?"

"Are you trying to collect from two clients?"

"Sure. Why not? Lawyers do it all the time."

She sipped more brandy. "How much do you charge?"

"Two hundred a day plus expenses." The back of my neck itched when I said it. I knew better than to scratch the itch. Pacific-Continental had charged two bills a day for my services, but they paid me closer to forty for the same services. I thought I was worth the money, but then I didn't have to pay it.

"That's a high price for blackmail."

"It's not blackmail. A private investigator exercises the same confidentiality that a lawyer does." Sort of.

"What do I get for my money?"

"That's hard to say." I tried to remember the non-

sense Pac-Con told potential clients. "You get confidential services, if it's possible, which is to say legally
permissible."

She hadn't been listening. "What expenses? You're
to keep Dani's name out of the newspapers, not solve
some imaginary case."

"Sometimes it costs money not to be published."

She opened the desk drawer. I tensed, wondering
what she would come up with. Absently she pushed the
pistol away and came up with the checkbinder and the
pen. "I suppose you need a retainer," she said.

"That would be nice," I said.

She was hiring me to keep the family name from the
headlines. I was the stooge who kept things under
wraps. The one who had to sling the red herrings. There
were a lot of old families like hers in the city. It's just
good PR to hire someone to put your name in the paper
and hire someone else to keep it out.

I could understand that. But why was she worried
about Dani's name appearing in print? It didn't make
sense. Nobody cares about such things nowadays, except gossip freaks, and nobody cares about them. You
can do anything you want nowadays, and five minutes
later nobody remembers you. Unless Catherine figured
Dani had been up to something best kept out of print.

Sure, maybe Dani smoked marijuana or had an abor-
tion or blew 'the family fortune on chrome-plated
vibrators. If I came across something like that, well,
that's what I was being paid for. I wouldn't turn
anybody in for that. But Catherine had to know I
couldn't cover up anything illegal. I wasn't putting my
ass in a sling so a client could come out smelling like
roses.

Of course Dani might not be involved in anything.
Maybe my presence upset her sister. A lot of people do
foolish things when they hear a private investigator's
been around. Some people, you don't have to do
anything, and already they're paranoid.

Catherine stared at the completed check. Maybe she
saw a written confession. Whatever was troubling her

was something bigger than a simple toke of weed or an interrupted pregnancy. It need not even be illegal, though the odds favored it. I tried not to think what it could be. Only a fool tries to second-guess a woman.

She resented giving it to me. "I hope I can trust your discretion."

I glanced at the amount. She had written it for five hundred dollars. One helluva retainer. I hoped it wouldn't be too hard to earn. I'd hate returning it. I just passed thirty and I'm tired of being poor. I asked her where Dani was.

"I don't know where she is."

"Where did she go after she left Joey?"

"She hasn't told me."

"Then you have seen her?"

"I told you I did."

"No, you didn't."

"Then I'm telling you now."

"How is she fixed for money?" I asked. "Does she have any of her own? Does she receive an allowance? Does she work for a living?"

"She has some. I don't know what she does with it, though."

"Could she have left town?"

"San Francisco?" Catherine hadn't heard me right. "She was born here. She wouldn't leave San Francisco. Maybe a vacation, but certainly not permanently." She was a golden pain in the ass.

"Could she have gotten a place by herself?"

"I don't know. She might've."

"Any friends she would've gone to live with?"

"Oh, you'd have to take it up with her."

"Does she have any friends?"

"Mr. Brennen, must you—"

I cut her short. "How did Dani do with the boys?"

"I don't follow you."

"Was she popular? Was she a wallflower? Did she chase the boys, or did they chase her? Was she a lesbian? How did she do with the boys?"

Catherine didn't flinch. She bristled. "I don't believe

in discussing my sister's sex life with a private detective."

"Why not? Nobody else'll have those qualms. They'll tell me every piece of dirt they can dream up, and they do dream up a lot."

"Do you like wallowing in filth?"

"Sometimes. Not always, mind you, just sometimes."

"You're such a noble man."

"I like knowing the truth, that's all."

"Does it show itself to you often?"

Like water, I sought her level. "Does Dani fuck a lot?"

"Fuck you." She drank a lot of brandy then.

The black maid came into the library and said Catherine's lunch was ready in the solarium. Catherine rose to her feet.

"One last thing. Does Dani have a car?"

"Yes, she does." She hesitated. "A 1955 Thunderbird. She has personalized plates. They spell out her name."

"D-A-N-I? On a '55 T-Bird?"

"Yes, that's right." And then she scooted past me and disappeared down the hallway towards the staircase.

The maid had stayed behind. Her eyes were sullen and bored, as if she hadn't reconciled herself to life among the honkeys. I could sympathize a little. I didn't like living among the honkeys, either. But then I felt the same towards every ethnic group. I like living alone.

"Is she always like this?"

The maid didn't smile. "Sometimes."

I sighed and tucked the check into my wallet. Catherine Anatole would be a difficult client. She was probably lying, and she certainly could sling the red herrings. Listening to her got me nowhere fast. I was glad I was leaving.

I followed the maid down the hallway. She was silent, showing me where to go. I didn't care. I felt like talking. "She's a real liberal," I said, eyeing the hedgerows of braided black hair. "I bet she even gives you a ride home after dark."

Over her shoulder: "I take the 22 Filmore bus home."

The maid faced me as she opened the huge door. She didn't say a word, just held open the door. Feeling stupid, I walked out into the chilly afternoon. A faint mist was already falling on Pacific Avenue. I buttoned my coat and pulled up my collar.

A Mercedes 450 LSC with a ski rack was parked in the narrow drive beneath a clump of Monterey pines. A bumper sticker said the owner was a member of the Far West Skiing Association. There was a current *turista* deal on a side window.

I went out to the garage and peered through a dirty window. The garage was empty, but there was an oil stain on the concrete. It might've come from the Mercedes. I found my car and drove around the block twice. There was no sign of a 1955 T-Bird with or without personalized plates.

I drove down Steiner Street to Geary Boulevard and jumped on the Skyway south. Just before the Army Street turn-off, the mist faded away, and dollar-sized raindrops pelted my hood. They made a drumming sound, like bullets falling from the sky, then trickled away into silence a few moments later. The raindrops steamed on the hood for a while, and then they too were gone.

CHAPTER 6

O. Anatole Fish Company was the last building on a dead-end street down in Butchertown. Back in the Forties, when San Francisco was butcher for the West Coast, there were scores of slaughterhouses down here. The city's health department closed down a bunch, and the rest moved east to Stockton, leaving behind a rat's nest of junkyards, food processors, mills and machine shops, freight transfer warehouses, truckstops, plastic factories and beer distributorships.

The building itself was old brick and butted against the China Creek piers. It was painted a bilious aquamarine, like the inside of a health club swimming pool, and a giant dolphin in drag leered down at me.

A loading dock for long-haul semis ran the length of the north side, and there was a parking lot for employees and visitors on the south. The lot was filled with delivery vans and pickups. I drove through it, looking for Dani's Thunderbird.

A black man in black rubber boots and a red rubber apron was hosing down the loading dock. Fish innards moved sluggishly with the jet streams of water. Gulls swooped and darted around him.

As I came nearer, he turned his hose away from my path and aimed it at a large gull a few feet away. The soaked bird raked its claws and feinted at the black boots. The man tried to kick the bird, but the dingy-feathered gull scuttled away, cawing and hissing its hatred.

"Goddam scavengers." He sprayed two others who fought over a fish head. "Flying rats. That's what they are. I wish this was a gun."

"Stop feeding them. They'll go away."

"I ain't feeding them."

"Where can I find the boss?"

"Upstairs." He gestured with the hose. "Elevator's over there."

A woman waited for the elevator. She was in her mid-thirties, a pale-cheeked housewife with average looks and not a hair out of place. Her black raincoat hung open, and she was brushing water beads from the cloth with short, choppy motions, as if they were dog hairs. Under the raincoat, she wore a black wool pantsuit with a cream-colored blouse. There was a pea-sized diamond ring on her third finger, left hand.

We entered the elevator in silence. There was no button for the second floor. She punched the third floor button, and the doors closed on us. She make a point of retreating into the corner furthest from me. I didn't think I was a carrier or contagious, but I suppose one can't be too sure nowadays.

She glanced my way and her eyes were nuggets of ice. There was no life in them, a vagueness behind them, a disinterest with the real world. I've seen that look before in downer freaks. It comes from viewing the world through a barbiturate haze. There were other explanations, too. You see those same eyes on topless dancers and starving waifs and female impersonators. Maybe she was trying too hard. Most women who wear black during the day are.

The elevator opened onto a brightly lit corridor. There were several doors on the right, and a single one on the left. The woman scooted through one on the right. I moved slower and read the letterings on each frosted window. I learned O. Anatole Fish Company was the sole occupant.

I came through the reception door. Two grizzled-faced men in mackinaws and jeans were shouting at each other. The receptionist, a middle-aged woman with short mousy hair, managed to keep them separated. She told both to sail up to the Standard pumps at Fisherman's Wharf. "Pick up your ice and five thousand gallons, then go fishing first tide tomorrow. And use those credit cards we gave you."

The sailors filed out together, grumbling and arguing over how to split up the last five hundred gallons of December's diesel fuel allotment.

She turned my way. "Can I help you?"

"I'm here to see Mr. Anatole."

"Riki's in conference right now, but if you'll just have a seat, I'll tell him as soon as I can."

"Riki? Is that his name?"

"That's his nickname. It's short for Orestes. That's what the O stands for in front of our name. He was named for Orestes Anatole, the founder."

"Was that his father?"

She shook her mousy hair. It made a rustling sound. "Great-great-grandfather. We've been in business since the Gold Rush."

"Orestes?" I didn't believe her.

"Orestes," she corrected. "Only nobody calls him Orestes. They call him Riki."

"Is Riki any relation to Dani?"

"They're first cousins," she told me.

A door opened behind us. A young man backed out of Riki Anatole's office. His long black hair was tied in a ponytail, and he had a stack of ledgers under an arm. He was all beef and solid. Fifty pounds heavier and a couple inches taller than me. When he turned and passed us. I saw he was Chinese and soft-featured. If I were a barkeep, I'd think twice about checking him against the legal drinking age.

"He's a big boy," I marvelled.

She looked over. "That's our bookkeeper."

"He should be a bodyguard."

"He's a fairy." She decided to be professional and

asked if I wanted some coffee. I said I'd read a magazine instead.

The magazines I found were about the fishing industry, of course. I opened one near the middle and started a technical article about tuna-seining. Within a couple paragraphs, I was rooting for the dolphins.

The outer door opened again. A young woman came in. She was dressed to kill, Thirties style, completely in red. A silk flowered blouse, calf-length flaring skirt, three-inch platform shoes. Her face was as pale as any kewpie doll. Curly red hair hung over her shoulders like a rouge Niagara. Red lipstick and red fingernails. And, in the midst of all that, standing out like a fire engine, were round eyes as cool and green as jade.

I set my magazine on the end table.

She asked if she could see Riki Anatole.

"And your business?"

"It's about a job."

"I don't believe we're hiring right now, but if you want to leave an application . . ."

"We met last night. He asked me to come by today."

"Was he sober?"

"What does being sober have to do with anything."

The receptionist didn't smile. "His wife's in the building."

The redhead's smile wavered. "He will see me, won't he?"

"Oh, I'm sure he will."

"Should I come back some other time?"

"That's up to you."

"I'll wait, I guess. I need this job."

"Whatever. And your name?"

"Gideon. Ruthann Gideon."

Ruthann Gideon came and sat beside me. She looked aroung for a friendly face. Finding none among the office help, she latched onto mine.

She was the kind of chick who's always cool and funky. The kind who considers quaaludes *très chic*. Her closets were probably filled with Thirties trash. Sex came both male and female. Four letter words were ad-

jectives. She probably swallowed diet pills with warm
red wine. She loved dancing till dawn, and staying in
would only drive her crazy.

I slumped in my chair and tried looking suicidal and
disgusted. She twisted and turned so her spine faced me.
I straightened and smiled to myself. I felt pretty good.
Young girls with jade eyes and no job can be poison
when you're carrying a thousand dollar bill.

The receptionist said Riki would see me now.

I woke from my reveries and went into his offices.

Riki Anatole rose slowly from his paper-cluttered
desk to give me a hearty handshake. "Pauline said you
wanted to see me." He was a big man, forty pounds
heavier than me, but not athletic. He was a hulk beset
by his own inertia. "Your name is . . . ?"

"Brennen. Michael Brennen."

"Please have a seat, Mr. Brennen. I don't have a lot
of time to talk with you. We're running a little slow
today. Our trucks are waiting to go out on deliveries,
and they should have been out this morning."

He was a good-looking man in his late thirties. Salt
and pepper sideburns and a wavy forelock that hid a
receding hairline. He wore a red blazer, dark doubleknit
slacks and white patent leather shoes. There was a Linde
Star Sapphire on his left pinky.

Maybe it was his smile, the way he extended his hand
to shake mine, or maybe just the red blazer and the
white shoes. He didn't impress me as the head of a
prosperous company. His type didn't run companies.
They were doormen or waiters. Then I remembered his
ancestors had done the hard work. They had founded
this company. Riki was heir to their fortunes. That was
his birthright, not anything he had earned.

"Business sounds pretty good," I said.

"This is my fifth Monday this week."

"That's a long week."

"And this is our slow season." He gave me a great big
grin. "It'll pick up after the New Year's."

I smiled back, sharing his good fortune. "I bet you
say that to all your creditors."

His hearty smile froze solid.

"I'm a private investigator."

"Pauline didn't mention that."

"I didn't tell her." I passed over my photostat.

He was too polite to glance at it. He gave it back immediately. Maybe the grey had always been in his face, hidden by rosy cheeks and big white teeth. Anyway, the grey was there now. Maybe he was afraid I was here to confiscate the books.

"And whose husband do you represent?"

The voice was husky and feminine and right behind me. It belonged to the woman in the black raincoat. She had been silent in the shadows until now. Now she stepped from them like a dowager queen approaching her court.

Riki's chin started twitching, a faint and irregular pulse. "It's not about me," he told her.

Her mouth made a small "oh," but no sound came. She walked around me to his side and took his forearm in a wifely gesture. The way she held it reminded me of tourniquets.

"Mr. Brennen, this is my wife Lilian."

"Pleased to met you, Mrs. Anatole."

"Why are you here?" she asked.

"I'm trying to locate Dani Anatole."

Her ice eyes flickered at the name. A smirk rode her tight mouth. "And whose husband do you represent?"

"This isn't a divorce case," I said. "I've got a message to relay to her, and that's all."

"You were hired to relay a message?" She was impressed. "It must be important then."

"Somebody thought so," I said.

"Have you tried Sausalito? She lives there."

"She moved out. No forwarding address."

"She must've worn him out." She smiled. "Maybe my husband knows where she is."

"I haven't seen her," he said.

"Haven't you?" she suggested.

"No, I haven't," he snapped. "Now that you've struck out, could you let us discuss this privately?"

If eyes could have thrown spears, Lilian would have been skewered on the spot. But self-righteousness is a powerful armor. She had won her point and could turn her back on us. Like a cat sometimes turns its back on a cornered mouse. She walked in a slow circle around the desk and busied herself straightening the watercolors on the walls.

Over her shoulder: "I need that money."

"What about your credit cards?"

"Magnin's won't accept them."

"None of them?"

"If they did, would I be here?"

Riki stared at his wife's spine. "I guess we better do something about that." He spoke softly, angered with her.

She walked to the window. "I'm sure we will."

Riki's face hardened. He wanted to say something to her, but he forced himself to face me. "Let's get outa here," he growled. He left his desk slowly, like a bear coming from hibernation, fighting inertia all the way.

I had just lit a cigarette. I stubbed it out.

We left his office and Riki told the receptionist he'd be on the first floor. Without waiting for a reply, he turned and walked into Ruthann Gideon. He almost wet his pants. He mumbled something, then scooted through the door.

He stalked the corridor like a man chasing down money. Swift and purposeful. And maybe that is the mark of a successful businessman, but I knew there was more he feared behind him than anything he might face ahead of us.

"I'm sorry about Lilian," he said.

I said nothing. Who cared?

"She didn't have to insult you like that."

I hadn't felt insulted. I hadn't felt a thing. I thought she'd been insulting him. Which shows how much I know.

"She's a good woman," he told me, "but she's always watching television. All those soap operas. She thinks life's a melodrama."

We hiked the corridor to the last door. It opened onto a narrow staircase. The brick stairs were steep and slick with dampness. We started down them.

"I understand that redhead needs a job."

He shook his head. "Goddam cunts nowadays. They're always trying to use you. You gotta hire them before they'll shack with you."

My sympathies went right to the redhead. So what if she collected cocktail napkins from the all night disco joints in the gay neighborhoods, waiting patiently for a slumming rock star to mistake her for a groupie? Anybody could get laid. Jobs are a lot scarcer than virgins.

"Why do you want Dani?" he asked. There was concern in his voice. More than I might've expected. He wanted no one interfering with her life. I felt, maybe wrongly, he could be trusted with the truth.

"She walked out on Joey Crawford," I told him. "He tried to hire me to find her for him. Try and bring her back to him. He died before I could refuse him."

"He's dead? Are you sure?"

"He gets air-freighted to Spokane tomorrow."

"He was from Spokane? I didn't know that." His mind was playing tricks on him. Doing what it could to avoid the scent of death. It lasted less than a moment. "How did it happen?"

"An auto accident on the Golden Gate Bridge."

"Dani doesn't know about it?"

"I don't see how she could. It only happened this morning. It hasn't made the newspapers, and probably won't, unless it's a dead day for news. It was a routine accident. She won't be notified because she isn't next-of-kin."

"Where do you come in?"

"I was hired to find her, bring her back. It's a little late for that now, but I hope I'm the one who tells her he's dead. I figure I owe Joey that much, and she should hear it from somebody soon."

"I wonder how she'll take it," he said to himself.

"How close was he to Dani?"

"I don't know. I didn't think too much of him, myself, but I wasn't sleeping with him."

"How long did she live with him?"

"Three or four years, I guess."

"Why'd she stay with him so long?"

"Why does anybody stay with anybody? Maybe she loved him. Maybe she got used to him. Maybe she didn't like living alone. Maybe he was the lesser of two evils."

"When was the last time you heard from her?"

"It should have been at Christmas. The family was supposed to have a little get-together, but right after Thanksgiving she called, said she couldn't make it. Which turned out to be a blessing. Lilian and I went to Hawaii. Our first vacation together in years."

"She left Joey about a month ago. Would you know where she went after she left him?"

Riki didn't know. "Have you talked with Catherine? That's Dani's sister."

"She said she doesn't know where Dani is."

"Oh. I thought she might."

"And why is that?"

"Well, she is Dani's sister."

"Are they close?"

He gave me a broad grin. "Catherine thinks they're the best of buddies. She's always talking about how close they are. But they couldn't agree on the sunrise."

"Were they rivals when they were younger?"

"Not in the usual sense. Catherine always wanted to live on a pedestal. The opera, museums, that part of Society. And Dani, well, Dani has her friends, and they're more important than any museum. In a way, she's always been the more social one. She likes to get out and meet people."

The second floor was storage space. Derelict file cabinets and outdated files and cannibalized truck engines. Spare fishing nets and surplus camping gear. Our voices had echoes among the dust.

A window looked down at the China Creek piers. Several trawlers were berthed alongside the brick building. A rusted black freighter under the Panamanian flag was being unloaded by longshoremen on the other bank. The Bayshore Freeway and the low rent tenements of Portolla Hill were background.

The mist was back, and I cursed it. I've always hated the rainy season. These coastal storms had no squalls, no noise, no lightning. They were long and monotonous. They came and sat on the city like paid weepers.

"Could she have gotten a place by herself?"

"She could've. She's done it before."

"When was this?"

"Four years ago, maybe five. She went up to Seattle. Just dropped out of college and went north. Didn't tell a soul, either."

"How'd you hear about it?"

"A postcard. 'Don't worry. I'm okay. See you around sometime.' "

"How did the family react to it?"

"Those assholes," he said. "They stuck their heads in the sand and acted like nothing happened. If you want something done, you have to do it yourself."

"What did you do?"

"I got on the phone, started calling everybody I knew up there. Friends, business associates, anyone. This buddy of mine, a salmon packer up there, he calls me back and tells me she's working as a filleter in his cannery."
nery."

"And you caught the next plane north."

"She looked like a scarecrow." The memory still horrified him. "Scabs on her legs, scabbies in her hair, her face all broken up, she had lost all kinds of weight."

She sounded more like a junkie than a scarecrow, but I waited for him to go on. I hadn't seen her for myself.

"She was pissed. She wouldn't even talk to me. Like I was pulling a dirty trick on her. Like I busted in on her. Busted in, hell, I'm her cousin. I did it for her, not for me."

"That's what cousins are for," I said.

"Yeah, that's what we're here for."

"Did she come back with you?"

"She said she was staying."

"How long was she in Seattle?"

"Six, seven months. Then she came back like she had never left. But now she's got this boyfriend in tow."

Everybody kept using the same phrase. *When Dani brought him home with her.* It sounded like a pet following a kid home, and now her parents let the kid keep the dumb animal. Well, he was a runt. Maybe the runt of the litter.

"What did you think of Joey?" I asked.

"You shouldn't say things about the dead, but since I said them to his face, I guess I can tell you. I hated the little shit. He wouldn't shake hands with me."

"How come?"

"Because I run a fish company. Shit, there's nothing wrong with fish. People like it, and its's good for them. And that little shit had been working alongside Dani in Seattle, gutting fish the same way this family's been doing for generations."

I had to admit it made no sense. "What about the rest of the family? How did they feel about him?"

"Nobody could stand him. Nobody except my wife. She got the biggest laugh outa him. Dani the snob hanging out with a punk like him. She and Dani never hit it off."

"What about Catherine?"

"Oh, God, the way she treated him. She'd ignore him until he got nervous. As soon as he started to fidget, she'd level her eyes at him in that high society manner of hers, until he stopped. Then she'd ignore him until he got nervous again. Then she'd start all over again. God, it was cruel. But that's Catherine. She can be such a cruel-hearted bitch."

"Would Dani go back to Seattle?"

"She might go anywhere. Lake Tahoe, maybe. The family owns some property up there. She'd be close to grandfather, too."

"When was the last time you talked with him?"

"Just after we got back from Hawaii. A couple of days before Christmas. We were coming in the door when he called. But he would've told us if she was there."

"He's the founder, right?"

"His grandfather was. My great-great-grandfather. But it's really his company more than anybody else's. He ran it the longest and built it up to where it is now. You know, he kept it going for forty years, just by himself."

"He's retired, I suppose."

"Sort of. He keeps his fingers in the business, but that's mostly to keep him busy, stave off death, so we humor him. He had a heart attack several years ago, so he sold off a lot of his holdings, set up the trust funds and moved up to Stateline."

"Trust funds? For his grandchildren?"

Riki had another hearty smile. "After the heart attack, he discovered he couldn't take it with him, and the state would grab most of it, so he decided to settle accounts before he croaked."

"So who owns the fish company?"

"Well, we all do. All the cousins, in one way or another. He divided the shares into thirds. He sold one third outright, kept a third for himself and gave us, his grandchildren, the last third in the form of trust funds. Plus, of course, the money he made from selling the first third."

"So you wouldn't have to spend the rest of your life scaling fish."

"Yes, well, that's right, I guess."

"How's Dani set for money?"

"That's hard to say. She's got some, probably not that much. A hundred grand, maybe a little more."

"You don't think that's a lot?"

"That's not much divided over the last ten years. She owns that houseboat, for one thing. A hundred grand doesn't do much nowadays. In fact, she tried borrowing from me recently. Some kind of investment, I guess. I didn't ask her about it, because I didn't have any to spare myself."

"When was this?"

"November. Sometime around then."

"Well, at least she doesn't have to work for a living."

"Oh, she had a job. She sang in a band for almost a year. More heart than talent, but she got paid for it."

"Where did she sing? Any special place?"

"She sang in a lot of places. But there was one joint she worked maybe two, three times each week. It was down near the airport. One of those cocktail lounges. Arroyo Grande. That's it."

"Does the band still play together?"

"They broke up. October? No, it was November."

"The guys in the band? Did any have names?"

"Oh, I never met them."

"Is there anybody else who might . . . ?"

"My kid brother. He might know."

"How can I meet him?"

"He works down in the smokehouse." Riki looked at me. "You've heard of smoked salmon, haven't you?"

CHAPTER 7

Workmen in red rubber aprons and black rubber boots. Filleters and slicers and gutters. Concrete floors and fish heads. Dirty windows and cakes of ice and puddles of water. Weight scales and fish scales. Long aluminum tables with running water and hosing troughs. Mounds of salt everywhere. Staple guns and cardboard boxes.

"We're the biggest in the Bay Area," Riki told me. "We supply most hotels, most restaurants, even the supply centers for the Armed Forces."

Fish defrosting in daylight. Malaysian shrimp and shark fin. Dover sole and rex sole. Flounder and abalone and salmon. Kippered herring and Alaskan lobster and rock cod and perch. Butterfish and ling cod and prawns. Kingfish and oysters and steelhead trout. Dungeness crab and malefic squid and mackeral and clams and scallops. Smoked salmon and salmon caviar.

"You can't catch all this by yourself," I said.

"Oh no." He had a hearty laugh. "We have a fair-sized fleet here, and most of the fleet's up north in Coos Bay and Vancouver, but we could never get all this from the sea, not even with a thousand boats."

He ran it down for me. Each company sent out its own fleet, and each fleet caught what the sea gave up. What a company couldn't catch, it bought from its competitors, who were in the same boat.

The Anatoles caught salmon off the Oregon coast, but bought Peruvian tuna for its Portland customers. The tuna fleet based in San Pedro bought Alaskan king crab for its Southern California customers. The Florida shrimpers sell to the Japanese who have shark fin, but need smoked salmon.

"There's competition, of course," he went on, "but a lot less than most industries. We have to cooperate or we lose our customers." He stopped in midstep. "Shit. I almost forgot."

A Chicano workman had caught his eye. The man was filling plastic bags with what looked like and rattled like slate shingles. The slate shingles were frozen fish fillets. When Riki hailed him, the man left his plastic bags. Peeling off his heavy gloves, the man left a trail of frost behind him.

"There's a case of Johnny Walker upstairs," Riki told him. "Dump it for me in my trunk, okay? Oh, and after that, five pounds of rex sole in freezer paper."

The smokehouse was dark and dry, a desert cave. We had to duck our heads to enter. Salt made a crunching sound beneath our shoes. There were long tables and giant fans, galvanized ovens and buckets of salt. The slabs of smoked salmon sat in their trays like red hot coals on a rack.

There was a large fish on a metal table. It was pink and grey and over four feet long. The eyes were shiny and lifeless, and the jaws gaped like a cry that's gone unanswered. There were rings of fresh blood around the jaws. I asked and learned it was a sturgeon.

"You awake, Jack?"

"Why should I be asleep?" Jack Anatole was a good-looking man and could be a knock-out in some crowds. Prominent cheekbones and a square jawline and white teeth. The Anatole eyes, pale blue and piercing, were almost hidden behind shaggy dark eyebrows.

"Brennen, this is my brother Jack."

"Pleased to meet you."

Jack was almost a decade younger than Riki Anatole, nearly my age in fact. He weighed as much as his brother, but he was the real athlete. He was huskier and taller, muscular as a swimmer with strong forearms and a thick neck. His legs were solid and his shoulders were broad. He looked like he could move quickly.

"Did I tell you Jack's a war hero?"

"I was no hero, Riki." Jack was patient, almost brotherly. "I was either sitting on my ass or making one outa myself. Nothing to be proud of, either way."

Riki objected. "He won a Bronze Star in Vietnam."

"I also spent time in the stockade," Jack told me. "He never talks about that. He's not interested in any time I might've pulled. Just the medals."

Riki was embarrassed. "You were cleared." His twitch was back again.

"The charges were dropped."

"Because you were innocent," Riki insisted. He was beginning to realize he couldn't salvage this situation. "It was an accident. It was years ago."

"I got a record." Jack's anger was sudden. "It's on my discharge."

I pulled up a stool and asked what happened.

"I was a gunner on a chopper," he said. "A guy fell out of it. A South Vietnamese colonel. They said I pushed him, but they couldn't get anybody to testify against me."

"You should forget it," Riki said. "It was just bad luck."

Jack said nothing. There was the hint of a smile on his face. His smile was bittersweet and sad around the edges, as if too many dreams had soured for him. I've seen that smile before on others my age. It comes from sitting in limbo. They feel obsolete before they get started. They're not waiting for their ship to come in. They'd settle for the tide.

The Chinese bookkeeper came in with a problem he couldn't solve and Riki went off into a huddle with him. While Riki scanned the ledger pages, looking for a solution, Jack watched his brother. There was little love in his eyes. Only a lingering sorrow. Theirs was an old argument, and one they would never resolve.

The bookkepper was huge. I couldn't get over his size. He was fifty pounds and a half-foot taller than me. Chitown keeps growing them bigger and bigger, as big as any race can be. If his ponytail had been a pigtail, the bookkeeper could have stepped from the old Tong alleys of San Francisco. With a hatchet, he'd be the stuff nightmares are made of. His eyes were rocks, hard and unswerving, black as night. But he only had eyes for Jack.

I'd seen sharp eyes like his before. Young male hookers plodding the midnight pavement around the Union Square hotels, rubbing their eyes to keep away the dawn, waiting for a fifty dollar sucker. Those of us who worked late night surveillance with Pac-Con always called it the garbage detail.

Jack was oblivious to those eyes.

"Is Riki always like this around you?"

His smile didn't fade. "Always."

"Maybe he's proud of his kid brother."

He sloughed it off. "It takes no brains to be a hero. That day I had no brains at all." From another man, it might have been a back-handed compliment. But Jack said it absently, as if he had said it before and knew no one understood.

I've known men like Jack Anatole before. You don't spend your army time as an MP and not know them. Or back down from them, either. The Vietnam Vet was the American Itch. The hero came home and found everybody chasing Patty Hearst. He could give his life for his country, but his country acted ashamed of him. As if everyone expects a vet to be two years behind everybody else. Why haven't they caught on yet?

"Maybe it was just bad luck," I suggested.

"Look at me," Jack said. "Baking dead fish for sportsmen. Slice them and soak them in brine, wash them in cold water and dry them in the air, then into the oven for smoking."

He toyed with a thread on his rubber apron. He tugged at it, and it came free in a long string. He looked at it as if it were the thread to his future, and dropped it quickly, as if his future frightened him.

He snorted. "I see the old guys, the union men, working on their pensions, and I see how wacked out they get. How do I know I won't end up like them? How do I know I'm not going to be doing this forever?"

Riki came back. He said he had to leave us for a while. We said it was no problem, but he apologized anyway. I waited until Riki left, then started again with his brother.

"Does Riki know how you feel?"

"It's my problem, not his."

"You can't talk with him?"

"He's turning forty next month," Jack said. "Forty can be hell when you're insecure."

"I noticed that."

"It's his wife. She loves his ass. She's like some crazy parasite, sucking him dry with love. She can't walk across the street without his help."

"His wife's upstairs," I told him.

"Lilian? Jesus, remind me not to go upstairs."

"You don't hit it off together."

He shook his head "The way she spends money, you'd think she was Jackie O. Sure, Riki's got some bucks, and he gets the rest next month, but if he were on his deathbed, you'd have to call I. Magnin's to get her to come home."

"Nobody's that money hungry."

"Let me straighten you. She doesn't chase money. She just spends it. She doesn't know where it comes from. If it weren't for Riki, she'd be on welfare."

"Doesn't she have any of her own?"

"She had some. She was cut off when they got married. Riki almost got cut off, too, but Grandfather spared him."

"They had marriage problems?"

"Oh yeah. She'd been married before, and it didn't work out. She and Riki were childhood sweethearts and she latched onto him like a barnacle. Nobody wanted them to get married, but they wouldn't listen. You can't fight a marriage made in heaven.''

"He didn't have much say in the matter?"

"That's about it. She swept him off his feet. He liked her well enough, but he never expected to marry her.''

"Is that why he chases women?"

"He doesn't catch them."

"Not ever?"

He had a sad grin. "Have you ever seen a dog on a leash humping another dog? That's how Riki chases women. He's just going through the motions."

"So why does he bother?"

"He can't get it at home." Jack's smile held more irony than humor. "She's turned to ice."

"She's frigid?"

"That's about the size of it. Some kind of psychological hang-up. He told me about it once. He had too many scotch-overs."

"So why does he stick with her?"

"He's got his reasons." Jack looked over, as if noticing me for the first time. "I forgot your name."

"Brennen. Michael Brennen."

"What are you doing here?"

"Looking for Dani," I said.

His eyes tightened. "Are you a cop?" He had old eyes in a young face. Cold eyes that had seen too much blood and death and violence. He had eyes that would die for friendship, eyes that make few new friends. A man would have to be a fool or a madman not to back down from them.

"I'm a private investigator."

He was wary now. "What do you want with me?" He had been too long in the stockade. He was toughening up.

"Whatever I can get. Probably more than you plan on telling me. It doesn't have to be the truth. Whatever you feel like saying, it'll be more than you plan to say."

"I want to tell you nothing."

"I can see that."

"Look, I don't dig somebody following her around,

trying to find out what she's been up to. Who gives you the right to interfere with anybody else's life?"

"I get paid for it. Sometimes I do it for nothing. This time around I'm getting paid to find Dani and I'm going to find her."

"Like hell you will."

"You're not very cooperative, are you?"

"Why should I be? I'm not following people around, prying into their lives, bugging relatives and friends, just so I can make a few bucks. Why should I help you?"

"Joey Crawford's dead."

He took the news well. Only his eyes made any movement. They flickered for an instant, then stilled like the ocean at night. "How did it happen?"

"Auto accident on the Golden Gate this morning. He was in the city, heading back to the houseboats. There was a car stalled in the right lane. He never saw it."

"Does Dani know about it?"

"Probably not. How close were they, anyway?"

"Oh, they were close," he said glumly.

"Why did she leave him?"

He weighed a ledger. "She thought leaving him was the only way he could straighten up." Jack looked at me. "Joey was bleeding her for money."

"Why did she stay with him so long then?"

He didn't want to remember. "He helped her out when she was in Seattle. This was several years ago. She had a lot of things on her mind then, and he helped her get her mind off them. She was grateful to him for that."

"D'you believe that?"

"Hey, she's my cousin. If that's what she wanted, I'm not going to tell her anything different. Maybe she thought she could make it work." His concentration was wandering.

"Tell me about her," I said.

"What's there to tell? She's my cousin. She's got blue eyes." He cast around for other obvious truths. "She has trouble keeping them closed when she's sleeping."

"Did you get along together?"

He bristled. "We get along fine. We grew up together. Went to the same high school, went camping together in the Sierras. We get along fine."

"Does she do a lot of dope?"

"That was in Seattle. That was years ago." He was vehement. "Sure, she was strung out pretty hard, downers and speed, but she's off dope these days. Just a little weed now and then." What he was saying sunk in. "Who put you up to all this? Where do you come in, anyway?"

"Joey put me up to his. I was his best friend."

Jack smirked. "He had no friends."

"That makes me his best friend." My eyes kept going back to the sturgeon on the long table. The long fish fascinated me. It was like a corpse in the morgue.

Jack saw me watching the sturgeon. "You said Joey was dead." He was tightening again.

"He wanted me to find Dani. It was his last wish, I guess."

"What do you expect from me?"

"Do you know where she is?"

He had the lazy smile all prisoners cultivate. "I wouldn't tell you if I did." He looked bored, but anxious men act the same way when they feel threatened. He'd probably be happer talking to a drill sergeant.

And then the fish quivered. A shudder ran down its spine. Its gills and jaws moved like a drowning man, and I thought, of course, a fish would drown in the air.

The quiverings and twitchings were just nerve spasms, reflexes, and all corpses do that for hours after death. There's nothing mysterius about rigor mortis. Still, I needed a cigarette.

I started to light up.

"You can't smoke in here. Health Department." He bolted upright from his stool. "Let's get outa here. I can't think in this goddam place."

I didn't mind. It had been hard talking with him over

the whoosh of the giant electric fans that dried the fillets of salmon. The sturgeon's eyes seemed to follow me. Its jaws quivered again, calling me back. I shut the door firmly.

The clowns from upstairs were on the pier. They were still hollering at each other, this time over whose trawler would sail up the narrow creek first. Their crews scurried, stowing gear. Behind them the rusted black freighter coughed, emptying black oil and water from its bilges into the bay.

The mist had thickened into a gentle rain. Those storm clouds from the Pacific Northwest were closer, changing into large purple ones. I figured I had ten minutes before the downpour began again.

Jack watched the sky, too. "This is the shits," he told me. "This weather won't let up, and the boats want to go out." He was still a fisherman in a seafaring family.

"You're sending them out, aren't you?"

"First tide tomorrow." He looked determined. "We have to send them out, even if it's snowing. We need the fish. Shit, we're supposed to be wholesalers, but all we've been doing is buying fish from every other fish company on the coast."

"Has business been that bad?"

"Business has been okay. It's this goddam weather that's been keeping us in. Two weeks since we sent a boat out."

A trawler lolled at the end of the pier. It was a big ship, nearly seventy feet long, and twice the size of the other Anatole ships. Workmen scrambled around her decks.

"Is that part of the fleet?"

Jack brightened. "She will be soon enough. The boys just finished overhauling her engines this morning." He thought of something. "Riki wants to take her out himself, see how she feels, but God knows when he'll have the time."

"Riki looks like he belongs in an office."

"Yeah, I know." He couldn't believe it, either.

"Some guys are like that. They got their whole lives in some office, but what they really want to do is play Marlboro Man."

"She looks like a fit ship."

"She oughta be. She's powered by a 275 Cat V-8. Her cruising range is twenty-five hundred miles. Seventy-five feet long. All the rest are thirty-footers, warped hulls and all."

"Do you still go out in the boats?"

"Oh no. I'm retired from the sea. Doctor's orders. I got a bullet through the elbow in 'Nam, and it acts up in bad weather. Like arthritis, only worse."

"That's a shame."

He didn't think so. "This is a dying business. Like sardines down in Monterey. They've been fished out for forty years, and they'll probably never come back. Anchovies are nearly gone, herring's just about gone, king salmon's weighing less every year."

Above our heads a pair of broad-winged seagulls chased each other in wide arcs over the narrow estuary, fighting for a piece of fishmeal one had scrounged.

"It used to be," he told me, "you could fish a school for two full weeks. These days you're grateful for two days over a school. And those goddam Russians, they got giant trawlers, whole fleets of them, dragging the ocean for a dozen square miles at a time. No, it's a dying business, that's for sure."

"The way I understand it, you have enough money—you don't have to do this unless you want to."

"Where'd you get that idea?"

"Riki. Something about trust funds and your grandfather."

"Hey, I'm doing this because I have to. Orestes, that's grandfather, he figured none of us would scale fish, not if we could help it, so he set it up so we collect only if we work. We don't and he cuts us off."

"How can he do that? You got your money. You can always drop out, can't you, and live off what you've already gotten?"

"But there's not enough money to live off of. The

funds are gradual. You get some every few years, whenever you reach a certain age. When you reach twenty-one, you get ten percent. You get another ten percent every fifth bithday after that, and the balance when you reach forty, if you've been working in the fish company. You only get what you work for. Orestes is always preaching self-reliance.''

"Self-reliance? More like locking you in."

He agreed. "That's why everybody hates him so much."

"Well, it's his money to give out."

He had no answer, and it pissed him off.

"What happens to the money if you don't scale fish?"

"It reverts back to him."

"Not to the other cousins?"

"He said he loves us too much for that. He said, if it didn't, that would promote Murder Incorporated. Like signing our death warrants."

"Like an insurance policy, right?" It made sense in a macabre way. The more cousins who died, the more money the survivors would get. But it was a gruesome way to view your family. "Does everyone get the same amount?"

"Oh no. His favorites get more."

"Why should they get more?"

"Because they don't need him."

"Oh yeah? Who are his favorites?"

"Dani and Catherine." He looked over. "Have you met Dani's sister yet?"

"Yeah. She's got a nice pad."

"Nobody else wanted it." He snorted his contempt. "She doesn't associate with the family much. We smell like fish."

"How does she get off not working?"

"When she hit twenty-one, her fiancé invested her share in Mexican imports. A couple of years after she married him, he's suddenly an asshole and she can't stand him, so she divorced him. But those import companies still make good money for her."

"How does she get along with Dani?"

"Their parents died when they were in high school. Dani took it worse than Catherine did. She went into herself, didn't come out for anybody. Catherine figured she needed another mother."

"And she took the job," I said.

"Dani just wants to live her life in peace, but she's always had to fight for it. Dani only wants to be left alone."

"How come she's grandpa's favorite?"

"Orestes spits in our eyes, everybody's eyes. We don't spit back, no matter what he does. Dani hates him just as much as we do, but she's never cared about his money, so she's never tried to appease him. That makes her look like her own person, and that makes her his favorite."

"That's crazy."

"No, it isn't. Dani left home and worked in a fish company in Seattle. She didn't use her right name and she didn't tell anybody about it before she went and did it. And she bought a houseboat when she came back. It was just coincidence, but she's always led her life just the way he wanted her to lead it. She's just the person he always wanted her to be."

"What did the old guy think of Joey?"

"Oh, he hates him." Jack was matter-of-fact. "Joey was a little shit coward. Orestes almost cut her off, just because she was living with him."

"Why didn't he?"

"She's his favorite. And he hates the rest of us more."

"Could she have gone back to Seattle again?"

"Maybe. But it wouldn't be like the last time. If she went back again, it would be a positive thing."

"Which means what?"

"The last time she split to escape. She needed to get away because everyone was pressuring her. It was tearing her apart." He stopped and doused his cigarette in the creek waters. He straightened like a man facing a firing squad. "You never stop pushing, do you?"

"Do you know where she is?"

He was amazed. "You're a leech."

"Do you know where she is?"

"No, I don't, dammit."

"Thanks. That's what I wanted to know."

Riki came up behind us. He carried a parcel wrapped in freezer paper. "Looks like the two of you had a good time." He turned to me first. "If there's anything else we can do, we'll be glad to do it, but we all have to get back to work now."

I stamped out my cigarette. "I get the hint."

"This is a holiday weekend," Riki said. "New Year's Eve and everything, and we're very busy. The trucks haven't gone out yet. They should've left early this morning."

We headed back towards the smokehouse, and the rain began pouring down on the piers. The two captains were cursing their crews, while the men scurried like hose-drenched seagulls.

"Did you learn anything?" Riki asked.

"A couple of things." I looked at Jack.

"There's nothing to learn here," Jack said.

I laughed. "There's one thing I've learned as a private investigator," I told him. "There's an infinite number of sides to every story. You don't expect to know every one of them. You settle for as many as you can get. If you get enough, you even know what's a lie and what isn't. It all comes together in a crazy pattern. Juggle the pieces long enough and the puzzle solves itself."

Jack hated my guts. "So what's that mean?"

"There was enough," I said. I told him I'd be seeing him again. Then I followed Riki from the smokehouse.

Riki sensed my thoughts. "He's changed a lot since Vietnam." He slumped his shoulders. "The army did that to him. He came back a volcano. It's always simmering beneath his skin." He sighed. "When he erupts, it's with the wrath of God."

"How stable is he?"

"Oh, he's gentle. Unless you say something that

strikes him wrong. He's just seen too much. If he could just look on the positive side of life . . ."

I turned and looked back. Jack was dialing out on the telephone outside the smokehouse. I wondered who he was callingm I hoped it wasn't Dani.

We cut across the plant towards an exit. Riki's step had quickened and his spine seemed straighter. Maybe it was the bustle of his employees. Maybe he felt more at home with them, or more in control. Maybe he just needed a lot of people near him.

We found the exit nearest the parking lot. The rain was coming down heavier now, and we were both silent facing it. Riki seemed to be wrestling with a problem, and I was just chicken to race the rain.

"This is yours." He passed me the parcel. "Enjoy it."

"What is it?"

"Five pounds of rex sole."

"Is this a bribe?"

His laughter was almost hearty enough. "Just good business." He tried being familiar with me. "I wish I could give you some of that Johnny Walker, but that's for tonight's party. I know how you private eyes like booze, if you know what I mean."

I knew what he meant. "Thanks for showing me around."

"Any time." He had pinned his problem before I had found my courage. "Do you think you'll find her?"

I didn't know. "Oh yeah."

"She's very independent," he said. "You might never find her if she doesn't want to be found."

"I'll find her."

"Well, I wish you luck." He shook my hand, told me again to come back any time, then headed back towards the smokehouse.

My car was on the leeward side of the building. I sprinted through the rain to it, jumped inside and rolled up the window I'd forgotten earlier, then stuffed the fish into the glove compartment.

Across the lot some Anatole fishermen and workmen

stood beneath a catering truck's awning. I ran over and ordered a cup of coffee and a patty melt. The boiling coffee tasted like motor oil. The sandwich came infrared warm. It tasted like plastic explosives. I dumped the sandwich and headed back to my car.

CHAPTER 8

I opened my vent, and a woman called out. I looked around. The redhead stood by the elevator doors. She called again and waved her hand in the air. I rolled down my window.

"Are you heading up towards Market Street?"

"Sure. D'you need a lift?"

"Oh, could you? Just up to Market?" She rushed from the doorway, her red skirt billowing in the breeze. Skidding between raindrops, she ran around to the other side and hopped in beside me. "This is awfully nice of you."

I told her to forget it. Damn my charitable hide.

"Oh, I can't wait to get home."

"You had a long day?"

"Well, if I don't get home and feed my cat . . ."

"Here. Hold my coffee for a second."

"Oh, where did you get this?"

I hit the ignition. "A catering truck. Help yourself."

She took a big sip. Then another. And another. When she passed it back, I told her to keep it. If she could drink it, she deserved it.

In my rear view mirror, a beige Coupe de Ville with a white vinyl top was rounding the corner of the Anatole building. It was the kind of car you'd see ten years from now cruising past the jazz clubs in the ghetto.

It picked up speed and whispered past like a ghost. Its windows were starting to defrost themselves, and I could see the outlines of Riki and Lilian Anatole. I put my car in gear and followed them out to Third Street.

The Coupe de Ville was doing fifty when it reached Third Street. There were few cars and fewer traffic lights ahead of him. I gave him a block headstart and followed at the same speed.

"How did it go in there?"

"I didn't get the job." She looked up from her coffee. "His wife was there." She frowned at the windshield. "God, she's a bitch."

"Oh yeah? What did she say?"

"She accused me of adultery. Right, adultery. Like I've been shacking with her husband for years. I only met him last night. I didn't know he was married."

"Where'd you meet him?"

"On Union Street. One of those disco places where the cab drivers take the tourists. He was the only guy who didn't make me feel like a piece of meat. He seemed lonely, like he had no one to talk to."

"But he was married."

"Yeah. A married man. Just what I need."

"D'you go there often? Union Street, I mean?"

"I'll never go there again," she promised.

Maybe she was different. Maybe staying in didn't drive her crazy. Maybe she wouldn't settle for any slumming shark in the Union Street ocean. Yeah, sure.

"Do you pick out your own clothes?"

"What's wrong with what I'm wearing?"

"A job interview isn't a disco party."

"It was the girl across the hall's idea. She thought maybe I could shame him into giving me a job."

"Then there was no promise of a job?"

"Let's just say I don't get to quit the one I have."

"It could have been worse," I told the windshield wipers. "He could've led you on, made you believe you could share the wealth."

"He's got that much money?"

"His family does. Which means he doesn't sweat rent."

"I didn't even know he was married."

I slowed for the China Creek bridge. Two high-pitched whistles came through the rain, followed by a third one at a deeper tone. A watchman left his shanty to lower a guardrail behind us.

"They must be going out," I said.

"Who's going out?"

I pointed over my left shoulder at the two trawlers dieseling up the narrow estuary. "The weather's supposed to change tonight, so the boats are going out fishing tomorrow."

"They're going fishing?"

"Right. Tomorrow. The first tide of the New Year."

She twisted in her seat. "Are you a fisherman?"

"No way. You'll never get me out on the ocean."

"Then you're a salesman."

"Self-employed businessman." Maybe I was. I didn't know.

Riki knew the city well. He stayed on Third Street, not jumping over to the freeway downtown. The freeway was probably bumper to bumper with this rain, and that made Third Street the quickest way downtown.

I stayed well behind him.

"You said you have a job. What've they got you doing?"

"I'm a babysitter," she admitted.

"Where do you babysit?"

"The hotels. I move from one to another, wherever a tourist needs me."

"Sounds like a drag."

"Oh, it's not so bad. Most of the hotels have closed-circuit movies on their televisions. It costs three or four dollars, and the movies are played all day. The folks I sat for yesterday, they paid for the whole day, and I saw *Gone With the Wind* three times."

"Was this job through some agency?"

"Yeah. Some agency. They made me a babysitter."

"Is there any bread in it?"

She told me. A nickel more than minimum. "And if you know any girl who needs a job, could you let me talk with her? It's not much of a job, but if I can find anybody else, I get a commission from the agency."

I didn't know whether to laugh or cry.

The headhunter hires a staff of temporaries. He pays them a nickel more than minimum wage, then charges the tourists twice that for their services. Then he gives his temps a commission if they locate any other suckers.

A hotel guest slips the bellboy a ten spot to find him a hooker. The hooker gives the bellboy a ten spot for calling her. The bellboy gives a fin to the bell captain for letting him work. The hooker gives twenty to her pimp for letting her work. And prostitution's illegal. Maybe it is, but sometimes I wonder if the Yankee slave traders ever gave their slaves a commission for finding new slaves. Not that I was much better off. I had worked for Pacific-Continental for forty bucks a day.

I glanced at the jade-eyed woman. She was busy unfastening her pierced earrings. "When did you get out of college?"

"A couple of weeks. . . . How did you . . . ?"

"What did you take up in school?"

"English."

"Good luck. No teaching jobs out here."

"That's what everybody keeps telling me." She sounded bitter. "Well, if I can't teach anywhere, maybe I should be a cocktail waitress."

"Cocktail waitresses make good money in this town."

"I know. That's why I'm on a couple of waiting lists already. You know, there's a two year wait for openings at most hotels." She twisted my way again. "I was talking with one girl, and she told me she makes seventy-five bucks a night. Winter or summer. And that's for a six hour shift. That's real good money, isn't it?"

"That's real good," I admitted. I get that much weekly from my unemployment claim.

The rain was coming down in sheets. My car rode

roughshod over the chuckholes, and for a while, it was touch and go. Ahead, the beige Caddy splashed through the puddles, hydroplaning, splashing up gullwings of water. Somewhere far away, an ambulance began its mournful song.

It was twilight in the city. The moment before the streetlights and the headlights come on. When the night begins with rush hour and after-Christmas shoppers, and the car radio fills up with static and out-of-town stations.

"Why are we following that car?"

"What car? Following who?"

"That one. That beige and white one."

"I'm not following it."

"Oh yes you are."

"I'm a private investigator," I confessed.

She didn't speak for two blocks. "I've never met a private detective before."

"Investigator's a better label." I waited for her to tell me how interesting my work must be. That's the one-liner most women seem to latch onto first.

She was filled with surprises. "What are you working on?"

"I can't tell you."

"I won't tell anybody. I promise."

"I can't tell you. It's embarrassing."

"You don't want to tell me, do you?"

"That's right."

"Well, do you work for an agency?"

"Not any more."

"Then you have your own agency."

"Maybe I do." I mulled it over. "Against my own better judgment."

"You don't want to be a private eye? I mean . . . you don't want to be a private eye? Then why did you go into it?"

"I had a wife and two kids to support," I told her. "I grabbed the first job I could find."

"Oh. You're married."

"Divorced."

"Who did you work for? I mean, would I know them?"

"You might. Pacific-Continental."

Recognition came to her eyes. I wasn't surprised. Pac-Con is one of the biggest, and there's a Pac-Con office in most phone books. Everybody sneaks a look at the Detective Pages. It's like looking up dirty words in a new dictionary.

"You left them? Why'd you quit?"

"They asked me to leave."

"Oh. What did your wife say about it?"

"She asked me to leave."

We neared Market Street. The policemen and their shrill traffic whistles. A trolley lumbering down Mission, waddling beneath its overhead electric lines, scattering sparks as it crossed from one line to another.

"How about if I drop you here?"

"Where? Here?"

"You can catch a bus easily enough."

She sucked some air, but she said nothing.

I pulled behind a city bus as it was pulling out. The fumes from its exhaust put a cloud of soot on my windshield. The rain and the wipers tried their best.

I glanced at Ruth Gideon. Her eyes pleaded like a dolphin on a sandbar. Jade-eyed women are hard to resist. But I wasn't running a cab service, and she was a luxury I couldn't afford. "There'll be a bus along in a minute."

"Are you sure?"

"You'll be okay." I wondered why I had to play detective.

She got out, glanced around, and didn't believe me. I couldn't fault her eyesight. This was no-man's land. Neon and no expectations. Down where the pawnshops are numbered by the dozen. Barber colleges and liquor stores. Tattoo parlors and bus stations. Cheap hotels with fire escapes like facial scars. I wouldn't want to wait for a bus here, either. Even the pimps and the hookers stay away from Market Street. They cruise further north towards the Hilton and Union Square. They knew lowlife when they saw it.

I caught up with Riki and his wife on Kearny Street. They were moving slowly, wedged in the maze of homebound commuters. My lane was the left-turning one, open more often than theirs. I stayed a full block behind them.

Sometimes there comes to rush hour an unearthly silence. Pedestrians going about their business. Cars running as silent as any submarine. No brakes screeching and no overbearing horns. No cursing and no shouting. No newspaper hawkers. No fender-benders, and every engine seems tuned. The complete absence of city buses. No cable cars rattling up or down the hills. Just the patter of rain on wet streets. When all the elements mesh and everything is routine.

You know the shit's about to hit the fan.

A pregnant woman jaywalked in front of my car, determined to cross in the middle of the block. I stopped an inch shy of her. She gave me the finger, as did the guy behind me. Then a Volvo stuttered into my lane. The clown wouldn't pull over and he wouldn't pull ahead. Finally I passed him, almost nailing a mail truck double-parked with its emergency flashers on. By the time I could swing out and around, I had a full cab behind and an empty one ahead.

I drove up to California Street, then circled the block. But the beige Caddy had disappeared. I'd done it again.

I came back by Montgomery Street. It was soggy with calendar sheets. They'd been thrown New York City style from the office buildings of the Financial District, an annual year-end celebration. But there were fewer pages on the pavement this year, just as there were more high rises with windows that never open.

I circled Mission and came up Third. I saw her before she saw me. She was crouching in a telephone booth, trying to hide from the wino who was rifling the coin changer in the next booth. I tooted my horn until she turned my way. Her face unfroze and she scrambled from the booth to my car.

"Oh, thank God! You came back!"

"I couldn't leave you here, could I?"

We headed out into the Market Street traffic. Market Street still celebrated Christmas. Christmas music blared from the pawnshops, and the liquor stores were all brightly decorated. The Salvation Army played *Adeste Fidelis*, and gospel shouters, with their bugles and their Bibles, still preached the birth of Christ. Chinese school-girls, giggling and serene, compared their sugarplum visions at the bus stops.

But Christmas on the streets has little to do with the Season of Giving. It's a con game, and the suckers never get what they deserve. The poor people of the streets, those goddamn trusting fools, splurge on gifts to show their relatives and friends how well they did last year. A sign of their prosperity.

I wasn't any different. Christmas brings out the lonesome in me, too. Last June I put two little boy outfits on lay-away, just so they'd be paid off by Christmas. No, I wasn't any different, just luckier. This week I didn't have to pawn my own presents to repay my loans. I could thank Joey Crawford for that.

"Where to this time?"

She gave me an address on Sutter Street. A residence club she had found her first day in the city. The jobless lived in those places until they found work or went away.

"It's godawful," she told me. She shook her head, as if she could sweep away the club's filth and its lunatic residents.

"Why don't you move?"

"I can't afford to. No yet, anyway."

"Are you broke?"

"Oh no." But she fell silent too soon.

"How about if I buy you dinner?"

Her head swiveled like a chair.

"A real meal," I said. "No a hamburger joint."

She was hesitant. "I promised the girl next door I'd be home early tonight. She's making supper for both of us."

"Okay. Not tonight. Some other night."

Her voice was softer. "I'd like that." Almost too soft.

"How have you been eating, anyway?"

"I've been fasting."

"Was that her idea? The girl across the hall?"

Ruthann glanced out her window.

"Are you trying to lost weight?"

"That's right," she said.

Aw Jesus. The little dunce. She didn't have a brain in her head. She was fasting to lost weight because she had no money. I decided to cough up for more than one decent meal.

"What's she like? The girl across the hall."

"Why should you care?"

"I don't. Forget it."

She glared at me, considering obscenities, then turned away, deciding not to. "She's from Iowa, Ohio, one of those states. She's been here a couple of years already. She's been cooking for both of us because I've been out jobhunting or babysitting. I get fried rice and Mexican beans with every meal. And I'm getting sick of fried rice and Mexican beans."

"Can't she cook anything else?"

"Yesterday she burned a batch of marijuana cookies."

"Remind me not to eat her cookies."

Ruthann went silent. She shook her red hair, fluffed it once or twice, then turned to stare out at the rain. I was mystified, so I counted the traffic lights ahead.

"Maybe I shouldn't have told you," she said.

"About what? Burnt cookies?"

"No. Not that."

"Well, what is it?"

"Marijuana's illegal in California, isn't it?"

"Sorta. A hundred dollar fine for an ounce or less. But nobody gets excited about it." And then it dawned on me, and I started laughing. "You mean, you shouldn't have told me about the cookies because you're afraid I might turn you in. Is that it?"

She stared at the rain, said nothing. She thought I was mocking her, and now she was upset. When I spoke to her, she wouldn't answer. The car was quiet until we reached her residence club. It shook when she slammed the door.

CHAPTER 9

There was an empty space in front of my apartment building. I was in it in a flash. I locked my doors and went inside and took the elevator to the third floor.

I headed right for the refrigerator. It wasn't Mother Hubbard's cupboard, but the hoarfrost had an echo. I found a sirloin strip steak cowering behind the Best Foods mayonnaise. The little sucker didn't have a prayer against a private eye.

I cut it into long strips, then stuffed them down the neck of a liter carafe. I poured a couple of inches of brandy after them. I threw in a lit match for a kicker.

After a while the blue flames died. I tugged out the strips of brandy-soaked steak and threw them on a plate. With dinner in one hand, a beer in the other, I went to the living room. I plugged in the tv and switched it on.

The Treasure of Sierra Madre was on *Dialing for Dollars*. Fred C. Dobbs was splashing water on pyrite, thinking he had found the Mother Lode. And the doorbell rang.

I turned down the television, swigged a little beer for mouthwash, then went to peep through my landlady's peephole.

A man in a business suit was outside. He was small

and frail and Chinese. I couldn't decide if he were the oldest man in the world, or a cadaver who'd escaped the crypt. He was scrawny, boney, shrunken with age. Like many old people, it was a struggle for him to stand. Any minute he could fall into a fetal crouch. His spine was curving forward, like a hunchback's, and his shoulders were sloped. They looked as if they might someday touch, if they didn't collapse before then.

He pressed my doorbell again. He was impatient. Maybe he was afraid he'd croak before I answered the door. Then his body had a spasm, like the land above the faultline, and his face twitched with pain. I couldn't have him on my conscience, or on my landlady's carpet, so I opened the door.

"I am Tan Ng. May I come in please?"

He came ever-so-slowly through the doorway, hesitant and arthritic, using an umbrella as a cane. He had a thin chicken neck and his face was gaunt with loose skin and wrinkles. There were hollows where his cheeks should have been, and harpy lines flared down his nose. His hair was blizzard-white, but not as white as his skin. It was pale and anemic. Too pale for most Chinese. So anemic, he'd need a touch of jaundice to pass.

"I do not wish to disturb you."

"Don't worry. You're not." I noticed his shoes. There was a raindrop or two on the shiny leather, but they weren't as wet as they might be. Tan Ng had come by car. Maybe a chauffeur was downstairs.

"It is still raining," he apologized.

"Let me take your umbrella."

He shook it out, splattering water on my face, then passed it over. I set it upright and open to drip on the carpet. His watery eyes roamed my apartment like a Methodist minister casing a massage parlor. Nothing escaped him, not even my supper. "You were preparing supper?"

"Just a little snack."

"I am sorry. I must leave. I will come back later."

"Forget it. If it doesn't bother me, why should it bother you? In fact, I'll set a place for you. You look like you could use a good meal."

He didn't like that. "I have eaten."

Tan Ng came on like a career woman. Prim and proper and fastidious. Asexual, almost, determined not to show emotion. His every word was precise and slightly minced, as if he had spent time listening and imitating career women and their speech. But there was one answer. Like career women, the Chinese have to work twice as hard to get half as far.

I wondered what his game was. He might be as old as Chinatown, but he had spent too many years here to be playing the poor immigrant. His business suit was too well-tailored, even for his ill-fitting body. And his snowy hair hadn't been trimmed in any Chinatown shop. It had no cowlicks, for one thing, and it was neater, fuller, more rounded than the butchers of Chinatown could ever do. His teeth were just crooked enough to be real, and white enough for fluoridated water. He was thin enough for malnutrition, but a lot of rich folks diet and exercise for that look.

"Something to drink? Beer, wine, coffee, tea, brandy . . ."

"A little tea perhaps."

I went into the kitchen. The old man followed at his own pace. Gingerly, he sat at my kitchen table. He watched me set the kettle on the gas stove. I let him select his own favorite. He chose jasmine, and I turned up the heat.

He still stared at my tea rack. "You drink Po Lee tea?"

"My wife bought it."

"It is from the Mainland."

"If it's good enough for Nixon . . ."

"Please do not mention his name. He has done us much harm in Chinatown."

"All of us, my friend. Not just Chinatown."

"Had he never set fool in Peking, the Maoists in our city would have no say in community matters. Because of him, they now feel their voices should be heard on every street."

"Why should you care?"

"I am a lawyer. I have many clients in Chinatown. They are old and I try to help them live within the white man's world."

"Where do I come in?"

He faltered, then caught the thread. "I have been in practice for many years. More years than you have already seen. And I have been a good citizen all those years."

"I'm sure you have."

"On occasion, I have associated with the police department. And on occasion I have asked their assistance. But a matter has arisen that is not easily remedied by their intervention. That is why I wish to hire you."

I had to laugh. "Who put you up to this?"

"You are a private investigator?"

"Until May, I am."

"What happens then?"

"My license comes up for renewal."

"But you will renew it."

"Maybe. I haven't decided."

"I trust you will."

I made a small noise. It was a fifty buck fee. Fifty bucks was fifty bucks. "Who told you about me?"

"Oh, you were well-recommended."

"I'm not in the phone book."

"I would rather not say."

"And I can name a hundred better than me."

"Please do not humble yourself. I have been to many detective agencies over the years and have spoken to many men in your profession. You have been highly recommended."

"I'm not even in business for myself."

"That works very much in your favor." He tried being conspiratorial. "For one thing, you are not associated with the police department, as most others are. I have need for a man who is not already connected

with them. A man who will not run to them when the
journey becomes difficult.''

"I don't break laws for anybody else," I told him.
"If you want them broken, go break them yourself."

"I am not asking you to break any laws, or ignore
anyone who is breaking them. I merely wish that you do
not feel alone in their absence."

"You're a slick old fart," I marvelled.

He chose to ignore that. "I need a solitary man. A
man not indebted to his employers. A man who would
tell me more than he would tell them. I do not want my
problems discussed by secretaries."

"That's no problem," I said. "I got fired from my
last job."

He understood. "Many clients must be very difficult."

"That was no client. My company fired me."

"Was there good cause?"

I thought it over. "Yeah."

"May I ask why you were fired?"

I thought it over. "No."

"Oh." He was shook. "Are you working on a case
now?"

"You might say so. And you might not."

"May I ask who your client is?"

What the hell. "That's privileged information."

"Perhaps if I knew his name . . ."

"It's none of your business."

He didn't take offense, dammit. He took a hundred
dollar bill from his wallet. "Again I ask you. Who is
your client?"

I stared a while. I wanted to laugh. This had to be
someone's idea of a joke. I wondered where Sidney
Greenstreet and Peter Lorre were.

He folded away the bill. "You are a most ethical
man. You will not reveal your client's name. You
respect that which is confidential. A man who refuses to
be corrupted."

"Nobody's asked me yet," I snapped.

"There is another reason, of course. Your fee."

"I charge the same as anybody else."

"And how much is that?"

"Two hundred a day plus expenses."

He didn't flinch. One point in his favor. "There are some in the city who charge more."

I decided to re-evaluate my charges at the earliest possible opportunity. Maybe that would keep the clowns from my door.

"Perhaps it is negotiable," he added.

"You want a rebate on the fee?"

"I simply mean it may be more negotiable than for others who have more expenses, such as office rent, electric bills . . ."

" 'Fraid not. And if you're thinking about tax breaks, you better forget it. I still declare my income tax, which means you would have to, too."

"Do you carry a gun?"

I stopped breathing. "Am I going to need one?"

"Oh, no." His face flushed. "What kind is it?"

"Oh, it's an ugly old thing."

"You do not wish to say."

"I can't see where it's any of your business."

He sat back, satisfied. "No, Mr. Brennen, there are not many like you. Perhaps you are the man who can solve my problem."

I had to say one thing about the crazy old man. He thought fast on his feet. He was determined to prove I was qualified faster than I was trying to disprove it.

I should have kicked him out then, but, like the cat, curiosity's going to be my downfall. Unlike the cat, I had only this life. "What's your problem?"

"A valuable jade necklace has been taken from my house. I wish to commission you to have it returned to me."

"When was it taken?"

"Sometime earlier this week. I cannot be more precise, for I was in Sacramento when it was taken. When I returned to the city, I discovered it was missing."

"And the police?"

"They have not been informed. The Chinese community has learned much from the white man's police force. We prefer to handle our own affairs and we hope they will do likewise."

"Have you heard from the thief?"

He thought that was funny. "I do not expect his call."

"I mean, the ransom. Have you received any note, any instructions, on how to pay it?"

"That will be your job. You see, the young man who took the necklace did not take it for ransom. Nor do I believe he will try to sell it. There is no place where he can sell it. It is too valuable for most dealers, and he is too intelligent to try the pawnshops."

"You know who took it?"

A faint smile. "I believe so."

"Why did he take it?"

"Revenge can be the only reason."

Oh boy. Start at the beginning on this one. "Do you have any photographs of the necklace? Maybe a drawing? Any detailed description will do."

"They have never been necessary. It is one of a kind."

"What's it look like?"

"Do you know the symbols of the Chinese zodiac?"

"A little. Twelve animals, right?"

"Yes. There is the dragon, the hare, the tiger, and so on. Certain craftsmen of the T'ang dynasty arranged the twelve animals in order from clasp to clasp on this necklace."

"A charm bracelet, right?"

He didn't like that. "It is a necklace."

"How old is it?"

"The T'ang dynasty . Around 700 A.D."

"And the value of the necklace?"

"Oh, it is priceless."

"Sure. How much is priceless?"

He pursed his lips. "It could well be part of the Brundage collection."

That was priceless. I asked what estimate the insurance company had placed on it.

He was hesitant, reluctant to speak.

"It is insured, isn't it?"

"When something is insured, it becomes noticeable."

Oh boy. "You mean, it's a hot rock."

"I do not understand."

"First you swiped it, then it was swiped from you."

"No, no. This is not stolen property. There is a bill of sale. It was brought from the Mainland. That is why it is uninsured."

"Who had it before you?"

"That should not be your concern."

"It is. Who had it?"

"A childhood friend from Kwangtung province. When the Mainland fell, his family came with mine to Taiwan. They had much art, valuable art. Some pieces were sold, but most were stored until the family could return to the Mainland. The government of Taiwan said that day would come."

I saw where he was heading. "And then Nixon went to Peking, right, and they started selling off their collection."

"He accepted my offer," Ng said.

"How did the necklace get here?"

"Oh, it had a very difficult passage."

"Was any customs duty paid on it?"

"Perhaps at a later date."

The rock wasn't hot, but it was lukewarm. No wonder the old man didn't call in the cops. "What would the police say if they knew that the necklace came into the country the way it did?"

He hadn't thought of that. "It would be most unfortunate." He startled himself. "They would take it away from me."

"That's right. And who has it now?"

"His name is Lim Song." He spelled it for me. "His family is also from Kwangtung province. His father has been a close friend for many years. I arranged for the youth to come here from Taiwan. He was enrolled in the public school system. Later, when he could read and write English, I offered him a part-time job with my law firm. It was a lowly job, and the pay was little, but for a young man of diligence and enterprise, there could be much achievement and steady promotion.''

I had heard that line before. That meant the kid had no papers, that he was an illegal alien, that Tan Ng brought him into the country to work eleven hours a day, seven days a week, for a buck less than minimum. Without his green card, the kid didn't have a prayer. It was a coolie's job, pure and simple, and the kid had been caught in an ugly trap. Maybe Tan Ng got his start with the railroads.

"What makes you think he took it?"

"After he had been with my firm for several months, it was brought to my attention that he had a police record. I investigated and found it was true. I had little choice. I dismissed him.''

"What had he done?"

"He was caught taking items from the retail merchants in Chinatown.''

"A shoplifter?" I didn't believe it. "A shoplifter?"

"Is that not enough?"

I didn't think so, which shows you how much I knew. "How long was this crime spree going on?"

"Two years. He has been in San Francisco that long.''

"Just how old is Lim Song?"

"He is seventeen years old.''

"And the jade's been missing since he was fired?"

"That is right.''

"How did he know about it?"

"I told him to consider my home his home. The necklace was in a display case in my study. On several occasions, I have found him in front of the case. It is very beautiful. He was moved by its beauty.''

"And so he took it, after you fired him.''

"It could only have been Lim Song. And that, too, is

part of your commission. I must know if he did take the necklace. If he is not the thief, I must make amends to his father."

"And if he did?"

"I wish merely its return."

"What if you have to pay for that?"

"I will pay it."

"How much will you pay?"

"Whatever is necessary."

"You know, shoplifting isn't much of a crime, especially when the criminal's only seventeen. When he's older, his juvenile record is sealed . . ."

"We Chinese are a law-abiding race."

"Yeah. Sure. But what else has he done? Maybe not illegal things, but things which still upset you. Maybe he's got a prostitute for a girlfriend. Maybe he hangs around the mah jongg houses. Maybe he smokes a pipe of opium now and then. There must be something else."

"It is his choice of friends," Ng confessed. "They are from Taiwan, from Hong Kong, but they do not work. They say, why should we work, there are no jobs, there are no good jobs, you do not pay us well enough."

Understandable. "Go on."

"I do not know where they get their money, but they have fast automobiles. The back of the car is high above the ground, much higher than the front end. They drive so fast through Chinatown."

I knew the type. All-American Boys. Sorta.

"Will you help me, Mr. Brennen?"

I lit a cigarette and thought it over. The old man didn't like the threads of blue smoke that came up, so I cracked open a half-inch of window. The smoke was sucked outside, where it mingled with the monotonous rain.

"You'd better find yourself another boy."

"You are refusing me?"

"Oh yeah."

"Perhaps for two hundred a day plus expenses."

"There's no way I'm taking on this case."

"You wish more money?"

"I don't want your money. And I can give you a dozen reasons why I shouldn't even be listening to you."

"May I hear those reasons?"

"First, there's the hot rock. That necklace came into the country illegally. You didn't pay any customs on it. That's smuggling, and Uncle Sam's a poor sport about smuggling. Which means I can never call the cops, no matter what kind of trouble I get into. Secondly, the necklace isn't insured, so nobody can even prove it exists. Part three, there's Lim Song. You've just about admitted he's an illegal alien, that you brought him here to be your own personal coolie, yet you fired him for shoplifting, which is chickenshit. Maybe he took the necklace, and maybe he didn't. Maybe he still has it, and maybe he doesn't. But there's no way I'm going into Chinatown to mess with a Chinese juvenile delinquent."

"He is just a young man."

"No, he isn't. He's a Tong."

He was bewildered. "There are no Tongs."

"Yeah, I know. They were just a turn-of-the-century fairy tale. Nobody uses that word nowadays. So the Tongs must be gone. Well, maybe you were one when you were younger, and maybe there are no more Tongs around, and maybe they're gone for good, but anywhere else Lim Song would be just another punk. In Chinatown he's a punk in Chinatown, and what the punks in Chinatown got is gangs. They're either Maoists, or part of the Chinese Mafia. Either way, whichever he is, it's no dice because, if I can help it, I'm not getting caught in that crossfire."

Tongs. Punks. Street gangs. Juvenile delinquents. Hoodlums. Gangsters. The awesome horror of murder is somewhere among all those labels. The proof is in any morning edition. A yellow-skinned high schooler is gunned down by a slant-eyed sharpshooter. The next night, a week later, a month or two goes by, then an ignition bomb explodes against a firewall, splattering blood and flesh and skin and bone through a maroon GTO.

No race differs much from another when it comes to revenge and greed, when it comes to slaughtered innocents and murder. Each race kills close at home, its own people, and no blood is exotic when it collects in puddles on the streets. The Chinese are no special breed.

"There could be a bonus for recovery."

I had to laugh. "It's not a question of money. You want me, a white man, to follow Lim Song, a yellow man, through his own neighborhood, a yellow man's ghetto, and pretend nobody's gonna notice. I've got to wonder if you're sober."

Tan Ng was silent for a long time. He looked like I felt the day my wife confronted me with my infidelity. Finally his watery eyes found mine. "Is it because I am Chinese?"

He had lost me again.

"Is it because I am Chinese?"

A while before I answered. "It's not because you're Chinese. It's because Lim Song is Chinese."

He rose from his chair. For a shrunken old man, he stood tall, with dignity. "I am very sorry you feel this way." A red and gold packet came from his pocket. "A small token for your trouble."

"You don't owe me anything."

"I have stolen your time. Time is most precious. It is a jewel in a man's life. No man should give freely of his time, when another man can pay him for it."

He went the way he came. Slowly and hesitantly. And every step must have been hell, for every step was a baby's step. I'd have carried him by the armpits, if it hadn't been for his fierce dignity.

When the elevator finally swallowed him up, I went back to my dinner. But I was too wound up to eat. I pushed away my plate. The old man had thrown me for a loop. He had a great little speech. Well-rehearsed, too, but I didn't buy it. God knows where he came from, what his game was, why he had chosen me. Maybe he thought he could get away with this silliness. Maybe I was supposed to see through this little charade. I didn't understand why it had to be me, but I had a feeling he had some wolves he wanted me thrown to.

The sound was down on the television. I stared at the silent movie for answers. The movie was almost over. A dust storm in the ruins ouside Durango. The gold had gone back to where they had found it.

I pulled out Tan Ng's packet. It was the size of a small thank-you card. There were florid designs on each side. A firebreathing dragon and a tiger with golden fangs.

The Chinese call these packets "lucky money" and give them to their children and grandchildren during the weeklong festivities for Chinese New Year.

I opened the packet. A folded one hundred dollar bill was inside. So much for the movie. I went and put my dancing shoes on.

CHAPTER 10

The Arroyo Grande was a cocktail loucge down in the older half of South Airport Highway. It was surrounded by freeway on-ramps, car rental agencies and commuter flight motels. Like most of its neighbors, it could have been a bowling alley.

The barkeep was washing glasses. He was a small man with bushy eyebrows, no hair on his head and a sunken forehead. He looked like a shaved Neanderthal. "What'll you have?"

"How about a Millers?"

He shrugged and went to the cooler.

The only other drinker in the lounge was a man at the other end of the bar. He was busy mooning over a row of shotglasses. He could have been a thirsty conventioneer waiting for the next flight out, or a traveling salesman too cheap to flag a cab into the city. His face had the pinched look of a man who had seen no way out.

I had expected a raised stage with a few upright microphones, some speakers maybe, or even a set of drums left over from last night's show, but there was only a jukebox playing a country and western ballad. The box shimmered with pastel lights, and the bare spot in front of it was probably somebody's idea of a dance floor. A little crepe above the bar mirror was the only concession to Christmas, and a few cheap New Year's Eve decorations hung down like scalps.

The keep brought a cold bottle. "A buck'll do it."

I gave him the money. "That sign up there says Dancing Nightly."

He looked at me. "We got a jukebox."

"I thought you had a band."

"We got no band." He rinsed more glasses. "They quit a month ago. Didn't give us two weeks notice, either. Just called up and said they weren't coming in no more. That's why we got the jukebox. What do we need a band for, anyway? Only costs us money."

It made sense. You didn't need a band to work this dump, to soothe the losers here. If the band were any good, they'd brighten lonely hearts. The bar didn't mind losing a band. That cut costs and kept the suckers stewing in their brew.

A middle-aged woman with broad shoulders and no chin came from the back room and looked over the twilight trade. She looked like she wanted to spend New Year's Eve elsewhere.

I asked if Dani Anatole was around.

He stopped the faucets. "What do you want with her?"

"I heard she worked here."

He narrowed his eyes. "How'd you know that?"

"A guy told me. He said she was working here, so I thought I'd drop by and say hello. She does work here, doesn't she?"

"She don't work here no more."

My face dropped. "And I drove down here for nothing."

His brows arched. "Where you come from, pal?"

"Sacramento."

He felt like talking. "She was in that band that quit on us. She was the singer." He looked down. "She can't sing for shit."

"She can't be that bad."

"She ain't gonna be missed none, that's for sure."

He didn't look at me when he said it. He sounded like cuckolded love talking.

"How long was she singing here?"

"About a year, I guess."

"About a year," I groused. I set my half-empty beer on the bar and glowered at it. "I must be getting soft."

"You shoulda been here last week."

"I shoulda been here last week. She's been here a year, and I shoulda been here last week. What was I suppose to be doing here last week?"

"She came in last week. Her and that Chinaman."

"A Chinese guy? Is that her old man?"

"He's just the drummer, as far as I know. That's why they came in. They were picking up their last checks."

"And when was this again?"

"Last week. Day before Christmas. Davey Huie. That's his name. He played the drums in her band."

I asked if he had her address.

The woman without a chin stepped from the shadows and shouldered her way past the barkeep. He hadn't noticed her, and he almost jumped through his skin. "What do you want her for?" she asked. She had a voice like a cat being sandpapered.

"I want to see what she's been up to."

"You wouldn't be her boyfriend, by any chance?"

"I didn't know she had one."

"She sure does. He calls here every day about her."

"If he's got her," I asked, "what's he calling for?"

The barkeep told her she talked too much. She gave him a go-away look, and he buttoned his lip and went to wash ashtrays. It must have been an old story between them.

"Maybe you are him." She tried being sly. "Maybe she don't like you no more. How do you know her, anyway?"

"I knew her back in college."

"You knew Dani in college?"

"I think we're talking about the same girl." I pulled out my wallet and showed her the print Joey Crawford had sent me through the mails.

Her face soured like green apples. "That's her," she regretted admitting. She still couldn't believe it. "She went to college?"

"Yeah. Mills. Over in Oakland."

"That school's for rich girls."

"Her family's loaded."

"Then what was she doing here?"

I shrugged. "Maybe she needed the money."

"What makes you say that?" Her face said she trusted only money and that she'd never seen enough.

"Everybody needs money." I gave her a grin. "Maybe she was slumming." I hadn't liked her when I met her, and she hadn't improved with age over the last couple of minutes.

But she wasn't listening, dammit. She was lost in thought, digesting the news. I figured she was planning some way to get Dani's family to donate to her pension. I didn't wish her any luck.

The woman wanted to talk. "Every time she got a check from us, she made us go over the books again. Just so what we took out for Uncle Sam matched what the books said."

"So what?" I wouldn't trust this shrew, either.

"What'd'ja mean, so what?"

"Uncle Sam's got big teeth," I told her. "When he bites, you feel it. Nobody wants to give him more than a mouthful."

"It was more than that." She cleared her throat. It sounded like the bile had backed up and wanted out. "We paid them union scale, and we never did that for no other band that played here."

"They belonged to the union," I suggested.

"No, they didn't," she said.

I held up a hand. "So they got paid what they should have, and they didn't have to pay union dues. There's no right-to-work laws in California. None that I know of, anyway."

"They had a contract here for a full year."

Now that was unusual. The Bay Area had more bands per acre than places for them to play. And Dani's band had been here for a year under contract. Yet she sang average-to-lousy, and the band couldn't have been much better. It didn't make sense. "How did they get that?"

"You ever seen a b-girl wheedling drinks at the front bar for the customers?" She had picked up a set of keys somewhere, and she rattled them impatiently against the varnish. "She did that to the boss, and that's what got her that contract."

I wanted out from her green apple ways. "You got her address?"

She made up her mind. "It'll cost you five hundred bucks," she told me. "That's what she owes the lounge here. She don't show up for a full month, then comes in saying she couldn't make it because there's this guy following her. She gets her check, then bums five hundred bucks off my old man. Maybe you're the guy that's following her. Well, that's what it's gonna cost you for that address."

The keep had wandered back. He caught the last exchange. He snuffed his cigarette out in an abalone shell ashtray. "She was broke." His eyes flickered between us. "That's why she borrowed the dough."

She ignored him. "You ask me, she's a masochist. She likes men who beat her up, put bruises on her face and hands. Now, what kind of man is that?" She was staring at me.

"She fell down a flight of stairs," he told us.

"That's what you say," she said.

He looked like he was choking on cigarette smoke.

"She's a real hungry woman," she told me. "She's just about a stomach when it comes to men." She didn't like the sound of it, even. "A stomach."

"That's not true, Merle." His voice was softer than velvet. "The poor kid's close to nervous exhaustion already, without you always picking on her."

She waved a thumb his way. "My old man is a sucker for blue eyes," she sneered. "Maybe I should get contact lenses. Maybe he'd give me five hundred bucks once in a while."

He bowed his head against her voice, like a man with an umbrella before the rain. "Lay off her, will you?" He rubbed his forehead. His knuckles were bulging. He looked like he wanted to erase the sight of her.

"Five hundred bucks," she hissed.

"I'll get it back," he snapped.

She hadn't forgotten me. "All those hippie chicks in Sausalito, they're all the same," she went on. "So long as they ain't pregnant, so long as their old man ain't around, they're on their backs, got their legs in the air, stepping on ceilings."

"You're ruining her reputation," he argued.

"What reputation? Only difference between her and a prostitute is prostitutes got sore feet from walking around all night. All she ever did was stand in that corner there, flashing those blue eyes at any man dumb enough to sit up close."

He was mad enough to tremble. "That's enough, Merle."

"What's enough?" she sneered. "I seen her doing it. Maybe you was too busy tending bar, but I seen her. I seen what she done."

He was disgusted. "You got a big mouth."

"They went outside," she told us. "Only they went out separately, so nobody'd notice them. Out there in the parking lot, steaming up the windshield. One of them vans painted up like a French whorehouse."

"Why don't you shut your goddam mouth?"

"Who says it was free love? You saying it, old man? What did you know about her?" Her key ring rattled loudly, violently, out of synch with her ramblings, and she had to raise her voice to overcome their clatter. "Maybe free love ain't so free. Maybe she gave nothing away for free."

His face was glowing. "I told you to be quiet!"

"Maybe she don't owe five hundred bucks," she said. "Maybe she paid it back in trade already."

He grabbed her by the forearm and shook her violently. Her keys rattled like a cable car climbing uphill.

"You lemme go, you bastard!"

He gripped her tightly and stared into her face. She tried biting him to get away, but he shook her like a hound shaking fleas. Then, without releasing her, he shoved her into the back room. The door closed behind them.

There were loud voices. Then, nothing.

The barkeep came back alone. There was more sadness than anger behind his furrowed brows. This had been another in a series of pyrrhic victories.

He saw me and went the other way and started uncrating some cases of imported beer. He looked up at the drunk. "What's wrong with the jukebox?"

The drunk focused. "Nothing's wrong with the jukebox." His eyes were quiet and lifeless. His words slithered out like an old whore from between the sheets.

"That song keeps playing and playing."

"I played it five times," the drunk moaned.

The keep asked him where he was from.

"Back East. Detroit. Murder City, USA."

The keep nodded, as all barkeeps do in the twilight hours. "I was afraid the box was broken." He counted the row of shotglasses. "It costs a lot to fix them."

"Nope. Just me. Just the way I feel."

I got up and went across from the keep.

"You need another beer?" He didn't want me around.

I asked him for the Chinese drummer's address. He wrote it down on a cocktail napkin and gave it to me. It was off Clement Street in the Sunset District of the city.

"She ain't living with the Chinaman."

I turned back. "You know who she's living with?"

"The guy that plays the rhythm guitar."

"You got his address?"

"Yeah." He used another napkin.

"It's a houseboat," he told me. "Over in Sausalito."

I tucked the paper away. I think I thanked him.

"When you see her . . ." But his hope had fallen with his face. "Forget it. It wasn't important."

"I'll tell her you said hello."

"That's good. Tell her I said hello." He thought of

something else. "You want I should say you were here?"

I said it was up to him.

I left the lounge and found the on-ramp. I was a mile down the Bayshore Freeway a couple minutes later, fighting the last round of rush hour. Traffic moved at its normal speed, but the rain made a difference. Not exactly bumper-to-bumper, but the holes were few and far between. Changing lanes was impossible. I turned the radio louder to drown out the wipers on the windshield. The radio played a song about moving to Mexico. I was trapped in the slow lane on the freeway.

CHAPTER 11

There was a bedroom light onboard Dani's houseboat. I went down the gangplank. The tide was in, and the boat lolled at the end of its lines. A rubber hose extended from a porthole. A steady stream of water came from the hose into the bay. And a shadow flittered across the frosted bathroom glass.

I gripped a railing and pulled on the aft lines until the houseboat slipped near enough so that its tire fender rubbed against the slip. I slipped aboard without a sound. The craft drifted back to the end of its lines. Small waves played pattycake on the hull.

I went to the front door. The hinge screws were out, but the deadbolt had been slipped. Someone didn't want to be disturbed. Not that a burglary on New Year's Eve in an uninhabited dwelling was likely to be discovered.

I still had to get inside. Maybe through the skylight.

The roof was an easy climb. The latch to the skylight was clasped inside by a clothespin. I jiggled the skylight with my fingers, and the clothespin fell to the living room carpet. The latch lifted easily, and it was a short drop down.

The living room looked like Moving Day. The stereo system sat on the floor by the door, alongside the melon crate of albums and the portable tv. The cable spool and the hatchcover table were beside them. Most plants and

113

ferns had been taken down from the rafters, but a few still swayed like pendulums on their macrame ropes. The paperbacks were stacked in boxes, and the rug was rolled tight as a joint. The bamboo shutters were still up. They'd be the last to leave.

The night visitor was busy in the bathroom. From his heavy breathing, he was a hard worker. He sounded like an asthmatic after a mile race.

I peeked inside the bathroom. A bulkhead had been removed, and a man had his head in the bilges. His upper torso and both arms were wedged in the gap. The man in the bilges wore brine-soaked tennis shoes.

The bathroom was a mess. The floor was soggy with bilge water and its disgusting inhabitants. The brass towel racks were gone, and even the fuck books and the *Penthouse* magazines sat in a small pile by the bedroom door. A rubber hose snaked from the bedroom to the porthole, and I could hear running water. I had a hunch the waterbed was being drained.

I went and stood behind Alex Symons. He suddenly grunted success. His hand snaked up from the bulkhead and dropped a discolored plastic baggie in a water puddle. The baggie was water-tightened and filled with flowers, leaves, sticks, stems and seeds.

Joey's private stash. Maybe a pound's worth. Its absence had bothered me this morning, though I hadn't known it at the time. I'd been searching for contraband when I came up with cigarette papers.

Joey had been dealing. The CHP found none on him, which meant he'd just finished selling some wares. He had to have more. At least his own stash, if not some for future customers. Even if it were only weed, it had to be hidden somewhere.

Alex began to edge his body from the hole.

I kicked a foot out from under him. He went sideways, and his other leg went off-balance. Cursing and swearing, he caught himself and tried boosting himself up. He wanted to know who the hell I was.

"I just came back from the Arroyo Grande."

I kicked his other leg out, he went the other way, and

his feet churned crazily. His other reflexes worked fine. Bitching and yelling, pissing and moaning. His free hand waved the air behind him, and he tried to stand, to back out of the hole.

"You didn't say you were a musician, too."

I grabbed his heels and shoved. He went deeper into the bilges. He tried kicking me as he fell forward, but his heels swung through empty air, and he only went deeper.

"A little sneak thief, that's what you are."

I grabbed an ankle and tried stuffing him in sideways. I knew it wouldn't work, but it kept him off-balance. I think his hair touched bilge water then, for he let loose a shriek the devil wouldn't touch, and his one free arm and both legs thrashed like pinwheels.

"Does your little actress friend know you're a scavenger?"

He tried to shout, but it came out muffled.

I pulled him back by the belt. "I can't hear you."

"He's dead! He don't need it!"

"Dani might need it," I said.

"Fuck her!"

"It's not nice talking like that about a lady."

"Lemme outa here!"

"I thought you liked her."

"I hate her! Lemme up!"

I dunked and hauled him out a couple of more times, then took pity on the mired man and grabbed both ankles and pulled him out. He came free looking like hell. He dripped greenish salt water and small sea critters. His shirt, neck and shoulders were coated in green slime, and across his face were dirt marks where he had rubbed against the inside of the bilges.

As his feet touched ground, he tried spinning on me. I stepped aside and kicked a leg out from under him. He fell flat on his face in a puddle. When he tried getting to his knees, I planted a foot on his butt and pushed. He lurched forward, smacking his head against the bathtub. I pressed my foot on the back of his neck. He resisted, so I pressed harder.

"You hated her?"

"Yes! Yes! I swear it!"

"Yet you shared your boat with her. That makes you out a liar."

"I'm not lying! I hate her!"

"Yeah. Sure. And cops are allergic to coffee."

His hand snaked around and tried to pull my other leg. I shoved down at him, then took my foot from his neck and stomped on his hand. He shrieked until the devil wouldn't have him. My foot was already back on his neck.

"She's been staying with you, hasn't she?"

"Oh God no!"

"Her mail wasn't at the houseboat."

"Hnnn." He gasped for air. "So what?"

"Somebody had to be saving it for her, or collecting it, or forwarding it to her. If it had been Joey, he would've known where to find her. So it figures she was getting it from the mailbox, sometime between the time the postman came and Joey went out for it."

"Maybe she came by herself . . ."

"Maybe. But it had to be checked every day, and how would she know she'd be in the neighborhood every day, unless she were living here on the houseboats. Right under Joey's nose."

"That doesn't mean she's been living with me."

"It points a finger in your direction."

"She could be living with anybody out here."

"But she knew you. You saved her life, remember? And how could a girl like that forget a guy like you?"

"Where do you figure in all this?"

"The first time you met her, you were screwing her."

"That's a lie!"

I pressed harder on his neck. I heard a small bone crack like a knuckle. He moaned. I eased up the pressure. "In my book, you're the liar," I said.

"I didn't fuck her until the party!"

I had him. "When you saved her life. Sure."

"I did, man, I did."

"Sure, you did." I lifted my foot a few inches, then

slammed it down again. His head jerked like a puppet called to task. His teeth jarred the linoleum. "Where is she now?" I demanded.

"I dunno! I swear it!"

"Okay. How long was she here?"

"A month. She left Christmas Day."

"Where did she go?"

"I don't know. I swear I don't."

"You haven't seen her since?"

"I'll kill her if I see her."

Interesting. "All right. You can get up now."

I removed my foot and stepped back. He lay for a moment without moving. Then, gingerly, he pressed his fingertips against the floor and started to do a push-up. He managed to get to one knee, then the muscles in his back tightened.

He was going to try me again.

As he started to make his move, I kicked his butt, and once again he flew into the bathtub. His head made a bell-like sound against the porcelain. His lungs collapsed with the impact, and he whooshed out air like a bellows.

"Move slower," I said. "I get nervous easily."

His back to me, he slowly got to his feet. I sensed, rather than saw, his shoulder blade tensing again. He wanted to about-face me.

I slammed him hard while he was still off-balance. He clutched at the shower curtain as he fell against the rim of the tub. His feet flew out and he flew forward, tearing the curtains from their rings. They fell with him into the bathtub.

I picked up the plunger and held it like a club. "I told you to be cool." Then I dropped the toilet lid and sat on it. "This time you stay down. And no more lies, right?"

He fingered his lips. They weren't bleeding. That seemed to surprise him. He looked up, nodded his assent. There'd be no more lies. At least not tonight.

"When was the first time you met Dani?"

"Right when they moved in. I bought her a drink. I told you about that. But I didn't score. She's a pricktease. She'll sweet talk you, then tell you she's got an old man.''

"She wanted to stay with Joey?"

"Yeah. And she gave me a raincheck."

"A raincheck? For what?"

"There's no such thing as forever, is there? People are always leaving their lovers. Maybe she'd leave Joey, and then maybe I could use my raincheck."

"And you fell for that?"

"Yeah. I fell for that."

"And no hard feelings?"

"Like I told you before, if she's not the one, she's not the one. Women are like the tide. They come and they . . ."

"I know how it goes." I shook out a cigarette. "What happened that you got a raincheck?"

"Her old man walked in on us."

I grinned. "I see why you two never hit it off."

Alex went sour. "Joey used to xerox dollar bills and pass them at the coin changer in the laundrymat. He was nothing but lowlife."

"How long before you and her were good buddies?"

"A year or so. Yeah, that's a long time, but Joey always bird-dogged her. We just said hello and left it at that."

"When did she start her band?"

"Her band? It was never her band. She said she could sing, so we let her. We figured a chick gave us a little class."

"So you hired her."

"She didn't want money. She just wanted out of the houseboat once in a while."

"You worked the Arroyo Grande, right?"

"That goddam dive."

"They paid scale, didn't they?"

"We bought our own drinks, too. That manager's a goddam ape. Knuckless dragging the ground. He looked like the Missing Link."

"He got along all right with Dani."

"Yeah. Any time she needed anything." He stewed in

his anger. "Treating him like a human being. A goddam ape, that's what he was. That's how come we got a year-long gig there."

"Did Joey ever come to the gigs?"

"At first he did. He'd sit down front, mooning over her like a groupie. And she sang right to him. It was disgusting."

"Why'd he stop coming around?"

"Because she had no room to mess around. He kept her straight, when he was there, but if he didn't show, she'd find somebody else, some turkey from the sub-urbs. The turkey would buy her a drink, and the next thing you know, she'd come up stage and say she'd be missing the next set, so why don't we sing around her."

"Where'd she go with the turkey?"

"The parking lot, mostly. Maybe over to his place, if he lived close enough. Maybe the hotel across the street. She knew how to cover her tracks. Like she never walked out the front door with a guy, and never walked in with one. She always made it seem like she was just going out for fresh air or a cigarette."

"Were you messing with her then?"

"No way. It was strictly business."

"Your decision or hers?"

"Both of us."

"How long did that last?"

He hesitated.

"You're not going to deny you did?"

"No. No. I did. That party was the first time."

"How much of what you said is true?"

"All of it, man, all of it."

"I don't buy that. I didn't when I heard it. For one thing, you said you were on deck taking a leak, watching the lights of the last ferry, when Dani ran past you."

"That's the truth."

"You also said it was last spring. May or June, right? But in the springtime, the last ferry stops a half hour before sunset."

"You checked with the ferry?"

"I didn't have to. I live in the Bay Area, too. I know how those ferries run. I've been on them once in a while. I've played tourist in Sausalito, myself."

"I got it. Sherlock Holmes. That's who you are."

"Can it. When was the party?"

"Thanksgiving. The day after. Thanksgiving Friday."

"And how much of what you said is true?"

"Most of it." He glared at me. "Hey, I did save her life."

"You said you didn't go to the party."

"Yeah, well, ah . . . ."

"But you were there, weren't you?"

He admitted he'd been at the party.

"How did you save her life?"

"Just like I told you. She ran past me. I went after her and I caught up with her on the Bridgeway and pulled her out of the traffic."

"Why was she running?"

"Joey went berserk and tried smacking somebody. She was stoned, she was freaked out, so she took off running. The only thing she could think to do."

"She wasn't committing suicide?"

"She didn't even see the traffic out there. She was just running for the sake of running." The edge of his mouth tried to curl into a smile. "She tore her blouse on the fence. Her titties were hanging out." He had forgotten me. "She took my hand . . ." He remembered me.

"So you took her back to your boat."

"Hey, she wanted me real bad."

"What about your date?"

"She was passed out." He caught my eye. "It was that kind of party."

"Did Dani stay all night?"

"No, she went home. I thought that was the end of it. Well, it wasn't. She came over the next morning. She wanted to talk."

"Did Joey come with her?"

"Naw. She told him she was just gonna tell me to get

my date. She was still passed out on the couch. She had slept there all night.''

"What did Dani want to talk about?''

"Leaving Joey. He was doing a lot of speed. He was going downhill fast, and she didn't want to go downhill with him.''

"What was your advice?''

"I told her to think it over. If she wanted to leave him, she'd better leave him. And if she needed a place to crash, she could stay with me until she found a place of her own.''

"When did she move in?''

"A week later.''

"Weren't you taking a chance? After all, Joey was living down the boardwalk.''

"I didn't think she'd stay the whole month.''

"Why'd you let her stay so long?''

"Those blue eyes.'' He wasn't ashamed to admit it. "Her eyes were so big, she couldn't keep her eyelids closed. Even when she was sleeping, her eyes would be open.'' He shook his head. "They were spooky, I tell ya.''

"Why did she stay so long?''

"She thought it was the safest place to hide. You know, like that story by Edgar Allen Poe. You hide where everybody's looking.''

"Oh, was that her reason.''

"I told you she was a bitch.''

"Maybe you thought she had another reason.''

He didn't answer me. He pretended to be fingering his head for blood. Maybe he had fallen for the blue-eyed girl. Maybe he hadn't, and he was putting on a show.

"Maybe you thought she cared about you.''

When his eyes met mine, they were brittle and carefree. "She never cared about me. I admit it. But I didn't know that, not when she came on board. I didn't know what a bitch she was. And she used me good.''

I played a long shot. "Is that why you hit her?''

"I didn't hit her." He gave me a filthy look. "She fell down the stairs."

"On a houseboat?"

"Hey, that's what she told me. She was over at her sister's house, and she fell down the stairs. Maybe she tripped on a roll of money. How should I know?"

"Did you kick her out?"

"She took off on her own. Christmas was the last time I saw her. Christmas Day. Merry Christmas. I got back from the 7-Eleven store, and she was already gone. Just moved out with all her stuff. She even took my stash."

"So you thought you'd liberate hers." I picked up the plastic bag of grass and hefted it again. At least a pound inside. "You got carried away, right?"

"She can afford it."

I asked him who Davey Huie was.

His eyes blinked. "He was our drummer. Why?"

"He picked up your last paycheck from the Arroyo Grande. Dani was with him. You think she's staying with him?"

"No way. He's a lush."

"Where does he live?" I listened to his recitation. It matched the address from the Arroyo Grande. I shrugged. "Maybe I'll give him a call sometime this weekend."

Alex seemed to relax at that.

I stood up to leave. He shifted in his bathtub, and his eyes brightened for the first time. As soon as I left, he could climb out and stand on his own two feet again.

"One last thing. Put everything back where you found it. Because if you don't, the heat'll be on you so fast you won't know what hit you."

"She won't miss it."

"I would. And I fight dirty."

I watched him. Reluctantly, he agreed. I turned on my heel and left the houseboat. No sense asking for another skirmish.

I waited outside behind an overturned dinghy. Someone nearby had their fireplace going. Woodsmoke mixed with the fog, and a little mist drifted down the waterfront. The houseboats were almost sinister in the fog. The creaking of weathered wood: the boardwalk, the pilings, the houseboats. A hundred vessels swayed not as one with the currents and cross-currents.

Five minutes later I went back onboard. I didn't bother trying the door. I clambered up the roof again and lifted a half-inch of skylight. A great way to spend New Year's Eve.

Alex came from the bathroom. He had spent the time cleaning himself up. He went to Dani's telephone and started dialing. I couldn't see the numbers, but it was a local call, either San Francisco or Sausalito. He let it ring for a few seconds, then started talking.

"It's me. Right. I'm over here on my boat. Brennen's just left, and he's still after Dani. Listen to me. He wants to talk with Davey. How should I know? Listen, Davey'll be down at Jardin's Saloon getting loaded. It's New Year's Eve, remember?"

Before Alex hung up, I slid down and hiked to my car. I threw Joey's pound of grass in my trunk, then headed off towards the freeway and the bridge.

The holiday traffic crawled across the bridge, and storm clouds and fog haloed their headlights. Red flashers on the span announced there were four south-bound lanes. They also announced CAUTION and AC-CIDENT. A northbound Maverick had sailboated into a southbound Plymouth.

I huddled in the far right lane. The Golden Gate Bridge is a lethal weapon. There is no retainer wall be-tween the lanes of traffic, just small rubber pods every dozen feet. The newspapers call it Blood Alley.

I thought about Joey Crawford's last ride.

Then there was a clear patch in the clouds. Over the eastern railing, the beacon flashed from Alcatraz. Six seconds later it flashed again. Then the winds off the Pacific brought more fog through the Gateway.

Maybe Joey had been lucky. Maybe he had gotten off cheap.

CHAPTER 12

From the Bayshore Freeway, which rises on steel girders above them, the San Francisco flats are just another commercially zoned district of single-storied buildings whose rooftops carry billboards for cigarettes, scotch whiskey and economy cars.

When you leave the safety of that freeway, drop down beneath its elevated security, you've entered the place where no city has a skyline. The flats are warehouses, train sidings, loading docks. Vacant lots and dead-end streets, broken glass and peeling paint, locked doors and towaway zones. Even the muggers steer clear of the flats. There's no business for them here.

But there is a nightlife under the overpass. A few neighborhood bars where night people by temperament or circumstance can find safety among their own kind and live out their fantasies. When the sun goes down, the nightcrawlers come from the long shadows to these lice-ridden firetraps. Nothing from the daylight world can threaten them there, for there is only loud music, dancing partners, chemical madness. They come to dance. The chemicals make it bearable.

Jardin's Saloon was the raunchiest roadhouse in the flats. It slouched at the intersection of Monterey and Missuola streets like a hooker on an off-night, a babyshit brown building catercorner to a welding supply company.

There was enough loud music coming through the walls to scare off any fire inspector dumb enough to be slumming in this part of town. And the blast of hot air that came from the swinging doors stunk of sweat and cigarettes, wet clothes and booze.

I took a deep breath and ducked inside the funhouse. The transvestite working the front door was too busy buying a handful of amy nitrate spansules from a black man in pink pants to check me against the legal age for alcohol. Yeah, this was not the daylight world, and it made sense best on chemicals.

The band was screaming *Gimme Shelter*, and the bodies on the dance floor glistened and smelled. Half looked like runaways from the Vacaville mental wards, and the others like Quentin graduates. I was the only joker in the house with a full set of teeth.

There were bikers and bearded ladies, leather boys and acidheads. Dragqueens in short skirts and juice freaks getting fixed on warm red wine. Tenderloin trash and hippie nookie. Methadone junkies and panhandlers. There were six races and as many sexes drying their clothes with the dirty boogie.

I saw my quarry at the back bar. Davey Huie was half-wasted and talking to a man with two black eyes. He was dressed western style and both hands were taped with athletic bandages. He was a little clean for this crowd. His hair wasn't that long, though it touched the nape of his shirt and covered his ears. His jeans were faded and fringed, but they didn't seem holey, and his flowery cowboy shirt had all its pearly buttons. He wore a patched levi jacket and a powder blue stetson. There was even a shine on his Frye boots.

I shimmied through the crowd as fast as I could. When I reached the back aisles, I scanned the back bar. Davey was still there, but his black-eyed buddy was gone. The empty stool by Davey beckoned. Maybe Davey knew where Dani had gone.

I pushed through the aisle and flopped onto the barstool, as if I'd stumbled onto a gold mine. The barkeep danced towards my end of the bar. I told him to bring me a beer.

"Anything else?"

"I can't think of anything."

"I bet you can if you try hard." He was a middle-aged leather boy, slim and wiry. He flexed his muscles with the beat of the rock band.

"Just the beer."

"Suit yourself." He pranced off.

I reached for my cigarettes, then matches. They weren't in my shirt pocket. They weren't in my jacket. I waited, cigarette in hand, for the bartender to prance back.

A pack of matches sailed through the air and landed by my hands. I lit my cigarette and then passed back the matches. "Thanks, man."

"I've seen you before," my benefactor said.

I shrugged. "Maybe you have."

"My name's Huie. Davey Huie."

I introduced myself. "But I've never seen you before."

"You useta live in Berkeley, didn't you?"

"Yeah, in Berkeley," I lied. "How'd you know that?"

"You remember me, don't you? I useta sit over on the benches in Sproul Plaza by the Student Union. I was the guy always playing the congas."

"Sure. Over by Sproul Plaza. Right by the Student Union. How come you got your hands bandaged?"

A wry grin. "Too much congas."

Davey was a lovable old mutt. His face was round as any basset's, with long black bangs over big dumb eyes, an eager-to-please mouth, and a permanently forlorn expression. Another guy trying to be everybody's pal.

I should've felt better. He had broken ice first. But he came on like a fruit trying to land another fruit. He didn't seem like a fruit, but this was San Francisco.

I noticed his glass was empty. It sat near mine like a tin cup from a beggar. The Chinese cowboy was another mooch, cadging drinks off the dumb. If he'd been female, he'd be a B-girl.

The bartender brought my beer.

I turned to Davey. "Whatcha drinking?"

"Tequila Marie."

I told the barkeep to get one. The barkeep gave Davey a hard, cold look—a woman's look at a rival—then went to the coolers. I felt like a nickel waiting for small change.

"So what've you been up to?" I asked.

"Oh, I was in a band for a while. It was bullshit, but a gig's a gig."

"You still doing it?"

He shook his head. "Our chick singer split on us. Everybody was fed up, anyway. I couldn't work with those people. They were all maniacs. How about yourself?"

"The same old shit. Just hanging around."

"Yeah, I know that scene. It's everywhere."

"One thing, though." I peered around, looking for someone. "I've been trying to locate this chick. She was s'pose to be here tonight, but I don't see her. That ain't saying much tonight with this crowd, but she said she'd be here. Maybe you seen her. A plain jane in her late twenties. High cheekbones, a few acne scars, an oversized nose, brown hair cut short, big blue eyes."

He cut me short. "What's her name?"

"You wouldn't know her. She's from Sausalito."

He set down his drink. "What's her name?"

"Dani Anatole. Why? You know her?"

"That's the chick who split on us."

"That singer you were talking about?"

"Yeah. That's the chick."

"I'm sorry I brought it up. I didn't know she was a bummer."

"No, it's okay. What do you want her for?"

I tried being reluctant. "I'm just looking for her, that's all."

"Hey, you can tell me, man."

I backed off, suspicious.

"I'm no cop," he told me.

"So what? Neither am I."

"So a cop can't lie to you, not if you ask him if he's a cop. If he lies and busts you, that's entrapment, and they gotta cut you loose. It's the law."

I had a hard time keeping a straight face. Davey thought cops couldn't tell a lie. Expecting undercover cops and operatives to reveal themselves on request was worse than naive. It was downright stupid. Any lawyer could've told him that. Oh, maybe for a hooker, busted for soliciting, but not in any other kind of undercover work. Undercover boys didn't have to tell the truth. They just couldn't force you against your will to break the law.

"Dani was buying a stereo receiver from me," I said.

"Oh yeah? What kind?"

"Sherwood." I thought fast. "Sixty watts per channel."

"How much are you asking for it?"

"Four bills."

He whistled. "You got any more at that price?"

"Only this one. Dani's got first dibs, but if she doesn't show up, or if I can't find her . . ."

"Is it hot?"

"Nope, it's just like new. Only got a cigarette burn on the right side. That's why it's for sale. It was a demo."

"A cigarette burn?" He smiled like a co-conspirator. "What are you getting in the deal?"

"I score a little weed."

"Four bills buys a lot of weed."

"A key of regular."

"A good price," he agreed.

"Well, we're both doing okay, since there's no money changing hands. It's a trade, a little barter between friends."

"When did you set this up?"

"Last week sometime. Just before Christmas. She called me up and asked if I still had it for sale and how much I wanted. She said she had some weed, so c'mon over to her houseboat. I went and there was nobody there."

"When were you in Sausalito?"

"Last weekend and this morning. Nobody at home."

"Wasn't Joey around?"

Davey had gone with Dani to the Arroyo Grande. He knew she had split from Joey Crawford a month ago. No sense climbing out on a limb. "Who's Joey?"

"That's her old man."

"He wasn't there. Nobody's been there for days. This cat next door, he told me she split, he didn't know where."

He rubbed his jaw with a bandaged hand. "Far out," he muttered. "Maybe she left him."

"So she left her old man. So what? How do I do this deal, if I can't find her?"

"I've never known Dani to do any dealing before." He looked me over. His half-wasted eyes had smelled trouble. "Usually it's her old man, not her, who's dealing. He deals mostly in coke."

I gave him a sharp glance. "Say what?"

"Maybe you're trying to score some coke."

Suddenly a lot of things made sense.

Cocaine was rich man's dope. An ounce of coke cost as much as a pound of gold. Not many can afford a hundred dollar gram, but that doesn't stop those who believe it's magic. They'll swallow coke-filled rubbers to get it across the border. The dumb hunger for gold was nothing compared to coke fever.

Coke dealers were just as crazy. Like used car dealers or insurance salesmen, they needed a gimmick, a strong selling point to impress their suckers. Maybe flashy clothes, bleeding nostrils, a Rolls pimpmobile, a guru's smile, or maybe a thousand dollar bill for snorting.

Just the show for a guy like Joey Crawford.

I had to say something. "Maybe I am. There's nothing wrong with it."

Respect rose up in his eyes and walked away, going elsewhere, far away. "What do you want with coke?" He sounded like a social worker at the detox clinic.

"I wanna get high. That's what I want with it." I tried sounding confident in the face of adversity. "She's got the coke, I got the Sherwood. And there's this guy down in Palo Alto, he's gonna give me a good price on it."

"You're gonna resell it on the Peninsula?"

"I'm getting a good price."

"Yeah, a little easy money. Right. You gotta be outa your mind. I useta do coke myself. I don't do it any more. You know why?"

"Cos it's expensive."

"You know what coke does to you?"

"Yeah. I know what it does. It gets you off real quick."

"I grew up in China Camp. A Chinese settlement up in North Bay. When I was a kid, there was this old man next door who had a pet raccoon. Coke makes you crazy as a pet raccoon."

"That's bullshit, man."

"Don't tell me it's bullshit. You start doing coke, you start losing days."

"Now what's that mean?"

"You start and you want to do more. Pretty soon you want to do all you can. You start doing it earlier and earlier in the day."

I threw up my hands. "What's wrong with that?"

"It's so good, you don't want to slow down. You start staying up all night to do more, and nine a.m. becomes overnight. Then you start doing other shit, upper or downers, all sorts of shit, trying to maintain your everyday style. And then you get strung out on all this shit, and you can't get your head together no more. You wake up and you got no friends. Or maybe you do, and those friendships, they're only fingernail deep. Then what do you do?"

I stared at my drink, weighing every word.

"The devil made coke," Davey said. "And when he made it, he made it too good, almost too good to believe."

"What do you think I'm going to do? Get hooked on it? I'm gonna sell most of it, keep a few lines for myself. I just want a little freebie for myself."

"Go ahead, but be cool about it."

"I'm always cool."

"Keep your eyes open, too."

"What are you saying? You sound like somebody's gonna burn me? Nobody's gonna burn me. Dani wouldn't. Would she? I mean, she does have good coke, doesn't she?"

"If she's doing the dealing."

"Dani and me. That's it. Just us two."

"She won't burn you. If she says it's good coke, it is. But her old man would sell you shit that's been stepped on a dozen times already. It's coke, but it's also talcum powder. Or maybe sugar. He's got a sweet tooth."

"I know good coke when I see it," I bragged. "Nobody's gonna burn me."

"What about after you done a few lines of this, a few lines of that, a few more of this stuff? You won't be able to see straight."

"So I'll come back and break heads."

"And the goons'll break yours."

"What goons?"

"He's got juice," Davey cautioned. "They both do."

"City, state, or federal."

He didn't laugh. "It's bigger, and they get theirs from the top."

"The Syndicate?"

"It's got a lot of names." He stared at his glass. "They're both amateurs, not professionals like the Mob, but they got connections. If you play the Big Leagues, you gotta have connections. If you don't, you don't live."

I didn't believe him. If the Syndicate is half as powerful as half the people claim, how could it bear up with so many fourth-rate punks taking its name in vain? But I told him it was worth considering.

"You gotta consider it, if you're messing with dope. Like Dani's old man, he deals a lot of cocaine, and he . . ."

"What's he deal?"

"Mother of pearl. Rock crystal. Whatever's around."

"You know where he gets it?"

"Columbia, Peru, Bolivia."

"No, man. Where does he buy his stash?"

"Why do you want to know?"

"If I can get it wholesale. . . ."

He frowned at my greed. "You're gonna end up just like him." He tried to explain. "Joey's crazy. Done too much coke. That son of a bitch tried to kill me one night. That's why I don't want to do none any more."

"He tried to kill you? Where was this? When?"

"One of their houseboat parties. Right around Thanksgiving. The first time I'm ever on his goddam boat, and the son of a . . ."

"They throw a lot of parties?"

"First one I ever went to. And the last, too." He tapped a matchbook to the band's music. "See, I walked into the bedroom at the wrong time. Dani, Joey, a half dozen others, all sitting around, doing one line after another. They had a mason jar filled with coke."

I gave a low whistle. "A lot of coke."

"I stuck my head closer, too, just like you would've—maybe join in, if I can. But Joey starts screaming and he jumps me." Davey gulped some tequila and went on. "He's shoving tables all around, there's chairs slamming on the floor, booze and weed flying all over, and I don't know what's happening. This was the first time I ever met the dude."

"So what did you do?"

"I started shoving tables back and forth, yelling, spilling shit on the floor. I told him to throw the first punch and make it his best one, because if he let me live, I'd kill him. Which was bullshit on my part. Shit, I'm no fighter. And that's when it got freaky. This other dude, Dani's cousin, he stands up for me, telling Joey to shut up and fuck off. Parnell does the same thing then, and he don't know me from Adam."

"Parnell." I squinted at the rafters, trying to place him. "I never met him," I admitted.

"He's this freak Dani useta know in Seattle. They're still pretty tight. He's an okay guy. That was the first time I met him, and he's coming down on Joey like Joey's done that shit before. Like it's nothing new that this guy becomes a maniac and wants to kills you."

"Maybe he knew this guy in Seattle."

"Maybe. Him and Jack Anatole got it on together, you know. Yeah, they started duking it out on each other, to see who got first punch at Joey. Joey was bug-eyed as me. I mean, somebody standing up to you is one thing. But two guys at once, and they're fighting over who gets to deck you first. Dani couldn't take it. She just freaked and started screaming. Hysteria, that's what it was. She got hysterical and took off. I can't blame her, though. That's a heavy scene. Her cousin and her old lover fighting over who's gonna deck her old man. That's insane."

"Where did Dani go?"

Davey didn't know, didn't care. "I just wanted to join her."

I had a good idea where she'd gone. She had taken off down the boardwalk, and Alex Symons had followed her. Later he had taken her over to her houseboat.

No wonder they had made beautiful music together. They had both been coked out of their minds. On cocaine, any combination of humans can make beautiful music together.

"Did you end up fighting him?"

"Oh no. I'm just as chicken as Joey was."

"He wouldn't fight?"

"No way. He's just a show-off. A little guy with a big mouth. Scary, like any maniac big-mouth, but he's just chickenshit in front of you."

A strange story. Maybe it was believable.

"I think I appreciate this." I gave a weak grin.

"Who needs appreciation?"

I got the hint. I bought him another drink. The barkeep gave me a dirty look. I waited until he left us alone. "What am I suppose to do?" I wondered. "I still gotta find Dani."

"Maybe Symons." He hesitated.

"Who's he?" I wondered how Davey would handle

this. He knew Dani was living with Symons. Since he had ignored that, it was his problem. And if you see one flaw, look for others.

"There's this guy, Alex Symons. Dani and him had this thing going. An off-and-on-thing."

"Because she had an old man?"

"Ah, yeah. Maybe he knows where she is. You can find him over in Sausalito. He lives on a houseboat near hers. It's called the *Mal de mar.*"

"What's the name of the boat?"

He was shaken, but he repeated it.

"That's where I was. She told me to meet her there."

He was confused. "She told you she lived there?"

"When she called me. But nobody was home. The dude next door, he said she took off, and he hasn't seen anybody since."

Davey seemed genuinely puzzled. If he didn't know Dani wasn't living with Alex any more, then probably he didn't know where she was now.

"I don't know where she is," he admitted.

"What about Parnell?"

"Maybe. I don't know."

"How do I get in touch with him?"

"Who? Parnell? Oh yeah. You can try him, I guess. He lives up in Point Reyes. Inverness. Just a couple hours north of here."

A floorboy came to the stage, cleared his throat a couple times into the microphone, then called for everybody's attention. He read aloud my license number and asked the vehicle's owner to come to the front bar.

I pushed my way across the dance floor. A stuttering lunatic blocked my way and started badgering me about his gall bladder operation. I gave him a buck and told him to get me a beer. He disappeared faster than cocaine at a biker's wedding.

I asked the floorboy about my car.

He tried to remember. "Somebody sideswiped it, or somebody's stripping it for parts." His eyes looked like optical illusions. "I'm not really sure. It's not my car."

"It's my car." I grabbed his shirt. "Who told you this?"

"Just a guy." The floorboy brushed away invisible dirt. "I don't like being touched."

I took off towards the front door. I couldn't believe anybody would steal my car, but someone could have sideswiped it in the rain. I went outside. The rain came down in thick sheets. Visibility was zip. I pulled up my collar and scooted across the street.

My car was right where I had left it. It didn't look damaged, though someone might've thought so in the rain. It does have more dents than a Yellow Cab. Maybe I had been sideswiped. I couldn't tell, and it probably didn't matter. It wasn't much of a car. It had cost me as much as two Rolls Royce hubcaps. Which is what you'd expect a legal bachelor on unemployment to own.

I started back inside. My skull roared with thunder, and my eyes went pigeon-toed. I tried to kiss the wet concrete. I know I reached for it, thinking it was a good idea.

The rain went on forever. It stung my eyelids, my face, my hands. My skin went rubbery with the rain. It sounded like popcorn popping.

A raindrop ran up my nose. I woke up coughing and choking. Vertigo came like a jackhammer. I'd woken up too soon. My head felt like the silver ball in a pinball machine. The dry heaves came, had a good time, then went away.

I was in a basement doorway, beneath a wooden staircase. Dark and cold and moldy. It stunk like a toilet. A flooded drainpipe was emptying itself into my shoes. The rain coursing down the pipe sounded like popcorn popping.

When the vertigo was more manageable, I had a long talk with myself. Somebody had trashed me and stashed me here. What was I going to do about it?

At times like this, I wish I had a partner. Maybe then I wouldn't feel like such a wallflower, an old maid. Maybe a partner could keep me awake. Maybe he could lift me off my butt. With a partner, I could double my chances for standing up. Maybe even for getting out of these messes.

I gripped a beam and pulled myself upright. My arms were tougher than my legs. My legs were jello. But my arms could hold jello upright—I could stand, and that was a big step towards the future.

I had more guts, too. I wobbled up the stairs to the sidewalk. There, I tried to decide. Jardin's Saloon was two doors down, my car was across the street, my apartment was across town.

I went towards the bar, and I was proud of my reflexes. They clumped down the street like I'd walked with them before. I didn't bump anything or break anything or run over anything or crash into anything. I was real proud.

I went back inside the funhouse. The band had finished a set, but the dance floor crowd wasn't about to disperse. They had come to dance, and they waited for the jukebox. I looked them over and decided Damon Runyon had tunnel vision.

And then the jukebox started up. Suddenly the music was too loud. Suddenly there were too many people, and they all were moving blurs. Somebody asked me what time it was. I didn't know what day it was. I asked what year it was. They asked what time it was. And I wanted to die.

I headed right for the men's room. A dragqueen just leaving held open the door. I stumbled through without saying thanks. Some cowboy was pissing in the sink. He looked at me, gulped part of his drink, zipped up and left me alone.

I was better off in the basement doorway. The men's room was a good shooting gallery for any junkie. Naked lightbulbs and broken porcelain. Broken tiles and filthy walls. The mirror was cracked, and the paper towel machine had been ripped from its hinges. There were shreds of toilet paper everywhere, like the calendar pages in the Financial District. Puddles of water, murky and brown and algaed, like the mudflats at low tide. The smell was the same, too.

I found my reflection. My eyebrows were frowning, and my eyes were redder than the squiggle of blood trickling down my forehead. My hair was plastered like greasy leather, and there were grease streaks across my face and hands.

No worse than any wino in the Tenderloin. Maybe even better than most. But this was the night-before, not the morning-after. I didn't look like me, and I felt worse than I looked.

There was an icicle lost inside my head. It felt like an icicle, anyway, making a few stabs in the dark. Maybe it wasn't an icicle. Maybe it was a needle looking for a haystack. Maybe my head boomed with the sound of my own pulse.

It took a long time to clean up. A real long time. Finally I felt ready to face the real world. I hoped it was ready for me. I headed out to see what I could see.

I called the bartender over.

"What happened to you?"

"A mud puddle in the men's room," I didn't care what he thought. "Gimme a couple of fingers of brandy."

"The good stuff?"

"Make it rotgut." I drank down the shotglass. The cheap brandy burned like iodine on a wound. I was wider awake than anytime since breakfast. Now I was smart enough not to drink this crap. I looked around the back bar. Davey was missing. I asked the bartender if he'd seen the Chinese cowboy.

"He's not here any more."

I wondered if I was slowing down. Of course he had split. Whoever had conked me had gotten Davey out fast. And Alex Symons had talked with that one on the telephone.

"Did you see who he left with?"

The bartender hadn't noticed. "He wasn't what you need." He had his hand on his hip, Bette Davis style, and he stared with brazen eyes at me. His thin smile was pulled tighter than his britches.

I was tired. Too tired to get upset. "I like women."

We looked over the women who sat at the back bar.
They were all flat-chested, and their fat buttocks spilled
over the barstools.

"Should I try and get you one?" he asked. Then he
pranced away looking for his midnight love.

It was New Year's Eve. I needed someone.

I thought I knew where I could find her.

CHAPTER 13

The desk clerk was sleeping beneath a Chinese newspaper. I rapped knuckles on the desk. He came awake slowly, like a streetsweeper on doubletime, set aside his paper and ambled over.

"You wanna room?"

"Yeah. Ruth Gideon's."

"No visitors after nine o'clock."

"What room is she in?"

He said it again. No visitors after nine o'clock.

I was in no mood to play games. My head throbbed and my armpits stunk. My clothes were masquerading as sponges, my socks squeaked in my shoes, my shoes were buckets of rainwater.

I put a dollar on the counter. I told him he looked like a man money could buy. He didn't call the cops and he didn't kick me out. Nothing flickered in his eyes. I threw another dollar after the first. Something flickered, but he was still the Rock of Propriety.

"If there's another," I said, "you're gonna eat it."

The wisdom of Solomon is knowing when to pass the buck. "Two-two-seven. Second floor."

The second floor was like tuning a car radio. I heard every station in town. I could almost smell every restaurant, too. Curry powder, oyster sauce, boiling cabbage, garlic, tobasco sauce, even the autumnal

smells of burning marijuana. It was strongest in the hall
be Ruth Gideon's door. Maybe the girl next door was
baking cookies again.

I knocked on room 227. Footsteps came from behind
the door. They came reluctantly, a woman's footsteps
when she's alone and not expecting a knock on the door
at night.

She wore a green robe that she held tightly with
folded arms. She looked at my water-softened face, my
dirty clothes, my mud-streaked hair. "Oh my god!"

I sighed. "Maybe I could come back tomorrow."

"Oh no." She told me to come in.

I shambled in on rubbery legs.

Her room was munchkin-size. Two people made a
crowd, and the far wall was closer than the ceiling.
There was a single bed, a dresser, a wall closet. She had
tried covering the bleak walls with two-dollar travel
posters. She wasn't going anywhere, but she had hopes.

"What happened to you?"

"I got mugged," I said.

Her jade eyes. "You were robbed?"

"No. Just mugged." A spell of vertigo came over me.
I sat on the bed and waited it out. Neither of us knew
what to say. She just stared, and I felt stupid.

"Is there anything I can do?"

I shook my head. The icicle rattled against my ears. I
held my head until it stopped rattling. I wondered why
the icicle didn't melt. It had plenty of time to melt. I
looked up at Ruth. She looked concerned. Maybe she
didn't want me getting sick on her bed.

Finally I could talk. "How come you're not babysitting tonight?"

Her smile was faint. "A girl needs a night off once in
a while."

"It's New Year's Eve," I said. "All those tourists in
town. You could name your own price, almost."

"Money isn't everything." Her smile grew. "Besides,
I've seen every movie on the hotel tv."

"You're going to stay in all night?"

"Nobody asked me out."

"I will. Right now."

She folded her arms again and tucked her hands under the folds. The hardwood floor must've been cold, for her bare feet rubbed at each other. "It's late. We won't be able to get in any place."

My throat was dry. "We can go to my place."

She debated it. "All right."

I almost passed out from relief.

"I better get ready," she said.

She took off her robe and hung it inside her small closet. She wore only panties. She had a healthy body. Slender hips and lean thighs. She didn't mind me watching. Maybe she wasn't worried about a sick man. There weren't many clothes in her closet. Another person who could throw all her belongings on the backseat of a car.

When she was dressed, she lifted me and we left.

The desk clerk stood by the front door. He watched us like old folks watch the rain. There was nothing he could do about it.

She wished him a good night. He was silent, wearing the look the Chinese cultivate around round-eyes. It's not inscrutable, but it's better the round-eyes don't know what it means.

She stopped me on the steps. "What's wrong with him?"

"He's thinking you've ruined the joint's reputation."

She cocked a disbelieving eye at me.

"Scout's honor," I lied.

"Are you sure he's not jealous?"

I looked back. The desk clerk had his hands in his pockets and he was playing with himself. "You might be right," I told her.

She was shivering from the gusts of wind. The storm was almost a squall. The fog-shrouded buildings on Sutter Street were no windbreak against the wind and rain. The rain came sideways like hailstones. It was bitter cold.

"Where's your car?"

"Just up the street by the fireplug."

She took my car keys and took off running, dodging

the rain by ducking under awnings and into doorways. I was already soaked, so I lagged behind, getting water-logged.

San Francisco is a city of colors. White buildings and green palms and blue skies and the ocean in every breath. But the city when it drizzles is a broken promise. All big cities are ugly in the rain, except maybe Paris, so I'm told, but San Francisco must be the ugliest in the rain. Everything is grey and moody and fogbound, and the clouds seem to hover around third floor windows.

She had the car and the heater running when I got inside. They didn't seem to matter much. The winds howled between my windows and around the doors. Cold seeped through the floorboards.

"Anything to drink at your place?"

I'd forgotten that.

"There's a liquor store up ahead. Next to the gay bar."

I drove the half-block and pulled into a yellow zone. We went in together. She picked out two bottles of wine. The Arab shopkeeper told me they cost nine dollars. I searched through Joey's bankroll for a tenner.

"Is that all yours?" Her eyes were wider than a rookie cop with his first book of tickets.

"Evidence. A case I'm working on."

"Would anybody miss some of it?"

"Probably not." I grinned. "Why? Are you planning on rolling me?"

"If I could, I would. How much is that?"

"I won't tell you, so you won't be tempted."

"You better put it away. I'm tempted now."

I thought how tempted I was. I didn't know why I was holding onto it. With this dough, I could live down in Mexico and miss most of the rainy season. Instead I bought two bottles of wine.

The rain was forming wide pools across Geary Boulevard. Cars were sailboating from lane to lane, and emergency brake flashers dotted every other block. One car ahead went into a 360 degree turn, sideswiping a small foreign car, then finally colliding with the median barrier.

I wasn't too happy, either. My wipers were worn. Just as they'd clear a swatch of glass, some joker would roar by me tossing rooster-tails of rainwater back onto my windshield, and I'd be blind again. I felt like I was steering a submarine through rough ocean swells.

But, somehow, my car managed to cut a wake through the floods. Somehow we weren't sideswiped or drowned. The car began to smell of wet clothes drying. A muskiness that increased the tension between us. Ruth resolved it by moving closer to me.

I parked in front of my apartment building. There was no one on the streets, and no lights were on in my building. Even my landlady's apartment was dark. New Year's Eve, of course. Everyone was out partying.

We took the elevator upstairs. When we got to my flat, I reached inside and snapped on the overhead light. Ruth walked in first. She gave a low whistle. I stepped around to see why.

Someone had broken in and had searched my place. They'd done a great job, too. My apartment looked like a hippie van after a customs check.

My newspapers, the ones I'd been too lazy to throw out, had been pulled from the closet and thrown everywhere. My couch had been overturned, and the lining had been ripped with a knife. The back panel of my television set had been removed. Every cupboard had been emptied, and most of the foodstuffs were scattered over the counter. The ice trays had been defrosted, and even the wall plugs had been removed.

The telephone rang. I answered it.

"Brennen?" A man's voice. Throaty and low.

"Yeah? What is it?"

"If you don't quit this case, they'll do you just like they did Joey Crawford."

I gripped the phone. "Who is this?" He had hung up. On a hunch, I drew back the drapes and looked up and down the dark street.

A man slithered from the phone booth by the hamburger joint on the corner. He scampered through the rain and jumped into a silver Porsche. The engine coughed, shook itself awake, making more noise than a power lawnmower. The headlights snapped on, and the car spun out onto Geary, then disappeared.

Ruth was straightening the furniture.

"I didn't bring you here to clean house."

"Why don't you grab a shower?" she said.

An idea whose time had come. I needed a shower, a good long one. And tonight with everybody in the building out partying, there just might be enough hot water.

The bathroom had been hit, too. My toothpaste tube had been squeezed dry, and there were fluoridated squiggles all over the sink. The toilet paper holder and the shower curtain rod had both been torn loose, on the off-chance one or both were hollow. The Boston fern on the tanktop had been unpotted, and dirt covered the tile floor.

I cleaned what I could, gave up before the room was clean, then shucked my clothes and hopped into the shower. The needle spray was a thousand pine needles. Slowly the fatigue washed away from me. I almost felt human again, not a puppet managed by a nitwit.

The shower curtain was pulled back. Ruthann came into the shower. She was very much naked. Red ringlets glistened like copper below her navel.

And there was time for kisses and caresses, splashing feet and make-believe falls, giggles and babytalk and laughter.

Later, when she pushed my hands away, we rinsed off the soap and stepped from the shower and toweled each other dry.

There was a full-length mirror on the inside bathroom door. Our reflections were half-hidden by steam. We seemed to fit together, like the chords of some song.

I held her close and kissed her. I could smell the creme rinse in her hair. It smelled like vanilla extract. "I'm glad you're not babysitting," I told her.

She opened her eyes and stared into mine. Her jade eyes were deep and a mountain lake. A man could get lost in them. I looked down at her long fingernails. Red nails lost in the darker curls of my chest.

She took my hand. I led her to my bed. We made love like all first-time lovers. We were clumsy, awkward, too much aware of our bodies. And it was over too soon as it always is.

I didn't fall asleep when she did. I couldn't sleep. I peeled away the covers and left the bedside. She didn't waken. A man leaving bed in the middle of the night was not a strange feeling for her.

I pulled back my landlady's drapes and looked out across my city. The rain had stopped, and the storm was busy moving eastward. Fog was blowing in from the Golden Gateway. This was not the white fog of summer, but grey and serpentine. Winter fog meant the rainy season had settled in. A lone searchlight from the harbor patiently flailed at it, like a man knifing a ghost.

I opened the window. Cars sluicing through the rainwater on Geary. Fire sirens from the downtown districts for an instant. And behind them all, reverberating, the foghorns on the bay.

I watched a tomcat doing a tightrope on my neighbor's fence. My neighbor's kitchen light flicked on. Then I heard a burst of high-speed Cantonese. A young boy's voice, then a man's deeper tones. The cat crouched with bright fearing eyes.

I waited until it came. A string of firecrackers. Then several shots from a deer rifle. Lastly, a shotgun's double barrel boomed through the moist night, erasing for a moment the foghorns.

Ruthann jumped from the sheets like a startled fawn. She grappled me from behind, and her body shook, chilled by the noise and the randy evening. Her voice was shrill, noise to my ears. "Gunshots! Those were . . . !"

"Take it easy," I whispered. Her waist in my hands. "It's just my neighbors celebrating the New Year."

"New Year?" She was startled. "It's midnight?"

"Yes, it's midnight. Come to bed."

She gawked at my neighbors. "They're Chinese!"
She leaned over the ledge. "Don't they have their
own?"

I coaxed her back to bed. I calmed her shaking body.
I palmed her pubic hair. Her flat stomach fluttered with
my touch. A moment later she caught her breath, and
her body slowed from its tremblings. A moment later, it
found another rhythm.

"Mmmm. Again."

"You like that?"

"Yes. I like that."

Midnight. The last day of the year.

I brushed a red hair from my lips.

CHAPTER 14

From my bed I watched the moon set behind the Farallones. The islands, thirty miles out in the Pacific, are rarely visible from the city. Too much haze on the water, usually. But last night's storm had cleared the air, and now those granite rocks were bathed in moonlight and daylight.

The Chinese celebrate New Year's Day as the time when debts are paid, when accounts are settled, when grudges are forgotten. I wasn't so civilized. I wanted to do nothing today. It was my holiday, too, and I wanted to enjoy it. I wasn't going to play detective today. Not when the moon was setting in the Pacific, when the skies were clear and the sun was warm, when a fine woman shared my bed.

For six months I had slept alone. Now Ruth Gideon slept beside me. Her legs were curled around mine for warmth, and her long hair had fallen on the pillow like a rouge Niagara. She looked lovely in the moonglow, in first light. Better than I deserved. I wasn't sure what to say when she awoke.

I was a damn fool to get involved with Dani Anatole's life. It wasn't my business some female grew apart from her boyfriend. It was natural, normal, an everyday thing, and I didn't have to play detective for a living.

I had joined Pac-Con for a job. Not because I wanted

to be a trained investigator, but because I needed a paycheck every two weeks to put food into my kids' mouths. The job paid forty a day. It paid the landlord, the pediatrician, the finance company, the supermarket.

There's nothing wrong with the nine-to-five existence. Nothing wrong with a paycheck every two weeks. Nothing wrong with two weeks paid vacation, major medical and dental, pension points and group insurance.

I just never made it as a company man. I was embarrassed by what I had to do. The job was a snap, even for me, and I have no illusions. I'm not much of an investigator.

But I couldn't quit. I had a family to support. But then it became easier and easier to quit, harder and harder to stay. So I let myself get fired. The easiest way out.

I lay there a full hour, watching the moon falling into the sea, watching the new year rising with the sun. Smoking cigarette after cigarette. Her cigarettes. I didn't know why I was back in the game.

Her cigarettes eventually made me sick.

I slid from bed and found some clothes and grabbed my car keys and wallet. There was an Arab mom-n-pop ten blocks away that was open every holiday, even the Arabic ones. I didn't bother leaving a note. A quake wouldn't budge Ruth, and I'd be back within a dozen minutes.

When I reached the streets, the early morning westerlies off the Pacific tousled my hair. I didn't bother raking the tangles. The winds were warm and this was a Farallones holiday. A great way to start off the new year.

I got into my car, started the motor and rolled down my window. There was a lot of sunshine and ocean breeze today. I wanted my share.

A late-model Camaro lumbered down the street. Its ass was higher than its hood. A large decal said *Camaro* in block letters on the rear window. It drove past slowly, then reversed itself until it was almost alongside.

There were four Chinese males inside. They didn't look intimidating. I'd seen their kind before, usually cruising Broadway near the topless clubs. Just teenagers trying to keep back the boredom. Voyeurs with little money and too much time.

The driver left his car and came over. He was moustached and near my age. His eyes were black glass, unflinching, like rattlesnake eyes. He said something that I didn't catch. Thinking he needed directions, I asked him to repeat it.

He kicked my door. "You cut me off on Geary."

I said nothing. I wasn't worried about my car. It had plenty of dents. One more was nothing. This goon hadn't confused me with anyone. I was being ambushed. Like teenagers baiting hookers, these Chinese were out baiting the white folks. Looking for trouble and hoping they had found it. They couldn't have timed it better. The world was hung over, and there'd be no witnesses today.

"I'm talking to you, round-eyes."

I watched his three buddies. They had left his Camaro and were fanning out around me. They moved like men who had been drinking warm red wine by the jug all night. Not drunk, just weary from steady drinking. I got a little worried then. These guys could be crazies. With a little heat in them, they might try anything.

One had chipmunk cheeks. He brought two woods sticks from his jacket. Two short pieces of wood held together by a short swivel chain. He came head-on, and he had eyes for my windshield.

The other two were younger. They looked sleepy-eyed. Maybe they were up too early. One sidled around the right side. I looked around and behind. The doors were locked. He wouldn't get in that way. The other disappeared behind me. I heard a jarring sound, felt the car rock. The goon was on my trunk, crawling forward. I didn't bother to look.

The circle was closing in.

The sticks registered then. They were nunchukas. A vicious pound of steel and wood. They were more than lethal. They had been used in karate classes until the state outlawed them.

Whip them forward and reverse, and they could crack a human skull or break an arm in two. In the hands of a pro, they're twice as fast as cheetahs. But you didn't need to be a pro. A little natural coordination, five minutes of instruction, another fifteen of practice, and you can take on the world. Just right for street punks with inferiority complexes.

And the goon wanted my windshield.

I set my foot on the brake and slipped the gearshift into low. The car moved imperceptibly. I wanted to be ready to fly. I lifted the door handle. The door was open. It would swing freely.

Rattlesnake Eyes had been talking. I hadn't heard one word. I looked up his way just as he called me a "lackey dog." I told him to go fuck himself.

He blew up then. Unleashed a burst of short jabs at me. It was hard fending the flurry of fists with just my hands. I did my best, then popped open my door. I slammed it against his knees, nearly toppling him.

It didn't stop him. He lunged through the window, got a grip on my neck and tried throttling me. I grabbed a wrist and twisted it with both hands. I peeled his fingers off, but his other hand still peppered my face.

I caught a glimpse through the windshield. I shouldn't have looked. The maniac with the nunchukas had the sticks swinging in a fast circle through the air.

I grabbed Rattlesnake Eyes by the wrists and twisted. Chipmunk Cheeks whip-snapped his wrists. I closed my eyes and stomped on the gas pedal. The windshield shattered. I felt slivers driving into my face. The car shot forward, hauling ass down the street. I held onto the wrist and dragged him with me. The goon on the trunk tumbled off. I could feel the wind roar through the hole in the windshield. The car dragged Rattlesnake Eyes down the street. He had a heart-rending scream. It was louder than the engine's roar, the roar of the wind. And he was so hard to hold.

Someone shouted not to shoot.

Oh Jesus. They had guns. I had to get outa here.

I slammed on the brakes, let go the wrist, slammed down again onto the accelerator. The car hesitated, almost stalled, then leapt forward like a startled fawn and howled down the street.

I opened my eyes. My windshield was a huge hole. The rim looked like Jack Frost etchings, like fossil leaves. There was shattered glass on my seat, on my clothes, on my eyelids. I tried the rear view mirror, but I couldn't see. My face was lathered in glass, and blood was running through my eyes.

The car screamed up the street, around the corner, onto Geary Boulevard. I moved into the right lane of the divided highway and kept the pedal on the floorboards. I started crashing red lights.

I hoped the cops would stop me before the goons did. Or before I had an accident. I wanted a hospital more than a cop shop. My skin prickled with glass slivers, and blood makes a lousy eyewash. I was still too far in shock to feel anything.

I had the streets to myself on the only day I could have the streets to myself. I crashed red light after red light and never slowed down. I couldn't see, but I didn't dare stop. I had to assume the goons were after me. Meanwhile, last night's amateurs were home in bed, hospitalized, or cold in the morgue.

Two blocks from the hospital, I spotted a low-riding police cruiser stopped for a red light ahead of me. I hurtled towards them. Just as I came up behind them, they hit their siren and made a U-turn around the barrier and flashed back the way I had come. My neighbors had probably called them.

I found a parking space in front of the hospital. I locked the doors, then noticed I had no windshield. Then I stumbled around and opened my trunk. I left behind Joey's stash, but took my gun and its holster. If a holiday couldn't keep the muggers from my door, should it hinder the car thieves?

Wandering the hospital's corridors, I came upon a telephone booth. I found a dime, then couldn't remember my own telephone number I pulled out the phone book and tried looking up my number. Blood droplets fell on the white pages.

I remembered my number. It seemed to ring forever.

Her voice was whiskey-throated with sleep. "Lover!" Soft and husky and eager. "But where are you?"

"The hospital. I want you outa there. Right now. You're surrounded by killers. Get going. Right now."

"Wha?"

"Just grab your clothes and leave."

She hung up when it sunk in.

Maybe I was melodramatic. The goons had their wounded, too, and they had to expect the cops, so they were probably gone with the wind.

The hospital was quiet. The walls were white and the lights were bright. My head hurt. The icicle had come back. I wondered why it didn't melt. I leaned against the booth. I watched my blood cloud my eyes. I felt it sliding down my face. It tasted salty on my lips. I thought I heard it fall to the floor.

I heard someone shout. An intern was coming down the corridor with a security guard behind him. I felt my gun slipping from its holster. It fell to the floor, clattered like a dish. I stared stupidly at it. I think that's when I gave up.

CHAPTER 15

The cabbie dropped me by Washington Square. I gave him a buck more than meter. Any cabbie who'd pick up a man with a dented face on a holiday morning needed the dough.

I hiked across the mall towards Mama's of North Beach. A young Chinese boy, ten or eleven years old, stood outside. He had rifled the newspaper machine and was hawking half-price morning editions. I gave him a quarter for his enterprise and went inside the restaurant. A cute high schooler took my order. I found a seat by the window, spread out my newspaper and did my best to forget I was a private investigator. According to the paper, the New Year had started off like any other year. There was trouble everywhere in the world.

Someone rapped on the window. I glanced up, set aside my paper and waited for the rolypoly teddy bear with rumpled fur to float in. I wasn't too surprised seeing Doug Lacjak this early. Not even in jogging clothes and canary-yellow sneakers. He'd always had this thing about long walks and hangovers.

He slid opposite me. "You and your damn phone calls." His anger vanished. "What happened? You look like Frankenstein's monster."

I almost touched my face. "I got thugged by some Chinese goons."

153

He winced. "How many stitches?"

"A couple of dozen." I tried to smile. "You ain't so hot yourself."

He smelled of stale cigarettes and stale alcohol. There was a purple bruise over one eye, and his left cheek was puffed like a pigeon's chest. There was tobacco or marijuana in the scruff of his beard, and the whites of his eyes were red. His mouth was so slack, I doubted he could swallow coffee.

He shook the beard. "Yeah, it got a little drunk out last night," he confessed. "I don't even remember passing out." He'd been staring at the stitches. "Do they hurt?"

"The doc's got me on codeine."

"Lemme have one," he said. After he used my coffee to drink it down, he remembered I was here. "What did they use on you? A Waring blender?"

"Nunchukas. Karate sticks." The waitress brought my breakfast, and I settled in to devour it.

"You know what you oughta do." Doug leaned forward. The chair bitched about that. "File with the state for damages occurring during the commission of a violent crime."

"You think I could."

"Sure. One of our caseworkers got drunk and tried picking up a hooker down in the Tenderloin. The hooker was a dragqueen and got upset when he got upset. She pistol-whipped him and took all his money. Now he's filing for damages."

"Will it pay for fixing my car?"

"You were inside your car?"

"They got the windshield, not me."

"It's just for personal injuries."

"Too bad. The VA covers that."

"File anyway. Compensation above and beyond." He noticed the bulge beneath my jacket. "You're carrying heat?"

"I never said I was smart."

"Chinese kids." His brow went up. "Any connection with that phone call?"

"There's gotta be," I said. "I might know one of them. A character named Lim Song."

"No shit." He was impressed. "You picked a good one."

"What do you know about him?"

Lim Song was born in Taiwan. He got his green card when he was ten. He was purse-snatching before he was twelve, joyriding before he was thirteen, mugging B-girls coming off the night shift before he was sixteen. For his sixteenth, he joined with some other kids and expanded into the stolen car racket. Their favorite haunts were the automotive garages after closing. They'd hotwire the cars left outside, drive them behind Telegraph Hill, and strip them for parts.

If Lim Song and his boys hadn't gotten greedy one night, they might've grown wealthy. But they rolled a drunk tourist walking the wrong way back to his hotel. Some other tourists saw it and took pictures. The SFPD busted the boys in less than a week. Lim Song was sent away until he was twenty-one. He came out with a high school diploma and a barber's license.

The Sixties were a boomtime for higher education. Uncle Sam wanted everybody to go, and he helped anyone with the guts to try. Lim Song's parole officer helped the boys enroll in a local junior college. Like a lot of street punks, they majored in Bonehead English and other remedial courses. And they learned it was easier filling out National Student Defense Loan forms than rolling drunks or snatching purses. They decided to stay in school.

And they were good students, too. Not the best grades maybe, but better grades than anybody ever expected. And they were good students because somebody gave a damn, or maybe because no one gave a damn. Some even took Asian studies. They read about the railroads, the vigilantes, the massacres, the Exclusion Acts and the Anti-Queue Laws.

Then graduation rolled around, and the boys found out they'd been short-changed. They had degrees but they were obsolete. Uncle Sam forgot to compute when the labor market was glutted with college kids.

But the boys had always expected the worst. They went back to the streets of Chinatown and their old ways. At least the streets were predictable. What went down went down every day.

They had changed, too. No more boosting cigarettes. No more stripping cars. They'd been politicized by Kent State, SF State, other campus turmoil. With their heritage, they found their own reasons to become Maoists. They turned their backs on tradition and went after the Chinese Mafia. Like modern Robin Hoods, they'd hit a fantan parlor or a mah jongg house, shoot a few holes in the ceiling, then skedaddle with the loot. Unlike Robin Hood, they'd also shake down the hookers for protection money and freebies for everybody in the gang.

I set down my coffee. "He's Robin Hood, and I'm the Sheriff. Great."

"Maybe you need a beer." Doug swiped more bacon.

"Maybe after breakfast." I wasn't feeling my best. I watched his darting fingers. "How about saving me some bacon?"

"Sure." He downed my orange juice. "I need a favor."

"More orange juice."

He fished in his pockets and tossed me his house-keys. "I'll be gone a week, so how about watering my plants?"

"Sure. How come?"

"Oh, a couple of guys are driving down to Moro Bay. One of our caseworkers got busted for abalone poaching."

"That's gonna take a week?"

"We're gonna do some diving, too."

"Okay. Sure, I'll water 'em. Hey, I got your car keys, too."

"Oh, I'm not driving. I'm drinking."

"Well, okay then." I pocketed the keys, then realized

what they meant. "I'm gonna use your car while you're gone."

"What happened to yours? Oh, yeah, the windshield." Doug didn't mind. "Where're you going to?"

I stopped at the door. "I gotta see a man about a charm bracelet," I said. "Enjoy my breakfast."

CHAPTER 16

Like most peoples, the Chinese will celebrate any holiday they're offered. But, unlike the round-eyes, they don't sleep them away. Everyday is Market Day, and, though the rest of the world might be hung over, the streets of Chinatown bustled with crowds of shoppers. Like barnyard hens, fat matrons in babushkas and slacks haggled over fresh fish and vegetables, while their husbands, weary-looking men who had forgotten how to smile, sat in their cars, practicing the ancient oriental art of double-parking.

I found a phone booth on Stockton Street. Tan Ng wasn't listed in the SF book, so I borrowed the Chitown directory from a harried shopkeeper. The white pages gave Ng's home address on Nob Hill and his law offices on Jackson Street just above Grant Avenue. I wrote both down, then tried calling my own apartment. There was no answer. Not that I expected one. If Ruth had any more brains than a sand flea, she'd be long gone.

Ng's law offices were one flight above the Chitown draft board. The door at the top of the stairs was unlocked, but no receptionist was on duty. A large oil painting of Sun Yet-sen behind the desk gave me a dirty look any receptionist would approve.

An interior door opened. "Is someone here?" Tan

Ng's voice, shrill and wavering, came from inside. Tufts of snowy hair appeared around the door frame, followed by his pale face. "Oh, Mr. Brennen, I am so surprised to see you." He opened the door for me. "Won't you please come in?"

"So this is where you work."

You could park a car in his office. For a minute, I thought I was in the city council chambers. The ceiling was almost as far away, and the ornamentation was just as dreamy. A huge crystal chandelier hung over a mahogany conference table.

"May I ring for some tea?" he wondered.

"This isn't a social call."

The old man actually smiled. "Then you have decided to accept my proposition." He had a smile like Godzilla.

"Why don't you cut the bullshit?" I snapped.

His body had a spasm. "I do not understand." He gave me the Chinatown Faker look. A peculiar expression the Chinese use when they suddenly don't understand the English language as spoken by round-eyes.

"Sure, you do. You tried to hire me to track down Lim Song and a missing necklace. I told you I wouldn't because Song was a juvenile delinquent. Well, I was wrong there. He's no juvenile delinquent. He's not even a juvenile. He's a raving Maoist maniac with his own private army."

"Who told you this?"

"That crazy sonovabitch tried to strangle me this morning."

Ng sat down abruptly. "Oh no."

"I walked right into an ambush. And one of his goons shattered my windshield and put these dents in my face."

His dull black eyes leapt upward to the cuts and bruises, seeing them for the first time. "He did that to you?"

"Him and his Red Guards," I stated.

His skull tightened. "I am so very sorry." He didn't look sorry. He looked like he wanted to sue.

"Why don't you tell me why you tried to get me killed?"

"I had no idea this would happen."

"You wanted me to follow him."

"I didn't think you would."

"Then why try to hire me?"

He sucked his gums a while. "I'm a lawyer," he began. Then he stopped and ruminated over that.

"I know what you do for a living."

He nodded his old head. "One of my clients called me yesterday afternoon," he said. "My client said a private investigator had been to see him. You were that investigator and you made references to creditors."

"You mean Riki Anatole, right?"

"He wanted me to find out about you. You see, this is a critical time for his company's finances. He thought you might be a forerunner for a take-over bid. He asked me to see what I could do."

"So you came to buy me off."

"That was merely an excuse to meet you. I came to investigate you. To find out whose interests you represent. To find out who your clients are. My nephew suggested that we hire you."

"The missing necklace was never missing."

"We never expected you to take our proposition seriously. I knew I was not fooling you. We both knew that, Mr. Brennen. But it could have been an effective way to gauge you. We thought the jade necklace would be a harmless diversion."

"What if I had taken it seriously? What if I had agreed to try and locate the necklace?"

"We would have found something much safer for you."

I swore beneath my breath. Sure, they'd found something safer. Like maybe wrestling junkies to the floor of City Hall. The little weasel was just trying to sound humble, contrite, sorrowful.

"What about Lim Song? Where did he come in?"

"Believe me, Mr. Brennen, I had no desire to involve you in any serious trouble. Lim Song is well-known in

Chinatown. We felt you would know him through his reputation. I felt satisfied that you knew who he was. You acted as if you knew him when you talked about Chinatown gangs.''

"Who told him about me?"

"No one did."

"Somebody told him. Look at my face."

"I can't believe that," he said firmly.

"You think these stitches are a lie?"

"Please forgive me. I do not question your honesty. Merely that I believe no one informed him about you."

"Then how did he know about me?"

"I can only assume I was followed to your apartment." He splayed out his fingers on the table. They were all knuckles and bones, and they had more than their share of liver spots. His fingers were long and thin, sheaves of wheat on wood.

"You were followed. Sure."

"I am followed everywhere these days," he told me. "When Lim Song discovered I had been to see a private investigator, perhaps he saw you as a threat to his security. Perhaps he felt he should take some measures to guarantee that security."

"Why should you be any threat to him?"

"I represent many interests the Maoists wish to discredit. I am legal counsel for many elderly Chinese. I try to help them live within the white man's world. The Maoists reject that. They preach radical change and violence. I am opposed to violence in any form."

"And that makes you threatening?"

He gave me a wry smile. "They think so."

He might've been the disillusioned patriarch with that blast of white hair and his ancient features. He might be happier waiting for his monthly pension check. It seemed plausible. Yet I had to go slow.

"Are you a threat to the Maoists?"

He shook his head. "I am a very foolish old man who should have retired long ago. My clients will not let me retire. They will not listen when I say I am too old."

I was right. He thought he was indispensable. I wondered what time warp his clients were in. And remembered the Anatoles were clients.

"So what are you going to do about this?"

"About what?" Confused again.

"That madman tried to strangle me. One of his goons used karate sticks on my car. The same clown who put these marks in my flesh. Take another look at what he did."

He went to his desk and started rummaging through it. "I accept full responsibility for any trouble you have had." He came up with a business checkbook. "I will make amends for any damages done through my foolishness." He paged through his checkbook for the last check he had written. "I should never have listened to my nephew."

I told him to stop.

My anger startled him. "I must make amends."

"I don't care about that," I told him. "I want to know what you're going to do about Lim Song."

"I do not know what I can do."

"I don't want that maniac camping on my doorstep."

"But what can I do?" he appealed.

"You can't call him off?"

"He does not listen to me." Tan Ng struggled for words. "There is little I can do. He is like the rain, everywhere. How can I stop the rain? If I approach him, he will become violent. I am no match for him. I am a very old man."

"Try a little harder."

He tried. "I can loan you some bodyguards. I can urge you to move elsewhere." His words tapered off like a junkie's heartbeat. They didn't start up again. Maybe it was my cue.

But I'd had enough. I walked out on him.

I went looking for Doug's car.

CHAPTER 17

I drove out California Street to the Sunset District. I knew the neighborhood well. Before Pearl Harbor, this area had been sand dunes and sand fleas. But the war brought people west, some to carry guns, others to make them. Many stayed on after peace to build homes and raise families.

Three decades later, their city days were almost over and retirement had come. Over the years, their homes had skyrocketed in value, and it was a seller's market for these castles in the sand.

The new buyers were happy paying hard cash. They were solitary people who had sweated and slaved and saved for their share of the American Dream. Their skin was tallow and their eyes were sloped. Like any immigrants, the Chinese wanted to move up. Like any ghetto people, they wanted to move out. Now the realtors were calling this neighborhood Chinatown West.

The address I had for Davey Huie was a dentist's office just off Clement Street. No doctor has office hours on a holiday, but I knocked on the front door anyway.

A middle-aged Chinese housewife in pink slacks and pink curlers came from her garage next door. She carried her plastic garbage bags out to the treelawn. When she dumped them, they clattered like pent-up whiskey bottles. She saw me and came over the lawn towards me.

"He's not there on holidays," she said.

I stepped from the porch. "I'm looking for Davey Huie. They said I could find him here."

"Davey? He lives around back. A studio apartment. You have to walk around back to find it." She gave me a nervous look, the kind neighbors reserve for strangers. "What do you want with him?"

"He ripped off my stereo."

"Davey?" She was startled. "He really ripped you off?"

"Naw, I was just bullshitting."

She flushed, but I was already gone, hiking around the stucco building, dodging shrubs and small trees.

There was an enclosed porch behind the dentist's office. I found a rickety pair of steps and stepped up to the warped wood door. I knocked twice and no one came. I knocked again, and again there was no answer. I tried the door and went inside.

Davey's studio was something you'd give an overnight guest with many apologies. Or you put a washer and dryer up front and use the rest for storage. You don't rent it out. Not unless you're one helluva greedy landlord.

The room was barely fifteen by ten. Nothing more than an add-on room. The dentist, or his landlord, had enclosed a back porch with fiberfill and plasterboard, dabbed on a couple of coats of paint, and rented it to the first sucker. The room was dinky enough for warm thoughts about my own landlady.

Davey was home, but unavailable for comment. He was stretched out across a single mattress on the floor. His eyes were closed, and he was breathing slowly, regularly. He wore a terrycloth robe and his stereo earphones. Bare feet pointed in different directions. There were powdery rings around each nostril. His bandaged hands lay by his sides, and a small hand mirror lay beside the mattress. Several lines of whitish crystal sparkled on it. A razor blade and a thin-rolled dollar bill were alongside.

My shoes had an echo in the room. Even the empty streets outside were noisier. A faint whirring sound from the tapedeck was the only threat to silence. I've found this same silence in other hip dwellings over the years. Davey was just another cokehead catching tunes on his stereo.

There was just the single mattress on the floor. It had no boxsprings or bedframe. No sheets, either, just a sleeping bag. There were no windows, either, though the room needed some desperately. A partition cut off several feet of space, and two doors were cut into the plywood. If one was the closet, the other was a bathroom. There was little else in the room. A hotplate on a ledge. A set of drums in one corner. A chair piled with last night's cowboy clothes. Turntable and tapedeck and amplifier and speakers.

I punched the *on* button for the external speakers. A few riffs from the rhythm guitar came through the speakers. Downhome country and western music. The female vocalist was throaty, but average. Whenever she hit a flat note, the harmonica man crooned mournfully and almost covered her goofs.

I pushed the *power* button off. The tape deck slowed, then stopped. The music died.

Davey's eyes fluttered, but did not open. A few creases almost came to his forehead. His lips parted like a thirsty man, but nothing came forth.

I bent over him. His face was damp with sweat, but there was no fever. His pulse had weakened, and his breathing was getting shallow. Both seemed to be slowing. I lifted an eyelid. The pupil rolled like a marble on glass. It was receding fast. There were bruises below each sideburn.

I called the cops. They said they'd hurry.

I covered him with his sleeping bag and placed a cold wash rag on his forehead. There was yesterday's coffee on the hotplate. I forced some down his throat. He gagged and tried to retch. I gave him more. I shook him and shouted at him and smacked his face.

I was giving him mouth-to-mouth resuscitation when the medics came. They tried cardiovascular drugs and electroshock.

After a while, they gave up and carried the cooling meat outside on a stretcher. Doors opened and closed on an orange-trimmed ambulance, and it took off down Clement Street. The meat wagon didn't bother with its siren. The streets were deserted, and the flashing lights woke no one.

CHAPTER 18

I looked down at my fingers. My cigarette was still unlit. Somebody up there was telling me something. I sighed and slipped it back into its pack. I asked if I were under arrest.

"We'd just like to hear it again."

"You're Curtain, right?"

"I'm Howard."

I couldn't tell them apart. They were both detectives with SFPD, and they could have been twins. They both had styled hair and brown beards. They both wore imitation leather jackets and earth shoes. Their shirts were open at the throat and their shirt collars hung over their jackets.

"What do you know about this guy?"

"He was a nice guy," I said. "I liked him."

"How long have you known him?"

"I never saw him before last night."

"You two hit it off fast."

"I make friends easily. I guess he did, too."

"Where'd you meet him?"

"A bar down in the flats. Jardin's Saloon."

"Why did you go there?"

"I wanted a drink. New Year's Eve and all."

"What made you pick that firetrap?"

"If it's a firetrap, why isn't it closed down?"

"Why did you go there?"

"I like the people. They never ask questions."

"What did you do when you got there?"

"I bought a couple drinks."

"Did you know he'd be there?"

"I never saw him before last night."

"So why did you strike up a conversation?"

"He started it. I was at the next barstool."

"What did he say to you?"

"He said he had seen me before."

"And what did you say?"

"I said I'd never seen him before."

"And then what did he say?"

"Nothing. He mooched a drink."

"What else did you talk about?"

"Just bartalk. Same as everybody else. Then he left."

"Where did he go?"

"I dunno. He didn't even say good-bye. Of course, it was his turn to buy a round . . ."

"What did you do when he left?"

"I had another drink and then I left. I went looking for a woman. New Year's Eve and all that. Am I under arrest?"

"We're almost finished," one said.

"Why'd you come over here today?" the other said.

"I thought he might be home."

"Did he say he'd be here today?"

"I never asked him. You see, it's a national holiday. A good day to visit people. You know where everybody is. Everybody stays at home on New Year's Day."

"What did you want to see him about?"

"He owed me a couple drinks. I thought I'd collect."

"What did you talk to him about?"

"He was in a coma when I got here."

"The woman next door said you had to ask where he lived."

"Like I said, I've never been here before."

"She also said the Chinaman ripped off your stereo."

"I told her I was bullshitting."

"Why did you lie to her?"

"I didn't lie. I was bullshitting."

A snort. "Big difference."

"Yeah, there is," I said. "You boys should know. You're both cops."

"Why did you say that to her?"

"It was none of her business."

"How about telling us why you came here?"

"I told you. He owed me a couple drinks and . . ."

"There were bruises on his face."

"They weren't there yesterday."

"Maybe somebody pistol-whipped him."

"He was an easy guy to pistol-whip," I said.

Anger. "Where do you come off saying that?"

"He wanted to be everybody's buddy. He was open and friendly and easy to please. People like that are easy targets."

"Do you know who did it to him?"

"I have no idea who did it to him."

"Maybe you pistol-whipped him."

"Sure I did. Then I made him snort cocaine until he went into a coma. Then I waited before I called the ambulance."

"Maybe you did."

"I was here less than a minute. Then I called you. You can check with the woman next door. She knows what happened."

"You got bruises, too."

"Yeah. They hurt when I talk too much."

"Where'd you get them?"

"I had an auto accident this morning." I watched the cop playing with the childproof top. "That's where those pills come from. And you can check with the VA hospital on Geary. I was there about three hours ago."

"Did you file a police report?"

"Not yet I haven't."

"Why haven't you?"

"My car was the only vehicle involved, there was little property damage, and I figured it could wait until Monday."

"Where were you before you came here?"

"Breakfast at Mama's of North Beach."

"Did anybody see you there?"

"Yep. Doug Lacjak, a lawyer for the city and county."
county."

The detective looked over the tiny studio. "What do you think caused the Chinaman's death?"

"A toxicologist could tell you that."

"What do *you* think happened?"

"Heart failure from an overdose of cocaine."

"Did you know he was an addict?"

"I don't know that now," I said.

They exchanged knowing looks.

"I don't know how anybody can get addicted to cocaine," I went on. "It's a stimulant, not a narcotic. There's no physical dependence, no withdrawal symptoms . . ."

"You're saying he wasn't an addict?"

"I've never met one yet. Oh, I meet people who use it a lot. But they can take it or leave it. If they can afford it, they save up and buy some. If they can't, they don't. People who use cocaine think of it like fine wine. Something they save for special occasions."

"What makes you such an expert?"

"I used to work for Pacific-Continental Investigations. We studied drugs. You never know when your investigation crosses paths with drug users."

"This guy died from cocaine."

"I agreed. "And it's the first I ever heard about."

"Others have died from coke," he insisted.

"Yeah. Those clowns who swallow coke-filled rubbers just before they go through customs. Their stomach juices eat away the latex, and they poison themselves. This is the first time I've ever heard of a regular OD."

"Do you know where he got it?"

"I don't know where he got it."

"Did he mention cocaine to you?"

"Last night was the first time I ever met him."

"Did he mention it last night?"

"He said he used to do it, but he didn't any more."

"Did he say why?"

"He said coke makes people mean."

"So why was he doing it today?"

"That puzzles me, too," I said.

"Why do you think he told you that?"

"Maybe he was paranoid. Most dopers are. They don't mind saying they've used it, but they won't admit they're still doing it. They're afraid of getting busted. Which reminds me. May I ask a question now?"

"Okay. Go ahead."

"Why am I being detained?"

"We need a statement from you."

"I gave you my statement before. I got here too late to do anything. By the time I got here, he was already in a coma. Am I under arrest?"

"What do you want, Brennen?"

"A little distance from you."

"We can get your license pulled."

"Don't bother. It expires in May."

"How about a little cooperation then?"

"I'm cooperating as best as I can."

"Then maybe you should try showing a little respect."

"You mean, caution, don't you? First you imply I know where he got the shit, then I gave it to him, then maybe I pistol-whipped him. I tried to save a guy's life, and you're grilling me for an alibi."

"You're making our work more difficult."

"You make it sound like I'm holding back, like I'm keeping you from making an arrest, but you don't even know if a crime has been committed. You're trying to convict me. Am I under arrest?"

"How come you keep asking us that?"

"If I'm not under arrest, then I'm free to go. That's the way the law reads, doesn't it? Am I under arrest?"

"No. You're not under arrest."

I stood up. "Since I'm not under arrest, then I guess I'll leave." Even the lab boys heard me and looked up.

"The cop frowned. "Okay, Brennen. Move on."

"Don't you boys know anything besides 'move on'?"

"Get going, Brennen."

I stopped at the door. "One last thing."

"Yeah? What's that?"

"Happy New Year."

CHAPTER 19

Once upon a time, Point Reyes was just another island in the Pacific Ocean. Right around the death of the dinosaurs, the North American continent drifted into it, wrinkling the land into hills and valleys, making it a peninsula separated from the mainland by the San Andreas faultline. Much is still rugged coastline and wilderness, a national seashore an hour's drive north of the city.

Inverness is the only village on the former island, and it's smaller than most wedding parties. The village doesn't have a traffic light or a stop sign, just a slow-to-20-mph sign. Most homes are hidden away beneath the dense Bishop pines on the Inverness Ridge behind the main highway. A grocery store and a gas station and a post office cater to the handful of rustics, seashore tourists, backpackers and weekenders from the city.

The grocery store was open, so I parked and went inside. A rack of postcards caught my eye, especially one of spouting grey whales. The legend on the back said the whales could be seen this month from the lighthouse at the national seashore. The whales were going south for the winter. I saluted a great idea.

The countergirl was a surfer blonde with floppy breasts. As she rang up my purchase, she asked if I were from San Francisco. When I admitted I was, she nodded her head. She had known it all along.

"I used to live there," she said. "I liked it. But everything moves too quickly down there. That's why I came up here. Nobody lives up here."

"You live up here."

"Yeah. My old man, too, sometimes. He don't like this place too much. He drinks too much. He smokes too much. Always staring at the walls. Only time he's happy is when he's off chasing tuna."

"A tuna fisherman?" I tried remembering the magazine article I'd started at the fish company. "I thought the tuna fleet sails from San Pedro."

"They do. And they sail as far south as Peru and as far north as Alaska. Wherever the tuna goes." She told me his albacore boat had passed through last week on sea trials. She was glum. "By the time he got this far north, he was a hundred miles offshore."

"Where's he now?"

She didn't know. "Wherever the tuna is." Her eyes were quiet and lifeless. They'd given up on life already.

I asked if she knew Parnell.

"Oh yeah. He comes in just about every day." She twisted behind the register and peered out the store windows. "He's outside right now. The guy loading groceries in the pickup truck."

I paid for my postcard and went outside.

Parnell was a long-haired blond with a bold moustache. He looked like Yosemite Sam on junk. At one time, he might've been a college footballer with those broad shoulders and his barrel chest, but those days were a dozen years and many missed meals ago. He was a half-foot taller than me, but thirty pounds lighter. There was little meat fleshing his bones, and none hid his ribs. He looked like a linebacker gone to speed.

I walked to his pickup. "Parnell?"

"That's what they call me." His voice was low and deep and distant, a foghorn on a rainy night. "You look like you've been kissing thistles."

"Auto accident." I introduced myself.

"What do you want with me?"

"Joey Crawford hired me to find Dani Anatole."

"Is that what you want me for?" He snorted his contempt. "He's better off without her."

"Maybe. But I'm not giving up yet."

He hefted another bag. "And why is that?"

"Joey's dead, and somebody has to tell her."

"Aw Jesus." He set down the bag as if it were the weight of the world. "How did it happen?"

"Auto accident on the Golden Gate Bridge yesterday."

"That little asshole." He noticed me again. "They never go the way you think they'd go."

"No, they don't," I agreed.

His eyes inventoried mine. They were pale eyes, clear and clean, like California wine. "All right. We'll talk about her, if you want." He grappled with another bag and shoved it onto the truck. "Only we'll do it at the ranch. I don't want this food to spoil."

I followed his pickup south. He drove like a man with his thoughts elsewhere. Just beyond the entrance to the town, he made a right turn onto a dirt road. The road led several miles into the uplands above the national seashore. After a few miles, the road forked, and we came upon a cyclone fence. A gate blocked us.

Parnell motioned me onto the shoulder. While I locked up, he unlatched the gate and pulled his truck through. After I closed the gate, I joined him in the front seat.

His face was drawn, and his eyes avoided mine. "Did he suffer much?" he wondered.

"Probably not. Probably never saw the other car."

He seemed relieved. Then he hesitated. "Was it pretty bad?"

"As bad as they get."

Silence for several miles. Parnell lost in thought, while I wondered whether I had paid my burial insurance. He drove like a junkie heading for a fix, and his truck stirred up enough dust to make a cowboy homesick. There was a ravine on one side, of course, and a hillside of boulders on the other.

His fist slammed the steering wheel. "That dirty little cunt." He slammed the truck into a lower gear. "I told him to look out for her. I meant take care of her. He shoulda done it the other way. He shoulda steered clear of her."

"He wasn't with her when he died."

"He didn't have to be."

"Are you saying she caused his problems?"

"He wasn't a burn-out when he met her."

"He had a police record when he met her."

"Oh big shit. Joyriding and possession of grass. Half the kids in this state have that before their senior prom."

"How long have you known him?"

"We grew up together in Spokane." He pressed down on the gas pedal. The pickup scooted like a jackrabbit. "He was a good guy until he met her."

"What was he like?"

"Joey was the smallest kid in school. Always getting into fights, and not just the bullies, either. Everybody picked on him because he was so short. He never won a fight, you know."

"Being short preyed on him?"

"That's why he did so much cocaine. You see, cocaine's a cinderella drug. It makes every dream come true, for thirty minutes. It gives you guts, stamina, brains, whatever. And Joey was in heaven. Coke made him feel six feet tall, which was all he ever wanted from life."

"Did he do a lot?"

"The last I heard, he was getting off it. He was pretty strung out in Sausalito. Mostly coke mixed with speed. But that was before Dani left him. He might've been doing some after she left, but not much. Another couple of weeks, and he would've given it up for good."

"Why didn't he quit sooner?"

"He could've easily enough, I s'pose, but he liked it.

Coke's an upper, not a downer. He was Superman on nose powder. It maintained his fantasies, and Dani could afford it. When she left, he couldn't afford it like before, and there wasn't much reason to keep on doing it.''

It made sense. Joey Crawford had never been dependent on cocaine. He had been dependent on Dani. When she left, she took the pleasure of cocaine with her. People can take it or leave it. He had been trying to leave it.

"You introduced them, right?"

"Yep." He glanced out the window. He didn't want his face seen. "I knew her six, seven years ago, back in the city. I was living just below Union Street and Telegraph Hill. I met her in Vesuvio's over a beer. Maybe I shouldn't tell you?"

"It's up to you." I watched the road. He might know it well, but we were moving fast, and the road was shitty with ruts and chuckholes. I lit a cigarette.

"Better put it out. Even with all this rain, there's always fire danger.''

I used the ashtray. "If you can't trust a private eye, who can you trust?"

"What's that s'pose to mean?"

"What happened at Vesuvio's?"

He missed a tree somehow. "She walks up and asks me if I want to sleep with her. We went to my place and she stayed a week."

I grinned. "Sure she did."

"Go fuck yourself. That's what she did."

I stared out the window and counted trees as if they were out-of-state plates. After a couple of dozen, I looked back at Parnell. He was intent on the windy road.

"It's your story, not mine."

After a while he agreed. "I left for Seattle when she left." He looked like he had tasted something bitter. "I heard the rest when she came up to Seattle." He almost slowed down. "She was at Vesuvio's with some other guy. She was bored, I guess. She told him she was leaving with the next asshole who walked through the door.''

"You were the next asshole.''

"I wasn't the only one.'' He glanced over. "The other guy had just proposed to her.''

We drove along the hillcrest until we crossed into the next valley. There was a ranchhouse below us. It was single-storied and rambling, like an old hunting lodge, the kind the Big Money Boys built after the railroads. I doubted they'd recognize it now.

The road seemed to sink, and we downshifted towards the ranchhouse. Tan fields and tall grasses stretched ahead of us. A pack of mongrels came from the tall grasses and chorused our arrival. We parked near a stone cistern behind the house. Naked children splashed water and shireked at us. Chickens ran loose.

Within moments, the commune came to unload the groceries. The men were lean and rangy, like their dogs. Most carried knives and leather stash bags on their broad belts. Long-haired and bearded, they all went shirtless, and their bodies were baked by the sun. The womenfolk were all baby machines, chubby-cheeked and broad-haunched. They wore billowy skirts and no make-up, and their long hair hung to their spines.

"When you got a commune,'' Parnell said, "it's like running a restaurant. No matter how you plan ahead, you still gotta go shopping every day.'' He asked if I were thirsty.

"I'm always thirsty,'' I said.

"We make our own beer up here.''

I told him to lead the way. We didn't help with the unloading. Our long strides scattered chickens.

A narrow dirt path beyond the cistern and headed uphill, an alleyway of eucalyptus on either side. The path made a half-turn after a hundred yards, and the trees began to thin. Some toolsheds were hidden beneath some sycamores.

He threw open the doors on a toolshed, flooding it with sunlight. The shed was a cover over a dirtwall cellar. The floor was inch-thick sawdust, and the walls were beams packed with dirt. The cellar looked like a liquor wholesaler's warehouse. There were cases of unlabeled beer bottles stacked against every wall.

We went down the stairs. I found an empty case and sat on it, while he opened a couple of bottles.

"We don't use the chemicals the commercial brewers use," he told me. He said they collected rainwater into earthern crocks. Malt and yeast were added, as was sugar. After fermentation in a real toolshed, the beer was siphoned off, bottled and capped, then stored in the coolness of this dirtwall cellar.

The beer was sweet and cool and mellow and light.

He told me to nurse it. "It's potent stuff. We get a higher proof, too. Almost thirty percent higher. You can get off on one bottle." He chugged in celebration.

"You said you knew her in Seattle."

The pleasure left his beer. "She was in Seattle. She dropped out and came north. She was in pretty bad shape when I found her. Staying in crash pads, shoplifting supper at the supermarket. She had lost thirty pounds in two months. She was skinnier than me, nothing but elbows and knees. Her face was breaking out. She was even losing her hair."

"Sounds like a lot of dope."

"It was. Mostly uppers and downers. She was strung out bad. Taking anything around. She had the stutters for a while, like speeders get. Their mouths work faster than their brains. And sometimes she'd be in a downer frame, and you couldn't get a word out of her for days."

"So you introduced her to Joey."

"And that same night she took him to bed. It was his bed, but she took him there."

"Love at first sight," I said.

"He felt sorry for her, for what she was doing to herself. He thought he could straighten her out, get her off pills. Dani, well, she needed room and board, and she thought it was pretty funny. Here's this little guy from the wrong side of the tracks playing social worker to the debutante."

"Sounds like a perfect fit."

"It was. He let her move in, got her a job at the cannery where he was working, even made sure she worked alongside him, just so he could watch out for her."

"Did you see them often?"

"Once after that in Seattle." He shook his head like a man shaking off a panhandler. "I got a letter from these people." He indicated the commune outside. "They needed a brewmaster, and they wanted me. I decided to accept the gig, so I went over to Joey's place to say goodbyes." His lips were wet with beer. "Dani wasn't home, but Joey was. He was in the kitchen heating a spoon over the gas burners."

I lowered my beer. "Smack?"

"I knocked the spoon out of his hand. Called him every name in the book. Then I walked out on him." His face was sad for his little buddy. "It wasn't very strong stuff. Kool-Aid strength maybe. But he was skin-popping it, and that stuff's easy to go for again."

"Where'd he get smack?"

"Dani. Nobody else could get him to try it. He couldn't wipe his ass unless she said it was okay."

"D'you think he kept trying it?"

"After what I said to him?" But Parnell wasn't a hasty man, and he tried being reasonable. "I doubt it. Maybe." He looked sadder. "We better start heading back."

I told him I hated to leave. "D'you make house calls on this stuff?"

He knew it. "It is good beer."

I bought a case for five bucks. He threw a six pack in.

"For the ride home?" I wondered.

He didn't smile. "This stuff you can't drive on."

The sun was glacier-white when we came out. Across the valley, some people from the commune were finishing the first half of a geodesic dome. Its mylar exterior was a mirror of sunshine against the tan hills and green trees. A hawk coasted on a thermal.

"Have you seen either one since then?"

"Last month. The Friday after Turkey Day. I hadn't

seen them for ages. Not since they moved down to Sausalito. Then I get this postcard inviting me to a Thanksgiving party. I guess they wanted me to see how well they were doing. I know that's why I went. I wanted to see how they were doing, too.''

"How were they doing?"

He didn't know. "They were blasted out of their minds.'' He smiled like an old fan listening to a has-been comic working for laughs in an empty lounge. "I've never seen so much cocaine at any single party.''

"They were both doing coke?"

"Lots of coke. Line after line.''

"Did you talk to Joey about it?''

"I tried a couple of times. He wouldn't listen. Why should he? He was in heaven on coke. He never saw what it was doing to him, what he was doing to others. I told him, if he kept it up, he'd find himself picking beets on a state prison farm.''

"Why was Dani doing so much coke?''

"Dani likes the party scene as much as her sister does. Coke brings out people to a party. The more coke you got, the more guests. Dani dug the attention everybody gave her.''

"Did you talk with her about it?''

"Not about coke. She came up to me early and got the point across that she wouldn't mind rekindling whatever had been between us. Even though she was still living with Joey. I told her to get fucked. If she wanted me, she had to dump him. I wasn't trying to be cool, I was just trying to help him out. If she cut him loose, he might've had a chance.''

"How did she react to what you said?''

He didn't know. "That's when the fight started.''

"Between who and who and over what?''

"It was really stupid. Joey baiting a poor Chinaman. Accusing him of switching flour with his cocaine. The poor kid didn't know what was going on. I tried step-ping in. So did Jack Anatole, Dani's cousin. We almost got it on together. He wanted to smear Joey's face, just knock him flat. I wanted to get Joey out of there.''

"Why save Joey's hide?"

"He didn't know what he was doing. He had done so much coke, booze, weed, whatever that night, he couldn't taste a cigarette. He was only fighting because the Chinaman was his size. Why fight when you can't stand up?"

We passed more communards coming back. The womenfolk sang or hummed to themselves. My presence seemed to put them off slightly, but they could still smile and whisper hellos. The men kept to themselves, as if they'd been poaching deer in the lowlands. Only their heads would nod when our paths crossed. There wasn't a black or brown or yellow face in the whole crowd. There were no teenagers, either, and no one looked middle-aged or older. It was as if certain generations had been deliberately skipped.

"Dani was here last week."

I stopped in midstep. "What day was that?"

"Oh Christ." He watched the sky. "A couple of days before Christmas, I think. She told me she'd left Joey. She said he was impotent from doing so much coke. I think she got tired of cheating on him, got bored with guilt. She wanted to move in with me right then and there."

"Just like that?"

"Yep. That's when I hit her." He wasn't embarrassed. "I'm suppose to be a pacifist, but she pissed me off . . ." He realized the show he was putting on for my benefit. His voice trailed off.

"Where did she go when she left here?"

"Back to her sister's house, probably. She told me, if I changed my mind, to call here there. Not that that's likely to happen. Not after what she did to Joey."

He drove me back to the cyclone fence. He opened the gate for me, then came over to my car. I rolled down my window.

"How'd you know where to find me?"

"Davey Huie." I saw the name meant nothing to him. "He was that Chinese kid at the party."

"No kidding. How's he doing, anyway?"

"He's dead." I watched his eyes.

He was confused. "He was with Joey on the bridge?"

"An overdose of cocaine, apparently."

Parnell almost laughed at that. "You need a swimming pool full of it before you can overdose."

"Like I said, apparently an overdose."

"I don't get you."

"Maybe he'd been doing it for years and poisoned himself. Maybe he did one helluva superhuman dose. Maybe it was cut with Draino, or maybe it wasn't even coke. Maybe he had a weak heart. Maybe somebody jammed it into him."

Parnell was stunned. "But that would be murder."

"I don't know if it is," I said.

But he saw an answer in my eyes.

He stayed for a while in my rear view mirror. He looked like a man who had been left behind. He didn't look grateful.

CHAPTER 20

Daylight glowed on polished oak panelling. I looked over the library shelves. Not a paperback in sight, just bound volumes of century-old literature, none by any author I recognized.

"What are you doing here?"

I spun around feeling guilty.

Catherine and her goddam entrances. "Just what the hell are you doing here?" She wore a Jaeger blouse and embroidered jeans. Her tennis shoes were street-worn and holey. She still looked good, a living doll. She was unbearable, a golden pain in the ass.

"I came to see you." I forced myself to cool off. "Aren't you going to wish me a Happy New Year?"

She came on like a fertility goddess who had just caught her high priest messing with a sailor. "And what did you do to your face?"

I gave up being polite. "I want to see Dani."

"She's not here," she snapped.

"She's been here since Christmas Day."

She stopped dead. "Who told you that?"

"Aw, c'mon. Does it matter?"

She poked her face into mine. "Who are you?" she hissed.

I was surprised. She was afraid of me.

"I want to know who you are."

I almost snickered. "You know who I am. You hired me. You remember that, don't you?" She wasn't half so regal this close.

"His parents never heard of you."

"Whose parents?"

"Joey Crawford's, that's whose." She looked down on me. "Dani called Spokane, and they never heard of you."

"I never heard of them, either."

That stopped her. "But you represent them."

"I never told you I did."

She backed off. "Jack told me." She tried her information on me. "He called here yesterday after you left. He said you were out at the fish company asking about my sister. He said you were working for his parents."

"I never told him that."

She shook her blonde hair. "He said you did."

I said that to Alex Symons. "Mind if I smoke?"

"Yes, I do mind. If you must, use the back porch."

I shoved my smoke back into its pack. She was another goddam clean air freak. They were determined to bring back Prohibition. "What else did he say?"

"He said I shouldn't trust you."

"So why are you telling me all this?"

She wasn't flustered. "I want to know what's going on."

"Why didn't you tell me Dani was here?"

"Nobody was supposed to know." She was an older sister still keeping little girl secrets. "Joey was calling all the time. If he knew she was here, he'd start coming over, and Dani didn't want to see him." Older sisters get protective.

"If she saw him," I argued, "she could've told him it was all over between them."

"But she didn't know whether it was all over. She didn't know if she wanted a reconciliation. That's why she came here. She needed time to think it over."

And of course Catherine had agreed. She thought she could poison Dani's mind against Joey. "Why did you hire me?"

"I wanted to know what was going on. I was buying time. Time until I found out from Dani what was going on."

"Did you tell her about Joey Crawford?"

"Yes." She hated to remember. "She went up to her room." Her chin quivered. "She told me to leave her alone. She locked herself in."

Oh boy. So much for my case.

"And I told her about you," Catherine said.

Aw shit. "What did you say?"

"That you were here. And what Jack told me."

"Did Jack get a chance to talk with her?"

She didn't know. She couldn't remember.

"What did Dani say about me?"

"She didn't say anything." Catherine walked around the desk. "She called Spokane. His parents said he died in an automobile accident. Is that true?"

"As far as I know."

"You said it was murder."

"I said the police don't confide in me." I sighed at wasted time. "Where is she?"

"I don't know." Sounded like a probation officer called on the carpet because her prize trophy robbed a gas station and split town in a police car.

"You don't know where she is."

"I wasn't here when she left." She tried to explain. "She left sometime last night. Just packed up her belongings and left. Not even a goodbye note. I haven't seen her since last night."

"Why did she leave?"

"She said you'd know."

"What am I suppose to know?"

"She said you wanted to bust her."

"I'm not trying to bust anybody."

"I told her you said that. I told her you weren't from food stamps, and she said you didn't have to be. She said you had a good reason for following her. She said you wanted to bust her. Does it have anything to do with drugs?"

"I'm a private investigator, not a nark. I told you that."

"She has been involved with drugs?"

I hesitated. "It seems like she has."

"Oh lord." But she didn't doubt me. In her eyes, Dani was now Missing In Action. Her kid sister was as good as dead. Sometimes it wasn't that simple.

"Where did she go when she left?"

Catherine was deliberately vague. "She could've gone anywhere. She just packed some clothes and left." Her mind was starting a Disappearing Act. Maybe she was working on a breakdown. Maybe it was all a con.

I didn't buy her story. There were few places Dani could have gone last night. Most people were out celebrating the New Year. Either Catherine was hiding something or Dani didn't trust her sister any more.

Catherine began to rise, as if her body was a ghost. She looked like she had seen The Way and was tired of waiting. She was drifting to get away from me. Drifters and runaways always think the grass is greener somewhere else.

I wasn't finished. Not yet, anyway. "Where's your Baretta?"

"Uhn?" She stared.

"The gun you keep in your desk."

"It's in my desk." She came back to earth. She went around and opened the drawer. "It's not here." She looked up. "How did you know it wasn't here?"

"I went through your desk."

"You went through . . . ?"

"I didn't take it. Maybe Dani did."

She was stunned. "You think she might be in trouble?"

"I think she thinks so."

She puzzled over that. "For what?"

"Where would she go if she thought she was in trouble?"

"She'd come here." She couldn't concentrate. "She

was here. She was here until you showed up." She remembered me. "Why are you doing this to her?"

"Whatever she's been doing she started before yesterday."

"Yesterday." She remembered she had it rough yesterday. "Oh, you're driving me crazy with worry!" Her face twitched at the thought of more worry lines. "Why are you doing this?"

I was persistent. "Where would she go?"

She tried hard. "Riki? Jack?" She didn't know. "No. No. I don't want to hear any more of this." Her spine jolted upright. She bolted from the room.

Once again I was left alone with the black maid. She blocked the doorway as if I might chase and tackle her employer. Her sullen eyes said I was a bucket of shit with a rusty handle.

I waited until we reached the hallway. "Dani was here." Maybe someone had told her loose tongues sink ships. "What happened yesterday after I left?"

"Why should I tell you?" she said. "You fucked up New Year's Eve for me, and the way it's going, my whole weekend's going with it."

"You know I never meant to do that."

She hardened. "I ain't taking any more shit than I haveta."

"My job's the same way." I didn't care what she said. "Dani was here. Why didn't you tell me she was here?"

She decided what the hell. "She wasn't here when you was here. She was out shopping for clothes."

"What's with all this secrecy bullshit?"

"That boyfriend of hers. Dani didn't want him around no more. Catherine, she thought he was shit."

"What did you think of him?"

"He only come here once."

"So what did you think of him?"

"He was shit," she agreed.

"What's Dani been up to since she came here?"

"She don't do shit." She realized that wasn't fair. "Eating candy, rolling joints, playing records, drinking

Galliano like it tastes good. If I had her money, I'd be rolling my own. Only I wouldn't be drinking that Galliano. I'd get some good stuff."

"What happened yesterday after I left?"

"Catherine got into the bottles." She grimaced. It was a corny story. "She was feeling guilty about Joey dying like that. You know, unwanted. Jack, that's her cousin, he called up right after that and told her 'bout you and she went back to the bottles, only harder, like there was no tomorrow and she wanted to die, too."

"What time did Dani get home?"

" 'Bout seven. Catherine was drunk and crazy. The first thing she tells her sister, your boyfriend's dead."

"She's that bad a drunk?"

"Worse." The maid knew. "She drinks all alone and she drinks till she falls down." Her face held no respect for a drunk woman.

"How did Dani take the news?"

"Oh, she freaked out. You gotta when your boyfriend's dead, even if you don't love him. She ran upstairs, locked herself in, wouldn't come out for supper, even. I took some up to her, then she don't even eat it." The maid really couldn't blame her. "She hadda get her head together. When she does stick her head out, Catherine's gotta blow it again, telling her 'bout you being here."

"I heard how that went down."

"It didn't go down. Dani didn't know what to do 'bout you, or where you fitted in. She called up north and then she really got scared. Nobody ever heard about you up there. She thought you were the Heat."

"Where was Catherine all this time?"

"Crying and whining in her bottle. Half gone and all twisted around. Talking about the family name, like that means something. Even Dani got pissed at that. She went back upstairs and locked herself in again. She made *me* come up with her, made *me* pack an overnight case for her." She was pissed all over again. "Shit, I told her I wanted to go home, it's New Year's Eve, I had things to do."

"But she made you stay."

"She said she was gonna give me a ride home." The maid couldn't forgive that. "I musta been crazy waiting around for her to get off the telephone. That woman. I told her nobody stays home on New Year's Eve."

"Who'd she call?"

"Anyone she ever knew. Only they wasn't home."

"Anybody in particular?"

"Her cousin Jack. She tried him a whole lotta times, only she never got through. She got busy signals, then nobody was home."

"She never got through to him?"

"Not while she was here, anyway."

"What time was this?"

" 'Bout nine. Maybe later."

"Anybody else?"

"A long distance. I don't know who she called, but she said she'd be there by morning. She said she had a couple of things to take care of, and she'd be on her way."

"How did you know it was long distance?"

"She had the telephone book out, and it was open to the area code map, and I had to put it away."

"You don't know who she talked to?"

She smirked. "It was a man."

"How do you know that?"

"Dani was smiling. She's got a poker-face around women."

"Then what did she do?"

"We split."

"Did she say where she was going?"

"The airport. She was getting outa town for a while."

"Why didn't she tell Catherine where she was going?"

"She couldn't. Catherine had passed out. Shit, I hadda wait around until she put her sister to bed. We both done that before, you know, so it didn't take her long, but I wasn't the only one what was pissed off."

"After she dropped you off, she went to the airport?"

"I don't see how she did." She snickered. "She didn't have no money. She was in a hurry and forgot it." The maid couldn't believe white folks' foolishness. "The banks was all closed, cos of the holidays. She tried borrowing off me, but, shit, what with all the money this family's got, she ain't getting no money from me."

"Why didn't she come back here?"

"Cos she thought you was gonna show up here again. You was all she could talk 'bout. She wanted no part of you."

"She thought I was the Heat."

She gave me a foul look. "Dani's either a fool or a phoney, cos she shoulda known you ain't the Heat. You're too soft."

I ignored that. "Where would she go if she thought she were in trouble?"

"The first man she found at home."

The phone began ringing somewhere inside. The maid shooed me outside. The front door closing behind me sounded like an airlock closing. Maybe this branch of the Anatoles wanted out of Spaceship Earth. I couldn't say they were wrong.

The Mercedes was gone, as was the holly wreath on the door. I went to the garage and peered through dirty windows. The garage was empty. There was an oil stain on the concrete. It could've come from the Mercedes.

I started off downhill towards my car. It was peaceful on that shaded street. You could hear the limousines waxing in the sunlight. Wealth is a plateau above the daily grind, and in Pacific Heights the rich do look down on the poor.

Massive homes. Songbirds and trees and lawns in the city. There were no people around. They all led busy lives elsewhere. They were creative. They had taste. They hired interior decorators and subscribed to the opera. Their city park had tennis courts and flowers. The men could smile without showing their teeth, and their women could never be too lean.

Then I dead-stopped.

It felt like a steel rod. My whole spine curled up like a

question mark. You can never forget the feel of a gun in your back. You swear you can feel that metal circle. Only dead men and movie stars have guts at a time like this.

I started to raise my hands slowly.

"Put your hands down, stupid." It sounded like Riki Anatole. He poked me again. "Turn around slowly."

I moved slowly. Even then I thought I moved too fast. I made a conscious effort to slow down, and still thought I moved too fast.

Riki was half in the bag and dead serious. His boozed face was drawn and angry, afraid of me. He needed sleep and his clothes looked slept in. His tie was missing, and a collar point hung over his blazer lapel. He looked like a bear leaving a cave on the first day of spring. He had a Police Special in his left hand.

"What's with the gun?" I asked.

He tightened his grip. "I don't trust you, you son of a bitch. You've been following me."

"When was I following you?"

"Yesterday." His gun hand shook. "You bastard."

"If I did, I didn't mean to."

"I don't believe you." He wet his lips. "You wanted to follow me. I told my lawyer about you."

"Is Tan Ng your lawyer?"

"So what if he is?"

I pointed to my face. "He did this to me."

"That old man?" He swayed. "I just wanted to know who hired you." He remembered his gun. He poked it my way with a cokehead's phony bravado. He waved the gun through the air. "You think you're pretty tough, don't you?"

"Tough enough to handle you," I lied.

His chin twitched, a faint and irregular pulse, just as it had yesterday with his wife at the fish company. His twitch made him an easy win at poker and a dangerous man with a gun.

People like Riki Anatole have little knowledge of guns. Amateurs with a gun were the most dangerous. They knew nothing, and that is usually more than they needed to know. What was worse, they don't understand a gun and its consequences.

"Start walking across the street."

I went slowly, deliberately. I set foot after foot ahead of me, almost counting the steps. I resisted every impulse that told me to run. Nobody runs with a gun in his back. I found it hard to believe no one saw us.

His beige Caddy looked like a magazine ad beneath some umbrella trees. I followed his instructions and entered on the passenger side. He made me slide across the seat to the steering wheel. The big bear blundered in. He threw me the ignition keys.

I snapped the ignition. The steering wheel unlocked. Then the starter turned over. I forgot the gas pedal. The engine coughed, then died. I told Riki he needed a tune-up.

"Get on with it."

He was a bigger man than me, so the car seat was pushed back all the way. He helped me move it forward. The bear jarred me against the steering wheel when he helped the seat with his weight. That gave me an idea. I fastened my seat belt and my shoulder harness. Riki was nervous, too nervous to notice. He was left-handed, and he found it hard to hold the gun on me from the passenger side.

I started the car again.

"This time use the gas pedal."

The engine roared into life. Exhaust smoke billowed in the rear view mirror. The Caddy had a big engine.

"I suppose you're taking me to Dani."

"Why would I do that?" His laughter was coarse and laced with whiskey-courage. "You're a cocky son of a bitch. Never give up a cover story."

"What did you tell her last night?"

"I didn't say nothing," he said.

"Didn't she call you last night?"

"I wasn't home last night." He frowned. "Last night was New Year's Eve. I threw a party at the club." He started to shrink. "My wife drank too much. She was asleep before midnight." He sounded like a disappointed honeymooner. He raised his gun. "You're working for her."

"I'm not working for her," I said.

"She did hire you. Jesus H. Christ, she'll be the death of me." He looked over with bleary eyes. "You're fired. And you're gonna refund all that money."

"I'm not working for her."

"Slow down," he demanded.

We were almost going fast enough.

"My grandfather hired you, didn't he? Well, fuck him. You just tell him, I don't care if he does cut me off. I've done the best I could. Even threw a goddam party and that didn't help none." He was lost in self-worry. "I almost lost my wife last night. She shouldn't mix pills with her booze." His knuckles went white. "That crazy bitch. I'm not going to let that happen again."

I slammed down the accelerator. The car was sluggish, almost stalled, then overdrive kicked in and all 420 cubic inches broke free.

"Hey, I'm telling you, slow down!"

I pushed down my foot. "Go fuck yourself."

"Listen, I mean it." He shook his gun in my face.

"So do I. Go fuck yourself."

He leveled the gun. Both sides were blurring.

"Shoot and we crash." I pressed it to the floor. The car shot ahead at freeway speeds. We crashed a stop sign.

He reached for the ignition key.

I slapped his hand. "You can't take the key out. The steering wheel locks." There was a Rolls Royce ahead. I knew enough to pass him. He was just cruising.

"Oh Jesus, you're gonna kill us." His face was snow white. We flew through, passing a mail truck making a left turn.

"I don't give a shit." We scared the hell out of a lady curbing her Afghan between two cars.

Sweat rode his temple. "Aw shit." He lowered the gun.

"You wanna talk this over?"

He nodded dumbly, too scared to talk.

"Throw away the gun. Out the window."

He had forgotten it. It was useless to him now. His right hand blundered down and caught the power window buttons. The vent on his side began to widen. His left hand tried cramming the pistol outside.

We hit the crest at Lyons Street. My biggest mistake.

We jumped the crest at freeway speed and Riki screamed.

The homes alongside were small castles, brick chateaus. One of the most charming streets in the city. It's not quite the steepest, but it is paved with smooth red brick. The South Gate to the Sixth Army's Presidio is at the bottom of the hill. There's a stop sign, too. An Army convoy was almost through the gate.

And I had all four wheels off the ground.

I spun the power steering sharply.

Then we bottomed. The car went *whomp* and the shocks gave. Riki started screaming. The tires screamed back. But slowly, ever-so-slowly, the car angled off to the left. I slammed down the brakes. They locked and we sluiced leftward, hurtling down towards Presidio Avenue.

But we didn't hit the convoy. We hit a mailbox.

We hit like a jetliner nailing a beer can. The noise was incredible—a planeload of plumber pipes crashing. The hinges of the box squealed and broke free from cement. The Caddy was lifted into the air. I thought we'd fly like a rock skipping over water.

But the undercarriage caught on the mailbox. When my body slammed forward, my shoulder harness kept me from the steering wheel. Riki wasn't so lucky. He slammed into the dashboard, banging his head and shoulders. His gun went off, shattering the AM-FM radio. It was quiet like eternity then.

I sat and sat and stared and stared.

Riki was slumped like a ragdoll. His clothes were all bloody.

"Are you okay?"

He started swearing. His heart wasn't in it. He had a bloody nose.

"If you can bitch, you're okay." I cracked the door, hauled myself up, then stepped down.

The Caddy sat atop the mailbox like a boat on a reef, its prow dangling over a treelawn. The mailbox was crushed. It had broken free from all four metal hinges, cracked the cement and been thrown onto the lawn. Oil was soaking into the grass. The transmission and drivetrain were twisted like drinking straws. The front wheels hung down like a dead man. A corpse on a rock.

The convoy had stopped. Servicemen were coming our way. The other traffic on Presidio tooted their horns, impatient. Some neighbors closed the curtains and opened front doors.

I patted the prow and started off down Presidio.

"You're leaving me here?" Riki had crawled out.

"You don't expect me to stay."

His face changed color. "How do I explain this?"

"You were cleaning your gun and it went off and you lost control of your car."

His face changed color again. "I can't say that."

"You better say you were driving. I have no insurance, and your company won't like my version."

He realized that. "Oh my god." He was a tired man.

"Maybe Uncle Sam won't sue." I went off downhill. There was a coffeehouse down the street that sold imported beers. The walk would keep me from stiffening up until I was ready.

CHAPTER 21

Smuggler's Cove is a little seacoast town south of the city and west of the airport. Its name goes back fifty years, its buildings almost as far. The houses are mostly woodframe worn by the wind and tired of the ocean. The people who live here have faces like driftwood.

Although it has a primo location along the coast, Smugglers Cove has never developed a Gold Coast. People, like water, seek their own level, and the lowlands were subdivided and civilized a long time ago. The hills were too steep for developers, and the summer fog kept the tourists away. Headlights are no good in a fog that lasts all summer.

Smuggler's Cove had a single shopping center. It wasn't much, a couple of dozen mom-n-pops and a family-owned supermarket. There was no Sears, no K-Mart, no Penney's, no Safeway, not even a Woolworth's. The mall wasn't landscaped, a capital crime in parts of California. Most people didn't bother locking their cars in the lot. The market manager probably kept coathangers for anyone who did.

The mall was west of the coastal highway between two rugged promontories that stood a thousand feet high. A road circled those two cold rocks and the mall. Behind the mall, it skirted between sand dunes and the apartment building I wanted.

The apartment building wasn't much, either. A quarter of a century ago, someone had hollowed out a solid block of stucco, painted it like a sand castle, then partitioned it into a couple of dozen cavelike units. An outside landing had been tacked onto the second floor like an afterthought.

I took the access road between the apartments and the shopping mall. There were parking stalls on the building's backside. There were no backdoors, so the tenants had to walk around the apartment building to get inside. You could've bought any car in the wooden stalls for five hundred bucks. The majority would've gone for two hundred. Some a junker wouldn't tow for scrap. Only one stall was empty.

I parked curbside by the ocean. Every tenant had a carport, so there was plenty of street parking. The surf echoed against the rocky headlands, there was sand in the street, and the winds blew strong and constant.

A pair of seagulls flew in from the ocean, then flew up and over the roof. I looked over the blue water and white surf. There was a gold sun beyond. Surf on rock made a pleasant sound.

The building had weathered poorly. It looked tired. It faced the ocean as if it knew it was only a windbreak for a shopping center. Its walls were faded and chipped from blowing sand and salt air. There was the suggestion of a lawn, and the grass grew thin like hair on an old man's head. Nobody had plants outside their apartments. There were no hibachis, no briquets, no bookshelf bricks, no welcome mats. You mind your own business when you live here.

The lobby was open to the public. The mailboxes said Jack Anatole lived in an end unit on the second floor. I started up the staircase, passing a ten-speed bicycle double-chained to the railing. Just another sign of the times.

There were hedges of ivy along the wall. Some leaves were gunmetal grey. Up close, they were plastic, corroded by the salt air. I looked out at the cars in the street. They all had rusted hoods, fenders, grills. The blowing sand and salt air were hell on them, too.

I rapped knuckles on his door. Hollow doors to match hollow hills. There was a decal on the kitchen window. The black horse dancing. There was no answer from inside. I tried the door again, and still no one came. I had a hunch whose carport was empty.

The door wasn't flush against the woodwork. A push-button lock and no deadbolt. The windows and the patio door had aluminum frames, pop-out glass and simple latches. Why should a burglar waste time with the ten-speed? From a security standpoint, the staircase was probably the toughest nut to crack.

I wondered how Jack lived. My curiosity got the better of me. After all, Jack belonged to local Porsche club. I used an expired charge card like a knife, and the door swung free like a noose. Like the banks say, credit cards open new doors.

I had to duck my head entering. The air was stale and heavy drapes kept out the sunlight. The insides were dry and dark, like a desert cave and just like the smokehouse. The landlord had used the same paint inside, and the walls were sand, too. The surf was a pulsebeat beneath my feet.

I guess I expected Dani to pop from the woodwork. When she didn't, I felt stupid. Since I was here, I went from room to room. Maybe some of her belongings were here. Maybe some clue to where she was.

I started in the living room. Furniture from rental and some cobwebs above the drapes. A portable color tv with last Sunday's tv supplement. A fairly expensive AM-FM receiver, some speakers, but no turntable and no record collection.

The kitchen was next. A sixpack and a three dollar bottle of wine in the refrigerator. TV dinners in the freezer and ginger ale in the trash. Instant coffee and coffee cups. Some kitchenware. A few water glasses, but no eggs. A new calendar on the table, though the old one was still on the wall, stuck in the middle of last year.

Lines had been drawn through the first few days of December.

I went to the bedroom. There was a kingsize bed with rumpled sheets on one side only. A dresser and a nightstand and a closet. The closet had clothes neat on their hangers. A suit, sportcoats, slacks, jeans, workboots. Some camping gear on the shelf.

The nightstand had a clean ashtray, a clock radio, a fuck book about the last man alive on a planet of women. There was a *Car & Driver* atop the clock radio. There was a Porsche on the cover of the magazine. I paged through the magazine, came across an 8×10 enlargement of Dani, a duplicate to the print I carried. Once again I found myself falling into blue eyes.

I went through the dresser. A pack of condoms. A jackknife. Some stones from the ocean. A stack of photos. I laid them out in a row. Jack or Dani standing or sitting in front of a VW microbus. No other people in any photograph. In some, a small palm tree or a cactus nearby. The Mexican coastline was background for all of them. I shuffled them and replaced them and kept digging.

And what's a bachelor pad without an address book? I paged through it. Jack Anatole was a good-looking guy, a knockout in some crowds, but he lived a cold fish life. There were four names and addresses in the book. Cousin, cousin, brother, grandfather. There were no ladies listed. He had no warm numbers to crawl to at last call.

This was the cleanest bachelor pad I'd ever seen. There were some crumbs around the toaster, some cobwebs above the drapes, but the joint was cleaner than babyteeth. No clothes or shoes or newspapers on the carpet. No dust on the receiver. Not even scratches on the imitation wood chairs.

The cleanliness bothered me. Some folks are compulsive, but the cobwebs above the drapes said Jack Anatole wasn't one of them. A man's home is his castle, and seeing how he lives shows me the man. Jack couldn't be this unimaginative.

There were no posters, no paintings, no bookshelves, no plants, no souvenirs from Vietnam and nothing a cop could call paraphernalia. None of those homey charms people use to indicate they live somewhere. There was no mail, either, not even a Christmas card. Nothing, in fact, to signify the holidays.

There was no personality to this place, as if it were swept clean daily, down to the fingerprints. There was just enough and even less. I couldn't tell if he had nothing or just didn't want to be pinned down.

I couldn't live like this. It was like being in the Army again. A transient barracks. A man getting ready to ship out, or a man waiting for his discharge. A man who hadn't expected to live here this long and hoped he didn't have to live here much longer.

Guys in prison are this neat. Killing time was important to them. Jack had spent time in the stockade. Last year's calendar had days marked off, and Jack wasn't a man to doodle. Maybe, for him, each day was the same. Maybe he had no reason to mark the days any more.

A blur in the corner of my eye banged into the side of my head. It was like being jumped by a brick wall. It knocked me flat on the floor, and I hit it hard.

I lay there a while. I was breathing and I was alive. I couldn't remember how to stand on my own two feet again. It didn't seem that important. I told myself that if I just stayed still, somebody would find me.

I came back soon enough. Jack Anatole sat on the edge of his bed. My gun was in his hand, and it was pointed at me.

He looked me over. "You're a mess."

I saw a grocery bag with tv dinners and ginger ale. There was a battered clock radio on the bedsheets. Somebody had stepped on it with my head.

"Don't you ever get tired of this shit?"

"All the time." I had spoken too soon. My head echoed like a hall of mirrors. I wondered how my gun had been taken away from me.

He kicked my shin. "Did you have a nice time going through my apartment?"

"I was just returning the favor." I waited until I felt better before going on. "You went through mine last night."

His hand tightened, then relaxed. "Somebody's a liar."

"Where were you last night?"

He played it cool. "Celebrating New Year's Eve."

"Your Porsche." I had trouble swallowing. "Somebody saw it outside my place."

He was amused. "I wasn't driving it last night. Somebody borrowed it. Somebody from work, I think."

"On New Year's Eve?" I shook my head. It rattled. "Oh no, you'd be in it."

"You're pretty good," he admitted.

"I know." My skin felt like a drum being tightened. My pills had fallen from my jacket. I picked them up.

He raised the gun.

"Pills." I pointed to my face. "My face." I got to my feet slowly. "Don't go away." Then I stumbled off towards the bathroom.

He watched me pour a tumbler of water. He found my guts refreshing. "You're tougher than you look."

I swallowed two tabs. "Dumber." I didn't feel brave. Listening hurt my head and talking didn't help. Right now the codeine was more important than a bullet in the back.

He sat on the pot. "You keep a messy place."

"As if you didn't mess it up more." I looked in the mirror. The stitches were where the drumskin had stretched too far. There were still green and purple bruises from my windshield, but I didn't see any new ones. There wasn't even blood on my head. I held the sink for a while to keep it from shaking.

"You got a nice face there," he said.

I couldn't think of anything obscene to say. "Why should you care?" I threw water on my face. "What did you break into my place for?" It seemed like a fair question.

"I wanted to find out who you were."

I frowned. "Who do you think I am?"

He looked down on me. "Once you were a private eye. Now you're a bum collecting unemployment. You're broke. You need dough. That's why you're playing in this shit."

"I coulda told you that," I groused. The needle was back. It echoed like the turf. It had to be my pulse. I covered my face in a towel for a while. "Are you planning on pressing charges?"

He looked around. "What were you looking for?"

"Maybe I was just looking."

"As far as I can tell, nothing's been taken."

I tried to laugh. It hurt. "You got nothing."

He raised my gun again. "You're still looking for Dani." It was an old story. The man with the gun knows all the answers.

"I almost found her yesterday."

"Oh yeah?" He wanted to hear this.

"She's been at her sister's all week." I could talk a bit better now. "But you knew that. You called her after I left the smokehouse."

"I can still talk with my relatives, can't I?"

"You told Catherine Joey Crawford's parents hired me."

He snorted. "Why not?" He looked glum. "It's truer than what you told Alex Symons."

"Why should I tell that yoyo what I want Dani for?"

He jiggled the gun like a man making up his mind. "What do you really want with Dani?"

"Did she call you last night?"

He braked to a halt. "Why was she trying to call me?"

"She needed money. She was leaving town."

"Now you tell me how you knew that."

I made a cluck-cluck sound. "You shoulda called her back."

"What makes you think I didn't? I called her right after I left your place, but there was nobody home."

"And I drove up with a chick."

He aimed the gun at me. "Now you tell me what's going on."

It seemed fair enough. "After Catherine talked with you, Dani found out about it and got scared. She took off running. What do you think she was scared of?"

"You, chump." He had a point to make. "I'm sick of you chasing her. You're worse than a guy puppy-dogging a chick."

I let that pass. "You know of any places she might've gone?"

"A million places. I'm not telling you any of them. Why should I? I don't dog people around, trying to find out what they're up to. It's none of your fucking business where she goes or what she does."

"Where would she go if she thought she were in trouble?"

"She's not here." He was matter of fact.

"If she couldn't reach you?"

"You're a clown," he told me. "How did you ever get suckered into this? Don't you ever investigate your own clients?"

"I told you. Joey Crawford's my client."

"A dead man for a client." He shook his head. "Bullshit."

"He wanted me to find the girl who walked out on him. Find Dani, that was his last wish."

Jack reconsidered everything. "You said last wish. His last wish would be to see her again." That seemed to intensify him. "I can see why they hired you."

This should be good. "Oh yeah? Why?"

"You're stupid." He talked like a probation officer trying to save some punk's life. "You don't know who you're working for. You don't know it's shit you're playing in. You don't even know what's going on."

"I don't," I agreed. "Why don't you tell me?"

He edged forward. "You're a pawn in this mess," he said. "A pawn for the muscle. Your clients aren't playing straight with you, Brennen, and they're using you to get to us. If you knew who they were, you'd sooner kiss shit."

"Okay. I give up. Who're my clients?"

"Organized crime. Or working for them."

"What would they want that you got?"

"You really don't know," he marvelled.

"I don't even know why I'm talking to you."

He had a face like a fortune-teller. "They're gonna do you just like they did Joey Crawford." To him, the future was a rock so big even God couldn't budge it.

"Dead, you mean."

"Real dead." Vietnam was in his eyes. The VA hospital was filled with eyes like that. Superman could only see through walls.

"You don't think Joey's death was an accident, do you?"

He was patient. "They killed him and they'll kill you. My advice is to lay off this mess. Stay out of it."

"Is that why you called me last night?"

"I don't want you hurt. Stay out of this."

I got curious. "Are you threatening me?"

"Jesus, where do you get your lines? If you're standing in their way, they're gonna blow you away, so you better stay out of this. Tell your clients, too. They better stay away. They're muscling in where they don't belong. If they try anything, I will kill them."

"Is that why you got Davey out of Jardin's Saloon?"

He thought I was smarter. "Davey's no match for you."

"You sandbagged me, you sonovabitch."

His GI smile said sorry, Charlie. "I had no choice. I had to get him away from you. He's got a big mouth when he's drunk."

"Is that why you worked him over? To sober him up?"

He didn't understand. "When was this?"

"He had black and blue marks on his face."

"I didn't do anything to him. I'm not the Mob and I don't play by their rules. Go ask him yourself. Yeah, why don't you?" He had a better idea. "You're the private eye. Why don't you find out who did it to him?"

"Davey was a real pain, wasn't he?"

He was catching on. "Okay, Brennen, you're going to tell me what's going on." He knew my gun was a great persuader.

"He's dead. Heart failure."

He flinched, came close to pulling the trigger. "Heart failure? A heart attack? Don't bullshit me, Brennen."

"He ODed on coke this morning."

"I don't believe you." He almost laughed. "You don't die from doing coke."

"That's what happened."

He lost himself in thought. "I can't imagine him dead. Nobody dies from coke." He found no comfort in those truths.

"You were the last one who saw him alive."

He caught up. His face curled. "I oughta kill you for that." He sighted my gun at my heart. "Like putting you outa your misery." He sounded like a volcano finding a perfect excuse.

I figured I was dead. How do you save your life in twenty-five words or less? "You're talking just like the Mob. Don't play by their rules."

"You stupid shit." His hand dropped. "Get outa here." He wasn't even looking down at me. "Right now." He had seen too much of me.

"You got my gun."

He tossed it over. "Blow your brains out."

"Thanks for the advice," I told him. "I'll be sure to follow it someday." I stopped by the door. "By the way, where is Dani?"

"Fuck off, Brennen. She's not here."

CHAPTER 22

Baytown is a city of fifty thousand people south of the airport. A few years ago only Jesus could have walked these streets between the freeway and the bay. That's because the whole suburb is a manmade island built by developers.

They were already scarring the nearby hills with their tract homes, but what they wanted was their own island where they could sculpt in stucco and not have to deal with the law.

They bulldozed the dirt from the hills, trucked and dumped it on the marshlands below. Then prefab buildings were snapped into place atop the packed dirt. The law came to town after the last lot was sold.

Each developer left behind his own vision of the future. They clustered their tract homes together in little bulls-eyes and gave each bulls-eye poetic names like Sea Breeze and Sea Haven and Shoreview and Vista Mar.

But the pride of Baytown was Marina Riviera. Its two hundred townhouses were easily the most expensive, the most futuristic. They weren't along the shoreline, either, but at the center of the island, as if San Francisco Bay paled beside this developer's dream.

Marina Riviera was a photographer's dream, too. Each townhouse had two condos separated by four smaller ones. They were white stucco with gold tile roofs and blue awnings. Mineshaft modern with angled roofs and terracings. Manmade lagoons separated each half-dozen townhouses and each building fronted its own private marina. There were boat hampers on most back patios.

I followed a cobblestone path from the parking lot along the water's edge. The water was high and coots floated by. I wondered what the smell was like at low tide. There were only rowboats or kayaks in the hampers. Maybe the lagoons were diked in and had no access to the bay.

The Anatoles lived on a little peninsula. I suppose they needed to live near water, and I'm sure waterfront living impressed their friends. To me, they were attempting suicide by living in a prefab unit on filldirt in earthquake country, especially when the seismologists figure the Big One should come during the life of the mortgage. Filldirt never settles evenly, and in a quake it liquefies. The Anatoles were living in a coffin on quicksand. You can get better odds on a snowball in hell.

I went through an iron gate.

"Happy New Year, Mr. Brennen."

I heard Lilian Anatole, but I didn't see her.

"I'm up here." She stood on a Mussolini porch above me. "Why don't you join me?" A hand gesture indicated an outside staircase half-hidden by some half-grown trees.

I came up the tile steps. "Is your husband home?"

"I don't know where he is." Her voice was dry and husky—dry like my throat and husky like good whiskey.

"When do you expect him home?"

Her face told me to be serious. "He'll be home when he feels like coming home." On a day when most people couldn't see straight, she had her best looks on. She wore a black silk robe, the kind a man could listen to for hours. Her husband was a fool to leave her alone. "Would you like some iced tea?"

"Sure." I found a seat. Her husband was gone, and

she was dressed to kill. Some women have fantasies about private investigators.

Her porch was slightly smaller than my apartment. There were magazines, several lounge chairs, a pitcher of tea on a glass-topped table. Sliding glass doors behind her led inside, though a giant white Christmas tree blocked the view.

She poured some tea for me. "He's left me alone a lot lately." She was almost pouting.

"Maybe he's been busy at work," I volunteered.

She looked up. "Innocent until proven guilty?"

"Sure." I got curious. "Why not?"

"You should never defend the guilty."

"What if he's just being inconsiderate?"

"Men take women for granted." She looked down again. "They want us around for their pleasure, and the rest of the time they ignore us." She poured her own glass. "What do you take in your tea?"

"Nothing." I wondered where Riki had discovered this windfall. She might have been talking to me, but what she was saying you don't tell a PI. I wasn't near divorce court and I didn't need this. And she was so cold about it, too. What she was saying should only be said in rage, but these words came from her mouth like an arctic breeze.

"Redheads are chic this season," she told me.

I bummed a smoke. "Ruth Gideon?"

She undid the sash on her robe. "Oh, I don't know what her name is." Underneath she wore a two piece swimsuit of black mesh. "That slut at the fish company yesterday." Then she laid herself out on a lounge chair.

She had a dangerous build. Last year she had been voluptuous, appealing, sensuous. Next year she'd be dumpy and dowdy, overweight. A full-figured woman one step away from matronhood.

Her porch faced west, where the sun debated setting behind the coastal range. The porch was still room temperature, but she didn't have much time left.

"What makes you think he's messing with her?"

"How could he resist her?"

"Well, maybe she didn't want him."

She wasn't amused. "She'd do anything for a job."

"Maybe it got stopped before it got started."

She turned my way. Her eyes were nuggets of ice. "Is she the one who scratched your face?" In those eyes, I was a failure, too.

And then it dawned on me. Hers was a valium world, and she was loaded to the gills. She was working on a tan in the shade. And I had to show up for this. Oh joy.

I wanted out. "Maybe I should come back later."

"Have you found Dani yet?"

"Have you heard from her recently?"

"Yes, in fact, I have. She called here last night. She wanted to talk with my husband, but he had already left. We gave a party at the clubhouse."

"What did she have to say?"

"I'm afraid I wasn't listening." She reached up for her drink. "I was on my way out the door." She didn't drink more than a mouthful. "She sounded okay."

"Did she say where she was calling from?"

She shrugged. "A phone booth, I suppose."

"How was the party, anyway?"

She thought back. "I left early."

"Anybody at the party that I might know?"

She tried hard. "Creditors. Clients." She knew it was one or the other. There was so much she didn't remember. It had to be hard living under such a large dosage.

"Could Dani have left town?"

"Lord, you can't be lucky twice." She had only to glance at my confusion. "Dani went to Seattle a few years ago. Just up and ran away. She said she was trying to find her head." She had a sneer for the hip phrases of the counterculture.

"You didn't believe that, did you?"

"She did. Isn't that enough?" She had a lazy smile for her ice cubes. "Her head should have been on her shoulders. I can't imagine what it was doing in Seattle."

"Would she get a place by herself?"

"She might. She wouldn't live with another man

again, that's for sure. That was her first and only mistake. She won't repeat it."

"Where would she go if she thought she were in trouble?"

Her eyes still on ice cubes. "Someone she could trust. Someone who could help her." She twisted and turned the tumbler, as if puzzled by her own reflection.

"Any idea who that could be?"

"There's no one she could go to." She looked up. Something dark and feral swam through the glaciers and almost touched surface. "What do you want with her?" There was no love here for her sister-in-law.

"Joey Crawford hired me to find her."

She was vindicated at last. "To pin the goods on her, right?"

"It wasn't infidelity. I'm just a good Samaritan."

"You could have found someone better to help, someone who won't end up dirtying your hands."

"Hey, he's dead. Rest in peace, right?"

"He's dead?" Her head went sideways.

"Yeah, he's dead." I softened. "Day before yesterday. Auto accident on the Golden Gate Bridge."

"An accident." The glaciers almost parted. "I'm sorry to hear about that." The ice came back thicker. "I wasn't thinking of him, though."

"You mean, Dani?"

"Well, you don't imagine, if the roles were reversed, she'd be lying in bed drying her eyes out until she fell asleep waiting for him to come back to her."

"I never met her. I wouldn't know."

She faced me. "And I've known her since she was born." She realized the show she was putting on for my benefit. "Let's leave it at that."

"Let's not and say we did."

Her ice eyes could peel me apart.

"Hey, I'm new here, remember?" I couldn't keep a straight face. I tried to smile like her closest friend. "C'mon, you can tell me."

Her reluctance was pitiful. "She's had so many men in her life. One more, one less. What's that to a woman like that?'' There was no stopping her now. ''She's a slut.''

''How can you say that?''

''She wants my husband.'' She stared in her tumbler. The ice was blue in the almost-twilight. ''He's mine, not hers.''

''Why would Riki mess with her?''

''Men like seducing women.'' She thought I knew.

''Sure, but they're first cousins.''

''He did it once. He can do it again.''

''With Dani?'' I didn't believe her.

''I'm not sure, of course. I can't be everywhere. But I meant someone else.''

My face itched. ''Catherine?''

She had a smirk for Catherine. ''She belongs on a California postcard. One of those ones where she's riding a pony through the surf, silhouetted against the sunset.''

''You think Riki's been fucking her?''

She didn't blink. ''Anatole's my maiden name.''

''You lost me.''

''Riki and I are first cousins.''

I didn't get it. ''But you are married, aren't you?''

Her nostrils flared wider than her eyes. ''My marriage is legal,'' she insisted. She caught my confusion and mellowed. ''California is one of the few states where first cousins can legally marry.'' She took a deep breath. ''I went to a lot of trouble to get that man.''

I stared at her. ''Right.'' I wanted out.

The phone inside the house began ringing, thank God.

''If you'll excuse me . . .'' She put on her robe and went inside.

I was shivering on her porch. Goosebumps and everything. They didn't come from land losing heat to the night. Like the fool on the hill, I was listening to a dingdong, and she scared the shit out of me. Her husband was a fool to leave her alone.

The porch looked down on the causeway. Manicured

lawns and growing trees and the marina. A workman further down along the water's edge was the only human being I could see between me and the freeway. Nobody lived here. People only spoiled the symmetry. Only developers and photographers were allowed here.

Lilian came up behind me. "Depressing, isn't it?" She took my cigarette from me. "A retirement community for those who hate to paint their houses."

"Why do you live here then?"

She French-inhaled cigarette smoke into her lungs. "A birthday present from grandfather." She looked like she wanted him dead.

"A nice present."

"I was surprised myself," she admitted. She tried reading the brand name on the cigarette. "We won't be here much longer, though." She liked that thought.

"Where are you moving to?"

"Carmel Valley." She looked into the future. "Something like Catherine's house."

"It's a nice house," I agreed.

"It's fantastic." She admired it for a moment in her memory. "I had thought I might get it."

"Maybe you will someday."

She considered her odds. "He had a heart attack a few years ago," she remembered. And then she remembered more. "That was Riki on the telephone." Her eyes distant and brooding, she blew a smoke ring, a delicate one, towards the sky.

I asked what was wrong.

"He was in an auto accident in the city."

I kept a straight face. "I hope he's all right."

"It seems he hit a mailbox." Her voice told me what she thought of that. "I'm going to him now." She didn't blink. "He's my husband." It was that simple.

I pushed back my chair. "Goodbye, Mrs. Anatole, it's been real." I headed down the stairs.

The workman was a good half-mile away from her patio. He was pounding stakes along the water's edge. Sound travels slowly across water. The sound of his hammer on iron arrived just as he'd start his next down-swing. From where I was, he could have been hitting himself in the head.

I went through the gate and along the cobblestone path. I followed the iron signs staked in the mud. I didn't look back.

CHAPTER 23

The workman wore formless khaki pants with a paunch and a face like a mule. He was a little guy in his mid-fifties, and he had motor-mouth worse than any speed freak. He was chattering away like a parrot left behind.

"How come you're working today?"

He yelped and dropped his hammer. He was completely bald, and his dome was gold from the sun. His hands were monkey paws and old scars, and the skin was ancient and sun crisp.

"Are you okay?"

"I didn't hear you come up," he confessed. He enjoyed talking to himself. Audiences were rare on these manicured lawns.

"Sorry. How come you're working on a holiday?"

He dismissed it. "I'm on strike. The whole fleet's on srike. We can't get the prices we want. The boats come in, and the crabs from Oregon are cheaper." He didn't want me to get the wrong idea. "I'm not blaming the guys up north. They're so far from anywhere, they gotta drive sixty miles inland just to get to the freeway. They gotta sell for whatever they can get."

"So you're here for the duration?"

"I'm getting double-time, too," he crowed. "Today was s'pose to be my day off, but what with all the rain we been getting, this is the first chance I got to work."

He was grateful for this job. "I gotta be doing something. I'd be going crazy if I couldn't work."

"You're already talking to yourself."

He ignored me. "I was lucky to get this job. I know the manager here. I called him up, asked if he needed any work done. He said yeah, so I come by and do it maybe four days a week. I figure on working here nine months a year, fishing the other three." He looked over the causeway. "I was gonna retire, anyway." He looked over. "Fishing, I mean."

"Fishing's no business for an old man."

He didn't like that at all. "Well, it's no blessing for a young man, either." He knew so many reasons why. "There's no fishing on the Bay anymore. Pollution killed the oyster beds. Limits now on shrimp, salmon's down to five months, six months for crab, and not many of them left." There were so many heartbreaks. "Best crabs are in the Bay, but the government won't let you take them. You gotta set your crabpots out by the Farallones. That's about the closest you can get to the Bay." He shook his head in wonderment. "I can remember sailing out the Gateway at midnight, sailing by the light of the moon. Just a few miles. Phosphorescence from the sardines. You could throw a bucket overboard and haul up a bucket of sardines. There were billions of them."

He was glad to have an audience. He liked talking about the old days, and he had a million memories at the tip of his tongue. He was happiest wandering through them.

"You miss the old days," I said. After the Imperial Iceberg, he was a real treat.

He thought he was alone again. "There were forty canneries along the coast in those days. Sixteen men crewing every seiner." He could have been talking to a shadow. "The whole fleet was buddies then. They useta take Sundays off, take the family, friends, everybody, go sailing up to North Bay for picnics. There were camping trips in the Sierras, too. The whole family came along. Even the kids. All them kids was cute." He had grandfather eyes for the children in his past. "They never got into trouble."

"They don't sound normal."

He loved a good josh. "Aw, they got into trouble." He grabbed the first memory that came to mind. "There was one time, I was getting off-watch, I thought I was hearing noises, and not the ones you always hear at sea." His face was slowly souring. "I got worried about the kids, so I checked in on them." He wasn't sure this was the memory he wanted. "Both of them was in the sleeping bag." He didn't know what to say.

"What were they doing? Playing doctor?"

"Goddam them." Anger made him hiss it. "I got them both outa there, told them I never wanted to catch them doing that again, or I'd slap them like a crazy man and still tell their folks on them." The anger was still there, after all those years.

"What were they doing?"

"It wasn't right." He left it at that.

"You must know Orestes Anatole."

He did. "When I was your age, he was already an old man. I've known him forty years almost." He felt better. These were safer memories. "He raised three sons all by himself and he kept that fish company going all those years. He never let a man's family go hurting. Not once. He's a helluva guy. He ran hooch during Prohibition. Scotch from Vancouver, tequila from Mexico."

"I thought he was just a fisherman."

"Sure, but it was Prohibition. Everybody had to do their part." He smirked like a co-conspirator. "Orestes, he had to bootleg. He had all his money invested in the wine country, only nobody was buying wine then, only the priests. He'd'a gone bankrupt if he didn't."

"A fishing boat seems obvious."

"He never landed, not with booze in the hold. He'd switch loads with other fishing boats past the three mile limit. He'd come in with the fish and the other guys brought the booze ashore."

"That's pretty slick," I lied.

He remembered something slicker. "You know what the old man did with the money he made bootlegging? He bought more land up in the wine country. Nobody else was buying it. But that's how come he's sitting pretty up in Tahoe."

"D'you know Riki Anatole? His grandson?"

"Sure do. His wife, too. They live right over there." He pointed back the way I had come. "She thinks she's the cavalry. All she can do is charge." He liked his little joke.

"How long have you known them?"

"Since they were both little kids." His eyes weathered suddenly. There was only sadness there. "I got invited to their wedding." Maybe he was remembering kissing cousins.

"Did you know they were first cousins?"

He couldn't believe I'd said it aloud. "How'd you know that?"

"His wife told me."

He realized he was talking to himself and he wasn't alone. "Who are you?" He had his job to protect.

I showed my photostat. "A private investigator."

He read it like a man looking deep into hell. He found no loopholes. He stopped and his eyes plunged. "I got a big mouth."

"How well do you know Dani Anatole?"

He almost yelped again. "What do you want with her?" He'd talk to a ghost the same way.

"You know what she's been up to?"

"You better go see the manager." If he had a ten-foot pole, he wouldn't touch me with it. "He useta work for Anatole Fish. Still does now and then, whenever they need a good mechanic. He's been working on their new trawler, mostly." He wanted out fast, but he didn't want it to seem like a turn-off.

"Where can I find him?"

"Probably at the display model." He looked around for his bearings. "Take that path and follow the For Sale signs." He was glad he shut his mouth that quick.

"Thanks."

"There ain't nothing to it." He wouldn't wait for me to leave. He grabbed his gear and went to punch out. He disappeared faster than a church key.

I followed the cobblestone path along the water's edge. The display model was close to the parking lot. At least I was headed in the right direction.

The manager's wife answered the door. She didn't yelp when she saw me. She thought fast on her feet. "The Anatoles live over there, on the other side of that causeway."

"It's Pauline, isn't it?"

"That's right." The Anatole receptionist stared, still surprised, but she was flattered I remembered. "I don't remember your name," she apologized.

"Brennen. Michael Brennen."

"Oh, right, right." She was a little fieldmouse of a woman in her mid-thirties. She had round cheeks and big eyes and mousy brown hair. A lean face and a pointed chin gave her a slight overbite. "You don't want the Anatoles?"

"I came to see your husband."

She scratched her cheek. "What did you want to see him for?" She remembered her manners. "Come in, come in. Would you like some coffee?"

"I'm trying to quit."

"I just quit smoking," she said. "It's been seventeen hours now. They say the first twenty-four are the hardest."

The living room was bright white, like an handball court on opening day. The walls and ceiling had whiter paint and windows.

There was carpet and real-estate furniture. A sofa and two chairs, a portable display board and some pamphlets. A desk that collected paper cups and ashtrays.

The seventeen-foot ceiling looked shipwrecked. It was mineshaft modern, too. Rafters pointed in odd directions, beams went into tight angles, joints redoubled back like billiard english.

I stayed standing. "Nice place you got here."

"My husband should be back soon." She was standing by a small Sony on a tv stand. The set was on, but the sound was down. She had been watching one of the Bowl games. She wasn't very happy watching a football game on the first day of a new year.

"You both work two jobs." I was impressed. "It must be pretty hard on you."

"Well, he's not full-time at the fish company," she told me. "He helped them build a couple dragboats and he got called back to do some engine work. The fish company always calls him in. He's real good with boats." She had proud eyes for him. "Orestes asked him to run this place for him."

"Orestes Anatole? He owns this? Marina Riviera?"

"He owns half of everything." She was a respectable woman, but the lines on her face said she had never been favored. She sat alone a lot. She thought a lot about money.

"Your husband's doing the new trawler, right?"

"He just finished yesterday," she admitted. Her shoulders slumped. "Ready and rigged for sea trials." She looked up. "Yeah, he just finished."

"I hear Riki's taking the boat out on sea trials."

Her face changed. "Riki's not going out. He's never been on a trawler. He's a real sweet guy, but he gets seasick in a swimming pool. His kid brother takes them out. Jack's the only sailor in the family."

"He's that good a sailor?"

"When he wants to be. He was born at sea." She smirked. "Sea trials, that's all he's allowed any more."

"Because of his war injuries?"

She had the devious grin that comes with office gossip. "Jack was thrown off the boats for spending so much time on the piers, him and those longhairs down in San Pedro. That's why he's working in the smokehouse." She sunk like a rock. "He used to work there," she reminded herself. "'He don't work there any more."

I leaned forward. "Jack lost his job?"

"I just called him." She had a heart-broken smile. "Jack didn't believe me. He just got laid off. I just got laid off, too. They shut the plant down."

"Wing that one past me again."

She stared at the tv long enough to realize it was a tv. "Orestes called me this afternoon, said I better call the crew and tell them not to bother going out. He said the plant's shut down until further notice." She knew better. "Probably for good, that's my guess."

"I'm very sorry."

"I knew the company was going under," she told me. "They couldn't wise up. New equipment being used to send a five buck order down to San Jose. There's no money in that. My last paycheck from Anatole bounced higher than a basketball. Riki, when he heard about it, he paid me right out of his own pocket."

"He knew the company was in trouble," I suggested.

"It's not his fault," she insisted. "He tried his best, but everything was too new for him. He can't stop lay-offs when the company's hurting."

"He's new on the job?"

"He's only been here a couple of years. Most people at Anatole's are just as new. Bernice came in June, I came last February, and Candy, she's the file clerk, she came in September, I guess. It's all still pretty confusing for us."

"If Riki's family, why wasn't he here before?"

"He's just a cousin. He was brought in a couple of years ago, sort of a caretaker government after the old man sold out to a Chinaman." She had a low opinion of that deal. "If the old man was still around, I'd still have my job."

"What's the Chinese man's name?"

"Ng," she mispronounced. "Tan Ng." She looked over at me. "He's the one who laid me off. They all have funny names."

"Sure they do."

"They're buying up the whole town." Her lips were tightening into a thin white line. "I grew up on Clement Street. Ten years ago there were a couple of Chinese families scattered around the neighborhood. Then they started blockbusting. Now there's nothing but Chinese restaurants and fish markets."

"What about Tan Ng?"

She had hitman eyes for the tv. "He goes back to the old days, just like Orestes, only he's skinny, even for a Chinaman, and they're skinny because they eat all that rice." She remembered me. "The Anatoles did a lot of business in Chinatown. Still do good business now. Our best customers in some ways. In appreciation for that, the old man gave him a deal on the stock."

"And Riki was brought in?"

"That's right. As office manager."

"I thought he was president of Anatole Fish."

"Oh no. Office manager. Tan Ng's the president."

"Tan Ng?" I was talking to myself.

She remembered everything. "First thing he did, he reorganized everything. Fired a lot of the old-timers, put that big fairy on the payroll as accountant. He tried to fire Jack once before, but Orestes said he had his job as long as he wanted it, so the Chinaman transferred him to the smokehouse."

"He tried to fire the owner's grandson?"

"He laid off most of the working crew," she said, resentment in every word. "That's why there're only three dragboats working out of the bay, a skeleton crew downstairs—and upstairs we were always swamped with paperwork." There was too much to forgive. "That son of a bitch."

"You still have this job, don't you?"

She had forgotten that. "I was only working there because I got bored hanging around here." She looked over the shipwrecked room like a salvage expert. "There's some money in this. Not much. Maybe it'll hold us until liquidation."

On the tv, ten people were spaced like pie slices in a round bed. All were trying to sleep, but not with each other. They kept tugging at the one blanket for warmth, but the blanket was too short for the bed. When somebody was covering up, somebody else was always exposed. It was an oil company commercial.

"You think that'll happen?"

She didn't know for sure. "We called up my

husband's uncle. He said we better get a letter down to the Labor Commission and make a claim for those wages we lost."

"You might have been working for nothing?"

She knew her future was a car payment away. "They still owe my husband some money. Not much. A grand, but that's a couple weeks worth, anyway. My husband's uncle said we won't get more than six hundred back. And god knows when that'll be."

"You didn't know this was coming?"

"They didn't tell anybody. I guess that would be against the law. I mean, why should one person get paid over another? I feel sorry for the old-timers, though. Some of them, they worked thirty, forty years on the boats. They haven't been paid for their last trip, and already there's talk they might not get their pensions."

I decided it was time I saw the silver-haired devil himself. Flying up to Tahoe was a hard decision. Yesterday's rain had moved east and it would be snowing today in the Sierras. I hate snow.

I thanked her for inviting me in. "I better go now. I don't think I should talk to your husband today. Maybe I'll come back some other time."

She stopped me at the door. "About that bad check?" She was thoughtful. "When you see my husband, don't mention it to him. He was screwed out of a thousand dollar fishing trip."

I said her secret was safe with me.

"His uncle got laid off too. He had thirty years in with the company. His whole family used to work there."

The sun had sunk into the ocean. The coastal range was blue silhouettes with a white sky behind them. A fat mallard was prowling the black lagoon. He swam in lazy circles, took a dive and ate some weeds, then swam around some more. He had a pretty soft life in lotusland.

CHAPTER 24

The cabbie stopped rolling a joint long enough to hear the canyon address of Orestes Anatole. "That's a high class neighborhood," he agreed.

"I know a chick who lives up there."

He started his engine. "Tell her you want to move in with her."

"It's that nice a neighborhood?"

"There ain't no neighbors." He slapped his gearshift into drive and scooted off the airport stand. It was snowing at Tahoe City. He made some interesting turns on the iceslick road through the lakeshore town.

The Tahoe basin is the bordertown between Frontierland and Fantasyland. It has the usual bordertown amusements. Green gaming tables and big name entertainment, two bill hookers, and bars that never close. A fresh water lake is somewhere near the center of the action.

Mostly, though, the basin is choice quarter acre plots and choice quarter pounders—motels and hotels, slumber lodges and coffee shops, gas stations and summer cottages, campgrounds and second homes, A-frames and fast food carryouts.

The cabbie swung up a canyon road east of the airport. The road was a snowy snake uphill. The blizzard thickened and snow blew hard and fast across the headlights. The driver thought he was driving a plow. He hurtled through the drifts with half-closed eyes and a pinner between his lips.

I asked him to slow down.

He took the joint from his lips. "How would you like to have this crummy job?" he asked the rear view mirror. "Do I bother you when you're working?" But he slowed to fifty.

Finally his cab crested a slope.

"That's the crib, man."

Orestes Anatole's house bit the neck of the valley. It didn't impress me, but I'm no taxman. The building only had two stories, but it was a block long and lined with acres of tinted glass and bright light. It was a nice house if you have a big family. You'd go stir-crazy living there alone. There were no neighbors.

The cabbie wasn't sure he could wait for me. "This meter runs slower than pegleg when I have to wait for somebody. How about you double the difference between when you go in and when you come out?"

"How else could I get out of here?"

"You could always call a cab." he said.

"You got a deal." I gave him a ten to seal it.

A nurse answered the door. She wasn't much older than Catherine's maid, but her eyes were more placid. She had made a separate peace with her paycheck.

I gave her my photostat. "Is Mr. Anatole home?"

She told me to follow her. We went from room to room. Some rooms had paintings of trawlers and purse-seiners, and others had paintings of the ocean and the sunset. Every room had bright lights and tinted glass. There was plenty of central heating, too. The PG & E bills had to be hell.

After I had lost all sense of direction, she held open one last door and closed it behind me. I was in a solarium overlooking scrub pines and scrub land. The spotlights were on outside, and the swirling snow was confetti. A Christmas tree stood in the center of the solarium. It was decorated with tiny mirrors, strings of popcorn, candy canes, homemade bulbs. My two boys had one just like it.

I walked around the tree and found I wasn't alone. Sonething like a mole sat in a wheelchair watching the snowfall and the night. It was humanoid, genderless and old. Very old. Its soda straw legs were wrapped in a thick blanket.

I went closer and found a man. His face was puffy and one eye was permanently half-closed. A phoney birthmark covered a facial wart. Thick pink lips and chicken bone wrists. The jowls were thick, the chins were many, and his flesh was like chicken skin.

The mole shook himself awake. "Glacierization."

I smiled. "Right."

He looked hard at me. "Did you fall down?"

I was sick of answering. "Yeah. I fell down."

"The glaciers are coming back," he told me. "It'll be another Ice Age." Slipping dentures slurred his words.

"Take it easy," I told him. "The snow gets to everyone. You shouldn't stare at it so long."

His eyes went outside again. "When they found those mastadons in Siberia, they were flash-frozen, like breaded fish sticks." He ack-acked a few coughs.

"Don't strain yourself, old-timer." I wondered if the head nurse knew the old grey mole had tunneled from the funny farm.

"There were still buttercups in their stomachs."

"Buttercups are flowers."

"That's what I said." He was mad and his voice was shriller. He punched the power button, and the wheelchair spun half-left to face me. "You're pretty dumb, boy."

"I didn't get your name, old man."

"I am Orestes Anatole." His teeny eyes were watery and flecked with red, but there was no mistaking the Anatole birthright of blue eyes. "You wanted to see me."

No shit. "I thought I did." I needed a drink.

He looked at me as if I were a fortune being squan-

dered. "You've been snooping around." He hushed
me. "I know you have. I know you have a legal right to
do it, too. I don't know what you're looking for, or who
you're working for, but you saved me a trip. For that
I'm grateful."

"You were coming down to see me?"

"I couldn't find your office in the phone book."

"I don't have one." I had one once. A hot little room
in the basement of a bank. "How did you happen to
hear about me?"

"Oh, I've gotten more phone calls . . . ." He brushed it
aside. "Would you like some wine?" He pushed a portable wine cart forward. "They're from my own
vineyards."

I read off the the labels. There was zinfandel and
cabernet sauvignon, pinot chardonnay and rhine. All
were from the Mariana vineyards of Sonoma.

"Mariana sounded more Italian," he confessed.

"Sure." I poured myself a glass of white. I was still
numb. I couldn't believe it. This old mole was Dani's
grandfather. He looked like a mummy playing
charades. I saluted him with my wine. "Here's to the
Wizard of Oz."

He decided to hide his irritation. The wheelchair spun
to face the snow. "I came up here for my privacy.
Privacy is all I have left. I'm a harmless old man. Who
cares what I do, what games I like to play?"

"Your family does," I said.

He was not amused. "They don't admit that I exist,
and I try to keep it that way." But there was less thunder behind his words. He showed me wounded eyes.
"I've been very successful."

I tried to think straight. This old mole was Dani's
grandfather. I could see why nobody talked much about
him. Then I remembered. "You must've been a helluva
rum-runner."

"That was too many years ago."

"I heard you were Syndicate. Or had connections
with them, back in the days when being in the Mob
meant something."

"I was never in the Syndicate," he said. "Oh, I knew them. Every runner did. Maybe you don't know this, but the West Coast was never their exclusive. People like me ran the most. Amateurs. Free lancers. They tried to stop us, but even the Coast Guard couldn't catch us."

"You sold to the Chinatown bosses, right?"

"Yes, I sold them booze and why not? I sold to anybody who had the money. Does that make me Chinese? You got something against the yellow man?"

"Is that how you met Tan Ng?"

He waited before he spoke. "You're a pretty fair detective."

"Investigator's a better word."

He gave me the point. "We started out together. Back when Grant Avenue was Dupont Gai and Dupont Gai bought Anatole fish. He ran a fantan parlor and I sold him the booze."

"He's changed a bit."

"He's a slick old boy. Still a little fantan, but now he's a busy lawyer. He helped me out once with the Tong people. They never did have much patience with amateurs. But you didn't come here to listen to an old man's sinful past."

I lit a cigarette. "What did you want to see me about?"

He asked me to put out my cigarette, then pointed behind him. The oxygen tanks sat like torpedos, Bufano statues. I stubbed out my cigarette.

"We can talk better in the next room." He pressed his power button and the wheelchair scampered towards the door. "Can you hold that door for me?"

I did as he asked. He punched it and his chair surged forward and through. I wondered if he could do wheelies.

The next room was windowless and large enough for echoes. It had chocolate pile carpeting and mahogany paneling. Against the wall, a fireplace the size of my car did its best against a chunk of telephone pole. A crystal chandelier the size of the fireplace threatened the pile carpet. All chairs were leather and all tables mahogany.

"Are you married, Mr. Brennen?"

"I'm divorced."

"Why did she divorce you? No, you don't have to answer that." He pulled a file from a tabletop. "I know about you."

"You have a legal right to check me out."

"I didn't break the seal." He tossed me a pack of matches. "Would you like to burn it up?"

"Why?" I found a seat. "You have other copies."

He waited for his jowls to stop trembling. "No, Mr. Brennen, this is the only one."

"Why don't you get a refund?"

"What would you fight for, young man? What would you die for? You don't have to answer that. It's personal. Individual. But I can make a guess. Very little and certainly not for an old man like me. Not for a fish company, ever."

"I hope you're right," I said. "Dying for a fish company is stupid."

"You're very glib." He wasn't being hostile.

"Just being honest, I hope."

He wheezed his contempt. "That's my grandfather up there," he said. "He was the man who founded the fish company. He was a good businessman, too. He ran it for forty years." He glanced at me. "He came to San Francisco during the Gold Rush. He was twenty years old then."

I looked behind and above me. The founder's portrait mocked any other "founder's" portraits I've ever seen. Orestes Anatole the First was a real fisherman. He wore a fedora perched rakishly over a mop of curly hair. A wool overcoat. A stubby cigar in his mouth. He grinned as if he had just sung ten verses of a dirty sea chanty.

"A lot of ships were stranded in the Bay those days," his grandson told me. "Sturdy ships that sailed around the Horn. Their crews had deserted for the Gold Country. My grandfather and his partner bought one and started fishing."

I looked over. "What happened to his partner?"

"One day he disappeared." The old man sucked his gums. "They say he was shanghaied from a Barbary Coast saloon."

"That was convenient."

The old man went on without me. "He never lost a boat. He never lost a man. He made deals with the Chinese. He helped them sail the Bay and fish for shrimp. He bought land and held it in trust for them. He fought the oyster pirates with knives and guns. He bought land in Sonoma for vineyards when land cost ten dollars an acre. And when the Blight hit the French fields, he sold them cuttings and bought more land." He paused for air, a vital commodity at his age. "He foresaw the sardines and bought purse-seiners for the Bay. He forced us to convert to gasoline, and later to diesel. He was even the first to open a restaurant at Fisherman's Wharf, but he lost money there. He was a decade too soon."

"He sounds like quite a man."

"He died in the bathtub," Orestes told me. "Mother and I hauled him out. He looked like a beached whale. A rather ignominious end for a fisherman, don't you think?"

I shrugged. "It happens sometimes."

He wasn't listening. "His death was the first freedom I ever had." He was talking to himself again. He noticed me. "I tried to instill that in my family."

"By setting up trust funds?"

He came close to a secret smile. "If I didn't, they'd have shot me for their inheritance already." It would take a nitro pill to make him crack a smile.

"What makes you think they've changed their minds?" I ticked off some points. "Those shares are held in trust until you release them. You kept a full third of the voting stock, just so they would never gang up on you. They can't sell their shares until they're forty, and they can't live off the interest because it gets added to the pot. And since you can stop their money, interfere with their personal affairs, they can't tell you to your face how much they hate you. It sounds to me like it leans your way.''

"I thought that was reasonable," he admitted. But the truth gave him an itch. He tightened. "They're still my family. I had hoped they'd be more self-reliant, but those funds are the only way they can survive." He sounded like he believed it.

"They have to work or they get nothing."

"The fish company isn't important by itself. But it does serve one useful function. It keeps the family together. Maybe if they could work together, they might stop hating each other."

"Catherine doesn't work." I reminded him.

"She never could." He was still honest.

"She has her own money. She doesn't need yours. And yet you give it to her. You even gave her a house."

His guts rumbled. His eyes went glassy. "She got that house because she'd be a public drunk otherwise." He looked like old age was poisoning him. "You don't know how much money she needs to keep her drunk."

"Booze is her alimony."

"I suppose it is." He shook his head. "Too bad about her husband. He had a good head on his shoulders. Too bad the chemistry soured for them."

"Dani doesn't work, either."

"She's a damn good woman. Better than anybody else in the family. She deserves every dime she's ever been given."

"How did she manage all that?"

"You know what she did? She ran away from home, to get away from those vultures. When she needed money, she changed her name and went to work for a fish company."

"Did she call you last night?"

"How did you know that?"

I winked. "I'm an investigator, remember?"

"She's been the only one in the family willing to leave me alone." He looked around and noticed me. "She was supposed to be here now. She said she was coming up here today."

"Why isn't she here?"

"She could've had car trouble." He thought he understood. "She's a big girl. She can take care of herself."

I hoped so. "What about Jack? He says he's bored stiff."

The old man sobered. "I tried to give him the sea. He didn't want it. All he cares about is that Porsche of his. It's his woman." He snorted his distaste.

"Has he changed a lot since Vietnam?"

He looked down. "I didn't want him to go. He didn't call me to say goodbye." He tried ignoring the past. "He's been worrying me ever since he came back. He's killing time, waiting for something to happen. Something's missing from his life."

"Waiting for his ship to come in?"

He thought it over. "Are there many like him?"

I shrugged. "It seems like it." Anybody, not only vets, withers without a purpose. I guess there's no adventure left in the world. Without that, without something to challenge people, they become robots and they age before their time. "What did you think of Joey Crawford?"

"Dani's boyfriend. I liked him. Oh, not for what he was. For what he was for Dani." The old man wiped his nose for the simple-minded of the world. "He was good for her. He kept her mind from wandering back here. That was the only thing he was good at."

"I heard you hated him. I heard you almost went up the wall when she brought him home, that you almost cut her off, just like you cut off Lilian."

"I never cut Lily off." He was vehement. "She wanted no part of my money. She said there was a smell to it." He looked up at his grandfather's portrait. "She's willing to share her husband's and that comes from me. She's another one who can't work. Riki waits on her hand and foot. God, does that boy dote on her."

"I hear he's a devil with the ladies."

"You heard wrong," his grandfather said.

"His wife says he's a wanderer."

"She'd go berserk if he did."

"Why does he stay with her then?"

"He's a Catholic," he told me. "He doesn't love her. He's a kept man, kept by his own sense of duty. If he could, he'd leave her in the lurch." But he was holding back something. "My grandson is a coward."

"Riki? A coward?"

His eyes tried to pierce. "They call him Chicken of the Sea behind his back. That's why we put him in an office. Only place he can keep his legs going in the same direction."

"They're first cousins. She told me so."

He broke his barrier. "She shamed him into marriage. Now she makes him feel guilty for not giving her his heart and soul." He banged the arm on the wheelchair. "My granddaughter can marry my grandson, but I'm the loathesome pervert."

"Why tell me all this?"

He remembered. "I want to hire you."

"Aw, c'mon, cut the clowning."

"How much do you cost?"

"More than you'll ever have."

"I'm in the fifty-percent tax bracket."

"Okay. You can buy me. But why?"

He leaned forward. "Last month I received a phone call from a man who wants to but the fish company. He wants to make another cannery out of it, another Ghiradelli Square." Leaning forward was too much for him. He leaned back. "You know what they do. They partition everything off into restaurants, art galleries, clothing stores, taverns. He wants to call it the Fish Factory."

It was a new story in the city. New and ever-present. A company is sold and its employees who made good money go on the unemployment roles. They rot there until they settle for less or move on. A developer renovates the building into a maze of tourist traps. He's an absentee landlord, and his rentors hire the unemployed for minimum wage.

"Are you going to sell?" I asked.

"I have no reason to sell. I care about my employees. I pay them good wages. What's going to happen to them? Can you see them selling toys to the tourists?"

It seemed simple. "Don't sell it then."

"It's not that simple," he said. "That man is from Las Vegas."

I almost smiled. "That doesn't make him a bad guy."

"Where did he get the idea I wanted to sell?"

"I don't know." I raised my hand. "I swear to God."

He gave me filthy look. "There have been rumors my company's having financial troubles." His guts rumbled again.

"Rumors are made to be ignored."

"Not when they start up here."

"The gambling grapevine?" I thought it over. "You think somebody's pressuring you into selling."

"Do you know anybody who could be doing it?"

"Why don't you look into it?"

"I already started." He tapped the file on me.

"Understand this. I'm not hassling you or your company."

"Maybe. But until I die, I am the majority stockholder. I am the final decision. I must know what's going on." His anxiety hit his liver. He looked like an old man holding a hot wire. "We're supposed to be fish wholesalers. Now we're buying fish from other fleets."

"I heard that's because of the weather."

"Oh, it is." He rubbed his stomach. "But when I heard you were prowling around, I could see how fragile my company really is."

"Is that why you recalled the fleet?"

"Yes, and they're staying in until I find out what's going on." He tapped the file cover. "I told these people to speed up, too."

"You should be able to find out," I said. I picked up the file. The seal was red wax, a silly flourish, something a useless old broad might do. My old bosses used it on their wealthiest clients. It dawned on me. "You hired Pac-Con to investigate me?"

"They're about the best, I hear."

I was pissed. "This is my work record." I wanted to choke the old fucker.

He flinched. "Would you like to burn it?"

"Yes, I would." I threw the dossier into the fireplace. I watched the gold flames. They didn't burn high enough for me.

"I'd like to make it up to you."

"You don't have enough years left for penance."

"I'll double whatever they're paying you."

"Look. Let's forget this, okay? I'll just leave."

He gave me a check. "A retainer. I'll pay you triple wages." He was getting excited again.

At least the check wasn't written in crayon. Then I looked at the amount and gave a low whistle. With this much bread I could buy a sloop and sail south for a couple of years.

He had started to drool. "I'll pay you to do nothing."

"Why should you do that?"

He almost didn't know where to start. "Your presence feeds those rumors. They must stop. You're interfering with my business. I don't want you around any more, and I want you to stay away from my family."

I said goodbye to Mexico. "Keep it, old man."

He set his back to me, like an old woman in a huff, and started punching buttons on a nearby tabletop.

I stood up. "Does Tan Ng know what you've been up to?"

He glared at me. "He'd never use it as leverage."

"Why's that? What leverage do you have on him?"

"So you can blackmail him?"

"I don't blackmail people."

"You can't blackmail the impotent," he said.

He didn't laugh and I should have.

The nurse appeared. I left the room by the door she held open. Dani wouldn't let me sail away to Mexico. And no old mole in a wheelchair in a glass house is going to tell me what to do.

Then I was in the lobby again. The same lobby where

I had started from. I had been led around the whole house and had ended up one room from where I had started. The old man had euchered me. I turned around, but he was watching the snow again. The nurse closed the door behind me.

My cab was still outside. The engine was idling, but the cabbie had disappeared. I got behind the wheel, turned up the heater and lit a cigarette. The cab radio was working down the top 100 songs of the year. The deejay said there'd be an Instant Replay tomorrow.

After a while the cabbie came back from the tules. He looked at me, shrugged, went around to the passenger side. After he fastened his seatbelt, he asked me where to.

"Back to the airport."

The cab churned through the snow.

He lit another joint. "This is the way I always heard it should be."

CHAPTER 25

I caught the Gambler's Special back to SF International. There weren't many players on the plane. Only the losers fly home Saturday night on a New Year's weekend.

I found Doug's car and dead-headed home. Sure, I'd considered a motel for the duration. Lim Song's goon platoon might be considering some form of revenge, but not on a Saturday night. Besides, I'm not hiding out. Some motel maid might shortsheet me.

The freeway was crawling with crazies. Amateurs with love or money on their minds. Every night of this weekend was their night, drinkers and drivers both, and they were going to have the time of their lives tonight. I hoped they'd have a real good time. I wasn't going to come between them.

My apartment isn't much. Motel-thin walls and electric wall heaters and furniture returned from rental. I like living alone, but I don't like living like this, so I spend a lot of time at the window, looking out.

I called the residence club. They said she was out. Any message? I said there was none. I thought of one after I hung up.

I thought about Ruth. I thought about warm nights in Mexico, some warm beaches I wanted to show her. Mexico seemed like a million miles away.

I killed the lights and went to the window. The streetlights had a frosty halo, and the parked cars beneath were dewy and glistening.

One car below my window had a finish as dry as the street below its muffler. The driver was alone, slouched against an open window, smoking a cigarette. The engine grumbled like a tiger's stomach, and the exhaust coughed out patches like fog. The ass was jacked higher than the grill. Block letters on the rear window spelled out Camaro.

I heard a small faint noise, like a door sliding open in another room. Someone had opened the elevator door. It could have been for the other apartment on my floor. It was leased to three student nurses from Presbyterian Hospital. They came and went like small animals in the night. Sometimes they were even getting off duty.

I keep a starter pistol in my apartment for night noises. I made sure it was loaded with blanks. I wouldn't want to end those noises, but I might want to scare them off. My own gun was fully loaded, anyway, not with dummy cartridges.

I went and stood alongside my door. Someone was breathing heavily in the hallway. It might have been whisperings. In San Francisco it might be harmless, some weirdo with a kinky problem. I checked the peephole. There were shadows in the hallway. Not enough light to see whose, but there were at least three of them.

A credit card came out between the frame and door. It slipped about, found the lock, began fumbling with it. I grabbed the card and yanked it through to my side. Then I fired the starter pistol at the carpeting.

No more heavy breathing. The staircase door opened. There were no more shadows in the hallway.

I went to the window, slid back the drapes. The wheelman was cued on the lobby. He kept revving the gas, like his life depended upon it.

Three young men in levi jackets rushed from the lobby. They were young and frantic. What one said sounded desperate in Cantonese. They hopped into their Camaro, and the car roared off.

I looked at the plastic. Lim Song was embossed across the bottom. He was awfully careless with his Master Charge. I could be a thief. I thought about looking him up, returning it. Better I should burn it. I could always claim I saved his life.

My floor began pounding. My landlady lived directly below me. She had her broom out again. She was pounding on the ceiling again. Another quiet night shot to hell.

CHAPTER 26

I passed a cable car climbing halfway to the stars. The tracks rattled like cold teeth and the gripman drank whiskey from a paper bag. The city had long since given up its heat to the night and ocean air.

It was windy on Nob Hill. A daisy chain of yellow cabs were outside the big hotels. Their drivers stayed inside their cabs, not outside talking among themselves. For some reason, the winds blow coldest on the most expensive real estate in town.

I passed the building before I saw it. It was hunched against the winds like an old man at a bus stop. It was stone, like the Hill itself, a symbol of eternity for the poor people of San Francisco. A mailbox watched-dogged the front while two stone lions covered the flanks. The building could have been a neighborhood branch of the public library. All it needed was a bicycle rack.

The doorman doubled as a security guard. He was reading a tenant's magazine, but he had a pump action shotgun beside him. He called ahead, then said the elevator was being sent down for me. While we waited, a Doberman came from nowhere to sniff my fingers. Money takes its own time, of course. It seemed forever before the elevator doors closed on the drooling hound.

The elevator opened at the penthouse.

I thought I was in a mountain glade. There were ferns, generations of ferns, more ferns than a redwood forest. Tall and full and overflowng. Every inch of the spacious room had something cool and green. This was a garden of delights for a midnight date.

I saw hardwood floors and tan furniture and realized this was the living room. There was indirect lighting and central heating. I looked for the F.T.D. decal that telegraphed bouquets.

Tan Ng babystepped in, sleepy-eyed. He wore a bathrobe, pajamas underneath. His robe was Chinese red and Chinese gold, while his pajamas were blue-and-white checked. Both were too big for him, something the Incredible Shrinking Man was leaving behind. With his cadaverous features, he looked like a corpse gift-wrapped with Christmas paper.

He was courteous. "You honor my house." He didn't look like he wanted to see me twice a year, let alone twice the first day.

"Sure do." I walked past him. "Gung hay fat chow."

He was patient with round-eyes. "Chinese New Year's is in February . . ." He caught on. "Lim Song again."

"He tried to ambush my apartment tonight."

His eyes flickered awake. "Bloodshed?"

"Maybe next time. If there is one."

He was firm. "You should not take the law into your own hands. Report him to the police. Let them deal with him."

"You'd love that, wouldn't you?"

"There is nothing else I can suggest." He was grim, a lawyer who had tripped on his own sidewalk. He didn't like it, but he couldn't deny it.

"I want to know why you set those maniacs loose to kill me. So what if you are a lawyer. You can tell me the truth. Just don't bullshit me. That's all I'm asking."

He was stung. "I have no desire to have you killed. I told you that this morning. I am opposed to violence."

"Now I feel all safe and warm."

His face was lawyer-blank. "I did not know he was following me."

"Cut the clowning," I snapped. "You wanted me to follow him, remember? You didn't even care if I took the job. You knew Lim Song would find out about me. You knew he'd come looking for me. If I didn't end up dead in some Chinatown alley, I'd be screaming for police protection."

"What do I profit from that? He wantd to know.

"Having the cops swoop down on your enemies is a dandy way to get rid of your competition. Or maybe you just wanted to buy some time. This would keep both me and the red maniac occupied."

"I did not plan this."

I ignored him. "I can understand why you wanted Lim Song out of the way. He's poison. But why me? Why did you set me up? Or was I just somebody to run interference?"

"I did not set you up. I was asked by a client to investigate you. He wanted to know who hired you. This is a critical time in his company's finances. I told you this this morning."

"Riki Anatole was the client, right?"

"He has been a client for many years."

"He works for you, Mr. President."

"I own one-third," he conceded.

I understood. "It's your company's finances."

He sighed like a failing balloon. "You must understand my predicament. When his wife died, Orestes Anatole sold me a third of his company. It is not often a yellow man can invest in a white man's company. I stepped very carefully into it. Then he had a heart attack. He asked me to reorganize his company, transform it from a small family-owned business into one that could withstand modern competition. For two years I have tried. Then his grandson calls and tells me a private investigator has been asking about management and creditors. What am I to think? I am a businessman. I must protect my investment. That is why I tried to discover your clients and their motives."

"It is a critical time, isn't it?"

"You knew that." He was exasperated with me. He took control of himself. "However, it is a serious charge to say I had anything to do with mismanaging the company." He looked like he wanted to sue.

"Is that what I'm saying?"

"What else would you be doing here?"

"Hey, this is none of my doing."

He turned away and started talking. "This is how I am repaid for a lifetime of service to the Anatoles." He was talking to no one in particular. "This would not happen if I were not Chinese. Oh, I was warned." He sounded like a man yielding to his own better judgment.

A young man came up in the elevator. He was Chinese and wore his long hair in a ponytail. It was the bookkeeper from the fish company. He wore clean jeans, a leather carcoat, dress shirt and shiny loafers. He had bought them at the big-n-tall shops on Mission. He was a slick young man about town. He was a brisk walker. People stepped out of his way.

He stopped when he saw me. "What's he doing here?"

Tan Ng flushed. "I thought you left."

"I forgot my credit cards."

"This is my nephew," Tan Ng told me. "Louis, this is Mr. Brennen. He is that private investigator."

"We met at the fish company."

The old man caught on. "I arranged for him to work there." There was genuine affection in his voice. He was very proud of his nephew. "He is very ambitious."

Louis cocked his head at me. "What's he here for?"

His uncle spoke in Cantonese.

Louis answered in English. "Slow it down."

Tan Ng was pissed, but he repeated himself slower.

There was no resemblance and fifty years difference between them. Louis dwarfed his uncle. The boy was solid beef. He looked more like a bodyguard than a nephew.

Their conversation went on and on. I got bored and started counting ferns. There were seven framing my armchair. Louis' eyes kept coming back at me. I glared at him and he turned away.

Tan Ng found English. "He recalled the fleet."

"They didn't sail?" Louis thought that was stupid. "Why would he do that? We need the fish."

"He believes something is wrong."

"What could be wrong?"

Tan Ng didn't know. "The plant is shut down, the fleet will not go out until he finds the evidence he needs."

The young man didn't understand. "Because the deliveries are late?" He thought that was ludicrous. "Why would he do that?"

They both looked at me.

"I had nothing to do with this."

The old man knew. "You turned in your report."

"I reported nothing to nobody," I insisted.

"Please, Mr. Brennen," Tan Ng told me. "We know you are only doing your job. Orestes hired you to investigate me. You have investigated me. It is not your responsibility when a business must close its doors after many generations of family management. I do not blame you personally for that." He acted like he was letting me live.

I was stunned. "Is that what you think?"

"Why else would you be here?"

"You sound like Riki," I groused. "Except he's drunk."

"Forgive me." He gave me a point. "Old men should not have a young man's vanity. Why should I be the only one? Of course you would investigate him, too." too."

"Why put yourself on a cross if you got nothing to fear?"

The barb got through. "Yes. Nothing to fear. The allegations are very serious, though. The trucks do not make delivery on time. Expenses keep mounting. The creditors are clamoring. All of which means lost business, lost prestige, lost profits. It is obvious Orestes does not like the way I have managed his company. He mistrusts me. How else do I take the news?" My barb had quite an aftertaste. "You can tell Orestes his wishes are agreeablé to me. We will have the books ready for him on Monday."

"I'm not his lackey. You tell him."

He still tasted shit. He wanted to sue.

Louis started to leave. "If you'll excuse me . . ."

Tan Ng stopped him. "You go out again?"

"It's Saturday night." He was polite, but brisk.

"It is late."

"It's Saturday night," his nephew reminded. A young man has little time for old men on a Saturday night.

His uncle wasn't reconciled, but he was a realist. "You will be careful?"

Louis opened his carcoat. A .38 caliber Colt revolver was visible in a belt holster. "I'm okay."

Tan Ng frowned. "Please be careful"

Louis was impatient. "I have to go now." He went out to search for love or money. He was a young man on a Saturday night. He left at a brisk pace.

"He lives here with you?"

"Not every night." The old man was easily impressed."He is a young man in permissive times. They spend the night together on the day they meet."

"How well do you know Dani Anatole? What about her?"

"I am her lawyer." He wrinkled his face. "Why do you ask? Is she somehow involved in all this?" He looked like he was blaming himself for the bad news he was about to hear.

"It's confidential. You understand."

"She has her own houseboat," he knew.

"She's not there any more. She broke up with her boyfriend and took off running. That was a month ago, and she hasn't slowed down since."

He held his breath. "Is she in trouble?"

"Where would she go if she thought she was?"

"A man, I expect." He became very professional. "Women trust men more than they do other women." He might have been prepping for a jury selection.

"When was the last time you saw her?"

He thought back. "The first week of December. She had some difficulties with her banking. I gave her a letter to facilitate the transfer of some funds."

"She needed money? How much?"

He didn't know or wouldn't say. "She had made a large purchase, I believe. I did not ask her. A lawyer does not pry into his client's private affairs."

I understood. He had asked and she had refused. Vanity has hindlegs and Tan Ng was back up on them. I wondered what her large purchase was. "How desperate was she?"

"Dani is always desperate, always having trouble. She does not like reality. The grass will be greener somewhere else." He shook his head over such foolishness.

"Why didn't she go to her grandfather?"

"Oh, she would never ask him for money."

"Did you tell him about her money problems?"

"Dani is not a minor." He was very curious. "What do you want with her?"

"I have a message for her."

"Tell it to me. She will receive it."

"You'll guarantee she'll get it?"

"Of course." He had a horrible smile. All teeth, like a decaying skull.

I couldn't smile back. "Where is she?"

"Oh, I do not know."

"Then how can you tell her?"

"I cannot say." He looked like he would not say.

"Where is she?" I asked.

"I am her lawyer. I have my ethics."

I laughed in his face. "I know all about your ethics. They rate one stink lower than a dying rat. Back off from them, old man, and tell me where she is, or I'll drop a letter to the Califormia Bar about how you conspired to import curios without custom stamps, and how you tried to bribe me into stopping an investigation.''

"You are a fool," he insisted. "I could have you killed for this."

"Aren't you having it done already?"

He stood up, his old bones creaking like a houseboat. "I will not answer any more of your questions." He swayed like an old erector set in the wind. "It is time for you to leave. Do not come back."

The elevator took me from the garden of delights.

CHAPTER 27

The streets of Baytown are wide and well-lit, but there were no pedestrians and no cars either. Nobody walks since everyone has a car. I didn't understand, though, why there were no cars on the street, especially on a Saturday night during a three-day weekend. I'd hate to think it's because everyone had a television set.

I flicked my cigarette out the window. It sailed halfway across the street. Then the wind caught it, sent it even further, to the other curb. The best thing I'd done for an hour.

Even though I had a map, I was lost. My map was color-coded to each development, with the same pastel colors of the townhouses. Too bad the houses weren't well-lit like the streets. Too bad all pastels are grey in moonlight.

It wasn't hopeless, though. Somewhere along the way I had latched onto an ebony Datsun. The driver drove like any other suburbanite with time on his hands, but he seemed to know the streets and to have a destination in mind. I hoped he was headed for a gas station or the freeway.

Then the ebony Datson slowed. Its taillights dipped and swung into a driveway alongside a two-storied townhouse, parking just outside a carport. Headlights revealed a beige Coupe de Ville inside the carport. It had enough dents to be a wreck, enough dents to embarass the neighbors. The man left his car and went inside the townhouse. He moved slowly, heavily, like a dancing bear who had danced too many shows.

I drove past and around the block. When I returned, I doused my headlights and found an empty curb. This was a rotten time to pay a visit. I'd hate to think I'd driven for nothing, but Riki Anatole might think I'd been following him.

Just then Riki Anatole stormed out of the white townhouse. He hopped back into his wife's Datsun, then raged down the wide empty streets like a madman. Minutes later we both jumped onto the Bayshore freeway north.

I wondered where he was headed. There were only a couple of hours left before the last call. Oh, there were a few after hours clubs. Some hothouses and some stroke joints. A few gay and/or black dancehalls. But only the young and drugged went boozeless after the last call.

He howled through the downtown maze, grabbed the Embarcadero freeway to the Broadway exit. Off the freeway, he slowed like a Rolls-Royce on chuckholes and idled past the lady wrestlers and the female impersonators.

He found a parking lot next to a dirty movie house. I grabbed a space alongside a jazz club. A moment later he came from the lot and started up Broadway. I locked my doors and followed him. He stopped outside Brother Baxter's Nude Encounter Parlor, looked around for any familiar faces, found none, then went inside.

Riki was a bundle of surprises. If a trip to a singles' bar is a dreamer's trip, and a hooker is reality, he had settled for even less. Only the lonely found satisfaction in a nude encounter parlor.

It was the dirtiest game in town. The neon signs said Private Room With Naked Girls, but the advertising was deceptive. Once inside a mostly nude male could talk indiscreetly with a mostly naked lady, but prostitution was illegal, and the ladies took pride in selling only promises. They were professional prick-teasers who could con a bishop into self-abuse.

It was a big break for me, though. Brother Baxter was the king of the SF nudie parlors, and he had made a fortune in a business even the whores looked down upon. Like the other parlor owners, he lived on a tightrope an inch above the law. He had to watch every inch of that rope himself, or some rookie cop could bust him. He had to catch the prosties before the cops could. One mistake and his doors were closed for good.

He hired Pacific-Continental Investigations to help him out. Each prefab bedroom was bugged with Pac-Con equipment, and Pac-Con ringers went in with house dough to proposition the girls.

I'd been the first Pac-Con operative he had met, and after that he always acted as if I were the top man of the Pac-Con totem pole. In my book, that made him less than clever, though maybe he was just another dreamer easily impressed. He need not have known Pac-Con investigates its clients, too, but he should've known that in every business the newest employee always takes out the trash,

I went after Riki Anatole. I got as far as the front door. A pair of meaty hands pulled me aside.

"Just the man I wanted to see," Andrew Banagan said.

He was the last man I wanted to see. I tried to bluff it out. "How's it going, Captain?" I hoped I had a disarming smile. "Looks like they gave you a night off finally."

"A Saturday night off." Banagan sighed. "It's beautiful." He leaned forward and peered at my stitches. "D'you cut yourself shaving?" His breath was bad. "What happened to your face?"

"I cut myself shaving," I said.

He gave a drunkard's smile. "Who was holding the razor?"

Andrew Banagan was a short lean man in his mid-fifties. He was Captain of Detectives for the SFPD. Over the years his freckles had darkened into liver spots, and his red hair had thinned faster than it greyed. He was the toughest cop in this tourist town. Once he disarmed a would-be mugger by kicking him in the balls. The last man he had hit only spent four days in the hospital. Banagan had chanced upon me, and this was the first time I'd ever seen him drunk.

"D'you meet my boy?" He decided I hadn't. "Lemme introduce you two. Walter? Where is that boy?"

Walter was barely a teenager. He had no shoulders, bad eyes, a lousy haircut and a suit that needed a bigger man than him. He was just a mop of dark hair and marmot eyes. He was a long way from shaving, but he was having a fun time checking out the action on the strip. The kid had a real hard-on for the neon.

"This is Walter, my oldest boy. The world's greatest ophthalmologist. Did I say it right, Walter? This here's Michael Brennen."

"Pleased to meet you, Walter."

Walter almost noticed me. He was staring wistfully at the headlights on a surfer blonde in leotards who stood in the doorway of Brother Baxter's Nude Encounter Parlor. She was cajoling a red-faced Englishman with stories not from Sunday school. Her hair was green-gold in the neon.

"He wants to be an eye doctor," Banagan hissed. "An eye doctor." He couldn't believe his son would stoop so low.

"Not everybody wants to be a cop."

"Sure. You wouldn't believe the shit you gotta take." Which reminded him. "I heard you lost your job."

I shrugged. "It wasn't much of a job. A baboon could do it just as well. Better, in fact." I remembered my replacement. "A baboon's doing it now."

"Still, it's a shame. It could've happened to anyone." I grinned. "Not to a baboon."

He liked that. "Any plans for the future?"

"I'm considering opening my own shop."

"Going private? You'll starve to death. Say, have you ever taken the civil service test? The one to be a cop. You could be a cop, Michael. Maybe even a great one."

"I wouldn't know what to do with all the money."

He snickered. "The paperwork, you mean."

"That's what the job is."

"Except when you make it more."

I'd been afraid he'd remember. "Which means what?"

"Those were my boys out in the Sunset." He was souring fast. Most drunks do when they remember their beef. "I'm Captain of Detectives, remember?" He started poking me with his finger. "I hope you got a reason for that shit, because I'll ream your ass Monday morning . . ."

I tried another course. "Is the PM in yet on that stiff?"

He stopped in midpoke. "No, the PM's not in yet." His favorite beef. "We got one fucking toxicologist, that's why. The son of a bitch's booked solid."

"What about the prelim?"

"Oh, we got that." His mind clicked into routine. "OD by injection leading to cardiac arrest."

I faced him. "I didn't see any hypo."

"Nobody did, dammit." He gave me a filthy look. "If you were a cop . . ." He gave up on me. "Just be down at the Hall Monday morning bright and early."

"I'll think about it."

He glared and gave me a final poke. "You be there, Michael." He resented his own anger. "I'll see what I can do about that civil service test. Now, where the hell's Walter?"

His son was at a dirty book store window, gaping at the plastic peckers and pussies. His eyes were wider than the streets of Baytown.

"Get your ass over here, Walter, and stop acting like a tourist. Walter, my boy, let's go down to Enrico's, get some capuccino. Sounds good, doesn't it?"

Together they went down Broadway.

A column of blue came up beside me. It was the beat cop, and he stood as tall as Wyatt Earp. He hooked oversized thumbs into his gun belt and assumed Police

Stance. He looked me over and looked down at me. "You know the Captain?"

"You gonna roust me for it?"

He gave pause. "That's the best cop on the force."

"Drunk as a skunk, too," I marvelled.

He relented some. "He got carried away showing off his kid. The kid just graduated from Saint Ignatius."

"The kid's a jerk," I said. "He couldn't walk across the street without a wino spitting on him."

Captain Banagan and his son were listening to the street musicians buskering for midnight dimes in front of Enrico's Coffeehouse. The Captain had his arm around his kid. It might've been a touching sight, if the kid hadn't been gawking at the taillights on a jaywalking dancer in feathers and glitter.

"He wants me to get the kid his first blow job."

"How're you suppose to do that?"

The beat cop didn't know. "The kid's packing enough heat for the OK corral," he confided. "The Captain let him carry both guns."

"So disarm the little bastard."

His eyes watched traffic. "I'm the beat cop. He's Captain of Detectives." His drowsy eyes missed nothing. "I'll think of something." Suddenly he was on the move. He walked as slow as the traffic after his captain.

I went inside Brother Baxter's. Several young women jumped me instantly, suggesting sensuous raptures and seductive prices. When I said I was here to see Brother, their claws retracted and they drifted away into idle chatter and porno books. A bouncer with dead man's eyes opened a sliding door. I went upstairs.

Brother Baxter had a face a cop would stop, eyes that asked for trouble, a nose broken more often than not, and a red cracked neck. His real name was Brendon Montgomery, which didn't scan with his thick Georgia cracker drawl. The drawl was real, too, but he was from Tallahassee, not Georgia. He also had a heart of gold. Once he bought his father a week in a whorehouse. He paid for his mother's divorce after that, and even sent monthly checks so she wouldn't have to work.

He looked up from a plate of scrambled eggs. "Michael." He had his mouth full, and his hand ushered me inside. "Where've you been keeping yourself?"

"A little early for breakfast, isn't it?"

"A little late," he corrected. "Maybe. You want I should send out for more?"

"Nothing so drastic. I just need some information."

"Okay. Sure." He pushed away the plate, while his mind raced ahead. "Background or courtroom?"

"Background. From downstairs."

He sobered. "You want to listen in."

"If you'll let me."

"You saw him coming in here?"

"Right through the front door."

"You know which girl?"

"I didn't want him to spot me."

"What's he look like?"

"A good-looking guy, clean, a little flashy but a slow mover, hitting forty, six-foot-two, two-forty, broad shoulders and a beer gut, blue blazer and white shoes."

He swiveled around and slid back a cabinet door. There was a tv and a video machine inside. They were connected to a closed-circuit camera in the lobby and others in the bedrooms. He stopped the videotape that had been recording, then ran back the tape, occasionally cutting in to set the scene. I saw myself entering Brother Baxter's, talking with the beat cop, to Andrew Banagan. I saw the barker mouthing his spiel. I saw Riki Anatole coming inside.

"That guy right there."

He locked the frame and tightened the focus. "Every clown in the world," he grumbled. Then he went forward. A blonde's head appeared and led Riki away.

"Denise." Brother shrugged. "He's got some taste."

He turned off the videotape, then played with other switches. The screen stayed blank. He turned back my way. "You never been downstairs."

"I know what goes on."

"But you never seen it live." He hit the switch.

The picture wavered, came into focus, settled down. I was looking into one of the prefab bedrooms downstairs. Riki was naked, on his back on a daybed, and Denise was urging him to climax. He was masturbating, and she wore panties and a bra. They were ten feet apart.

I told Brother to turn it off.

"That's all she's allowed to do," he argued.

"I know that."

He indicated the screen. "It doesn't bother him. When a man needs an orgasm, he's gotta have one."

I looked back at the screen. Denise was bright-eyed, excited with her fun. I flashed on Dani. "And women, too?"

"We get women in here," he admitted. "They pay the same."

I'd had enough. There was no need to follow Riki any more. Home was the only place left for him. I said goodbye, then went the way I came.

Downstairs, a customer was arguing with the surfer blonde. "I paid ninety bucks, and I got nothing." The poor fool had fallen victim to these vampires in swimsuits. I had some sympathy for him. If I hadn't known better, I could've fallen once.

"Prostitution's illegal," the girl told him.

"I don't get laid," he said. "I just get screwed."

She had heard that line before. She was growing bored.

"Lady, I work for the state," he insisted, "and I'm going to file a formal complaint against you and everybody else. This is nothing but fraud."

The surfer blonde nodded green-gold hair. She was patient as she asked him to leave. The bouncer stood behind her. He was patient, too.

I left Brother Baxter's and started walking. I had goosebumps on my arms, and not from the cool night air. I felt sick inside, as if I'd been kissing a snake. Nobody's fault but my own. That's what you get playing peeping tom in lotus land.

I needed a drink. I decided to buy myself one. But not up here on Broadway. Not on this slimy piece of land. The path of least resistance goes downhill, as it always does in this city by the bay. My feet carried me to Chinatown.

CHAPTER 28

Fog writhing in the neon. White light overcoming the blue night. A giant mermaid with big breasts and a broad tail beckoned me inside for a drink. Her slant eyes were a tourist trap, but I decided to take her up on it. Maybe she swam in the same circles as the Anatole dolphin. I could always introduce them if they didn't. Maybe they'd even let me watch.

The old cashier checked me over and went back to counting receipts. He didn't bother taking his cigar from his mouth. He made his money by the busload.

The club was smaller than a five-n-dime and darker than a banker's heart. There were dim glowing hurricane lamps above the booths and tables. The club was nautical with a hint of Polynesian. There were several life-size tiki heads, a couple of navy surplus anchors, palm plants that needed watering, even a ceiling fan.

An all-girl rock band was on stage in the back. They wore white jumpsuits with leather fringes and they sang Top Forty ballads in jagged Cantonese. There was a small dance floor in front of them, chairs and flat tables on either side.

There were a few customers down in front. Middle-aged Chinese men in casual clothes, they were slumped against their chairs, half-heartedly watching the show. Locals, they had to spend their money somewhere.

A string of Chinese b-girls sat at the bar. They were young and pretty, mostly, and they all wore chang-shans slit up the side, just like the tourists see in store windows on Grant Avenue. The bar itself wasn't very long. Nightclub owners didn't want lingering sorrow. They wanted their customers buying drinks with the ladies.

I found an empty table and took a load off my mind. The stool was an oversized capstan with padded cushions, about as comfortable as a driftwood sofa.

A waitress left the string of girls and asked what I was drinking. She'd seen round-eyes slumming in Chinatown nightlife before. Their money was as good as any man's.

"Anything. It doesn't matter."

"How about a house drink?"

I took the list she gave me. The house drinks were all based on rum or gin, and they came in colors prettier than a rainbow. They had cutesy names, too, like Tahitian Tumbler and Tiki TNT. My favorite was the Outrigger's Rigor Mortis.

"You get to keep the mugs," she told me.

The mugs had little tiki faces. They looked like old men in a smoke-filled room. They could keep me from drinking coffee in the morning.

"A brandy and soda," I said. "No. Make it two."

She headed right for the bar. She was a good waitress.

A tour busload of Japanese businessmen came in just then. You'd have thought they were entering a church. Their silence was sudden and reverent. Like lost children, they huddled together, finding protection in numbers. Their tour guide couldn't coax them any far-ther through the foyer. They weren't going to follow the leader everywhere.

The Chinese women left their barstools and came to help them inside. The businessmen liked that. Their eyes went large at the smiling ladies. The ladies steered them to an empty section far from the local trade. The local trade counted its change and drifted out and went home alone.

The waitress brought my drinks and set them in front of me, adding mermaid coasters and a couple of gratis packs of mermaid matches. I poured the first drink down my throat.

She had a smile for me. "You needed that."

"Yeah." The second wasn't much slower going down.

"Would you like another round?"

"Yeah." I remembered my duty. "Can I buy you one?"

She was agreeable. She went to the bar and had the bartender mix more drinks. She brought back my twins and a drink for herself. She said it was cognac. It was probably cold oolong tea.

She was older than the others, nearly my age. She was a nice enough woman, but she had sad eyes. There was too much of life behind them. There was too little, too.

She still stood there. "Mind if I join you?"

"Glad to have you." I started the second drink.

"My name is Suzie," she lied. "What's yours?"

"Michael. Michael Brennen."

She almost started to wait me out. "So tell me about yourself." She couldn't forget her duty. It was her paycheck, too.

"Oh, there's not too much to tell," I started.

"What do you do for a living?"

I thought it over. "I'm in the jade business." She didn't need to hear I was a private investigator, and I didn't want to be reminded of it. I remembered a cover story from work. "I'm from Paradise. It's near Chico."

She was amused. "So there is a Paradise in California."

"That's where crunchy granola comes from. It's mostly a retirement home for John Birchers. My grandmother still lives up there. She sends me apples every harvest. Jonathans and MacIntoshes." How did I get into this?

She wasn't listening, anyway. She only had eyes for the Japanese. I must've looked promising to her in an empty bar, but exercising her seniority rights had blown her cut of the action. At this hour I was a frazzled case, and those businessmen were spending money like tourists.

The Japanese boys had really loosened up. They were laughing and joking and telling stories, slapping their pants with excitement. They were in Frisco and far from home.

The Chinese women sat beside them. They laughed when the men laughed. When the men ignored them, they didn't talk to each other. They sat chain-smoking and inscrutable. Like waiters in a Chinese restaurant, they were counting their tips before they got them, almost before they spent them, years after they had earned them.

I feel pity in every tourist trap. Those who work for the Yankee dollar usually get the minimum wage, but these girls made twenty-five cents less than that. Legal in some California joints if the employee receives tips.

There's nothing like the minimum wage to breed contempt. That's more than these girls had time to feel. The struggle for survival in America's most crowded ghetto leaves little time for anything else. And what another might mistake for exotic or inscrutable is usually lack of interest doing battle with hunger.

My own waitress had the same eyes. I didn't bother asking how she had gotten here. I knew her story by looking at her. She was from Hong Kong, or maybe Taiwan. Maybe she had a green card. She lived in a nearby walk-up, a building with more families than there should be tenents. Her money was pooled. There were a lot of mouths to feed. It was an old story in Chinatown.

Which reminded me. "D'you know Tan Ng?"

She wasn't impressed. "Everyone in Chinatown knows him." She remembered round eyes. She became cautious, chose her words with care. "He's a lawyer. He helps the old people move out into the Sunset."

"Sometimes he lets them sink in the sunset," I crabbed.

"I don't know him very well." She toyed with her coaster. "Is he a friend of yours?"

"We're in the jade business together."

A while before she answered. "I can't leave until after last call."

Oh Jesus. Tan Ng could get you into more than a friendly fantan game. "What do I get for my money?"

"How much do you have?"

"How much is all night?" I countered.

"Two hundred dollars." She braced herself for the inevitable quibblings, but she was already reconciled to anything.

"What else can I get with it?"

Her smile didn't waver. "What would you like?"

"Black rice," I said. Right out of the blue.

"I don't know what that means," she confessed.

"It's an old story. Something to smoke."

Her smile was knowing. "I have some Oaxacan."

"Oh yeah? You have any to sell?"

She knew caution. "Maybe in the morning."

"How about nose powder? Tonight."

She said nothing. She waited for the pitch.

"I like staying up all night with a lady," I said. "Coke gets you up, keeps you up."

"Coke's expensive," she said. "Can you afford it?"

I showed her Joey Crawford's stash.

"That's a lot of money." She thought it over. "Lemme see." She left and went to the bar. I told her to bring another round.

The bartender had her wait until he was finished with the tour bus trade. Then he listened to her story. He gestured, it was no problem. She told him to look me over. He glanced over and saw round eyes. He started rapping hard in Cantonese, like telling her to stop being so greedy. She had started to chill off, anyway. They looked at me as if they hoped 86ing me would go easy. They were forgetting my drinks.

I threw a twenty on the table, reached over and took her drink. I tasted cold oolong tea.

She came back without the drinks. "That was my drink." She saw my empties and the twenty. "I forgot your drinks."

"Forget it. Where's the john?"

She pointed the way, then looked down at the twenty. She wanted it, but she didn't expect it. She didn't resent me, either. She was simply patient. Maybe I'd leave it behind.

"It's yours," I said. "Forget it." Yeah. I felt sorry for her. The other women were younger, and young women hustle best. A woman can make the most of it then. A hustler wears her age in her eyes. Pride was the first to leave them.

Her hand didn't move. The twenty disappeared faster than Saturday night parking. I knew Joey Crawford wouldn't mind.

The restroom wasn't built for broad-shouldered men. I was a bad case of elbows. There was graffitti on the wall. It was in Chinese. About what I deserved.

When I left the john, I started to push aside the beaded curtain, then remembered I needed cigarettes. A Chinese sugar daddy was holding up the cigarette machine, whispering sweet Cantonese nothings into his baby beancake's ear. I counted my change. I didn't have enough, anyway.

I pushed back the curtain. I saw a Chinese male at the front register with the old man. The kid had chipmunk cheeks. I ducked back out of sight, counted to ten fast, then took another peek.

It was the goon with the nunchukas. And another goon was behind the bar. The old man had his back to them. He was scooping money from the register and putting it into a white envelope. A couple of b-girls stood by with stupid looks on their pretty faces. Two other goons by the door were warming their hands in their hooded parkas.

It was a nice quiet shakedown. No visible guns.

There was a payphone on the wall. I called Central Station and said there was a robbery in progress on lower Grant. The duty officer took down the address and told me to wait around. I said sure, hung up, then slipped out the back door.

I knew the cops would find nothing there, and I knew less than nothing. The touring businessmen didn't understand English and the old man at the register soon wouldn't be able to. The b-girls had no green cards, and the owners had hired them. It was an old story in Chinatown.

I bought the next morning's paper from the Filipino hawker around the block. He was lame from Corregidor, but he took no medicine and never complained. He had a long face made longer by a stubbly goatee.

"How's it going?"

"It's going."

Four SFPD squad cars flew around the corner, their engines close to hemorrhaging. They flew past us. Their red flashers were on, but they had no siren.

"Somebody's in trouble," the hawker said. "Whenever I see those guys, I know somebody's in trouble."

The squad cars fishtailed to the mermaid club, scaring the hell out of a poor cabbie waiting for a fare.

A brace of coppers jumped fom the lead car. One leaped onto his car's hood to get closer. The front door began to open. The cop assumed Police Stance, used both hands to hold his gun, aimed it at the front door.

"Freeze!" Just as the Japanese were leaving.

They freaked. They hit the ground screaming. A couple of jokers in the rear took pictures. One drunk thought a Hollywood movie was being filmed. He started applauding.

The cops lowered their guns.

"What did I tell ya?" the hawker said. "Somebody's in trouble." His pale eyes said they hadn't seen it all, but they had seen too much.

We went on down the street together.

"How was your Christmas?"

CHAPTER 29

I knew the day was shot by the seventh ring. I tried thinking who'd call this time of morning. No one was worth talking to at this time of the morning. I lifted my eyelids, then answered the damn thing.

A man's voice. "If you want them, they're sailing with first light," he whispered.

I closed my eyes. "Good for them."

"You don't want them to sail without you."

I asked why not, but the sucker had hung up.

I hate telephones.

I was nearly awake by Third Street. Chain-smoking the cigarettes Ruth had left behind. My face felt tight, like my skin was shrinking. I popped a couple of codeine tablets and thought about hot coffee. But the all-nite gas station by the shipyards was closed for the holidays, and the vending machines were locked inside. The moon was just setting. It had a frosty halo. The fog had come in thick, like 100% lambswool. The only sounds came from the foghorns on the bay.

In daylight, the streets of Butchertown bustle with delivery trucks and semis. But only a paycheck keeps people here, and after office hours the streets are wide and empty, spooky with long shadows, home only for alley cats and squad cars. This section of the city is old, and the streetlights really are farther apart.

I parked at the head of the dead-end street. A faint light shimmered like a hand-held flashlight from the third floor of the fish company. Another night visitor? I unlocked my trunk and retrieved my gun, then hoofed it down the long shadows. Time for some alley-creeping.

I boosted a window by the loading dock and padded across the concrete. Harsh white light came from naked lightbulbs, and water puddles shared the reflection with dirty windows. I found the staircase and felt my way to the third floor. The corridor was lit with a single fluorescent panel. There were no lights inside the Anatole offices.

I went inside and the thin beam of my flashlight played across the shadows. A telecopier, a bookkeeping machine, a Xerox machine. Desk calculators, comptometers, typewriters and postage meters.

The soft glow came from Riki's office. I took out my gun and moved to one side. I felt for the knob, then shoved the door open.

"Who's there?" Her voice.

Ruth sat on the floor staring at my gun. She was surrounded by ledgers and journals. A long row of metal cabinets was behind her. The drawers were opened, and manila files stuck up.

"What are you doing here?"

"I work for Pac-Con," she said.

She waited. I had nothing to say.

She stared at my gun. "Old man Anatole's our client." She swallowed air. "He wanted somebody to infiltrate his company."

I put away my gun. I took my time. "You called him about me, didn't you, from that phone booth on Market. And he asked you to find out more about me."

Her jade eyes. "I had to. This is my first solo." Her eyes were bone-dry.

I said goodbye and went the way I came.

The long aluminum tables glowed with the moonlight that came through dirty windows. A cardboard box, soggy and crumbling, blocked my path. I stepped around, right into a puddle. Then I stopped. The plant was closed for the holidays.

I went back to the box. Chunks of shaved ice lined the insides. A path of water led towards the refrigerated storerooms. They looked like bank vaults in the night.

I followed the path. Only one storeroom was unlocked, and the path dead-ended in front. I opened the storeroom and went inside. The room was colder than a morgue photo and darker than death. A blast of frigid air almost sucked my breath away.

I found the light switch. A soft blue light glowed on the ice, and the ice became just as blue. I saw my breath was like cigarette smoke.

Frosted walls and mounds of ice. Shaved and crushed and in cakes. Cases and cartons dotted the mounds. Squid and dungeness crab. Shrimp cocktail sauce and kippered cod in sour cream. Tartar sauce and salmon caviar. Frozen carcasses of halibut, alabaster and headless like a mermaid's tail.

The path of water had frozen into a trail of ice that ended at a mound of shave ice. The mound was higher than any other mound, higher even than the cake ice.

I started shoveling with my hands. They quickly went beet-red, then pale with blue veins. As blue as the ice itself. I dug until I found a pale white leg, until I uncovered a pale blue thigh. I scooped ice away until I was brushing it from the dead woman's eyes.

Her eyes were half-open, vacant, a study in eternity. They were larger than robins' eggs, as blue as the Bay at dawn. I tried closing them. The eyelids slowly rose to half-mast. Blue eyes that wouldn't stay closed, not even in death. I had no coins to keep them closed.

She lay like a broken china doll. Unlike most stiffs, she looked younger than she was. There were bruises on the babyfat. The body was damp and rigid. She'd been here a while. The autopsy would say how long.

She had been shot in the temple by a small caliber pistol. Probably her sister's missing gun. There were a few specks of burnt powder around the bullethole. She had been shot at close range. Three or four feet at most.

There was no blood on the hole or around it. The body had cooled, melting the ice, and the icewater had washed the hole. Just a small black hole you could stick a pencil in.

I left her where she lay. I didn't bother closing the icehouse door or turning off the blue light. The police shouldn't scout dark shadows for corpses.

I found a telephone near the smoke house. The operator connected me with the Southeast District Police Station. The duty officer took my story and told me to wait around. I couldn't think of any place I could go to get away from Dani Anatole.

After I hung up, I pulled over an empty salmon crate. I lit a cigarette and waited for the meat wagon. It was too cold to smoke in the icehouse, and I needed a cigarette bad. It's always like this for me. Which is the way it should be. I never want to get used to the sight of a corpse.

"Put your hands in the air and don't make a move."

I looked up. "Hello, Alex. How's it going?"

He leveled the shark rifle. "Let's go."

"Sure." I stubbed out my cigarette.

Alex marched me outside to the China Creek piers. The huge trawler was the only Anatole boat present. A few interior lights overlooked us. The long black freighter was still berthed across the estuary, a mountain's shadow in the setting of the moon.

Jack Anatole studied charts in the deckhouse. He looked up as we filed in. "How did you know?"

"I got a phone call," I told him.

"Looks like we're going crabbing." He started folding his charts. "Was he carrying a gun?"

Alex swallowed. "I forgot to check."

"It's on my waistband," I volunteered.

I was frisked and Alex took my gun. He held it on me while Jack used sailor knots to tie my hands in front of me. I didn't try to resist.

"I thought you said you don't point guns."

"You didn't have to come here." Jack finished and looked over at Alex. "Get ready to cast off lines."

"What are you going to do about Dani?" I asked.

"We're not gonna forget her," he said. "She's just gonna have to catch up later, that's all."

Alex cast off the lines. The diesels cleared their throats, and the trawler began to drift. Jack opened the throttles, and we began to sluice up the long black channel. He blew two high-pitched whistles, then followed up with a third at a lower pitch. The bridgeman left his shanty to raise the Third Street bridge. He saw us and waved.

Alex jabbed me with my gun. "You're not fucking up Mexico for me," he hissed.

We all waved back. Then sailed into the Bay.

The sunrise was cold gold and glacier white, and the Bay at dawn was as blue as Dani's eyes. The city was a jewel, and the skyscrapers were like jagged glass. The streetlights on the Bay Bridge were a golden arc to Oakland. A rainbow of colors reflected from the water.

"How about some coffee?" Jack asked.

"What about him?" Alex asked.

"Take him to the galley with you."

Alex shoved me aft towards the galley. He had been simmering inside, and once away from Jack, he started poking me with my own gun, trying to get me riled. I was patient, docile, until we reached the galley. I was ready then to start changing the odds.

"Does Jack know you rifled Dani's houseboat?"

He forgot he had a gun and, with his other hand, he grabbed my shoulder and spun me around. He smacked me with his gunhand. I saw it coming and tried to roll away. He hit me hard, and the gunmetal slammed against my cheekbone. It jarred me and broke the skin.

A moment before I could speak. "You wouldn't do that if I were untied." I could feel the blood oozing out.

He laughed, surprised at his own strength. "I'm not dumb enough to fall for that crap," he said.

"Sure you are."

He was just pissed enough for showboating. He jabbed with his right fist. His body wasn't close enough to connect, so I didn't bother flinching. His fist swished the air inches from my chin.

"You're one of the dumbest monkeys in the world."

His fist swished past again. This time I flinched. He was angry and losing his touch. He was pretty good at swishing the air, though.

"You're a real toughie," I told him. "I can just see you as a teenager. Terrorizing old folks at the corner drugstore. But then Daddy bought your first car, and you and all the other toughies went off to the drive-in for strawberry pie."

He tried another right jab. I still outweighed him. I followed it and fell against him, making him fall back against the galley wall. He tried countering with a left hook. I grabbed his belt with both hands and pulled myself against him. His hook flew over my shoulder. Since he was so close, I kneed him. As he buckled, I slammed him into the wall again, pinning both arms against wood, knocking the wind from him. I used both hands to suckerpunch him. He crumpled, gasping and choking. I pulled him upright and shoved him into the wall again. Then I came up on the soft of his neck with clasped hands. He was out.

"That's enough." Jack had the shark rifle. "Over there," he commanded.

I waited in a neutral corner. Spent my time looking around the galley for miracles. I recognized the galley from Dani's houseboat. This was where she had gotten her design. No reason not to be home on the range.

Alex stumbled to his feet, saw me and growled.

Jack had no sympathy. "There's some booze in the locker behind you." He gestured with the rifle. "As for you, pal, the party's over. Upstairs."

"Dani's been on this boat," I said.

He corrected me. "Ship." Then he connected. "She's been here?"

I pointed both hands at the sink. A clean glass sat beside an empty bottle of Galliano. "That's what she drinks, isn't it?"

He was scornful. "She's not the only person who drinks that shit."

"Look at the bottle," I said. "Men don't wash their empties."

Jack puzzled over that, hesitated then gave Alex the rifle. "Here. Hold it on him." He turned back to his partner again. "And don't try anything while I'm gone. I might not be able to save you again." He went aft towards the cabins. He was back almost immediately with Dani's overnight case. "What do you know about this?" he demanded.

I had nothing to say. Dani was a corpse in an icehouse. She was surrounded by halibut and albacore. By now, she was probably defrosting. There was an APB out on me by now, too. I had to get home somehow.

He shook the barrel. "Okay, upstairs, then."

We sailed beneath the Golden Gate Bridge. The trawler seemed to pitch in all directions from the cross-currents. The bridge was clouded in swirls of tule fog.

CHAPTER 30

We sailed westward, away from the city and the continent. The sun rose and melted the fog into patches. The sky was icewhite, and the ocean was new denim. Sailboats, like shark fins, on the horizons.

Jack was the total sailor. He never took his hands from the wheel, and his eyes never stopped combing the waters. He sailed like a grunt on patrol, still looking for the enemy, and he was enjoying himself.

I spent my time watching the water shadows on the ceiling. They had made me sit on the deckhouse floor. It was damp and chilly. I was still tied in sailor's knots. I knew better than to test them. They'd been tied by a professional fisherman. I felt like a hound dog waiting for his master's kick.

Alex was just as uncomfortable. Restless, he paced up and down like a man outside Intensive Care. He had smoked several joints, taking quick puffs, not holding them in long enough. From the way he kept eyeing me, I should be stuffed down a sewer.

It was noon when we reached the Farallones. We sailed around the big island, away from the Coast Guard station. Jack cut the engines and we coasted. A western wind eased us along the leeward shore.

A million seabirds wheeled and darted above us, while on the rocks seals and sea lions worked on their

271

tans. Whole rookeries of gulls and cormorants roosted above them in the granite fractures. Grebes came up, got shy, dove beneath the boat, disappeared.

Jack saw the marker first. A long blue and white marker, not fifty yards from us, rising and falling in the slow swells. The trawler sidled closer on an outbound approach. Brown pelicans dive-bombed the waters near us.

Alex brought the marker alongside with a boathook and Jack helped him haul up its line. A kelp-coated crabpot came aboard last. They used a scaling knife to cut its cords, then brought a parcel inside. It was oilcloth completely sealed in inch-thick wax.

Alex disappeared down the galleyway. When he returned, he carried a cardboard box. He unloaded an icepick and a mirror, razor blades and test tubes, plastic straws and some aluminum foil, methanol and a propane camping stove.

He used the icepick on the parcel, then stuck a straw through the hole. The straw came out with an inch of whitish crystals. They looked like snowflakes, shiny and almost transparent.

He tasted the cocaine first. He seemed to like its bitter flavor. While he waited for his tongue to numb, he dumped more onto the face of the mirror. He spread it around, then broke the flake with the razor blade and formed it into a long thin line. He used another straw to snort his way down that line. It hit his mucous membrane like a gunshot. He threw back his head, snorted air in after it, then swallowed like a baby with a mouthful of ice cream.

He separated the rest of the cocaine. He dumped some into a test tube and filled it with methanol. As it started to dissolve, he lit the propane stove. He set the next sample on a swatch of aluminum foil and held it over the low blue flame. He was pleased at the way it burned.

"How's it going?" Jack asked.

Alex looked up. "Well, there's no bubbles," he told

us. "No rust in the residue, either." His speech was slurred. His tongue had numbed. He licked his lips and smiled at us. His eyes were bright enough for beacons.

Jack relaxed. He had little to do, just hold my gun on me. He lit a cigarette and waited for Alex to finish the cobalt test for color.

I watched Jack with his cigarette. He held it and took measured puffs with the coals cupped inside his hand. Some guys smoke that way when they step off the plane from Vietnam.

He felt me staring. A boyish grin appeared. "Just a little toot for me and my friends."

"How much is a little toot?"

"Fifteen kilos. Thirty-three pounds."

"That's a lot of toot."

"Coke's hard to get." His grin broadened. "You gotta buy it when you can." And he was one proud owner.

"What's the street value?"

"Uncut? Maybe a million."

"What did you pay for it?"

He didn't mind. "A little more than half that."

"All by yourself?"

"Dani and me covered half."

"Alex covered the rest?"

He smirked. "He couldn't get change for a quarter."

"Don't tell me it was Joey Crawford?"

"That little shit." The grin was gone. His face was brittle with anger. "He couldn't tell flour from coke." Jack was so angry, he was spitting my way with every word. "He ruined Dani's party because he couldn't tell them apart."

"Alex said we're sailing to Mexico."

"What?" He looked at his partner. His anger vanished and he laughed. "Why should we sail south? Who'd we sell this shit to?"

Alex was bent over a hot test tube. The liquid inside was becoming the same blue as cold steel. He mumbled something, then said he was too busy to talk. Maybe he was. He was sucking his gums, and there was sweat on his face. His eyes were brighter than headlights. He looked like a mad scientist hard at work.

Jack wasn't finished. "Our wholesale cost's higher than their retail," he insisted.

Alex leaned back. "Sweet baby Jesus," he crooned. He couldn't restrain himself any longer. "It's almost pharmaceutically pure!"

Jack froze. "No bullshit?"

"No bullshit." Alex giggled. "Cross my heart."

"Oh my god. It's all over." Jack could have cried from happiness, but he was grinning like an alkie who had just bought himself a wine cellar. "It really is. I never have to work again." He savored it with closed eyes, then remembered I was still here. He looked over at me. "You can tell your clients they were too late."

"And what happens to me?" I asked.

"We dump you first chance we get."

"Over the side?"

He went rigid. The muscles stood out in his thick neck. He raised my gun until it pointed at my heart. I looked into his eyes and froze inside. Only the grunts had gunfighter eyes.

We waited until his muscles relaxed.

"There's a lot of small islands up by Vancouver," he told me. "You might make it to civilization by spring, if you're any kind of woodsman."

"That's more than fair enough." I settled back for a long sea cruise.

Ruth Gideon popped up from the galleyway, assumed the Police Stance with a Police Special in both hands. The weapon was aimed at Jack's head. "All right, *freeze!*"

Jack exploded. "Who the hell are you?"

"I said, *freeze!*"

Alex stepped forward, thought better of it, then backed off. He wasn't about to assert himself. He was armed with a test tube. But he did suck his gums more.

Jack hadn't lowered my gun. He asked me who she was.

"She's a private investigator," I said. "Your grandfather hired her to look over the books."

"So what's she doing here?"

"Ask her." The shark rifle was leaning against the bulkhead. I leaned towards it.

"Hold it," Jack said. His hand was damn steady.

I stopped in mid-breath. I saw knuckles and steel and a black hole. The black hole was the barrel. You could stick a pencil in it.

"I said, *freeze*, dammit!"

"How'd you get here?" Jack asked.

"I followed him." She swayed with the boat.

I looked up. "What took you so long?"

Her chin quivered. "I came when the time was right."

"She was seasick," Jack guessed.

"What do you know?" She had a brave front. "I told you to put down that gun. Put it down. Slowly."

"Go fuck yourself," Jack said.

I was heartsick, but not over the man who held my gun on me. Jack Anatole was a veteran, and coolness under fire was his trade. He had a rock-steady hand. Ruth was the ringer, a ding-dong on her first solo. She had a green face. All guns are spooky, but amateur night in Tijuana was stupid. Somehow I had to get the guns down.

I asked Ruth to back down.

"He doesn't scare me," she said.

"He knows how to use that," I said.

She raised her gun. "Well, I know how to use this."

"Please don't be a hero." I tried being calm. "It never works."

"Because he's a man?" She almost spat the words.

I could've killed her for that crack. I tried being reasonable. "He can shoot me so fast, you wouldn't know what hit you, and you would be his second shot."

She mulled it over, then looked at him. "You got the Bronze Star, didn't you?" Maybe she was trying to be reasonable.

He didn't think he had heard her right. "So did a lot of other guys."

"But you came back," she said.

"Yeah. I came back. So what?"

"Did you give it back?" she asked. "Throw it on the steps of the Lincoln Memorial, like those other Vietnam vets did?"

He knew he hadn't heard her right.

"Did you give it back?" She was defiant as hell.

I told her to shut up. Jack was a short-fused man. He had a volcano for a temper. I didn't want him exploding near me, especially with my own gun.

"I didn't think you did." She was a smug little bitch. "I had you pegged right from the start. You'll never give up your Bronze Star."

"Shut up." His mouth was a thin line. Another Anatole trademark. He tried to be reasonable. "Listen to your partner."

She scoffed at that. "He couldn't keep his own job." She realized where she was. She pushed out her chest. "I told you to put down that gun."

"He isn't your partner?" Jack said.

"He was only after Dani," she snapped.

He was amused by that. "Was that all?" He peered down the gunsight at me. "If you had found her, you wouldn't be here right now."

I stared up the sight. "I never wanted this," I admitted. A bullet from my gun travels faster than the speed of sound. When it hits flesh, the bullet's shock wave can break ribs. At least I'd never hear my gun go off.

Ruth had no brains. "Oh, he found her."

I wanted her mouth zippered shut. I said a prayer to Our Lady of the Farallones.

"He did?" Jack was puzzled. "Where is she then?" He looked at me. When I had no answer, he looked back at Ruth. His gun almost moved up and away from my face. "Where is she?"

"She's back at the fish company," she told him.

"Alex!" My gun inched left. "Did you see her?"

Alex, confused, shook his head.

I tried to melt my body. I wanted to crawl on my back

like a sawbuck. I managed to get a couple of inches lower than the barrel. Now it would only blow off the top of my head. I tried shifting to the right.

"What was she doing there?" Jack asked Ruth.

"Don't play games," she snapped. "You're the one who killed her."

I closed my eyes and threw myself away.

A bullet struck the wood above me.

I went deaf. I thought I was dead. Being dead startled the hell out of me. I opened my eyes.

Ruth flinched at the noise.

A bullet punctured Jack's chest.

He lurched backwards, crashed through the deck-house door. My gun went clattering up the deck. He crashed against the railing, and went down hard and fast. He never heard the gun go off.

My ears came back. The echoes of gunfire flashed back from the rocks like ghosts come back to haunt. The seabirds went screaming into the airlanes. The seals and the sea lions roared with fright. They rushed hysterically towards the surf.

I burned off the sailor knots on the propane stove. Then I used a handkerchief and lifted my gun. I almost wiped the blood from the steel. But then I was the only one who could still think and function. I had a lot to do.

I went over to Alex. He shook his mouth several times. He had thrown up on himself. He didn't flinch when I frisked him. I found nothing on him.

Ruth still stood like a policewoman. She had wet her pants. I took the gun from her, careful not to smear the prints. I frisked her as gently as I could. She trembled and flinched from my fingers. Like so many others, she had just learned that murder comes easily. Just pull a trigger and a carcass starts to cool.

Jack was down for good. The bullet had hit him square in the chest. His pupils were gone, and only the whites of his eyes were behind his wide eyelids. He had said it took no brains to be a hero. Which was how he had become a hero. Which was how he had died. I frisked the body and found the keys to the chartlocker.

I went inside and unlocked the cabinet. Ruth followed me. She saw the bloodied gun. It meant nothing to her. It wasn't reality, and it made no sense. She was a caveman with a flashlight. She went and locked herself in the head. I locked the guns and the cocaine in the cabinet.

I found the radio-telephone. I let it warm up, then played with the buttons and the microphone. We were adrift thirty miles off-shore. I couldn't handle the ship, and Alex wasn't dependable help. One glance at the charts convinced me I needed a pilot to re-enter the Golden Gateway.

The marine operator connected me with the Coast Guard. I identified myself and asked for their assistance and gave them my location. "How soon can you get here?"

"A cutter has already been dispatched."

I blessed them. And Our Lady of the Farallones.

"Was that gunfire we heard?"

"Damn straight." I started to explain.

The Coast Guard interrupted me. "We advise you that injuring, shooting, maiming or poaching wildlife in this sanctuary is punishable by . . ."

I switched off the son of a bitch.

I found Ruth's purse in one of the cabins. I dumped it and started pawing through it. Cosmetics, birth control pills, her photostat from the Bureau of Consumer Affairs. A staff ID from Pac-Con that said she'd been with the LA branch for six months. A box of hollow-point shells. And a manila envelope marked evidence.

I paged through her evidence. The leasing bill for both of Riki Anatole's cars. A canceled check for floral arrangements for a neighbor's graduation. A restaurant receipt from a Third Street deli for three hundred bucks worth of grilled ham-and-cheese sandwiches for the Oakland As play-offs last year. A few scribbled notes from petty cash.

Her screwy evidence was legal proof that she was guilty of Breaking and Entering. That's all it was. The expense sheets might be sloppy management, but they were mostly legal or easily explainable deductions.

There was another envelope underneath. Inside were some photo-copies of some promissory notes Ruth had question-marked. Each note was for fifty grand, a year's loan to the fish company. They were dated thirty days apart, and the newest due date was next month. Each bore the same Chinese ideogram for a signature. The lender's name was typed below each ideogram. Tan Ng was the lender for all ten notes.

I went back on deck. The birds still shrieked above us. Jack's body was crumpled against the scuppers. He looked like he was remembering an old lover. The blood had stopped oozing out, most had drained into the sea, and what was left was already turning black from the salt air. My shoes made sucking sounds in the blood.

Alex was at the bow. He looked at me. "Mexico," he said. Not a statement or a question. Not a declaration of purpose or intent, not even a plea. Just the one word he could still say.

I told him we were heading back to port. Murder precluded Mexico. There was no way to sail there. And then I saw the Coast Guard cutter bearing down on us.

The Coast Guard came alongside and aboard. The officers were shaken by the carnage, while the crew was glassy-eyed over the cocaine. Alex was taken into custody. Ruth went aboard the cutter refusing medical attention. Jack's body went into a CG floater bag, then into the trawler's refrigerated hold.

I decided to stay onboard the trawler. An ensign gave me a receipt for the guns and the cocaine. A male steno took my statement. Finally there was nothing more left unsaid.

I went below and found a bottle of tequila in a locker. I swiped a lemon and a salt shaker from the galley and snuck aft to a cabin. I started drinking, thinking of Mexico. But there was no Mexico. No tequila sunrise. Just as there was no Santa Claus, no Easter Bunny. I was tired, or maybe it was the salt air, or maybe the tequila, but it didn't take long. Soon I was dead drunk, fast asleep.

CHAPTER 31

The Law was waiting in San Francisco. Uniformed officers came aboard and took custody of the guns and the cocaine. Jack's body was shipped to the morgue. Alex was read his Miranda rights and then led away to a four-wheeled cage. Ruthann disappeared in a black and white. No one seemed interested in me.

A late model blue sedan was parked at the head of the pier. Its engine had a lazy idle, like a government job. It had blackwall tires and a whip antenna. There were few dents or creases. Two men sat inside, each slouched against a door. They could have been twins. Their long hair was styled alike, and their beards were trimmed alike. They both wore open-throated shirts whose collars hung over their sportcoats.

I hiked over. "You're Howard, right?"

"I'm Curtin." He opened the rear door. "Captain wants you."

We started off towards the Hall of Justice. Though there was little traffic in the city, the detectives drove slower than a brace of hookers. Dispassionate and robot-like, their eyes kept scanning the sidewalks ahead, looking for whatever came next. Their eyes said they knew no buddies on these streets.

Halfway through the Stockton Street tunnel, the police dispatch began paging us. To me, it was all cop talk, laced with garbled words and winter static, but the detectives were cipher experts. They made a left turn onto Post Street, took Post to Kearny, then speeded north back the way we had come.

I asked what was happening.

"One-eighty-seven at the Orpheus on Broadway."

I leaned back and closed my eyes. 187 was police code for homicide, and the Orpheus Hotel was a last-chance flop located above the flashiest topless joint on the strip. I doubted I'd get any sleep tonight.

The streets of the Financial District were still littered with calendar sheets, left-overs from last year's going-away party. Once, when the city treasury was flush, the streetsweepers spent New Year's Day cleaning up the calendars. But the unions started demanding double-time, and now the streets stay filthy until the next regular workshift.

Broadway was just beginning to darken with sun-down, and the neon was already glowing above the jazz clubs and encounter parlors. We found a yellow zone and parked. There were a couple black and whites there, an unmarked car like ours, a meat wagon triple-parked with its emergency flashers on, even a television crew from a local tv station. A small crowd of early-rising nightcrawlers stood by, criticizing the show.

Captain Banagan had arrived ahead of us. He left his squad car and came curbside. "Hello, boys." He looked back at me. "We need that talk tonight."

"As bad as that?"

"The Chief says you're interfering with police work," he told me. He looked grim. "You've doubled our monthly homicide figures in a single weekend."

"The Feds'll love it," I said. "Now the city can apply for another grant." I ticked off the items. "More cop cars, more computers, maybe another toxicologist . . ."

"He's going after your license, Michael."

"Fuck my license. You think I wanted any of this shit to happen? You know what really happened out there?" I remembered what happened. I put my hands in my pockets. "I got lucky."

"You got lucky," he agreed. "What are you going to do now?"

"I don't know."

"Neither do I," he said.

No neon sign advertised the Orpheus Hotel. There was just a hand-painted one that fronted a bus stop. For five bucks, two people could stay all night. For thirty, they could stay all week.

We found an inspector with a beat cop.

"How's it going, Charlie?"

"Captain. Good to see you."

They shook hands and made introductions all around.

"Whatcha got for me?" Captain Banagan asked.

"I just got here myself," Charlie said.

"Let's go upstairs and check it out."

The hotel had stairs but no elevator. The carpeting was worn from dragging feet and shuffling shoes. Only the lonely lived here and not for long. They left town or found a plot in potter's field.

The police had taken over the second floor, and flashes from the police Polaroids lit our way. The hallway was a haven for burn-outs from the Haight or North Beach. Winos too far gone to rehabilitate and pensioners who had given up. Drifters building up courage for the long walk from town. Junkie hookers and part-time pimpsters. Lady wrestlers and bearded ladies.

The captain looked them over. "Well, get their statements anyway."

A fat transvestite, his wig off and his make-up on, jumped in front of us. "You'll find the killer, won't you?"

The captain walked around him. "Maybe."

"You're a real comfort," the tv said. "That's what you are."

Banagan looked back. "Yes, ma'am, a real comfort, that's what we are." His voice was as dry as the August hills.

At the end of the hallway, the medics were having the

devil's own time getting their stretcher through the narrow doorway. They grunted and heaved. Finally, tilting it sideways, they made their escape. They rolled the stretcher towards us, followed by a lady reporter hoping for a scoop. A Chinese cameraman tagged behind like a three-legged puppy.

The captain stopped them.

"Open it up."

The medics loosened straps on the morgue bag. Snooping for an exclusive, the lady reporter edged her microphone forward. The cameraman began filming.

"No kidding," Banagan said over the corpse. "Hey, Michael, you've seen this clown before, haven't you?"

I leaned forward. "Yeah, I've seen him before."

Tan Ng's wrinkled face stared up at us. He had the pained look of a vulture who's just discovered poison among the offal. Somebody had cut his throat, not quite from ear to ear, but deep enough to gash his neck to the bones. There was blood even in his ears.

"You know this man?" the lady reporter said.

"Since I was beat cop here back in the Forties," Banagan told her. "He was a big man in Chinatown. *Consiglieri* for the Chinese Mafia. He could spring them faster than I could book them."

She was interested. "Then it's a Chinatown gangland slaying?"

Banagan went grim. "He was a chicken hawk." As if that could explain it all to her.

She asked him just what a chicken hawk was.

"A homosexual who preys on teenage boys. This old guy was a master at it. He could find a teenager in a convent. But I didn't think he could still get it up."

She was startled. "This old man?"

Banagan shrugged. "Maybe those chinese herbs work."

"Well, he is a Chinese," she said.

"Fruit comes in all colors," he dead-panned.

She chose to ignore that. "Was he ever arrested?"

"For sodomy?" He sighed. "Never could get anyone to testify."

"The youngsters were threatened with reprisals?"

"It was never just sex, never just a one-night stand for this guy, or for the others like him. No, they take a real interest in their chickens. Sort of a Big Brother relationship, I guess."

She smirked. "Like a Little League coach?"

"Yeah, like a Little League coach." We walked on, and Banagan leaned over. "Too bad she can't say that on the Instant Eyewitness News," he whispered.

"She's gonna try," I said.

"You think so?" Banagan was amused.

Inside the hot little room, the Polaroid boys were packing their equipment, while the fingerprint team worked on the window ledges.

"Any prints, Dennis?"

The lab man didn't look up. "Millions."

"Millions, he says."

"And they're probably a match," Dennis went on, "with every wino, every junkie, every hooker who's ever passed through town."

"Keep collecting them," the Captain told him. "We can always start a scrapbook."

"Captain?" Charlie came up. "I talked with the bartender downstairs. A young Chinese male was here last night just after midnight. He bought a couple of drinks once in a while. The old man came in just before last call. He sat by the young male, they started talking, and both left about twenty minutes later."

"What about descriptions?"

"The bartender said the young male was Chinese." Charlie looked up from his notebook. "He said they all look alike."

"Anything else?" Banagan asked.

"So far that's it. Charlie spotted a waiting beat cop. "What have you got?"

The officer checked his notes. "The manager of this joint says a young Chinese male came in last night, paid his five bucks, then went out again. He didn't see him return."

"Any description?"

"Yep." The beat cop started paging backwards.

"Save it for the report." Charlie remembered. "Anybody checking with the next-of-kin?"

"Still trying," the beat cop said.

"Thanks, Charlie." The captain looked at me. "It seems straightforward, doesn't it?"

"Seems so," I agreed.

"This old man and the Anatoles were pretty tight," the captain said. "Any connection with you?"

"I think so, but I'm not sure yet."

"Care to talk about what you know?"

"Well, Orestes Anatole, the grandfather, hired Ruth Gideon and Pac-Con to check out some rumors. Ng's his lawyer and part-owner of the business—"

Banagan interrupted. "Were you messing with the chick?"

"Well, you see—"

"Ng didn't like you messing with the hired help?"

"Yeah, I guess so. He tried to hire me to chase down some Chinese who supposedly swiped a jade charm bracelet from him."

"You didn't fall for that shit, did you?"

"Oh no. I turned him down."

"A good thing you did, too," he said. "Not only is it too obvious, but you're not bonded any more, are you?"

"So what's the verdict?" The lady reporter had caught up to us again.

"The old man got lured upstairs." Banagan looked at me. "After that, it doesn't matter much. Either a lover's quarrel, or the old man resented getting rolled."

She seemed disappointed. "What was he doing here, anyway? I mean, why didn't he go down to some Chinatown bar, if he was trying to pick up a guy?"

"He was a Chinatown lawyer," I heard myself saying. "If he got caught in Chinatown . . ." I heard my voice fading away.

"But here? To bring him up here? After a topless joint?"

"A lot of fags work the topless joints," the beat cop told her. "They got radar for the closet cases. Con-

ventioneers, tourists, businessmen. Even their wives
don't know they suck cock.''

I needed out. "You need me any more?"

"What about our little talk?"

I pleaded. "Tomorrow?"

The captain was pragmatic. "Go get some sleep," he
told me. "Maybe you'll feel better tomorrow."

I took the stairs two at a time. I knew it wasn't going
to be any better tomorrow.

CHAPTER 32

Two portable news teams had set up shop on the opposite curb. They were photographing the grey mansion because no one would let them inside. Neighbors were watching from behind closed drapes.

The black maid blocked the door. "You fucked up my weekend." She wanted to sandpaper my skin.

"Sure, I did," I pushed past her. "How come they got you wearing a maid's uniform?"

"Cos we got company," she groused. She knew who to blame for that. She gave me another sour look. "Maybe you better come inside."

"Thanks." I let her lead the way.

The hallway stretched out like Death Row. If she were the warden, I must be the star of the show. I wondered what had happened to my last supper.

I felt like hell. There was tequila in my guts and death on my mind. Thank God I still had a heat on. I hoped I wasn't sobering too fast. I couldn't face these people if I were sober.

Orestes Anatole was alone in the library. He wore a three-piece suit beneath his blanket. His eyes were red with tears, and his chins were wet and stained. He sat in his wheelchair as if he'd been motionless for years.

He noticed me. He knew my name. "Brennen." He

spoke softly, slowly, fearing denture slippage. "Thank you for coming."

"I came when I could."

"You look tired." He thought it over. "You have been busy. And I've been waiting for the police to call."

I hesitated. "What did Pac-Con have to say?"

"They're going to call?" He sagged at the notion.

I frowned. "They haven't called yet?"

"No one's called." He amended that. "A television station. They wanted to interview me."

"I'm sorry they beat me here."

He waved a tired hand in the air. The silence of his heartache was oppressive. He was a newly haunted man. His grandchildren were ghosts.

He tried to be professional. "I called Las Vegas." Maybe he hoped that would override the agony.

A while before I remembered. "That guy who wanted to buy the fish company. He's still interested?"

"It's a fair price." Orestes took control of himself. "A very fair price." He couldn't forget the prices he paid.

Catherine came into the library. The artificial lighting made her look tired and frazzled. She had been crying. Her chin sagged and her face was pale and her cheeks seemed puffy. She stopped when she saw me. Her face said I was poison, but she said nothing. She went straight to the sideboard.

I asked the old man if he would sell.

He didn't know. "Why should I keep it?"

I told him to talk with his employees first. "They worked to make it yours. And after all the shit you've been through, there's still no justification for screwing the people who put their trust in you. They deserve first crack at buying in."

His chins quivered. He didn't want to remember.

Catherine forced herself to be polite. "Would you like a drink?" She indicated a liquor cart that had been brought into the room. She was already pouring Gran Marnier into a snifter.

I was wrong about her tears. She had tried to cry, but

she was too crocked. It was alcohol that had paled her cheeks, her remarkable tan, the blue in her eyes. She was so smashed, I wondered how she could stand.

"Why don't you have one for me?" I don't know why I said it. I had no reason being self-righteous. There were lots of living dolls like her. Lonely women who drank alone at home. Some were even quiet drunks. I wasn't a detox worker, and it wasn't my job to keep her from a bottle.

Her eyes flickered, then froze. "Blondes are people, too."

"I don't ever recall denying that."

"I like to drink," she told me. She hefted the snifter and downed several mouthfuls. "Why did you come back here?"

"I had to give my final report."

She refilled her snifter. "Why did you bother? It's in every newspaper."

"You were the one who hired me."

"Yes, I did, didn't I?" She tried to laugh, but laughter hurt. "I hired you to keep our name from the newspapers. Now it's smeared across every newspaper in the state." Her voice was brittle with self-pity.

"Your family name was smeared already."

She hadn't heard me. "Do I get a refund?"

"Do you want one?"

Her tan paled even more. "You're disgusting."

"If you want one, I'll give you one."

"Get out of here. Right now. Get out."

I threw her check on the desk. She stared at it as if it were shit. She made me feel like a dirty little boy.

I needed that drink after all. I went to the liquor cabinet. There was kahlua and white rum and creme sherry, Cinzano and Dubonnet. I found some Hunting Port and belted it down.

Her chin quivered. "Why did you do this to us?"

"They were smugglers long before I got here."

"This is all your fault," she said.

"And it's never yours, is it?"

She choked on a giggle. "Me?"

"If you had just told me Dani was here," I said, "right at the beginning, all this would've ended before any of it had a chance to get started."

She thought I was nuts. "If it weren't for you, she'd be alive today."

"He tried to kill me because of her," I said.

"No, you started this," she hissed.

Orestes punched the power button, and his wheelchair came to face me. "Is this true? Are you responsible?" His voice was an old woman's broken heart.

"Maybe I am. It's hard to say." I shrugged off the guilt. "Like I said, they were smugglers long before I got here. Sooner or later the local pros would've stepped in. Either they'd have let Dani and Jack join in, or they'd have cut them down to size. All I did was speed up the inevitable."

"You started it," she insisted.

I wasn't finished. "But if you're looking for somebody to blame, well, there's always yourself, for that matter."

"I never knew they were smuggling narcotics," Orestes told me.

"You told them about your liquor running days."

"What's that got to do . . . ?"

"They were amateurs, too," I told him. "They'd been smuggling dope a couple of years already, but nothing big until this last deal. Maybe a couple of pounds of weed, maybe a couple of ounces of cocaine. Maybe you thought they were listening to grandpaw's fairy tales, but to them it was proof that amateurs, free-lancers, could get away with it."

"They thought I gave them advice?" His eyes were glassy, and he had a hard time focusing.

"What did you expect them to think? They were just starting out. The Junior Achievement of smugglers. Well, smuggling's a family tradition. Who else could they turn to?"

"But that was years ago!" Catherine said.

"What does it matter?" I looked at the old man. "You were the amateur in those days. You went against the pros and got out alive and rich. What other proof did they need?"

"But they were smuggling *cocaine*!" he said.

I shrugged. "It's the modern hooch."

"You make them sound like criminals," Catherine said.

Orestes raised wet eyes. "Is there any more?"

"If you want to hear it." I didn't wait for him. "If it hadn't been for you, they never would have gotten as far as they did. You didn't even have to know about it."

They were both silent, lost in that puzzle.

"Once you were the Big Bad Wolf," I told him. "Tan Ng wasn't the only one who thought so. Maybe some people still think you are. Your name, even in the background, could've cooled the heat for Dani and Jack."

"Was somebody after them?" Orestes said.

I didn't hesitate. "They thought so."

"The Anatoles aren't criminals," Catherine butted in. "We don't go around pointing guns and shooting people."

"That's what they did," I said.

"They're not criminals," she insisted.

I held up my hand. "Maybe you're right. If somebody forced them out, they wouldn't steal cars or boost cigarettes."

She brightened. "That's what I mean." She was clinging to straws. She was one step away from imbecility.

I ticked off the other entries. "Mere possession of cocaine is a felony. It's a felony to use a gun during the commission of a crime. When somebody is killed during the commission of a crime, the charge is automatically murder."

Catherine was livid. "I told you to get out of here!"

I took another crack at the port. "You're just saying that to make me feel better." I went after the old man again. "Dani and Jack were lovers, weren't they?"

"Oh, why don't you leave!" Catherine cried.

"It wasn't her fault," Orestes said. His voice cracked

like celery stalks. "What happened . . ." His voice tapered off. " . . . anybody in her shoes . . . "

"Oh no." Catherine was crushed. She hadn't guessed.

His eyes were elsewhere. "She tried to stop it. She couldn't. There was so much feeling . . ."

"Is that why she went to Seattle?" I asked.

He was drooling. "He proposed to her. She was scared."

The gold woman closed her eyes. Money and looks were worthless now.

Orestes went on. "She was afraid she'd end up like Lilian."

It made sense. Jack was trouble, and Dani saw him coming. She left town to get away from him. She met Joey and moved in with him. She knew she had settled for less, but she made do, like most folks.

For one thing, there were drugs. Other drugs, at first, and then came cocaine. Up to a point, it prolonged sex, which made her life more bearable. When Joey became impotent from doing too much, she didn't leave him. She started seeing other men. She bought a vibrator.

Dani was predictable. When anything became too mechanical, too devoid of feeling, she left it behind her. When that happened with Joey, she wouldn't or couldn't cuckold him any more. She went to live with her sister. She tried more men, other arrangements. She was still resisting Jack. Maybe she did want time to think things over.

Then she heard Joey Crawford was dead, that a private eye was snooping. The cocaine deal was a natural target. She tried running again. She ran to the safest place she could afford. The family business closed for the holidays. She froze to death there.

Catherine walked out on us. Just breezed through the door like autumn's passing. You could hear her footsteps fading in the hallway, you could hear a cigarette burn in the silence she left behind.

I got up to leave. There was no sense staying.

Orestes stirred. "You might as well keep the money."

"It was never mine to keep," I said.

I found more to say when I reached the door, but the old man was staring at the bookshelves. I doubted they would answer his questions. There was nothing I could say to him, and I'm not good at watching old people cry.

I found my own way out.

CHAPTER 33

Chinatown was winter quiet. There were parking spaces, and the restaurants were deserted. A rising wind rattled the glass in store windows, rattled the Christmas trees on the curbs. Tomorrow the scavenger trucks would come and swallow those trees. In some places they had already come and gone. Tinsel left behind looked like droolings from a metal monster.

A light was visible in the offices above the draft board. I figured he'd be here, not at some joss house burning prayers in an oven. That was for tourists and grievers. I found the staircase and headed up. I was lagging and needed both railings to keep my momentum.

He sat behind his uncle's desk, bent over like some ancient Chinese scribe. A pocket calculator and an IBM Selectric took the place of owl ink and the abacus. Papers on his desk rustled like the rustle of windswept leaves. He had a nice collection of paper cups and cigarette butts.

"Brennen." He collected himself. "Come in."

"Hello, Louis." I found a seat. "How's it going?"

"I'm okay." He leaned back. "I hear you've been busy."

"I'm pretty tired," I admitted. "God, you must love your job. It's Sunday night."

He was calm. "Orestes Anatole wants the books done

294

by tomorrow. I had to bring them up to date for him."
He folded over some pages. "My uncle's reputation's at
stake."

I sloughed it off. "He never had anything to sweat."

"He'll be happy to hear that." He paused, played
with his pencil, started doodling on a file. "How can
you be sure?"

"I just came from Orestes Anatole."

"How's the old man doing?" He cursed himself as
soon as he said it. If he knew I had been busy, he knew
how Orestes was doing. Louis had slipped.

"He found a buyer for the fish company."

"Why would anybody want to buy it?"

"The guy wants to partition it off and make tourist
traps, like the Cannery and Ghiradelli Square. He wants
to call it the Fish Factory. He'll probably buy up your
uncle's shares, too."

Louis liked that. "My uncle will sell." It was a
foregone conclusion in his mind. He looked at his
doodles. "My uncle's not here right now."

"I didn't come to see him."

He looked me over with sharp eyes. Fag eyes that
never stop propositioning. "Should I ring down for
some tea?"

I wanted to laugh. "He's not your uncle." I knew no
polite way to say this. "You're a fag hooker. A street
whore. He picked you up off the streets of Hong Kong.
Or was it Taiwan?"

He took it well enough. He didn't hold his breath and
he didn't suck it in. He didn't even look at me. He went
back to his doodles. "You need proof. Where is it?"

I knew I had him then. "Cops are like elephants.
They never forget. Maybe you have a record. Let's call
the cops."

His eyes flashed hellfire on me. He had a record.

I looked at his scratch pad. Numbers. "He found you
working the streets. He liked you, took an interest in
you, fell in love with you . . . " I shook my head.
"Anyway, he brought you here and called you nephew,
so the neighbors wouldn't freak."

He frowned at a paper clip. "It's not what you think."

I didn't care. "You had a pretty good set-up. Tan Ng never had a son, no one to carry on the family name. Family is very important to the Chinese, to any immigrants. Maybe you did have the same name, which made you part of his family clan. He wanted you to step into his shoes some day, carry on that name. That was your part of the bargain."

He shrugged. "I'm not his nephew. But no one in this country knew that. Where'd you find it out?"

"I stumbled on it," I admitted. "I wouldn't even have considered it until you had trouble understanding his Cantonese. For me, it was like listening to a Chicano and a Chinese doing business together in English. You had problems with his accent. But then Cantonese has different dialects. Regional ones, right?"

He knew that. "We both came from Kwangtung province," he told me. "His parents were peasants. My family came from Canton. They're city people, not people of the dirt."

I had no respect. "You big snob. It's always the same old story. The hayseed gets taken by the city slicker. He wanted to help you. He gave you a job. A job in America. That was the biggest break you ever had."

"A job in a fish company," he advanced. He looked down at his pencil. "I don't have that job anymore." He threw his pencil with disgust into his papers. He had a good front.

"That's where you met Jack Anatole, wasn't it?"

"Of course." He frowned. "Why?"

"And through him, the whole crowd." I went on like I was reciting a dream. "They'd been smuggling small amounts of weed into the city. You thought that was a great idea. There's lots of money in dope, and dope's easy to unload. Your uncle had connections in Chinatown, so nobody'd question his nephew branching out."

He was motionless. "You're saying I'm a dope dealer."

"More than that. You and Jack were partners, smuggling partners." I couldn't wait any longer. "Alex turned state's evidence."

"Alex?" He glanced up. "Who's Alex?"

"Jack's crewmate on the trawler."

"I never met him." He was positive.

"He'll testify against you."

"With what? Hearsay evidence?" He shook his head. That was no problem in court. He had to whittle away his problems. "I should get my lawyer. This is slander."

"You split the cost, the up-front money, Jack brought it in and you unloaded it in Chinatown." I held up my hand. "That was fine for a while. Extra pocket money and all. But you got hungry and you went for the big time."

He had cooled. "What would that be?"

"Fifteen keys of coke. Raw coke. Pure coke."

"Fifteen keys." His nose twitched at that. "That's a lot of cocaine." He sharpened his eyes on me. "How much would that much coke cost?"

"A half-million dollars."

He lit a cigarette off the ashes of an old one. "You have to buy it before you can sell it. My share would have to be up-front, like you say. It would be half that, right? A quarter of a million dollars."

I grinned. "That's right."

"I'm a bookkeeper in a fish company." He stared and didn't blink. "I get a paycheck every two weeks." He could have been discussing the price of rice. He was already working on his legal defense.

"You're the bookkeeper," I agreed.

"You think I'm embezzling?" He smiled like an adult with a child. "That company's got serious cash flow problems. Do you know how long it would take to embezzle from a company that's having cash flow problems? You think there's a quarter million in petty cash? This is a fish company, not a bank."

"Dummy loans," I said. "A front for siphoning cash without fingering the till."

He shut up to hear the evidence.

"You fudged here and forged there until it looked like Tan Ng had loaned a half-million to the company. Dummy loans. The Big Money Boys bought them, maybe fifty cents on the dollar, and held onto them like claim checks. You got your cash advance. If anything went wrong, the fish company got screwed. Since it should be all profits, you could pay them back, retrieve the notes, and still never have to work again."

He looked up. "How long have you been at this?"

"Since Friday." I tried not to remember the weekend. "I just stumbled onto you. I was looking for Dani Anatole, Joey Crawford hired me."

"Is that all?" He lost composure. "Because she left him?" He looked like the Transparent Man. His secrets were floating away from reach.

"And you came at me with both barrels."

He knew now. "That was a mistake."

"You called your uncle and told him about me. He figured I was hired by Orestes Anatole to investigate his management. You talked him into hiring me to track down Lim Song. Then you called Lim Song and told him Tan Ng hired me. That way you could get me off on a wild goose chase, get Lim Song to take some heat off you, and save you the trouble of messing with either one of us."

His doodling kept on. His numbers grew larger, more dramatic. He couldn't decide whether to kill me now or later.

"Orestes never heard about the loans, but the Big Money Boys up in Nevada knew, and Orestes heard enough through the grapevine to hire investigators. They told him about me and he knew something was on. So he shut down the company and the fleet stayed in. And when Jack heard that news, he wanted his dope. He told you he was taking out the new trawler. You couldn't talk him out of it, so you woke me up and told me they were going sailing."

"But you said he was my partner."

"You couldn't trust him. You figured he was taking

off for good, so you threw him to the wolves. Maybe I was with the pros. They'd burn everybody and there'd be no survivors. If I were with the cops, the Anatoles wouldn't squeal. They wouldn't suspect you fingered them. And there was always hope for a shootout.''

"Why, if I stood to lose a quarter million dollars worth of pure cocaine?''

"Coke is risky. Mere possession is a felony. You wanted out already. You could afford to lose your investment if you could gain more by not getting caught doing it.''

He choked a laugh out. "What would I gain?''

"Everything your uncle has. This organization of his, for a start. When you heard Dani and Jack were dead, you thought you were home free. That's why you're forging your uncle's books right now. You want them to match the Anatole books. If the loans are in both books, then somebody has to pay them.''

"What about my uncle? What do you think he'd say about me forging his books?''

I almost hesitated. "Is Tan Ng your lawyer?''

"Yes, of course. Why?''

"That's going to look bad for you in court.''

Maybe he was counting heartbeats. "Has anything happened to my uncle?'' For an instant I thought I saw a spark of genuine regret. If it was, he got over it quickly.

"You sliced his throat,'' I said. "He's cold.''

"My uncle is dead.'' He was thoughtful. "You say I murdered him.'' He shook his head at that.

"You had to kill him. He was going to let the books be examined. With him dead, it was your word against a corpse. You step into his shoes and inherit his whole organization. He had no son. You were a natural.''

"When did I decide all this?''

"I don't know for sure. Probably last night when I was with your uncle. You overheard about the books. Or maybe it was when you were at the topless joint, looking for a pick-up. Anyway, it was there you called him up, told him where you were, told him to meet you there. And he came.''

"My uncle. In a topless club."

"Nobody'd notice two men talking together in a topless club. As for your uncle, he likes his privacy. He'd understand that. That's why he came. You told him it was important. Maybe the band was too loud for the old man, so you both went up to a hotel room. You thought that with his reputation, the cops would see it as a gangland execution. Lim Song and his pals were always available to take the blame."

He was quick. "What makes you think they didn't?"

I shook my head. "Something you never would've thought of. The cops never saw it as a Chinese gang killing. They knew he was a chicken hawk when he was younger. They think it's a lover's quarrel." I had to ask. "But it wasn't sexual, was it?"

"He was always an old man," Louis said. He was depressed, but he could still fight back. "Why would the cops want me? I wouldn't meet my uncle outside our own house. Why should they come here? They have no proof."

I felt sorry for him. "They have your name as next-of-kin. That means they have to notify you. They need your statement about your uncle's death. They will find you. Maybe the same hunch that brought me here will bring them here. They'll take you down to the Hall of Justice soon enough. And then you'll match the description of the guy who rented the flophouse room. They'll run a routine check on you and they'll find out you're not his nephew. The real investigation starts then."

He tried a different tack. "I rented no room. Suppose I don't match this description."

"You don't think you'll match?"

"Some people think all Chinese look alike."

"Yeah, but you don't look like many Chinese."

"Maybe somebody else rented the room?"

"A gofer?" I shook my head. "You couldn't trust anyone with that amount of leverage on you. No, you rented it yourself."

"I rented no room," he insisted.

"Was Davey Huie one of your gofers?"

He was startled. "I don't know who he is."

"You should. You killed him, too."

He looked worried. "Why would I kill a stranger?"

"He was your lackey. He helped you with your little coke deal. He kept an eye out for your interests. He told you I talked with him, that Jack Anatole rescued him from Jardin's Saloon. He knew about the cocaine. Maybe my clients knew the stuff was coming in, but not where or how much. You couldn't let me find out, so yesterday morning you went over to his house. Maybe you gave him a joint to relax. You sapped him. Easy for a big boy like you. You jammed pure coke into his veins. It was short, fast and clean enough for you, like putting a dog to sleep. You killed him to keep yourself out of the limelight. If it backfired, Jack could always take the blame. He probably told you he was the last man to see Davey alive."

He was busy shuffling some of his papers together. He came up with a .38 Colt revolver. He pointed it at me. "Is there more?"

I hate guns. "No, that's about it." I told myself it would be quick. I'd never see the flames from the barrel. I'd feel a flash of pain. At least it wouldn't be murder by torture. That's when you wait to die.

He stared at me. "Where do you come in?"

"I came to take you in."

"D'you really think you could?" he marvelled.

"I don't see any other way you can come."

He knew I was loonie. "Walk into a murder rap?"

I shrugged. It cost me a lot of guts. "Turn yourself in. Save the taxpayers some money."

"They'll go broke before that happens."

"Don't count on it. If the police don't find you, Lim Song will. And you know he'll come after you, if he finds out what the police want you for. He's got a lot of reasons after what you've made him do."

"My people can stop him."

"You're not your uncle's nephew. And when your

own boys find that out, how safe are you going to be? You're going to need protection from your friends and your enemies. You have no choices. There's nothing you can do.''

He still had one gun. "I can kill you."

"And make it three?" I shook my head. "I'm your only hope for staying alive. Turn yourself in right now. The longer you wait, the less time you have. It's late already. Things are in motion."

"Now what's that mean?"

"I called Lim Song," I said. "I told him everything. How you suckered us and played us against each other, so you could get control of the old man's business."

"You told him that?" He followed the lines to his future. "Why did you do that?"

"Revenge. Revenge against both you and Lim Song."

He stared. "Double-cross." He sighed, laid the gun in his lap. He was defeated for the moment.

I corrected him. "Killing two birds with one stone."

The outer door opened and I knew I was dead.

He was young and Chinese. He had a zapata moustache, and I didn't like his eyes. They were rattlesnake eyes. They were hard to read. They might go away. They might attack the nearest flesh. There'd be no forewarning. I wanted to leave before his fangs brushed against me.

He had four buddies with him. One had chipmunk cheeks. They could have been bored teenagers waiting for a ride home from Driving School. They could have been young men with customized campers and CB radios.

They were gangsters. Fear and terror were their favorite weapons, but tonight they carried guns. Lim Song had a Remington revolver. Chipmunk cheeks was empty-handed, but his jacket had suspicious bulges. The others had automatic rifles and a shotgun.

Louis kept his cool. "So you did set me up." He saw the death warrant in Lim Song's eyes. "A very nice job."

"Any time," I said. It didn't matter any more.

Lim Song didn't laugh. "We did not need a round-eyes to see your treachery." He indicated a young Chinese with a rifle. "He was out making collections. He saw Brennen at the Orpheus Hotel." He gestured towards another nervous face. "Then he was seen coming into this building." He looked at me. "We are sorry how you were treated."

"Sure." I didn't believe that for a minute.

"You will never interfere with us again."

"Sure." That I believed.

Lim Song didn't like me. "You can leave now."

I was afraid to move. "I can?"

He was patient, like a snake. "We learned a few hours ago that you tried to save David Huie's life. For that, we let you live."

"Davey worked for you?" I asked.

"What he was does not concern you."

A goon interrupted his leader. "He might call the cops," he whispered.

Lim Song didn't care. "We won't be here that long."

I had to ask. "What'll you do when I leave?"

"Are you partners with this running dog?" Lim Song was suave as a snake, too. He sickened me with the scent of his poisons. "You don't want to stay."

But I didn't move. "The cops want him for murder already," I argued. "If you kill him, it'll come back at you. The SFPD will come after you. If you let me take him in, you'll be left out of this."

He waited. "Are you finished?"

I sighed. "Maybe more ways than one." I heard the rattle of chain on wood behind me. I looked at Louis Ng. Beef against stick? But the animal was at bay behind his uncle's desk. He knew there was no escape for him. "So long, dead man."

"I can handle myself," Louis said. His hands were below the table. He sat like a patient man.

I remembered he had his revolver in his lap. "Maybe

you can,'' I told him. There would be bloodshed, and
not just his. I knew I'd better leave now.

Lim Song stopped me. "My credit card."

I opened my wallet and gave it to him.

"Goodbye, Mr. Brennen." He turned away, finished
with me, and started rapping hard in Cantonese.

Two goons came forward and took me to the outer
door. One went out to the landing first and the other
waited for me to follow. I had a hunch I wasn't going
very far.

I reached the landing and looked back. The door was
swinging closed after us. Lim Song got down to
business. He gestured to Chipmunk Cheeks. "Break his
legs first," he said.

And then all hell broke loose.

Louis Ng forearmed his desk and threw it at the
goons. Lim Song caught the brunt and went down
shouting in Cantonese. Chipmunk Cheeks went
sideways, around the flank. Louis had his gun up. He
shot a man. I heard him die. Then whirling sticks lashed
out like lightning. I heard bone crack. There was
another gunshot.

The henchmen on the landing ignored me, rushed
past me inside. Louis shot one of them. He had a
terrible scream. The door closed from the weight of his
falling.

A goon was downstairs watching the front door. He
had an automatic rifle, too. He came rushing upstairs.
He saw me halfway up and tried to swing his rifle
around.

There were railings on either side. I grabbed one in
each hand and launched myself feet first down the stairs.

The goon should have fired a burst. He swung at my
legs instead and missed. I flat-footed his face and we
tumbled together down the stairs. I landed on top of
him and he cushioned my jump.

Then I was on my feet again. He tried to grab me, to
trip me, and I kicked his face. His nose exploded with
blood. I took the stairs two at a time.

A white Dodge pulled up in front of the draftboard. Four Chinese men piled out from the car, and a fifth man joined them from the shadows. I ducked back and hid in the draftboard's doorway. They burst through the door, ran up the staircase and started shooting from the hip. Somebody started firing back. The plasterboard exploded with bulletholes.

I hit the bricks in a hurry. There was a phone booth across the street. I used a quarter and phoned Northern station. Speaking in pidgin English and faking a Cantonese accent, I told the duty officer there were dead men on Jackson Street. He asked my name and I hung up. There were longer pauses between the gunshots. They were taking time to aim now. They hadn't before.

I wanted out fast. I walked downhill and found a restaurant just below Grant. The restaurant was below the streets, down a flight of stairs. It was a real Chinese restaurant, one where the yellow man eats his dollar meals in peace. You must ask for chopsticks, the tea comes in tea bags, the menu is misspelled.

I found a booth near the back and sat with my back to the wall. A middleaged Chinese waiter came and brought me a menu. I don't remember what I ordered.

The waiter went off to the kitchen as the sirens came down Jackson. The reflection of flashing red lights wavered across the tarnished steel doors to the kitchen. They could have been Christmas tree lights. There was more gunfire. It sounded now like firecrackers. No one went outside to see the excitement.

Someone had left a morning edition behind. I read the front page comics first. The Farallones were tomorrow's headlines. Ruth was center-page photo. She said she saved my life.

I read the lead story again. Some facts were accurate, some were off-the-wall. I understood. The cops had their games to play. The newshawks had papers to sell.

The cops were upset because I'd lucked out on a coke ring. As if my feat had anything to do with ability, talent, good detective work. I got lucky. I knew it, they

knew it, even the newshawks knew it. I was grateful.
Only the lucky solve cases.

But the cops like tidy investigations. There was still
one loophole left to fill, and then the puzzle would fit
together like a pair of lovers. It was my job to find and
fill that hole before the cop shop crowd got upset with
an incomplete case. I needed to get myself off the hook
with them.

I needed a confession before their investigation
caught up with mine. I didn't care whether it was
thrown out of court by a clever attorney or a sensitive
judge. Cops are like elephants. They never forget.

The red lights still flashed against the kitchen doors
when the waiter brought my bill and fortune cookie.
The fortune inside said my salary would soon increase. I
paid my bill and left a dollar tip.

Outside a bright white light overcame the blue
Chinatown night. Black-n-whites filled both ends of the
street. The public servants held back the public. Two
more meat wagons arrived. The Instant Eyewitness
News team had their van double-parked near my
restaurant. A Chinese newswoman was talking into a
camera.

The Tac Squad boys came down the staircase with
their helmets off. They carried their rifles like hunters
after nightfall. They went off into small groups and
smoked cigarettes together. A stretcher came down the
stairs. One of the boys made the Sign of the Cross.

The wind had grown brittle and cold, a popsickle
taste against hands and face. The camera crew had
trouble with the stiffening wind. It pushed their spots
about. One shone up onto the windows above the street.
They didn't want to take pictures of the frightened poor
of Chinatown. Their color camera wanted blood
tonight.

I found my car. I turned on the heater, then the radio
to drown out the heater's whine. Some local station still
played its Top One Hundred. If I wanted to hear last
year again, the announcer singsonged, I should tune in
tomorrow. An Instant Replay would start at noon.

I drove down Clay Street to the freeway. The streets of the Financial District were still filthy with calendar sheets. Days thrown away. One by one they fluttered away.

I had the streets to myself.

CHAPTER 34

I walked up the cobblestone path, through the iron gate, and up the tile steps to the front door. I rapped on it, it started buzzing, I pushed it open.

The living room walls were glacier white, as was the ceiling. The furniture was the same shade, and even the carpet and drapes were bright white. Beams and rafters jutted down from the seventeen foot ceiling in sharp angles like icicles in a cave. It was like being buried inside a glacier. It was just about as cold, too. I wished somebody wasn't so shy with the central heating.

"It's about time you showed up." Her voice came on like a midnight date on a deserted beach. I could listen to it all night long. I just couldn't see the snow queen anywhere in her palace.

I tried for an echo. "It's Michael Brennen."

There was a long silence. "You're back again." She was on a balcony that overhung the far end of the room. The balcony was actually a bridge between the second floor bedrooms. She was still dressed in black, this time a cocktail dress like you see at happy hours at the Snob Hill hotels.

" 'Fraid so, Mrs. Anatole."

"I'll be right down." She started down the staircase. "I'm afraid you've missed him again. He's over at Presbyterian Hospital."

"What's Riki doing at the hospital?"

"Grandfather had a heart attack."

Sweet baby Jesus. "What are his chances?"

She didn't know. "He's in Intensive Care." Then she remembered. "He had one a few years ago." Her smile was warm. Another valium smile. She was loaded to the gills and she'd need a mood ring to know how she felt. She scared the hell out of me.

I told myself I could always come back tomorrow. But Dani wouldn't let my walk away. I saw a double funeral. Star-crossed lovers who never married, buried together in the family plot. A murderer among the mourners.

"Would you like to wait?" she asked.

"I didn't come to see Riki."

She hesitated, computed alternatives. "I'm flattered." She thought it over. "Very flattered. But I love my husband." She went bright-eyed. "We have a good marriage."

"You don't understand," I said. I settled myself in a chair halfway across the room. I knew better than to get too close to the Imperial Iceberg. She had frigid claws. "I was the one who found Dani."

An icicle snapped down over her eyes. "I know that."

"I don't think you do."

She waited for me. "What does that mean?" Her blue eyes stared back at me. Sometimes ice reflects the same color.

"I can't let Jack take the blame for Dani's death."

"You're accusing me of murder?"

"You did a lousy job."

She pursed her lips. "Why does it have to be me?"

"She was killed late New Year's Eve. The cops know what her last meal was. The autopsy will show what time it was. There had to be someone who answered her phone call that night. You're the only one who could've done it."

"Should I call my lawyer?"

"Probably." Though he was probably dead, I thought.

She had to know. "Would it help me?"

"How could it hurt?" I smiled like her closest friend. "He'll help you get all the facts straight. You should write them down now. And he should go with you when you turn yourself in."

She couldn't be sure. "Turn myself in?"

"The longer you wait," I lied, "the worse it looks."

She looked like she'd just woken up in a strange bedroom.

"Why don't you call your lawyer?"

She closed her eyes and furrowed her brows. I started counting to ten. Maybe she was trying to remember, or trying to get the facts straight enough. Maybe she was trying to remember her side of the story.

She came back at eight. "She was hysterical," she recalled. "Blabbering about narcotics and smugglers, murder, people following her."

"And you didn't believe her."

"She wanted my husband."

"Did she show you her gun?"

Lilian was taken aback. "She was daring me."

"So you took it away from her."

She got angry. "She was daring me."

"She was trying to convince you."

"Daring me!" She was turning nasty. She had her side of the story down pat, and this wasn't going her way.

"So you killed her."

She drew comfort from that fact. "I couldn't let her have him." She was earnest. People put old dogs to sleep with the same earnestness.

"Dani never wanted your husband."

"How could he resist her?"

"It was easy. He never wanted her."

She snickered. "That wouldn't stop her."

"Dani wanted Jack, not Riki."

"Jack?" Her mind caught up. "You can't believe that."

"They were lovers," I told her.

"No." She shook her head. "No."

"Too many people told me that."

"They're lying." She was sure.

"They were caught more than once."

A tiny gun appeared in her hand. It wasn't much larger than a track pistol, and it didn't light cigarettes. She fluffed her hair with her other hand. It was still in place. "And I say they were lying."

"Sure." I stared at the barrel again. I tried being calm. "I didn't think you'd keep that."

"Riki's left me alone a lot lately." She almost pouted. "He's got my car, too."

It was an effort keeping my voice steady and calm. "That's the final proof. The gun's registered to Catherine. Ballistics will prove it's the one that killed Dani."

She kept it pointed at me. "I suppose I should kill you."

I had to say something. "What will you do with my body? How about the mess it'll make? What about my car?"

She tossed them aside. "I'll think of something."

"You can't think of everything."

She started to speak, but her words froze. The gun in her hand went east, towards the kitchen.

Riki stood there, slumped against the door. God knows how long he had been there. From his expression, he had witnessed enough. He looked heartsick. She had gone too far this time.

I waited for the explosion. Maybe just a single shot. Maybe one right after another. But the shots never came.

She looked closely at the gun. She raised it, put the barrel in her mouth. She looked at me. Her eyes were haunted. She had lost him.

I told her to take it out of her mouth. Like an obedient child, she did. She set the gun in her childless lap. Then the dry heaves came. I took the gun away. She didn't resist. I wrapped it in a handkerchief.

Riki stopped me at the telephone. "You're going to call the police?" He had desperate eyes, blue with fear.

"What do you think I should do?"

"I don't know." His voice was grim.

"Is that your decision?"

"You should have let her kill herself."

"Then it wouldn't be suicide," I said.

"But she's homicidal!"

I tried to gauge him. "She's your wife."

"Yes, yes, I know that." He mumbled his words, as if mumbling divorced him from her. He had to know it wasn't so simple.

I wasn't finished, anyway. "She's your first cousin."

He winced like a man being nibbled. He seemed to shrink like a failing balloon. He looked weary of giving in to his own better judgment. He was almost a zombie from giving so much and going nowhere.

"Go to her," I said. "Go on."

He was in worse shape than I thought. He took a hesitant step. I shoved him when he faltered. He stumbled forward like a bear with a hangover. He cradled her in his arms, then hugged her tightly.

She didn't react at first. Then she started to whisper. She tried to hold him. Her hands stuttered and fumbled, as if trying to remember how they had fit together.

They held each other for a long time, as if it had been a longer time since either had held someone. Neither spoke. Neither wept. They didn't look at each other.

In the kitchen I found a dry bar near a gas fireplace. I scrounged through it, came up with a frosted bottle of cognac. I uncorked it and swigged a couple of mouthfuls. It was bitter, like gunsmoke in the lungs.

I tried to think of something clever to tell Banagan tomorrow. They never make it easy on you. I looked at the clock. It was last call. Mañana was here already. The end of the New Year's weekend. The freeway would be jammed with homebound weekenders.

Never enough money to get away.

CHAPTER 35

The autopsy said Dani Anatole was in her second month of pregnancy.